SEP 2009

LT Fic HUSTON
Marine One /
Huston, James W.
33341005045694

MARINE ONE

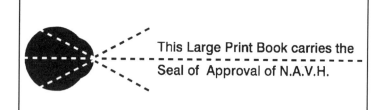

This Large Print Book carries the
Seal of Approval of N.A.V.H.

MARINE ONE

JAMES W. HUSTON

THORNDIKE PRESS
A part of Gale, Cengage Learning

GALE
CENGAGE Learning™

Detroit • New York • San Francisco • New Haven, Conn • Waterville, Maine • London

GALE
CENGAGE Learning

Copyright © 2009 by James W. Huston.
Thorndike Press, a part of Gale, Cengage Learning.

LIBRARY OF CONGRESS CATALOGING-IN-PUBLICATION DATA

Huston, James W.
  Marine One / by James W. Huston.
    p. cm. — (Thorndike Press large print thriller)
  ISBN-13: 978-1-4104-1849-4 (alk. paper)
  ISBN-10: 1-4104-1849-9 (alk. paper)
  1. Military helicopters—Accidents—Fiction. 2.
Presidents—United States—Death—Fiction. 3. Accident
investigation—Fiction. 4. Trials (Products liability)—Fiction.
5. Washington (D.C.)—Fiction. 6. Large type books. I. Title.
PS3558.U8122M37 2009b
813'.54—dc22   2009015397

Published in 2009 by arrangement with St. Martin's Press, LLC.

Printed in the United States of America
1 2 3 4 5 6 7 13 12 11 10 09

For Paul Michael Huston

Fiat justitia et pereat mundus.
Let justice be done though the world
should perish.

— Latin proverb

PROLOGUE

The rotor blades of Marine One beat against the rain and hail in the black thunderstorm as the helicopter fought its way from the White House to Camp David. The leading edges of the spinning blades smashed the hail into small ice bullets that slammed noisily into the side of the passenger compartment. An updraft bent the helicopter's blades down unnaturally as it raced upward, only to be forced violently down again.

The noise inside President Adams's helicopter grew deafening. The jet engines screamed and the metal bent in resistance to the invisible forces in the darkness. The floor plate in the passenger compartment suddenly buckled and fractured. Vibrations rippled through the sides of the helicopter, first in large waves, then in microscopic spasms that joined to break the aluminum skeleton.

The nose of the helicopter pitched up. The occupants cried out as the helicopter fought valiantly against the wall of water and turbulent air. The helicopter flailed as it rolled over and plunged toward the Maryland countryside below.

1

If my radio alarm had gone off, I would have known the president was dead. But we had lost power from the thunderstorm that still raged when I woke up to the beep of my backup alarm, my Ironman watch. I got up and didn't even bother to look out the window. I liked running in the rain, but not in a storm. I shaved in the dim bathroom while the rain pounded the roof. I listened to Debbie running around trying to get the kids ready for school in the dark. They ate cold cereal with warm milk and whined about how horrible everything was.

It was the worst storm I could remember since moving to Annapolis. My commute wasn't far, but the storm turned it into a complete nightmare. I sometimes wonder why I even bother. I have high-speed Internet at home that connects me to my office just as if I were sitting at my desk. But I actually *like* having an office. There's just a different feel to it when you put on a suit and drive to the office. It feels wrong to sit in my pajamas talking on the phone with a U.S. attorney in D.C., sounding tough about a criminal he's trying to put away. Probably my Marine training. I spent too much of my lost youth deriving comfort from mindless routine.

I drove through the downpour ignorant of the enormity of events that swirled around me. Everyone in the world knew about the crash except me. I sometimes listen to the news while driving, but I had become addicted to books on tape. That day I was deep into a John le Carré novel, which, when I started the engine in my Volvo XC90, picked up right where it had left off.

I got to my office a little later than usual and parked in my space in front of our two-story redbrick building. As far as I knew, it was just another day, with the Big Storm to remember it by. I opened the heavy door to our building and forced it closed against the wind. I put my umbrella in the brass stand near the door and shook the rain off my raincoat.

"Morning," I said to Dolores, our fifty-something receptionist, who was well-intentioned but didn't really get it.

She had an odd look on her face. "Good

morning, Mr. Nolan," she said, pregnant with expectation.

"How are you, Dolores?" I hung my coat on a peg on the coatrack and picked up my briefcase, waiting for the storm questions. Dolores was waiting for something else. *"What?"* I asked.

"Can you bel*ieve* the news?"

I quickly realized I hadn't heard any news. "What news?"

"You haven't *heard?*"

"Heard what?"

"About the *president.*"

The last time anyone had spoken to me like that about the president was when Reagan was shot by Hinckley and I was a teenager. "What?" I asked.

"I thought you must have heard."

"Power went off."

"I thought you'd listen in your car."

"What is it, Dolores?"

"The president's helicopter went down last night."

I felt a sudden dryness in my throat. "Was he in it?" I asked, afraid of what the answer was. I'm not, or I should say wasn't, a fan of the president's. Different parties, different perspectives on pretty much everything. But the idea of the president dying was about the office of the president, the disruption, not the end of a politician I didn't care for.

"Yes. On his way to Camp David in the middle of that storm."

"Why the hell was he flying last night? That was nuts."

"That's what everybody's asking. Nobody's answering, but —"

"TV on in the coffee room?"

"Yes, sir." She frowned.

I started toward the back of the office thinking about what kind of storm it would take to cause the president's helicopter to go down. Last night's storm was just the kind. Lots of wind, electrical storm, nasty rain, hail, maybe even icing. Lots of possibilities. "Anybody get out?" I yelled over my shoulder.

"No, sir. All killed. Pilots, Secret Service agents, president, everybody."

I shook my head. "Vice president been on television yet?"

"Just for a second — looked like he'd seen a ghost. He's being sworn in at ten. Mr. Nolan?" she said, forcing me to stop.

"What?" I said, stopping.

"There's something else."

"What?"

"Kathryn Galbraith called."

She was the vice president of Aviation

Insurers International, or AII as it was known, A-double-I. She was one of the people who retained me in cases, who made it possible for my children to eat more than saltines. A lot of what I did was to defend airplane manufacturers in lawsuits when planes crashed, especially helicopters — which I flew, and still did, in the Marine Reserves — and which, coincidentally, crash more than fixed-wing airplanes. In the Marine Corps, we said our helicopters were sixty thousand parts flying in formation, yearning to be free of each other. Sometimes that was more accurate than we liked to admit.

AII probably insured either the helicopter or one of the major parts in it, and they were concerned. "She say what she wanted?" I asked.

"Just that it was about Marine One."

Everybody from our small firm except Dolores was crammed into the squeaky-floored coffee room. A small, round table sat in the middle of the room, and the old television with a built-in videocassette player was in the corner on the counter. "Morning," I said to the group.

They all responded without looking at me. They were riveted to the live images of the crash scene. News helicopters battled each other in the rain overhead the crash site for the best angles to show the wreckage; several had their cameramen hanging out of the doors to zoom in better on the scene. One cameraman was standing on the skid of his helicopter, held on by a rock-climbing harness. They were about to make more wreckage if they weren't careful.

My law partner, Rick Berberian, said, "You lose power?"

"Yeah. All night. You?"

"Pretty much the whole western part of the city."

Two of our three associates were sitting in chairs, leaning forward. If the mood weren't so serious, it would have been comical. Rachel Long, the third associate — who worked exclusively with me — was standing in the corner with her arms crossed. She was also a Naval Academy graduate, surface warfare, who had resigned from the navy after a crushing divorce from a classmate. With her gaze fixed on the television, she said, "You hear Kathryn called?"

"Yeah." I nodded and stared at the video images of the crash scene that were being shown over and over as a variety of people spoke over the images. The wreckage still burned in the ravine. You could make out the skeleton of a helicopter and the path of

16

destruction where it had ripped through the trees. There was no trench in the ground or the trees. Marine One had come straight down.

A large, dark green tarp covered a large portion of the wreckage site. I couldn't figure out how or why they had erected a tarp, then remembered the news helicopters. A lot of sensitive evidence could be on the ground. Like bodies. Like the *president's* charred body. Not something for the news helicopters to feature around the world.

Rachel asked, "Think we'll get a case from this?" Rachel worked with me both on the criminal defense work I did, and aviation cases. She hadn't been a pilot when she started with me four years before, but had gotten her private pilot's license within a year. She loved it and was working toward her commercial license.

"Probably thinking about the security clearances. Lots of French workers didn't have the clearances the people at Sikorsky had. Remember all that yelling from Congress? They said if the contract for the new Marine One helicopter went to a French company, it would expose the president to assassination by helicopter. They picked the French company anyway. They're probably scared shitless right now."

Rachel stood up. "Maybe they did just kill the president."

"Well, maybe they're about to be our client, so don't jump to any conclusions. What do we know so far?" I asked.

Rachel sipped her coffee, pushed her black hair behind her ear, and said, "Departed the South Lawn around ten PM heading to Camp David. Secret Service wanted to drive, president wanted to fly. Marine pilot okayed the flight. Apparently he had a ton —"

"What was his name?"

"Chuck Collins." They all looked at me. "You know him?"

I knew him all right. Not personally as much as by reputation. Everyone in Marine helicopters, even in the reserves, was shocked when he was selected as the commanding officer of HMX-1 to fly the president. There had been a stunned silence in the Corps. We couldn't imagine how a pilot who was widely known to despise the president had become his chief pilot. Most had shrugged and put it down as one of the many ironies of life. Others had simply waited for something dramatic to happen, which they thought was inevitable. But what most expected was an anonymous book or article exposing the president as a fraud or a philanderer and Collins being fired in disgrace.

Rachel broke my train of thought. "So, *do* you?"

"Know him? Yeah, sort of. Not very well. Reputation mostly. Without a doubt, one of the best pilots in the Corps." He could fly anything. He'd flown F/A-18s, then transferred to helicopters. *Nobody* did that, but he did. He wanted to work with the grunts, get shot at and shoot back instead of dropping bombs. He had supposedly said he wanted to "watch 'em die" when he was in combat. None of this above-the-fray-anonymous-bomb-dropping-steak-eating existence for him. What a piece of work. But a great pilot. Several combat tours, highly decorated, brave, heroic even. But how had he become the president's pilot? Had the interviewers been so dazzled they didn't see what he was like? We had all wondered, but had frankly forgotten about it.

Rachel went on, "So he changed altitude a couple of times looking for clear air. Kept moving around. Last transmission to ATC said he was out of control."

"They interviewed the controller?"

"Yeah, and they've already recovered the FDR, even though it's pretty burned.

They've taken it back to D.C."

I felt stupid. If you'd asked me whether Marine One had a flight data recorder, I wouldn't have known. Airliners all have them, but most other planes don't. It made sense that they'd put one in Marine One, particularly the new model. "What about the CVR?" The cockpit voice recorder, a hard drive that recorded everything the pilots or crew said.

"Still looking for it."

"What's everyone saying happened?" I asked.

Rachel leaned back slightly. "First on was that senator from Mississippi —"

"Blankenship," Berberian said.

"He called a press conference at the Capitol. Said exactly what you just said." Rachel imitated Blankenship's voice: " 'I hate to say I told you so, but I said if we picked this *foreign* company to build Marine One, admittedly with an American company as the *front,* that there could be trouble. I'm now told we never even completed the security clearances of the European workers before this helicopter was delivered. Now it's come to this. I'm calling for a full investigation into the construction and security of the helicopter, particularly the parts made overseas.' "

Rachel said, "He said if it wasn't *intentional,* then it was a *defective* helicopter, and that's almost as bad. So he got two *I told you so*'s, which clearly pleased him. Then there were the usual experts. One former NTSB investigator said it was almost certainly the weather." The NTSB was the National Transportation Safety Board. They were responsible for investigating all major crashes in the United States, and sometimes outside the United States. They had trained investigators, one of whom was in charge of any investigation. Those investigators would often retire and go into private consulting work doing the same thing for private parties for a lot more money.

"Pretty good guess."

"Not if you listen to the *other* former NTSB investigator. He said this helicopter could handle that weather no problem. Wouldn't be comfortable, but wouldn't cause it to crash, and they were too high for a wind shear to knock them down."

"That's also true. What else?" I asked.

"Then there was the former helicopter pilot with a million flight hours who suspects foul play. Said these Marine One pilots are the best helicopter pilots in the world flying the strongest and best helicopter in the world. Wouldn't be maintenance, not with the way they take care of Marine One. He said it was either a missile or a midair by another plane that wasn't squawking."

"Squawking?" Berberian asked.

I answered, "Had their transponder turned off so Washington control couldn't see them on their radars, at least not easily. Might be the only way you could get another airplane close to the president in the air." I watched the video on the screen zoom in on a large rotor blade that was close to the rest of the wreckage. It was nearly intact. "It'd be pretty hard to shoot down a helicopter in the dark through a thunderstorm. Could be done with radar and fire control, but it wouldn't be easy. And I promise you not by some random guy with a Stinger in his trunk."

"Marine One have antimissile defenses?"

"Sure," I answered.

"What sort?"

"You're not cleared for that."

Berberian laughed. "You don't know, do you?"

I looked over his way. "Actually I do. But I can't talk about it."

He was puzzled. "Why the hell not?"

"Because I fly that helicopter every month, Rick. I know the Secret Supplement."

"The what?"

"The book that describes all the classified equipment."

Berberian wasn't persuaded. He wanted the inside scoop and was pissed I wouldn't give it to him.

Rachel poured another cup of coffee and headed toward the door while I watched the political commentators in front of the White House discussing the swearing in of the vice president, Donald Cunningham, the former senator from Illinois. "Shall we call Kathryn?" she asked.

"We?"

"Aren't I going to be involved?" Rachel asked.

"In the case, or investigation, whatever it is, probably; but not the phone call. I'm not going to make this call on a speakerphone."

Rachel was disappointed. She wanted to have more responsibility, the kind she had grown accustomed to as a navy officer. "I'll let you know what she says."

I walked up the stairs to my office. Rachel was right behind me. Her office was next to mine. I turned on my computer, checked a few news Web sites, and glanced at my e-mails. Dozens of e-mails from other Marine pilots in the reserves, most wanting everyone else's take on the accident. I could answer those later. I picked up the phone and dialed Kathryn's number.

2

The phone rang three times before Kathryn's secretary picked it up. "Ms. Galbraith's office." She sounded harried.

"Morning, Michelle. Is Kathryn available?"

"She's in a conference. May I take a message?"

I could imagine the pandemonium in her office on the fortieth floor at the south end of Manhattan. It wasn't too far from where the World Trade Center towers had been. Kathryn had watched the planes fly into the towers from her office window while she was talking to her twelve-year-old daughter on the phone. She said it had changed her life. They had debated moving their offices to New Jersey, but had decided that would be giving in and had stuck it out in New York.

"Sure, please tell her that Mike Nolan called."

"Oh, sorry, Mr. Nolan. I didn't recognize your voice. It's been pretty crazy —"

"No problem."

"She wants to talk to you. Please hold while I get her."

"Sure."

I waited for almost ten minutes, searching various Web sites for the latest information while I waited. Kathryn came on the line. "Mike, you still there? Sorry."

"No problem. Morning."

"It feels like ten o'clock at night. What a morning. Look, Marine One."

"Yeah, bad deal. Who do you have?"

"WorldCopter. They're getting absolutely hammered in the press. Did you see Senator —"

"I heard about it."

"What the hell does he think he's doing?"

"Grandstanding. It's what they do."

"It's *really* unhelpful right now."

I waited.

"Look, WorldCopter wants an attorney on this *right now.* They know they're going to be in everyone's crosshairs. They want someone who has tried helicopter cases *and* understands criminal cases, and they want a helicopter pilot. That's a small group of people. And not only are you a helicopter pilot, it's my recollection when we were working on that Bell case that you actually fly this same helicopter. The same as Marine One."

"True. The standard Marine Corps version."

"WorldCopter knows that no matter what happens, they're the target. NTSB investigation, Senate investigation, probably the FBI, maybe Justice, pretty much everybody in Washington will be after them. And they figure in a crash this big, somebody's going to sue them, one of the widows of the Secret Service agents, who knows? And they think when the investigations are all done, the government will never find pilot error; they'll try to dump this on them."

"They may be right." The NTSB's default logic is that the butler did it — the pilot. But when the butler is the *president's* pilot and the helicopter is mostly French, their default would probably be to find something wrong with the helicopter.

"So I gave them your name, faxed them your CV. It's a little bit of a hard sell because you're not with a big firm. They're not sure you can handle it. But for now I've convinced everyone. You know what I remember most?"

"What?"

"Remember that Whitcomb case? The one

you tried in Virginia?"

"Sure."

"I've never seen anyone cooler under pressure. That whole thing was falling down around your ears and you just got more and more calm. Everybody, including the client, wanted to cave and settle . . . what did our expert do?"

"He changed his testimony on cross-examination to support the plaintiff's case."

"And you cross-examined him, you impeached your own expert, then told the jury you had been wrong and changed your whole theory in the middle of trial. That took nerves of steel, Mike. If I weren't a woman, I'd say it took something else. But I think this case may take even stronger nerves, if that makes sense. Look, they're very impressed by your hours in this helicopter, and they like that you do criminal work. We want to retain you for World-Copter. Any conflicts?"

"No, no problem."

"Good. They want you on it right now."

"Fine. They want to meet?"

"No, I mean right now, as in at the accident scene."

That caught me by surprise. "The scene? Attorneys don't go to the scene until the NTSB is done."

"This is different. They don't trust *any-body*. They want you there, as an adviser at the scene itself. When can you get there?"

"I'm not sure the NTSB will even let me. And if I go to the scene, it might make me a witness. I could get disqualified if it goes to trial if I have to testify."

"I told them that. They don't care. They're willing to take the chance. How long to get out there?"

"Where is it?" I only knew it was on the way to Camp David.

"I'll send you the coordinates. It's where the hills toward Camp David start forming ravines. Supposedly there's a fire road about a thousand yards from the site. It's probably all mud by now. Do you have four-wheel drive?"

"Yeah, sort of. It'll take me at least a couple of hours. Maybe more."

She wasn't deterred. "I'll e-mail you the coordinates. Do you have GPS?"

"Yeah. I'll leave now and head in the general direction. E-mail me the coordinates and I'll punch them in."

"Make sure your cell is on." She hung up. She had never hung up on me without saying anything else.

I grabbed my suit coat and walked to Rachel's office.

She turned toward me. "What's up?"

"Let's go."

"Go where?"

"To the scene. We've been hired to represent WorldCopter."

"And they want us out at the scene?"

"Yep. Right now. Me actually, but I want you there in case I start yelling at somebody. You can tell them I haven't had my medication or something. Come on, we need to go right now. Meet me out at my house in thirty minutes. You remember where I live?"

"Sure. Do I need to bring anything?"

"Just your boots, whatever you've got that has Gore-Tex, and your new camera. Don't be late, or I'll leave without you. We've got to get out there before they rig the entire investigation to make WorldCopter look like a shitty foreign company that killed the president."

Rachel was on time. She climbed into my Volvo and we headed off. Kathryn had sent me the coordinates of the accident site and where the fire road intersected the state highway. I had grabbed my VFR flight chart out of my flight bag, which showed the fire road. It didn't show Camp David of course. Charts didn't show a lot of things the government didn't want on charts.

The GPS showed us as a triangle on a moving map heading out of Annapolis into the countryside. I put the coordinates in my handheld GPS as well.

The rain had slightly slackened. It was one of those confused times in March that could become winter or spring, depending on its mood.

The fire road was probably just a dirt strip between the trees and by now was surely just a muddy rut. Worse, it was probably obliterated by the fire and rescue trucks, to say nothing of the FBI, Secret Service, and NTSB vehicles. I had serious doubts I'd be able to get through the mess in my Volvo SUV.

Rachel asked, "You ever been out this way?"

"I've been to Catoctin Mountain Park — where Camp David is. It's a national park. I've been fishing there. Nice place. Lots of hardwood, some pine. Broke a good bamboo fly rod out there. Should have taken my little three-weight rod for the stream I was fishing, but I was in a hurry."

Rachel turned toward me in her seat. "What did Kathryn say?"

"WorldCopter's sure they're going to be the sacrificial goat. Too easy a target. They want legal advice from the first minute, at

31

the scene."

Rachel shook her head. "Nothing like a foreign company killing the president. Particularly a French one. This is going to be something."

"It's officially an American company, but I hear you." I handed her my BlackBerry. "Take a look at the e-mail Kathryn sent me. It has the names of the company reps that will be out there. Most are French, but they all speak English. They've got a power-plant guy, an airframe guy, an accident investigator . . ."

"Will the NTSB let them get involved?"

"Sure. They always do. They have company reps in all the groups. They need to know what the manufacturer knows. They have their best investigator on it already. I heard the name on the television."

"Who is he?"

"It's a she. Her name is Rose Lisenko." I looked at the GPS screen as Rachel copied the names from my BlackBerry to her pad. "One mile. Start looking for the fire road to our left."

The rain had picked up again. It pounded on the moonroof and ran down the sides of the windshield after the wipers tried to throw it out of the way. I leaned forward to see through the distorted images. My cell phone, which was also my BlackBerry, rang. Rachel was still holding it. "Answer it."

Rachel pushed the button. "Rachel Long." She waited and looked at me. "Hi, Kathryn, yes, he's right here." She handed me the BlackBerry.

"Hi, Kathryn."

"I wanted to let you know about a development." Her voice sounded wearier than the last time we had spoken.

"Sure."

"Where are you?"

"About a mile from the fire road."

"Still raining?"

"It slowed, but now it's pouring again."

"Hope you can get there."

"Me too. What is it?"

"The attorney general just went on the television. Justice is beginning an investigation."

"What kind of investigation?" I asked as I slowed. I pointed toward where I expected the fire road to be. Rachel nodded and started looking.

"Unrelated to the NTSB and Secret Service. He said he's looking into the bid process and how WorldCopter was selected for the presidential helicopter. And how *this* helicopter got into use when some of the people who worked on it didn't have clearances."

"Picked right up where the senator left off."

"He called for a meeting with the president of WorldCopter for tomorrow. We've talked to the president. He wants you to be there."

"Me? When?"

"Tomorrow. In D.C."

"Don't they have their own in-house guys?"

"Yes, but they want you to be there."

"Absolutely. Is it at Justice?"

"Two o'clock."

"We've got to prepare for that, Kathryn. You can't just walk into that buzz saw."

"You're set to have lunch at noon tomorrow at the Capital Grille. There's a room reserved in the back."

"Okay. I'll be there — There it is!" I said to Rachel as I pulled off the road. "Sorry, Kathryn, we're at the fire road. I've got to go."

"Call me later."

I never would have found the fire road if I hadn't had GPS. It was raining so hard I could barely see the Maryland highway. I turned sharply off the pavement onto the dirt and felt the wheels settle sickeningly into the mud. I selected mandatory four-wheel drive and pressed gently on the accelerator. The tires gripped enough to keep us moving, and we drifted through the water-filled shoulder onto a slightly firmer surface that led us into the woods. I accelerated cautiously knowing if we stopped, we'd never get moving again. We headed deeper into the woods following the now obvious ruts and tracks. The windshield wipers hurled the rain off the windshield just fast enough for me to see my way. I glanced down at the GPS screen. Fire roads aren't on the nav system so it wasn't of much help. It showed us gliding over a green forest with no road in sight.

We rounded a gentle curve and came upon an FBI roadblock. Several agents had set up a crude but intimidating barrier where the road narrowed. They motioned me to stop. "No visitors," one of the agents said. Others were standing in the woods with firearms protruding from their parkas.

"I'm Mike Nolan. I'm with WorldCopter. I'm their attorney."

He looked at a list on his PalmPilot. "ID?"

I handed him my driver's license. He examined it closely, then handed it back. "About a mile ahead. Watch out for the hill."

I nodded, accelerated gently, and pulled away. We regained our momentum and were making good progress. Suddenly the road made a sharp turn to the right and I found myself hurtling down a steep hill. I turned the wheel quickly to stay straight, but not fast enough. The Volvo slid sideways down the hill. I continued to try to compensate for the drift. Finally the wheels gripped and we headed straight downhill, only to see what had to be twenty-five trucks and cars parked at the bottom. I put on my brakes, which tried to help, but even with antiskid the tires couldn't grip the slushy mud. Rachel grabbed the handle on the side of the door as she braced herself for the impact and prepared to be punched in the face by the air bag. I could hear the word "Shit" forming in her mouth.

I was completely out of control as we plummeted down the muddy bank. As we careened to the bottom of the hill, I saw an area to the right of the parked vehicles that looked like mush. It was the only hope I had. I gently turned the wheels to the right, praying for *some* traction or at least steerage; the car moved sluggishly off the fire road into the high grass just shy of the trees. Rachel recoiled from the door, waiting for me to hit one of the massive trees on the right, now inches from her door. I gently braked, hoping to take off some speed. There was just enough room on the right of the parked vehicles and to the left of the trees for me to pass through and head up the other hill. I flashed past an international-yellow fire truck and slowed quickly in the mud beyond. I braked, came to a halt, turned the wheels sharply back toward the trees, and stopped. We both took a deep breath, and I said, "Let's go."

Rachel slowly removed her white hand from the door handle. I grabbed my parka from the back and pulled it over my head, got out, and opened the hatch. Rachel joined me underneath it, out of the rain. She looked for the location of the wreck and saw the tracks headed past the parked vehicles. She pointed toward the hill. I looked at my handheld GPS, which had the coordinates of the wreck, and nodded.

3

We crossed two hills and ravines. At the top of the third hill we looked down and could see the crash site. A flame was angrily burning in the pouring rain right in the middle of the wreckage. It hissed and sputtered like the eternal flame on another president's grave in Arlington.

The firemen and investigators at the accident scene must already have determined the flame was no threat. Extinguishing it would probably destroy more evidence than would be justified by the effort.

The site was full of people in blue nylon jackets with NTSB or FBI or SECRET SERVICE letters you could see from two hundred yards away. Some firemen were clearly debating whether the NTSB was right to let the flame burn.

I tried to see under the massive green tarp. From where we stood our view was partially blocked, but we could see a lot more than the helicopters circling overhead. I could see three bodies lying next to the wreckage. They were badly burned. I got a sick, brassy feeling in my mouth as I wondered whether I was looking at the burned body of the president of the United States. It was a disturbing image and a disturbing thought. Rachel saw me looking at the bodies. "Is that all of them?"

"I don't think so. I think there were seven people on the helicopter."

As we got closer, we could see that the damage to the dead was even more horrific. I wondered if they'd suffered, if they'd survived the crash and simply burned to death. In many helicopter accidents the occupants had only minor injuries but died in the fire. What a horrible way to go.

We trudged down through the mud and trees and approached the yellow caution tape that established the perimeter a hundred yards from the center of the crash. They didn't want anyone stepping on pieces of wreckage and burying them in the mud. A woman stood in the middle of the wreckage with her thick blond hair pulled back in a braid that went halfway down her back. I nodded toward the woman and said to Rachel, "There she is."

"Who?" Rachel asked.

"Rose Lisenko, the NTSB's investigator in charge — the IIC — for this accident."

Rose had seen us and was extremely concerned that someone was approaching her accident site. She hurried over to the caution tape and looked at me. "No press."

"I'm not with the press, Rose."

She looked at me more carefully as the rain dripped down her face. She wore no hat, no hood, and used no umbrella. Her incredibly thick hair absorbed 80 percent of the rain that was hitting her head but it was now saturated. The rain oozed out of her hairline onto her face and neck. She was maybe five feet four, thin, and not unattractive, but she had a hard face and dark eyes. She didn't want to be distracted, and whatever it was I wanted, she didn't want any part of it. "Do I know you?"

"Mike Nolan. I'm an attorney —"

"No attorneys here. *Absolutely* no attorneys."

She probably assumed I was a plaintiffs' attorney who had showed up to find out how to sue someone. "I'm here for World-Copter. They asked me to come out."

"They're here already, and they don't need any help. Thanks for dropping by." She turned and walked back toward the crash site.

Rachel looked at me with concern. I bent under the caution tape and walked right behind Rose. Rachel followed.

Rose turned around. "You think this is a game, sir? This is a controlled site! We're investigating Marine One here, not some student-pilot accident. If you stay here, I will have you *arrested*," she said angrily.

"I'll do whatever you say, Rose, but I've been requested to be here by WorldCopter. You know a party to an investigation can have whoever they want on their team."

She was already on to something else in her mind. She didn't have time for an argument. She threw her hand at me in disgust. She walked back to a group of NTSB investigators huddled under several umbrellas trying to examine photographs of a WorldCopter similar to Marine One.

I handed my camcorder to Rachel. "Videotape everything. I've got several tapes and three extra batteries in that bag. Use it all."

"Don't you want me to take photographs? You told me to bring my camera."

"Absolutely. Photograph everything. Do both. We can't have too many pictures."

I saw a man with a WorldCopter jacket and gestured to him. He approached. "Hi, I'm Mike Nolan. I'm supposed to talk to Marcel."

"Yes, he's right over there," the man said in perfect English.

"What's your name?"

"Jeff Turner, vice president of operations for WorldCopter U.S."

We followed him to where the other WorldCopter people were congregated. I looked at the wreckage up close for the first time. The fire had consumed most of the aluminum skin of the aircraft. Small pieces were identifiable, but most of what remained was a piled, blackened tangle of magnesium, aluminum, composites, and steel. The tail rotor had somehow survived nearly intact. It was attached to part of the tail boom and stuck up from the ground about eight feet. Just high enough for the blades to not touch the ground. It was eerie.

Suddenly the scent of burned flesh pierced my consideration of the scene. I had smelled burned flesh before. It's the kind of thing you never forget. While in the Marine Corps I had had the unfortunate experience of investigating two accidents. Both had been caused by pilot error and had resulted in the pilot and many others being — as Tom Wolfe would put it — "burned beyond recognition." The NTSB workers were sifting through the wreckage still looking for the other bodies or what pieces of them they could find. I saw a flash of white in one section of the debris that looked to be the back of a skull with the scalp burned off.

I looked up into the rain, blocking with my hand to try to see the trees through which the helicopter had plummeted. Most were tall oaks and hickory, with some pine. They were well over fifty feet tall and hardy. Branches that the blades had cut through lay around the wreckage. The leaves were still green and the cuts were fresh, but there weren't that many of them. The helicopter had come almost straight down. To me that meant it had lost power. The pilot might have tried an autorotation, where you use the rotor blades as an air brake to slow the fall of a helicopter that has lost power. It's something you practice from the first day of helicopter training, but that doesn't make it easy, especially at night, especially in a storm. The pilot might have lost power, descended in an autorotation, and misjudged his height above the ground. Possible, but really unlikely. This helicopter had three engines. It obviously had fuel because the fuel was still burning. The odds of losing power in all three engines simultaneously were about zero. It could have been contaminated fuel, or fuel-line blockage, but again, with Marine One, the best-maintained and best-protected helicopter in the world, I doubted it. Something else had happened.

Jeff was walking away from the bodies. "Jeff, I'll be right there," I said, peeling off and walking toward the tarp and the bodies, which had been laid side by side. Secret Service agents were standing around the bodies. I looked at every part of every body. I couldn't stop myself. I looked for identifying clues. But I had finally gotten close enough that one of the Secret Service agents came over to me and put his hand on my chest. "Who are you?"

I didn't have a badge or jacket or any other identification. Rachel stood about eight feet behind me. She continued to film everything, including the bodies. The same Secret Service agent that had me in his sights looked at her. "Put the camera down." While still touching my chest, he glimpsed over his right shoulder. "Greg! Watch this one."

Greg immediately came over and stood in front of me and began asking me questions, while the first Secret Service agent walked to Rachel. "Give me the camera."

"It's not mine."

"I didn't ask you who owned it. Give it to me."

"We're investigating the accident."

"Nobody videotapes a deceased president."

So one of the three bodies *was* Adams.

Rachel looked at me for guidance. I gave her a slight nod. She spoke to the agent, "Just take that tape. I need to record other parts of the wreckage, I won't record the bodies." She looked at the camera on both sides, turned it over, unable to figure out how to eject the cartridge. She looked at me for guidance. I put my hands up to the Secret Service agent, indicating I was backing away, and went back to Rachel.

I took the camera, ejected the tape, and handed it to the Secret Service agent. "We won't videotape the bodies. You have my word."

He glared at me and returned to his position, slipping the tape into his pocket.

I walked back over to the agent named Greg and stood beside him. He looked at me suspiciously. "What are you doing here?" he asked.

"I'm an attorney with WorldCopter."

He nodded. "They're going to need one."

He was probably doing what everyone else in the country was doing. Assuming it was the company's fault: either they built a shitty helicopter, or they let some maniac

45

who didn't have a security clearance sabotage the helicopter and kill the president. Either way, we lost.

"You may be wrong about that, but we'll save that for another day."

I went back over to Turner. "What do you have so far?"

He gestured me farther away from the Secret Service agents. I motioned for Rachel to walk with us. We stood near the yellow tape on the uphill side of the wreckage by ourselves. Turner said, "Helicopter's completely destroyed. But one thing . . ." He looked around at the others investigating the accident and glanced over at the nearly intact rotor blade that I had seen on the television screen.

"What?"

"That blade. The threads look stripped, but the blade is almost completely intact except for the end cap and the tip weights."

Rachel frowned and asked, "Can we go look at it?"

Turner considered her request. "Yeah, but act like you're just curious. I'll come over and explain it to you."

Rachel walked away looking around, taping the entire scene with the video camera, then stopped near the blade. She videotaped it, stopped taping, and called out to us,

"What about this?"

We walked over to the massive rotor blade, perhaps thirty inches across and forty feet long. Titanium shaft, composite core, and carbon-fiber skin on the outside. The shaft had a yellow-painted stripe near the attachment end that would tell us which of the seven blades this one was. Each had a different color ring: the blue blade, red blade, yellow blade . . .

I asked Jeff, "What do you make of it?"

"Come down here." He motioned, indicating the end of the blade away from where it attached to the helicopter. "Look at the end."

It was bare, with something of a concave look the entire width of the blade surface. I could see immediately what Jeff's concern was.

Rachel was puzzled. "The end looks odd."

"You know what tip weights are?" I asked her.

"Not really."

"They're little washerlike things that you stack onto those bolts there at the end. The end cap covers that and the rest of the end of the blade. You know the tiny weights that get tapped onto the rims when you get new tires for your car? To balance the wheel? Same idea. It's to balance a spinning surface. If a blade is out of balance, the entire helicopter vibrates. If it's bad enough, the helicopter comes apart."

Rachel looked at the size of the blade, glanced back at the wreckage where the main rotor head lay in the middle, and asked, "How do you balance it?"

Jeff said, "The Golden Blade."

"What's that?"

"Every blade is built to the same specs. But it's impossible to make two things exactly alike, to the thousandth of an ounce. So we balance every blade against the same master blade. The Golden Blade. It sits in a room all by itself and is never touched or modified in any way. It stays attached to a spinning rotor head, and every blade that comes in has to run in perfect balance and tracking with the Golden Blade. We adjust it by adding small tip weights. If they balance against the Golden Blade, they'll balance against each other."

Rachel asked, "So why is this blade here?"

Jeff looked at me with what I took to be extreme concern, maybe just short of fear. "Looks like it came off in the air."

Losing a blade in midair would almost certainly be the manufacturer's problem. A couple of things could cause that to happen that wouldn't be, but those were extremely unlikely.

I asked him, "Wouldn't the blade vibrate itself to death? Wouldn't it have thrown parts all over the countryside?" I stared at the blade, trying to listen to what it was saying. "And after coming apart in the air it just *happened* to land right where the rest of the helicopter crashed? I'm not buying it."

He said, "Me neither. But it sure came off somehow, and it's not as beat to death as the others, which are still attached."

I walked to the end of the blade where it would have attached to the helicopter. Jeff and Rachel followed me. I asked, "What about the threads? Are they stripped?"

"They look like it, but I can't say for sure. Have to put it under an SEM." A scanning electron microscope. He put his hands deeper into his parka. "I don't think I need to tell you how bad this is going to be for WorldCopter if we threw a blade in a storm and killed the president."

I didn't respond. The answer was more obvious than the question.

Just then another man with WorldCopter printed on the front of his raincoat approached the three of us. Jeff said to me, "Mike, let me introduce to you Marcel. Marcel is the chief accident investigator for

WorldCopter. Have you met?"

"No. Hello, Marcel." I extended my hand and he shook it vigorously.

Marcel said, "Thank you for coming, Mr. Nolan. We thought we would have much difficulty from the NTSB, but they've been very cooperative. We are able to work freely." He had a heavy French accent and was trying to be optimistic and upbeat, but the weight of what he was doing was evident on his rain-covered face. "Come over here, I want to show you something."

We followed Marcel to the main part of the wreckage. We stopped under the corner of the tarp. Marcel looked around nervously as he watched the government inspectors sifting. We followed his gaze and saw others walking up the hill looking over every square foot for any other evidence that wasn't in the central area.

Marcel leaned closer to me and said, "We are very concerned about this investigation. We are sure that at the end it will be shown to be pilot error . . . It is one of the reasons that I wanted you to come out here. I don't trust anyone." He looked around casually, then leaned toward me. "I am afraid the government will be listening to all my cell phones."

"Why do you think that?"

Marcel's face clouded. "Did you not see that senator?"

"Blankenship."

"Yes. His press conference at the Capitol. *He* is attacking WorldCopter. I think, as you Americans say, with a *vengeance,* a French word, which of course means the same thing in French, and we understand this. We *invented* this. And of course we have heard what you have heard, that the Justice Department also is beginning an investigation. As I recall, the Justice Department also includes the FBI, although I am not sure with Home Defense —"

"Homeland Security."

"Yes, but I am quite sure that they are investigating too. Many investigations, all with the purpose of making this our fault. So, if true, does that mean that they could listen in on our cell phones, Mr. Nolan? Hmm?"

This was already getting way more complex than the average aircraft case. It was the kind of case you long to have your whole professional life, yet also hope you never do. It's the kind of case that can make you and break you at the same time. "No, they won't be listening in on our calls. They know I'm an attorney. It would be privileged. I suppose they could claim they didn't know, so, yes, I guess it's possible they could be listening in, if they have a warrant. For other conversations, it wouldn't hurt to *assume* your calls were being monitored I suppose." If you want to be paranoid, I wanted to add, but thought better of it.

Marcel nodded. "Exactly. So you know about the Justice Department investigation? You will be there?"

"I'll be there. I'm taking Rachel too."

Marcel agreed. "Yes, it's good to have a woman there. Everything is different when a woman is there. They will be less aggressive."

"Don't bet on that. But she's going anyway."

A voice from behind us said, "Marcel." We turned and it was Rose. She was walking toward Marcel. We crossed to meet her. She spoke to him and ignored us.

"We found the CVR. Looks intact. We're getting it to the lab. If it's in as good a shape as it looks, we're going to play it tomorrow morning at nine o'clock. Just wanted you to know."

Marcel was shocked. "Where?"

"NTSB headquarters." She turned back to what she was doing to find the head of the engine manufacturer's investigation team.

Marcel almost smiled. "I am quite pleased we put these black boxes into the airplane. We should be able to find out what happened."

"It will certainly help."

He looked into my eyes to make sure I was listening. "I want *you* to be there too," he said, pointing at my chest. "At the playing of the tape. You're a pilot." Marcel returned to what he was doing, and Rachel and I were left alone. She was videotaping the NTSB inspectors doing their work. "Videotape everything, twice. I've got to look around."

I walked around the perimeter and just looked. I tried to absorb what it was telling me. An accident site speaks to you like a painting. You may not get it the first time, or even the second. And years later, when you look at it again, you'll see new things. That morning every blade of grass, every piece of metal, every pattern, had something to say, something about how this helicopter had ended up where it did and why it crashed. I wasn't an expert in accident reconstruction, but I had learned that when those experts did form their conclusions, I'd often notice something either by having been there or from a photograph that caused me to question their conclusions.

And sometimes it made a difference.

I walked away from the tarp and found pieces of wreckage a hundred feet and more away from the impact point. I was sure the NTSB would find every piece and create a wreckage diagram. I'd had bad experiences where they had missed things, but this was Marine One. They wouldn't leave anything undone. And if they needed an army to find things, they had the entire FBI at their disposal.

I looked at the trees and the ravine and tried to visualize what had happened in the dark night. I imagined the helicopter with its lights flashing and its blades desperately trying to keep the helicopter in the air as it plummeted through these tall trees in the dark in its dying seconds, in a hail of shattered blades, screaming jet engines, breaking metal, and death. I began to wonder if it had been on fire *before* it hit. That might explain everything. And I couldn't forget that it might have been shot down.

4

We got towed up the giant mud hill by a massive Marine Corps truck and drove back to my house in the dark. We arrived about eight, completely exhausted. Rachel went on her way, and I spent an hour explaining to Debbie what I had been doing all day. Later that night I typed the twenty-page to-do list that had been spinning in my head since the morning. It was more stressful *not* to write it down and run the risk of forgetting things than it was to stay up through my exhaustion and write it. At least I had the beginning of a plan, including responding to the investigations I knew about, and the others that were sure to come. The government investigations would be the heart of it. If they were able to hang this on WorldCopter, lawsuits and the collapse of the company would surely follow. We had to blunt the attack in the beginning. After finishing the list, I collapsed into bed.

The next morning I stood under my open garage door at 6 AM drinking hot coffee waiting for Rachel. The rain still poured down from the same massive storm that had been blowing on the South Lawn when President Adams had insisted on going to Camp David. Rachel pulled up and we climbed into my Volvo SUV. It was still coated with Maryland mud everywhere the rain couldn't reach. We headed off to D.C.

Neither of us spoke for the first fifteen minutes as we waited for the coffee to kick in. She looked tired and put her head back on the headrest.

I turned down NPR, which was covering the crash and the implications. "You okay?"

"Tired."

The rain slackened. "That's the first time you've ever been to a crash site, isn't it?"

"Yeah."

"What'd you think?"

She rolled her head toward me against the headrest. "It's also the first time I've ever seen a dead body."

"Really?"

"I've seen pictures, but I've never seen a dead body. Outside of a casket."

"Sticks with you, doesn't it?"

Rachel slowly moved her hand up and down the shoulder harness across her chest.

"I think I was up all night. I couldn't get the image of A3 out of my mind."

A3 was the nickname given to President James Adams, or maybe chosen by him. Although he was now simply known as "the deceased president," James Adams claimed to be descended from John Adams of colonial fame and his son John Quincy Adams. So he claimed to be the third Adams president, which everyone abbreviated as A3. Some in the political press claimed that one of the men in Adams's line of descent had been adopted and he didn't therefore count. But none of that stopped the usually critical press from making endless jokes about the Adams Family as just an extension of the television show.

President Adams had loved the nickname A3. He loved the historical resonance he believed he got from being in the lineage of two of the first six presidents of the United States.

Rachel continued, "All I could see was A3 lying there on the ground with his lips burned back over his teeth." She stopped as she studied the image again. "Like a big shit-eating grin. One of those things you wish you had never seen, but you can't tear your eyes away." She glanced up at me in the morning dimness, probably wanting me to say something deep.

I nodded. "I've seen enough dead bodies that I don't notice so much. But it's always different when they're burned. It's just more . . . obscene. Like they've been defaced. I don't mean that literally . . . I mean that it's like it burned away their identity."

Rachel nodded. "I just hope I don't start snoring when they're playing the cockpit voice recorder."

"Not likely. There are few things more riveting than listening to the cockpit voice recorder of an airplane that *you* know is going to crash but the ones speaking don't." I turned onto the freeway heading west to D.C. "Plus, I want you to do more than just listen. I want you to watch the other people in the room. Sit in the back, see how they're reacting. See when the people glance at each other like they've heard something significant or noteworthy."

"Do you have any more coffee?" Rachel asked.

"On the floor behind my seat."

She didn't move. "Maybe I'll just get some sleep on the way down."

"No way. We've got lots to discuss. I'll talk, you write." I handed her my to-do list.

Like the naval officer she used to be, she sat up without protest and got out her note pad. I handed her my typed to-do list, and we went through everything, from understanding the manufacturing process, getting diagrams and the maintenance manuals for the helicopter, to checking newspaper and Internet materials on every wacky theory that was already being circulated. I knew how this investigation was going to be conducted. Not only would no stone be left unturned, but each stone would be smashed open and examined from the inside, regardless of whose stones they were. Of course what was on everyone's mind, and what the NTSB didn't yet deny, was that maybe terrorists had finally taken out the president. The thought sent chills through the government and the entire country. No one had seen any evidence of terrorism, or even foul play, but a lot of FBI experts could be talking to each other about that very thing and not WorldCopter, or me, or the press.

I felt my BlackBerry buzzing. I grabbed it, pushed the phone button, and answered, "Mike Nolan."

"Mike, Kathryn."

"Morning."

"Where are you? I called your office and they said you were on your way to D.C., but I didn't think your meeting with World-Copter was until lunch."

"The NTSB is going to play the CVR this morning. Marcel wanted me to be there."

"Mike, you've got to keep me posted on what you're doing. I needed to know that. I might have liked to listen to the tape. What time are they playing it?"

"Sorry, I didn't think about that. Nine o'clock." I looked at the clock on the dash. "You might still make it if you left now."

"Too late." She sounded perturbed. "Look, I was talking to Richard in London, and he said he's glad you're aboard, but he may bring on some help."

Richard was the CEO of Aviation Insurers International, based in London. He was Kathryn's boss. I saw the car in front of me suddenly slow as the nose of the car dipped — he was braking hard. I hit the brakes and could feel the antilock brakes take effect as I tried to slow without hitting him. I tried not to fire off an expletive.

"What kind of help?"

"A couple of people, really. He mentioned Mark Brightman, on the civil side."

Everybody knew who Brightman was. The aggressive defense lawyer from New York City carried his New York attitude with him everywhere he went. "Seriously?"

"Yes, we're thinking about it."

"You said a couple."

"He was thinking of getting someone who has experience in Washington with these political witch hunts."

"Who?"

"Not sure yet. Some big names. I'm not sure what's going to happen."

I was annoyed but said nothing. "Just let me know."

I drove into downtown Washington with the familiar monuments pointing to the sky, which was beginning to clear from the lingering storm. The city now had a new president. Vice President Donald Cunningham had been sworn in as president of the United States the day before, while Rachel and I were out in the mud. All the news reports mentioned how his hand visibly shook on the Bible. Reporters were surprised by his nervousness. They took it as a reaction to the rumors that they had started and were now rampant that the vice president felt that he was in danger; he believed the president had been murdered. That was *really* helpful to us. Most of the talk was about "murder" by WorldCopter through their incompetence, their "uncleared" workers who undoubtedly sabotaged the helicopter, the dead rotor blade lying in the dirt, and the evil foreign corporations who had stolen this major contract from its rightful owner, the American manufacturer who had been making the presidential helicopters for the last fifty years. It was a classic example of what the press was so good at — taking a small piece of information, breaking it up into even smaller threads, and weaving a conspiracy. Really helpful.

We drove to NTSB headquarters and parked a couple of blocks away. We put on our suit coats and walked toward the building. The whole city felt different. It was hard to describe. It was as if the entire city were in a faint shadow of a massive object high above that was about to fall on it. The shadow would be there until the city knew what had happened to their president, or until the object landed on them.

The lobby was jammed with reporters and cameras. I said to Rachel, "Don't say anything."

The reporters looked at us, wondered who we were, and finally decided to ask. One reporter with a local Washington television station ran up to me and stuck a microphone in my face. Her cameraman had his Sony television camera on his shoulder with its red recording light illuminated. She asked me, "Are you here to listen to the cockpit voice recorder?"

"Yes, I am."

"And who are you?"

"I'm Mike Nolan."

"Who are you with?"

"I'm with her," I said, indicating. "Excuse us."

"Are you an attorney?" she asked to my back.

I didn't respond as I walked to the receptionist and gave her my driver's license. She looked at the list and checked my name off and handed me a visitor's badge. I passed through the turnstiles and took the elevator to the fourth floor, where I knew the large hearing room was. It was eight thirty and only ten other people were there, several from the NTSB, and several men who looked to me to be with the Secret Service. The room was government-stark. The paintings on the wall looked like photocopies of bad art in cheap metal frames. Two long metal tables were up front with fifty or so metal chairs placed like audience seats throughout the rest of the room with a narrow aisle in the middle. The only thing in the room that looked modern or new was a sophisticated PA system that had large speakers on stands at the ends of the two metal tables and a large amplifier in the middle of the table hooked up to the speakers. The charred CVR sat next to the amplifier. A technician was connecting its wires to the amp in preparation for playing the tape.

It wasn't actually a tape at all, of course, but a hard drive. The sound was recorded digitally. Tapes are too vulnerable to heat and pressure. The orange box that contained the cockpit voice recorder was designed to withstand one thousand G's — one thousand times the force of gravity — for at least five milliseconds, and eleven hundred degrees for thirty minutes. It had probably come close to reaching both of those in this crash. It was dented in one corner in particular and was more charred-black than orange.

Well before the clock actually reached nine, the room was full of parties to the investigation, from the engine manufacturer, to Marcel and his group, to numerous other component-part manufacturers who had been invited to participate. Rose came into the room with quite a flourish. Her braid was taut and long. Her face was humorless and full of determination. She waited until the crowd gave her their full attention, and the room finally grew silent.

She spoke to the group. "Good morning. For those of you I haven't met, my name is Rose Lisenko. I am the investigator in charge. Couple of ground rules. First, this investigation is ongoing. The press has not been invited because we don't know what's on the recording. We have checked to make sure that it is intact and will play. We have not listened to it. You will hear it at the same time we do. Because of that, we don't want the press taking this raw information and giving it to the general public, especially in a case as sensitive as this one. If we believe the recording should be released to the public, we will do so when that is appropriate. We therefore ask that everyone confirm to us that there are no recording devices in the room. Does anyone have a digital recorder or video recorder of any kind on their person?" She looked around the room and waited.

"Good. Second, after this recording is played, it will be transcribed later today, and each chairman of each working group will be given a copy of the transcript. If you are in a working group, you will also receive a copy of the recording. If you are not in a working group but believe you need a copy of the transcript or the recording, please let me know and I will determine whether you are entitled to a copy. We will also of course be playing the tape again later, and you can hear it at those later times. You will be given notice before the playing occurs. If you want to have the tape played after today, please let me know and we will determine whether we need to conduct a special playing of the tape."

She looked at one of the NTSB employees in the back and said in a fairly loud and commanding voice, "Secure the doors." He stood in front of the door as another NTSB employee exited the room. They took up posts on either side of the closed doors.

Rose continued, "I would ask everyone to refrain from making any noise whatsoever during the playing of this tape. Every little sound can be significant. We've cranked up the volume quite a lot, so that it may sound too loud to you in this room, but we, like you, are listening for background noises as well as the obvious information from the voices." She paused, looked around, and then said, "Play it."

5

I had only actually met Chuck Collins once, or maybe twice, but I remembered his voice. It was one of the first things we heard from the cockpit voice recorder, and I recognized his resonant sound immediately. Collins had been one of the best helicopter pilots in the Marine Corps. He had flown off carriers, desert pads, and roads. He had mastered every helicopter the Marine Corps owned, from the biggest cargo carrier to the smallest, fastest gunship. He had flown off steep, snow-covered mountains and floating platforms while working with special operations. He had even graduated from Navy Test Pilot School in Patuxent River, Maryland. He had flown several tours in Iraq and begged to go back for more, but he had gotten too senior to go blow things up. During his last tour as a helicopter squadron commanding officer, much of which was spent on a carrier in the Pacific, he was told he would be the first pilot to fly the president in the new presidential helicopters, the World-Copter 5, now known as the VH-80.

The CVR had captured the last thirty minutes of that evening's flight. It started with Marine One approaching the South Lawn of the White House through a torrential downpour. Collins was all business. Full of comments on the weather. His copilot was doing his job perfectly, monitoring the altitude, the air speed, and radios. They were talking to Washington control and the White House. It all sounded normal. Collins was a good pilot, and it showed through the recording.

I put myself in his seat and visualized what he was seeing, the instruments, the lightning, the rain hitting the rotor blades, and watching the White House grow bigger in the dark night as he approached. I'd never flown in Marine One, and I'd certainly never put a helicopter down on the South Lawn of the White House; but I had several hundred hours in this WorldCopter model and knew every switch that Collins was throwing and everything he was touching. I could do it in my sleep.

As they landed, everything continued normally until, just as they touched down, Collins said, *"Whoa."*

I focused intently. His copilot, Rudd said, *"What was that?"*

"I don't know. Might have been a wheel settling into the mud, but it felt like more of a thump. Maybe the strut bottomed out. We'll check it when we get out."

"Roger that."

We listened intently to the pilots' small talk while they waited for the president, listening for any indication of what we knew was about to happen, to see if just maybe they had a hint of what was coming. We listened for slurred speech, depression, anger, all the things anyone would listen for. But as the recording went on, it built its own story.

"This is an unbelievably shitty night to fly. Why we doing this?" Collins asked.

Lieutenant Colonel Rudd replied, *"You've got the final say. Just say the word. Ground us."* He waited for Collins to ground them, but he knew it wouldn't happen. They did what the president wanted, and the president wanted to go to Camp David.

"We're doing this because El Jefe says so," Collins said.

Rudd said, *"Plus we're just dumb-ass Marines who always do what we're told."*

"You're a dumb-ass, but I'm a smart-ass. So why am I doing this?"

Rudd replied, *"Because you've been trained since your earliest waking moments to follow stupid orders in shitty conditions. We're trained to* love *it. The stupider the order and the worse the conditions, the more faithful the Marine is for obeying it.* Semper fi. *You know that."*

Collins laughed into the ICS microphone. Probably only Rudd could hear him, but the crew chief might have been on the ICS line too. On a night like that, he would probably be outside checking the soggy ground in the pouring rain to make sure they wouldn't be pulling the earth toward the moon when they tried to take off, stuck in mud up to their axles. He was probably looking for the origin of the thump as well.

"At least we're in here and dry."

"Here comes the president," Rudd said.

I looked over at Rachel, who was listening with her mouth open.

"You've got the airplane. I'm going to talk to Secret Service." You could hear Collins moving out of his seat. I waited for the sound to cut off, but then remembered that they were using the new, encrypted wireless headsets. You could hear Collins belching as he made his way to the back of the helicopter. He was walking or moving, it was unclear, then he said, *"Hey, Greg."* Greg Marshall no

70

doubt, the head of the Secret Service detail on the flight.

"*Chuck,*" Marshall replied perfunctorily. We could barely hear the other voice, since it was coming through Collins's mike. If they hadn't had the speakers turned up so loud, we wouldn't have heard it at all.

"*What the hell are we doing?*" Collins asked. "*Can't you drive the president to Camp David?*" I could hear the noise of the helicopter engines in the background; they had kept the engines running and the rotors spinning as they waited for the president to board.

"*No comment,*" Marshall said.

"*You know what this is about, don't you?*"

"*Yes. One of many important meetings of the president of the United States.*"

"*Meeting. Right. Just a meeting. And who's he going to meet? Do you know everything you need to know about them?*"

"*You know something I don't know?*"

I found myself trying to see their faces in the speakers, wishing I could see their expressions and body language.

"*I've forgotten more about Adams than you'll ever know.*"

"*Right. Adams scholar. I forgot.*" Marshall waited a short time, then asked Collins in a tone that was half-annoyed and half-concerned, *"So what you got? Anything I should know about?"*

"If you don't know by now, I'm sure not going to tell you. Don't worry about it. I'll take care of it. It's nothing you can do anything about."

"You got something I need to hear, you know where to find me. Just don't kill us on the way."

"No guarantees tonight," Collins said. *"Your life will be in my very capable hands, but there are other forces at work."*

Collins's words were strange. Everyone in the room could feel it.

Marshall felt it too. *"You saying it's unsafe? Say the magic words, Chuckie, say it isn't safe, and we're headed straight for the limo."*

"Can't do it. I serve at the pleasure of the president. I do what I'm told."

"You can override any flight request."

"Never going to happen. How could it be unsafe when I'm the one flying? I could land this helicopter on the top of a flagpole." Collins chuckled. *"But you wouldn't mind if I flew ten feet above the ground to avoid the weather, would you?"*

"You know the minimum altitude." Marshall spoke to others we couldn't hear, then said, *"President's coming aboard."*

Collins sounded as if he had returned to

the cockpit, and you could hear some background noise. Rudd exchanged comments on the weather and the instruments with Collins, then warned him that the president was coming into the cockpit. A chill came over the room as we heard President Adams's unmistakable voice: *"Shit, Colonel — it's blacker than a witch's heart out there! Can you get us out of here?"*

There was a long, long pause while no one spoke.

Rudd filled in the gap: *"I believe so, sir. It isn't the best night for flying, though. Sure you wouldn't rather drive? You can borrow my car if you need one. Could be real bumpy, sir."*

The president laughed with a nervous, strained sound, then the voices faded. The cockpit was quiet.

Rudd's voice was loud: *"What the hell you doing, Chuck? You can't just ignore the president! He was talking directly to you!"*

"I don't really give a shit what he was doing."

"Don't let your politics get into this. They'll fire your ass. Show respect for the office if not for him."

"I don't have any respect for the office while he's in it. You see his face? He looked like he's about to crack."

"He always does. RPM?" Rudd replied as

73

they talked about the president and completed their checklist at the same time.

"Not like this. One hundred percent."

"Pretty close. Engine temps?"

"This is different. Engines are good."

They finished the checklist and were ready to take off. Collins said on the ICS, *"Ready in the cabin, Sergeant Olson?"*

"Ready, sir."

You could hear the rotor blades bite into the air as they pulled the helicopter off the ground. Rudd called out their departure on the radio: *"Washington Control, Romeo Uniform One Zero One airborne, northwest departure."* They were using an innocuous call sign. If some sniper or missile shooter was waiting for them to take off, he wouldn't know by the call sign, different even from the one they had used during landing.

"Roger, One Zero One, climb and maintain thirty-five hundred feet. Take heading three two seven. Squawk three five six five and ident."

"Roger. Passing two hundred for three point five. Squawking."

"Radar contact. You're cleared direct destination."

"Roger. Turning. . . . Washington Center, Romeo One Zero One. You have any PIREPs on the tops for this storm?" A PIREP was a

pilot report about the weather or conditions. It was highly regarded by other pilots. Real-time information, instead of some weatherman reading a scope or satellite picture.

"Stand by, One Zero One."

But Collins couldn't wait. *"One Zero One requesting seven thousand feet. The turbulence is too severe here."*

"Roger, Zero One. You're cleared to seven thousand or anywhere in between at your discretion. Report when level. Latest PIREP shows tops at twenty-five thousand."

"Roger. Leaving thirty-five hundred for seven thousand. Will report level. Thanks for the PIREP."

"No problem, Zero One. Wish we had better news for you."

Rudd laughed and said to Collins on the ICS, *"Maybe we should just stay at this altitude and see if we can get A3 to hurl."*

"Not a good idea. And knock off that A3 bit. He's not related to the other Adams presidents and you know it."

"Come on, Chuck; you got to get off that. One guy in his line like a hundred years ago was illegitimate or adopted or something. Doesn't mean he isn't a descendant."

"I'm surprised he doesn't claim to be the illegitimate son of Thomas Jefferson too. He's obviously comfortable with being a bastard."

The room was in disbelief that Collins could have such hostility for the president and was discussing what a fraud he was while flying him through a thunderstorm.

"Get over it, man. Why do you overthink this stuff? It just doesn't matter."

"I've looked into everything about him. I'm fascinated by him."

"Fascinated. But not in a good way."

They were talking over some radio conversation that would have to be separated out later by a technician. It was impossible for me to tell whether it was significant. The NTSB had the Air Traffic Control Center tapes too, so it wouldn't be hard to reconstruct what was said.

"You're just still dazzled by him. You'll get over it."

"You're right about that. I'm absolutely not ready to hear whatever it is you're talking about. There's seven thousand feet."

After a few minutes of silence, Collins said, *"Not much better here."*

"I think we're just stuck in this crap until Camp David. Thirty-seven miles. Look at the winds. They're westerly at thirty-five knots. If those are the winds at Camp David, we'll never get this thing on the ground."

Collins didn't respond for a long period, then transmitted, *"Center, Romeo Uniform*

One Zero One. No better here. We're going to head down to twenty-five hundred to find some smoother air."

"Roger, Zero One. Cleared. Take whatever altitude is best. No other traffic."

A series of rapid, unidentifiable noises followed. Something was happening, but no one could tell what, at least not without analysis of the sounds. The next thing we heard was a strained Collins saying, "We've hit severe turbulence."

He was fighting something.

Rudd asked, "You need any help?"

"No. I've got it." Noises . . . struggle . . . grunting. "Shit! This thing is out of control!"

"You got it?" Rudd screamed.

"No!" Collins yelled.

"What's going on?" the sergeant screamed from the back. "The president's panicking!"

The violence increased. The engines suddenly seemed loud in the usually quiet background of cabin noise. I thought I heard the blades. They sounded strained, as if they were working against each other instead of creating a smooth-spinning disk to keep the helicopter off the ground.

". . . out of control!" Collins said. "Check . . . hydraulics!"

"No light. Pressure's good!" Rudd said in what sounded like a mighty attempt to

77

sound calm.

The noise built to a crescendo. It sounded as if things were floating in the cockpit, hitting other things. I breathed harder just from listening. I tried to visualize what was happening, creating images that were surely only partly right. I didn't have enough information to complete the images, but my mind filled in the gaps.

"Pull up!" Rudd cried.

"I'm trying!" Collins yelled. *"Shit!"*

"The vibration . . ." Rudd reported

There was no response. Grunting, pulling, noises, small collisions, and metal doing what it wasn't designed to do. Then silence.

6

As soon as the NTSB finished playing the cockpit voice recorder, they played it again. The second time was even more riveting. As Collins's voice filled the room again, my mind jumped from one scenario to another as one small noise replaced another, each demanding immediate attention as the key to the puzzle.

I tried to listen to every single detail, but it was impossible. Too much was going on. I gave up taking good notes and just jotted down some of the things that were screaming at me. Ten things that might help explain what had happened. Some implicated my client, some the pilot, and some pointed to things outside the helicopter, which could be, as my law professor at American University used to say, either benign or malignant.

After the second playing, another NTSB technician entered the room with CDs for each of the party members of the investigation teams. The NTSB had loaded the data from the flight data recorder, the FDR, onto each disk. He gave them to Rose. Each CD box had the name of one of the principals on it. Rose looked down at the boxes, counted them mentally, then looked at the audience. "I have here the flight data recorder information. We thought that the FDR was damaged, but it was just the external box. The hard drive was fine and we had no problem getting the data out of the recorder. Since I know you are just as capable as we are of utilizing the software necessary to read the FDR, we're going to provide each of you with a copy of the data. Please do not duplicate it except for internal purposes, and please do not release it outside of your investigation team." She looked around the room. "Do I need to remind you that releasing information to people outside the investigation is *punishable?*

"In this room, tomorrow morning, at the same time as we met today, we will have the computerized animation of the data from the flight data recorder so you can see exactly what happened to the helicopter; many of you will be doing the same thing yourselves and need not attend. Now if you'll excuse me, I have to get back to the crash site. Please come up here after we're done and each of you can take your copy of the FDR data. That's all for now."

Those members of the teams that had been designated to pick up the FDR data made their way up front. Everyone else took the chance to discuss what they had just heard. Marcel approached me. He said quietly as Rachel joined us, "Are you going back out to the site?"

"No, I have to go to that lunch, then to Justice."

"Yes, of course, I had forgotten. You know who's coming to the lunch, don't you?"

"Yeah, David Tripp. He's the general counsel, right?"

"Yes, he is the general counsel, but he won't be the only one there."

This was news to me. In the e-mail I had gotten confirming the luncheon appointment, it only mentioned Tripp and the president of WorldCopter U.S.

Marcel leaned in a little closer. "No, as you might think, this has gotten the attention at the highest levels. They are very concerned about this accident and this investigation. The president of WorldCopter U.S. will be there, *and* the president of World-Copter Europe."

81

I was shocked. He was the man in charge of the entire multibillion-dollar corporation. There had been much speculation on the news about his whereabouts as he had not commented on the accident. Several senators were calling for him to make a statement, but he had not responded. Now he was here in Washington.

"Does anyone else know he's coming?"

"Only those who will be at the meeting."

I had never met either of the presidents of these two companies, and the Frenchman was legendary.

As Rachel and I left the NTSB building, I handed her my keys. "You drive."

She frowned, took the keys, and climbed into the driver's seat. I pulled out my black notebook and studied my notes from the CVR. I circled numbers next to the top ten things in the order I thought we should think about them. Listening to the CVR had caused me to rethink everything I had assumed about this flight. I didn't want to deny that this could still be my client's fault, but after listening to the recording, all I could think about were the malignant scenarios. And much of what I'd heard pointed to Collins.

The Capital Grille was on Pennsylvania

Avenue in the Northwest section of D.C. It was routine to see politicians, lobbyists, high-powered attorneys, and diplomats lunching there. I'd only eaten there a couple times. It was way out of my price range.

We walked up to the beautiful hostess. Rachel said, "We're here to meet with some people from Michelin."

As we headed toward the Fabric Room, a private dining room reserved for us, I saw the television over the bar in the back of the restaurant. It was a replay of the swearing in of the vice president, now president, Cunningham. I had watched it in detail the night before on my new high-definition television. I could see every bead of sweat on the vice president's neck being absorbed by his cotton shirt as he took the oath of office. I had wanted to see his face, and that television allowed me to see it better than I could have seen it if I were there in person. I could see into his soul. I looked for fear, excitement, anything that shouldn't be there. When he had been selected to be A3's vice-presidential candidate, the entire country knew the only reason he had been picked was his unmatched fund-raising ability. His agenda was to get power, and keep it. Pretty simple. But I wondered how far he would be willing to go. At this point I wasn't about to rule anything out. I had long operated by the idea that the more outrageous an explanation was, the more complex, the more it required a vast conspiracy, the less likely it was to be true. But like the saying about paranoia, the fact that most conspiracy theories were ridiculous didn't mean there weren't any conspiracies.

When I had first watched Cunningham's face during the oath, and later when he'd expressed his deep sympathy and personal grief, and the usual stuff about "moving on" and honoring the legacy of his predecessor, I didn't see much that looked out of the ordinary. But when I'd watched it again after my wife had gone to bed, I thought I saw fear.

Who wouldn't be scared to step out of the shadows of obscurity — from the job that wasn't worth a warm pitcher of spit according to Cactus Jack Garner, FDR's first vice president — into the infinitely bright scrutiny and endless hatred that goes with being the president? But as I now watched his face yet again on the television in the bar of the Capital Grille and saw that fear, the chord of recognition that it struck within me was far different from what I expected. Something was going on in his head that I needed to understand. It could be as simple as if this was an assassination, he could be next.

Rachel slowed, and I caught up with her as she reached the private room. Two doors separated it from the main area of the restaurant, and the only indication of its presence was a small bronze plaque that said fabric room. I followed Rachel as she pushed through the first door and then the second. She stopped as soon as she'd entered the room. It wasn't just private, it was secretive.

The large room had a table for ten set for lunch. Several men, none of whom I recognized, were speaking with each other in quiet tones. They stopped talking when we entered, which caused a rather awkward moment.

"Hello, I'm Mike Nolan, and this is my associate Rachel Long."

One of the men broke away and walked over toward me with his hand extended. A small man, perhaps five foot six, he looked pale and exhausted. "Hello, Mike, I'm David Tripp, general counsel for WorldCopter U.S."

We walked over to where three men were conversing. Tripp said, "May I introduce Mr. Jean Claude Martin, president of World-Copter, and Dan Lake, president of World-Copter U.S." I shook hands with both of them, as did Rachel, after which Tripp said, "Mike and Rachel are the attorneys our insurance company has hired." Martin was listening carefully and evaluating us. He had a serious look on his face.

I glanced at the third man who was standing nearby. Tripp hadn't introduced him, and I couldn't tell why. Finally Tripp could sense my curiosity and turned to extend his arm to invite the other man closer. "Mike, let me also introduce William Morton."

"Nice to meet you," I said as we shook hands. I recognized him. I'd seen him at criminal law seminars and on television. He routinely represented people in major political investigations.

I sat down at the table with Tripp to my left, and the two presidents to my right. Morton sat directly across from me. "Thanks for asking us to be here," I said to Tripp quietly, as the others at the table conversed by themselves. "I think you should just let Morton do the criminal side by himself. You're in good hands. Send me back out to the wreckage."

"No, for two reasons," Tripp said as he placed his napkin on his lap. "If the investigation results in criminal charges of any kind against WorldCopter, or a fraud case by the government, it might actually go to

trial. He has lots of trial experience" —
Tripp covered his mouth discreetly so
no one could hear him except me — "but
all of it on the other side of the table." He
glanced at Morton to make sure he wasn't
listening. "He has an amazing reputation,
but he's never tried a criminal case where
he actually *defended* someone. Usually
when he shows up, the government tries to
resolve it. That's what we're hoping for here,
but if they don't? That's where you come
in."

"So he prepares the criminal case and I
try it?"

"Probably together."

I didn't like the sound of that at all. Trial
work was all about setting a tone and selling your personal credibility. You can't have
two lead trial attorneys. "I'm not sure that
would work, but we can talk about that
later."

As the food was served by an army of
waiters, the French president of World-
Copter spoke directly to Morton and me.
He spoke softly but with intensity. His
English was excellent. "This obviously is a
catastrophe for my company, and for the
United States. One thing I can say with
certainty. This was not our fault —"

I interrupted, "I'm not sure we can say

that yet. We'd better find out what happened first."

"You do not understand." He leaned toward me. "No WorldCopter helicopter has *ever* crashed like this. There is no chance that this helicopter came apart in the storm. It is stressed to withstand ten times whatever this storm could produce. That simply did not happen. As far as the blade coming off" — he noticed my surprise — "I spoke with Marcel. That did not happen either. It has never happened, our balancing procedure is flawless, and we will not be held for the scapegoat for that. If this was our fault, they must prove it, but they will not. I promise you."

His promise was ominous. I had represented clients before who offered to "find" anything you wanted, and "unfind" anything you didn't want, and "promised" how things would come out, because they felt so strongly. Sometimes they'd give you a knowing wink at some appropriate time, just enough for you to know they'd taken care of it, and for them to deny it if you had an unexpected flare-up of your fading ethics. But his promise didn't change anything and wouldn't determine the outcome of the investigation. "We really don't know enough to say too much right now —"

"Yes, we do! That is my whole point! Our helicopters don't fail like this! I am *telling* you that, and I will tell the U.S. government that."

"That's fine," I said, glancing at the others at the table, not at all sure how to handle his intensity. "There's just a lot we don't know yet, and if we say that now, it will just sound like a denial, not a conclusion. And you're right about one thing: we can't just rely on the NTSB. They're good, but we cannot assume they'll get this right. You've already got your own in-house team on it, but you need to retain an outside accident reconstructionist and others. Metallurgists, aerodynamicists, lots. I'm sure the insurance carrier will help with that."

He waved his hand and nodded. "Yes, of course. Whatever you need. But the reason we're here right now is because of the meeting at your Justice Department this afternoon. This is where they start preparing the noose for me and my company."

Morton spoke before I had a chance even to prepare a thought. "Yes, sir, we will take care of you. I'm sure they will press on two things primarily: contract fraud — in other words, you delivered a helicopter that was not what they bought, i.e., defective — and breach of national security. The first one is simply going to be determined by what the investigation finds. The second one though is pretty scary. It's my understanding that . . ."

Morton said exactly what everybody needed to hear, that even though the lack of security clearances was probably caused by a lack of diligence on the part of the FBI, it left open the possibility that WorldCopter had an employee who was out to get the president and had placed something into the helicopter or otherwise sabotaged it so that at just the wrong moment, the helicopter would come apart.

"But what do we do *now?*" Dan Lake, the American president of WorldCopter U.S. asked. "What do we need to know going into this ambush?"

I answered while glancing at Morton. "Everything you say will be twisted. Every step you take will be scrutinized. They already think you're a criminal. They would love nothing more than to find an employee of WorldCopter who is responsible for this accident and put him, and you by the way, in prison and WorldCopter out of business. But they're a little torn. They have to consider an actual assassination, or terrorism, so they can't focus on you exclusively. They'll have a team of lawyers looking at you, and others looking elsewhere. I don't want to overstate it, but this could go very badly in a lot of directions."

Jean Claude nearly came out of his chair. "Prison? What do you mean?"

Morton jumped in. "The CEO of a company can be criminally liable for criminal acts of the company."

"Criminally liable?"

"You can go to jail. Literally. Just like a murderer."

"*I* can go to jail if the Justice Department decides? Me personally?" Jean Claude asked, furious.

"Yes, it's possible. Look, they'd have to issue an indictment, and if they couldn't get you to plea, they'd have to go to a trial. We're a long way from that, but Mike is right to let you know. Justice doesn't want to meet with you as your friend. They want to burn down your village. They can do real damage. They can ruin your reputation as a company, they can force you into bankruptcy, and they can put you in prison. And there are *hundreds* of young, ambitious attorneys at Justice who would like nothing better than to bring you down and hang this whole thing on a foreign corporation that stole business from an American —"

"We didn't steal the Marine One contract!

We competed for it against the American companies and won! We were selected by your government. How could anyone say we stole it?"

"They will, I promise."

Martin was deeply troubled about many things. He already knew this accident, or incident, or whatever it turned out to be, could ruin his company. But he had clearly not considered that it could ruin him personally as well. He turned to me. "What of the voice recording? Did you make any conclusions?"

"There were some interesting things. We'll need to study it, both —"

"What did *you* find interesting," he asked, pointing at my chest.

"Marcel would be the one you should —"

"No." Jean Claude paused until I looked him in the eye. "I want *your* opinion."

I hesitated. "Well . . . I . . . a couple of things. The pilot didn't treat the president with much respect. President Adams came to the cockpit and stuck his head in. You can hear the president talk to Collins, but he clearly doesn't respond. Later, right in the middle of a checklist, the copilot tells him that he just can't *ignore* the president. And Collins said, 'I don't really give a shit.' That's a remarkable statement by the pilot of Marine One."

Morton was frowning with his arms folded, but the president was interested. "What do you think —"

"I think it's —"

A young man walked into the room carrying a cell phone. "Excuse me, sir," he said to Jean Claude. "It's Marcel. He needs to speak with you immediately. He told me to interrupt. Sorry." The young man handed his phone to the president.

Jean Claude took the phone and spoke to Marcel, then listened intently. He looked around the room at us, knowing information that he couldn't share, but was anxious to do. He continued to listen, then a look of complete surprise or shock came over his face. He nodded, closed the flip phone, and returned it to its owner.

We all waited, anxious for this report that called for such an interruption. I watched Jean Claude's face carefully. It wasn't horror, and it wasn't pleasure.

Martin said, "He has reviewed the flight data recorder information. It is on our computer. He said everything is normal until very late in the flight. As the helicopter begins one of its descents, then something happened."

"What?" I asked, dying for the answer.

"We don't know. The flight data recorder stops."

We were all puzzled. Flight data recorders didn't just stop. Like the cockpit voice recorder, they ran on a continuous thirty-minute loop; there was no on/off switch.

"Did Marcel say why it stopped?" Morton asked.

"No. He is completely confused."

I couldn't imagine how that could happen. "Has Marcel checked with the NTSB? Did we get bad data — a bad CD?"

The president nodded. "That was his first call. The NTSB said theirs stops in the same place." He looked directly at me. "It now will be even more difficult to find out what happened." He leaned over, anger in his voice. "Get all the experts you need. Get them paid for by the insurance company, or if they won't pay, I will. But you must find out what happened to Marine One. You must solve this *before* the U.S. government does, because *we* will tell *them* what happened, not wait for them to tell us!"

7

By the time Rachel and I got out of the car near Justice, the sky had cleared. I asked Rachel, "What did the radio say about the funeral?"

"The parade, or whatever they call it, will be Friday. He'll lie in state at the Capitol Building. Closed coffin. Then there's a memorial ceremony at the National Cathedral on Sunday. Dignitaries from around the world . . . I don't remember the rest."

"Here we are." We walked through the sliding glass door, which closed behind us, leaving us locked in a small glass space that allowed the guards to see us. The glass was bulletproof. After about five seconds the other doors opened and we passed into the lobby. We told one of the guards who we were and were led to a conference room on the third floor at the west end of the building. The others were already there. No one was there from Justice yet. I wondered whether they were trying to annoy us by being late.

Morton said, "Let me take the lead on this, Mike."

Fine with me. Arguing with Justice wasn't my favorite sport.

Everybody was standing on the window side of the table except Morton and me. Suddenly the door was thrown open and three people walked in, two men and a woman. The one in the lead was in his late forties. He was clearly in charge and wanted everyone to know it. He was balding but wore his hair in a buzz so you couldn't really tell. He wore thin-wire glasses and had thin, angry lips. He placed the files he was carrying on the table in the middle, and the other two flanked him on either side. The woman was in her late thirties and attractive. The other man was remarkably tall and looked unintelligent. The one in charge looked around the room and said, "I'm Richard Packer. Deputy attorney general in the Criminal Division. I deal mostly with fraud cases." He let that sink in for a moment. "This is Alice Tomlinson, she's the assistant deputy, and this is Ed Wellenger."

We each introduced ourselves and Richard said, "Please, sit down."

He sat at the head of the table and opened

a folder in front of him. "First, I'd like to thank you all for coming. I know you've come a long way, and I want to get right to the point. We will have many details to work out, and we have many requests that we would like you to comply with immediately. But first, let me say, that at the direction of the attorney general, who is acting at the direction of President Cunningham —"

It was jarring to hear "President Cunningham."

"— we've opened a criminal fraud investigation into the contract that was entered into between the United States and World-Copter, relating specifically to the purchase of Marine One." He opened the massive briefcase sitting next to him on the floor and pulled out a document. "I have here a memorandum from the Pentagon which outlines the process by which this helicopter was selected, the representations made by WorldCopter both in the contract and outside of the contract, and concludes with the concerns that have been raised since the crash. I'm glad to see that you are represented by counsel," Packer said to Martin. "This prosecution could result in your personal incarceration as well as that —"

Morton spoke intensely but quietly. "There's no need to try to intimidate our clients. They get it. But they also know something you don't. There has been no fraud. So they're not afraid of an investigation. We'll cooperate, but we will not submit our clients to your browbeating. Clear?"

Packer ignored Morton and adjusted his eyeglasses in that way of officious bureaucratic men whose power is derived from something other than ability. "I have brought with me a list of things that the United States will need immediately." I loved it when they did that, acted as if they *were* the country and spoke for everyone in it. "We will need documents, e-mails, access to numerous personnel, samples of parts, drawings, blueprints, and access to your offices and manufacturing plant both here and in France. If you are even considering not cooperating and voluntarily producing this information, we will immediately issue the appropriate subpoenas, and then, today, this afternoon, I will call a press conference to announce that we have initiated a fraud investigation and that WorldCopter is not cooperating. How do you want to play this?"

Morton sat in stunned silence sticking his hand out for a copy of the list, which was not forthcoming.

I'd seen this kind of blustering dozens of times. "Would you mind if I asked you something?" I asked suddenly.

Packer looked at me with contempt. "And you are?"

"Mike Nolan, attorney for WorldCopter."

"I thought that Mr. Morton was representing them in this matter."

"We both are. So again, may I ask you a question?"

"Of course."

"Has the NTSB formed a conclusion on what caused this accident that I missed? Because if they haven't, how exactly do you find the nerve to begin an 'investigation' of one of the finest companies in the world with zero evidence of what you claim to be investigating? Isn't this because one senator — and really the press — have *demanded* an investigation? All you're doing right now is diverting resources from finding out what actually happened. I suggest you let the NTSB figure out what caused this accident, and *then* if you think WorldCopter needs to go to the woodshed, bring it."

Packer was unmoved. "I already know that WorldCopter failed in its obligations to the United States. The people who worked on Marine One, we now learn, never obtained the appropriate security clearances. They are in *violation.* So NTSB's conclusions, while interesting, will not determine the direction of my investigation."

I leaned forward with my elbows on the table, nearly standing. "And do you know *why* WorldCopter was in violation? Because the FBI didn't do its job. *Your* investigators failed to go to France. They were too *busy.* So they failed to do the job that they refused to entrust to the French government. They're the ones who delayed the security clearances, and yet at the same time, *your* Pentagon, which has given you that supposed memo about the contract, is almost certainly silent about how dicked-up the process was. They *demanded* that no construction be done until the security clearances were completed and, on the other hand, *demanded* that the helicopter be delivered on schedule or there would be massive late-performance penalties." I sat back and waited, then said, "I think we should just wait on all this until the NTSB investigation is completed."

Packer stared at me with contempt. He finally said, "No. Your client will produce these materials immediately." He slid the list across the table to me. I picked it up, glanced at it, slid it to Morton, and said, "Look, Dick, I'm here to tell you there's no call for this investigation. I fly that helicopter all the time in the Marine Corps reserves.

Do you hear them clamoring for an investigation? No. It's the best helicopter they've ever flown. There has never been a fatal crash in the history of its production. There has never been an accident of any kind since the Marines started flying it three years ago, and there's no reason to believe this accident is because of the design or any manufacturing problem."

Packer ignored me and said to Morton, "So let's go down this list and you can tell me which group of documents will be delivered to this office in ten days, and which ones will take thirty."

By the time Rachel and I got back to the office, Annapolis was quiet, lit only by streetlights and an occasional car. Everyone in the firm knew we were coming back, and several had waited to hear what had happened. We gave them a quick summary, then I went up to my office to drop off some papers before heading home. Rick Berberian followed me upstairs. He closed the door behind him. He never closed my door, so something was bugging him. He made small talk for a while while I packed up, then said, "This is an amazing case, Mike. Biggest thing either of us has ever had, no doubt."

"No doubt." I sat down waiting for him to say whatever was on his mind. We had started the firm together, expecting it to grow to maybe five lawyers, and knew each other well. We had counted pennies together on many late nights in the early days of our partnership.

He sat across from me and said, "So I've been thinking about this." He suddenly stood again and began pacing. "How are we going to do this? If you do the criminal investigation, represent WorldCopter in the international inquiry, it might take three or four lawyers to staff it full-time. And if you keep going on this accident investigation, and some civil case comes out of it, one of the Secret Service widows wakes up and realizes there's a pot of gold waiting if this helicopter truly failed, you'll need five or ten people. We don't have anything close to that. If it's not properly staffed, it could go completely off track, and the case could be lost."

"I'll take care of it."

He sat again and forced himself to fold his hands on his knees to look calm. "If we lose this, it will ruin us. Financially. Our reputation will be shot and we could be sued for malpractice, for not preparing properly. We don't have the experience, or the depth."

I stared at him in disbelief. I'd never seen him crack. He was absolutely unmovable in business negotiations and contracts, which is what he did. Now he was flipping out about what I was doing? I didn't need it. "What have you been smoking, Rick? I can handle this. If we need more people, I'll get more. And if it gets lost one way or another, it won't be because of me, I promise. Relax. And how could it ruin us financially? We're going to get paid whether we win or lose. Our regular hourly rate. Don't worry about it."

"You think if you lose a case this big, they won't look for a scapegoat? They'll sue us for malpractice."

"We have malpractice insurance, Rick."

"Yeah, twenty million dollars. That won't cover a tenth of this case. Remember I wanted to get one hundred million dollars in coverage?"

"Shit, Rick. That cost ten times as much. And if we make somebody lose a hundred mil, we deserve to go bankrupt." He was starting to bother me. "You've got to settle down. What's gotten into you?"

He rubbed his tired, stubbled face. "One of the legal reporters was going on about how outmatched you were going to be, no matter what you ended up doing. He said it was like starting a Single A pitcher in the World Series. He said you were going to get shelled, and you and your whole firm would come down around your head."

"Nice. And who was that?"

"I don't know. I'd never heard of him."

"And rather than shrug it off because you know me, because we started a firm together, starved together, you jump on that bandwagon and start pissing all over me? Damn, Rick!" I tried to control my anger.

He shook his head. "I don't know, Mike. It's just such a huge deal. Big firms in New York or Washington handle huge cases like this, not a small shop in Annapolis with two partners. It's a lot of weight to carry, that's all."

"No, it's an opportunity."

He stared out the dark window without saying anything for an awkwardly long time. He put his hands in his back pockets and turned again toward me. His face was lined with stress. "You ever do any reading into the Kennedy assassination?"

"Not much. Seemed like a UFO kind of thing to me."

"Some of it. I take it that you don't think the helicopter failed."

"Not sure, really. But I find it hard to

believe it did."

"Well, then, where does that lead?"

"Meaning?"

"Presidents don't die that often, Mike."

"And?" I said, concerned with the look that was forming on his face.

"And you're saying it wasn't from a mechanical thing."

"I said I don't know, but I doubt it."

"Then that means somebody wanted him dead. Right? Am I missing something? If it wasn't an accident, somebody was trying to kill him."

"I didn't say that. Could have been the weather."

"You don't believe that."

"No, I don't, but it's possible."

He waved his arm. "I'm talking about what *you* think. You say I should trust you? Well, I do. And I think that what *you* think is that someone wanted the president dead."

"I'm not ready to jump to *any* conclusion. Can't do that at the start of an investigation. Colors your thinking."

"But if you're right that it wasn't the helicopter's fault, then somebody else did it. That means somebody else killed him. As in *on purpose*."

"Is that what this is all about?"

"I'm just trying to think this stuff through,

Mike. Is my thinking wrong?"

"It's pretty far-fetched. I'm not convinced of that at all."

"If somebody killed him, and you're out there trying to prove it wasn't WorldCopter, then your only way out will be to find out who it was. Am I right?"

"Sort of."

"You ever think about that maybe they won't *want* you to find them? And that they probably already know who you are?"

"What, you think somebody's going to come after us?"

"I've read enough history to know that when the emperor dies, you don't want to be anywhere near it."

"There will be a rational explanation of this accident, Rick."

He wasn't satisfied. "What I'm saying is, I want you to — how do you always put it? Keep your head on a swivel." He jerked on the handle of my office door and walked out.

He was right about one thing. If someone killed the president, the last thing they would want was for me to find out what really happened. Fair enough to tell me to keep that in mind. We didn't know what was behind the curtain.

■ ■ ■ ■

I headed to the WorldCopter offices in Maryland outside D.C. the next morning before the sun was up. I told Rachel to stay at the office and do some quick research on federal security clearances for foreign corporations, and background research on the WorldCopter helicopter involved in this accident. I needed to know every other incident it had been involved in, the cause of every accident, and the helicopter's reputation. Now that I had stuck my neck out at Justice on how there had never been a fatal accident in this helicopter, something I was pretty sure about, I needed to know about every incident Justice might cite back to me.

Tripp was waiting for me in the lobby of the sprawling WorldCopter building. It looked like a factory but was really more of an assembly plant. WorldCopter made everything in France and shipped it to the United States for assembly. This allowed them to claim that it was an American helicopter. It was all about appearances. Everyone knew it was a French helicopter, or rather a helicopter made in France by a European consortium known as World-Copter.

Tripp gave me a badge and hustled me through security. "They've got it set up in the computer room."

"You watch it?"

"Not yet. Here we are," he said, opening a heavy steel door.

I was surprised at the number of people in the room. This was to be the first playing of the combined animation of the flight data recorder and cockpit voice recorder that anyone other than a technician would actually see. Even Marcel hadn't seen the entire thing; he'd just sampled it to make sure it looked right. Several technicians and engineers were standing around the computer console where the FDR had been loaded up. Others, including Tripp, stood against the wall trying to stay out of the way.

Marcel nodded his head to one of the technicians standing at the door, who dimmed the lights. Another one turned up the speakers connected to the computer. Everyone focused on the large, flatscreen monitor that had been connected to the computer and hung on the wall. I was anxious to see what movements of the helicopter coincided with the various noises I'd heard on the cockpit voice recorder. The background was dark blue for the sky and green for the land. There was no attempt by the computer to put any terrain into the images. The flight data recorder had no terrain information. The colors were simply background to help discern the horizon. The voices could be heard exactly where in the flight they were talking. Marcel had had the CVR transcribed too, so the subtitles went across the bottom of the screen as quickly as they were spoken.

Collins's voice was now familiar as the helicopter approached its landing at the White House. We stood silently and listened again to Collins's conversations with his copilot and the head of the Secret Service detail as they prepared to take off, then President Adams's approach to Collins and his shocking comments. None of that was on the FDR — it showed a motionless helicopter sitting on the lawn with the rotor blades turning.

Marine One took off and flew through what we knew to be the night. The turbulence was obvious in the bouncing helicopter in spite of Collins's attempts to keep it straight and level. He fought the storm and the turbulence the entire way, shifting altitudes in a vain attempt to avoid the worst. As he approached the final minute of flight, the room became deathly quiet. We looked at every movement and listened to every sound now correlated to movement as Collins searched for clear air. We heard his exclamations and watched him fighting the helicopter, cursing, then the flight data recorder information stopped. So did the helicopter in the animation, but the voices continued as we listened through to the end of the tape.

As the voices stopped, the screen went blank. Nobody said anything. We all had new thoughts, some things that confirmed what we had thought, others that conflicted. But not only was the puzzle not solved, the animation raised more questions than it answered.

The question foremost on my mind, though, was why the flight data recorder had stopped. I looked at Marcel. "You find the circuit-breaker panels?"

"Yes. But they're burned."

"Can you tell what circuit breakers are out?"

"Maybe. They have the pieces of plastic, and they're going to have to reconstruct the board. Some of the circuit breakers are still there intact, but most have been burned off."

I thought about where the circuit-breaker panels were near the pilot and what circuit breakers were on them. "Is there a circuit breaker for the flight data recorder?"

Everybody turned to me at once. The implications of the question were self-evident.

Marcel answered, "Yes."

"I know where the hydraulic-boost-pump circuit breaker is," I said. It was down to the right, just below the pilot's knee, and back a little bit on the right side. "Is the flight data recorder circuit breaker near that?"

Marcel stared at me. He nodded his head slowly. "Right below it. Unmarked. It looks like a dummy. Do you think he tried to pull the hydraulic breaker and got the FDR?"

I stood without answering for a minute. Everybody was looking at me, expecting me to say something, but it just didn't make any sense. Finally I said, "If you had a boost pump failure and had a circuit breaker pop out from the boost pump, he'd figure that out pretty quick and try to reset it. So he'd reach down, feel it, and push it in. The only thing I can imagine that would involve the flight data recorder circuit breaker would be if he decided to pull it out before he pushed it in and grabbed the wrong one. Seems unlikely."

Marcel threw his hands up. "Then why else would the flight data recorder circuit breaker have popped?"

"We don't know that it did. But maybe there was something wrong with the flight data recorder." Or he pulled it on purpose, I said to myself. "Did you load this flight data recorder info into the simulator?"

"Of course. It has been ready all night."

We headed toward the simulator room down a long hallway. I said to Marcel, "Does it have an FDR circuit breaker?"

"No, it's a standard helicopter, not Marine One."

"I want to fly it and feel what Collins felt."

Marcel held the door for me and the others who wanted to watch the flight from the control room of the simulator. The simulator room itself was enormous. It held three fully operational helicopter simulators on hydraulic stands. The cockpits were complete and identical to those operational helicopters. Each was surrounded by a dome that could project any image from mountains to bad weather to images of other aircraft.

We climbed up to the simulator that had been prepared, and I strapped into the right seat, the pilot-in-command seat, where Collins was sitting on the night of the accident. I put on the headset and Marcel took the left seat. An accomplished helicopter pilot, he had spent ten years flying attack helicopters with the French army. The cockpit was fairly dark, but the internal lights made the preflight routine feel like a normal night launch. I went through all the checklists from memory, and Marcel was right there with me turning on some of the systems to get us going. We could just have told the computer "go," and they would have put the simulator immediately in the air approaching the White House as Collins was at the beginning of the CVR. But I wanted to fly it from Andrews Air Force Base to the White House just as Collins had. I wanted to leave there with the same fuel Collins had and fly to the position he had gone to when we first encountered him. Then if things changed, if the computer put switches and settings different from where I had them, it would mean either Collins had done things differently from me, or he'd missed something.

Marcel and I took off from Andrews and headed for the White House. WorldCopter had actually flown the route from Andrews to the White House numerous times to film the route and get good video to put into the simulator to train the Marine One pilots.

I had asked them to plug in the actual visibility and ceiling that existed at the White

House when Collins made his approach; so we weren't seeing much on the way into Washington, just an occasional light from a monument. The synthetic aperture radar, though, made the terrain look like a moving picture. We could recognize the White House on the radar before we saw it.

I began my descent, nearing the point where the FDR and CVR would take over. I was right on track when Collins's voice came over my headset. I released the controls and looked for changes. A couple of things were set differently, different preferences for a couple of displays, but nothing significant.

The cyclic in my right hand — the stick, as nonhelicopter people might call it — and the collective in my left hand, which controlled the engine and the pitch of the rotor blades, moved as if possessed. Knowing it was duplicating the exact movements of a dead man made it even more spooky than it would have been anyway. I listened carefully again to Collins's conversations with President Adams and the others, then prepared for the moment when Collins lifted the helicopter off on its last flight. I placed my hands on the controls lightly, so I could feel everything he had done. My feet were equally light on the pedals that controlled the tail rotor.

Then Collins and I, together, lifted off from the South Lawn. He flew the helicopter with a confidence and fluidity I had never seen before. It was like driving in a car with a professional instead of just another driver. I tried to anticipate how he would handle the helicopter, thinking how I would get it to go where I knew he wanted it to go; but every time he would do it just a little differently from what I anticipated, and I would know immediately that his way was better. More efficient, smoother. Brilliant.

The White House faded in the mist and rain below us as we climbed aggressively to the northwest, away from the ground, where things were always the most dangerous. If you get tossed around at five thousand feet, it's just annoying. If you get tossed around at fifteen feet, it can be fatal. All those spinning blades and so many things to hit.

The flight was well-known to us by now, and we watched carefully as Collins took us through it. There weren't any new surprises en route. The simulator tried to indicate rough weather and turbulence, but was admittedly imperfect in doing so. Still, we could tell it was one hell of a bad night.

As we approached the last minute of the

flight, Marcel and I looked at each other, wondering what we'd notice from here that we hadn't seen anywhere else. The cyclic was moving much more than it had before. I could tell Collins was fighting what was happening. No doubt much of it was due to the gusting winds, which made me wonder if he was moving the cyclic or if it was simply being left behind in numerous involuntary jerks of the helicopter, like hitting the curb with your tire and feeling the wheel turn in your hands.

The final movements of the controls in the cockpit *were* like hitting a curb in a car. Abrupt changes, but in a short throw. Fighting something, back and forth, movement not obvious from watching the animation from any angle. Then one last thing before the simulator stopped moving — the nose of the helicopter pitched up dramatically. Again, watching on a screen didn't give you the full appreciation for the fifteen-degree nose-up attitude. You could certainly see it, but seeing it from the cockpit was much more dramatic. Something bad had happened right there. Before the FDR cut out. What it led to after that was impossible to say, but I knew something had happened. Not a gust of wind or turbulence. Something else.

The flight data recorder stopped and the simulator froze in its place. We checked the altitude, the heading, and the attitude — how the helicopter was situated in the air — and all the instruments. We looked at each other with the same puzzlement and ended the flight. The hydraulic platform hissed slightly as it returned to its resting place. We waited until it settled and stepped out.

We stood around the simulator on the smooth concrete floor and discussed what we had seen. There must have been ten of us. Lots of theories, lots of questions for Marcel and me. We told them what we could and suggested that they all go through the entire flight just as we had.

As we were walking back to the computer room to talk it out, I said to Marcel, "You feel that pitch up at the end? Right before the FDR went dead?"

"Yes."

"Any ideas?"

"No. I will give it much thought. I am sure you will too."

When we regathered in the computer room, there were many long faces. Everyone knew there was no conclusive proof about anything. We all had thought when we put everything together in the animation and the simulator, the answer would lie in front of us. I knew that was unlikely when I'd heard the FDR had stopped, but I was hopeful. Now I was as confused as any of them.

I said my good-byes and walked to my car. The movement of the controls had made me wonder about a lot of things. I still wasn't sure I could trust Collins. Great pilot, sure, but not a great guy. I had to know everything there was to know about him, and I had to keep it to myself. I couldn't exactly be telling people I had a vague suspicion that the pilot of Marine One crashed on purpose. Saying I suspected Collins was too strong. I simply allowed it to exist as a theoretical possibility. I was probably the only person in the world who did. The FDR showed someone fighting a storm. Or at least that's how it was supposed to look. Collins was smart, though, and knew the helicopter had a CVR and an FDR. If he had set this all up, he'd know we'd be listening. He could make it look however he wanted.

I had to find out more about him to put that crazy idea to rest, or to sound the alarm. I headed for my office to call Jason Britt, a Marine pilot I'd known for years and who was one of the pilots in my reserve squadron. He had flown with Collins in his last active-duty squadron before going to fly for the president. I had to talk to him before the NTSB did.

8

I needed to call Britt right away, but first things first. I asked Rachel and Justin, my unique, disheveled paralegal, to come to my office. We sat in a small conference room just down the hall from my office, between Rachel's office and Justin's carrel in the library. I said, "We need to get all the records we can on Collins. Justin, put together a Freedom of Information Act request to DOD. I want everything. Personnel files, fitness reports, test scores, discipline, go back to the Naval Academy — grades, infractions, demerits, everything. And get on the Internet. Look at everything that's out there since the crash. I'm sure they're already doing a Lee Harvey on him and accusing him of being somebody's pawn. I just want to know what's being said. Look at everything."

"Will do," Justin said as he wrote. He looked up at me. "You think the government will give all that to us?"

"No. We'll have to fight them over documents. Probably have to file a lawsuit to enforce it. But the sooner we get on it, the sooner we can force the issue."

Rachel asked, "Know anybody at the Pentagon who works in personnel?"

"Yeah, but I can't do that." I pondered for a moment. "We've also got to find out things about him that the government wouldn't even know. His personal life, his family life, everything. All the things he's lied about in his physical exams, or his background." I had an idea. I looked at their faces to see if they had thought of the same thing at the same time. "You know what we need to do?"

They shook their heads.

"Call Tinny."

Rachel said, "Well, if you want information and don't care too much about how you get it, he's the guy."

I said to Justin, "Dial it."

He reached over to the credenza, grabbed the phone, and pulled it onto the conference room table. He knew Tinny's number by heart. We used Tinny on nearly every criminal case we handled. Tinny gave me an advantage the prosecutors always underestimated. When they knew he was working on a case, they paid more attention, but I tended not to tell them until trial was imminent.

Justin dialed the number, and we heard Tinny's cell phone ring. He answered it in his recognizable voice with the one word he always said when he answered his cell phone; "Byrd."

I spoke loudly into the speakerphone, "Tinny, Mike Nolan."

"Hey, big shot. What's up?"

He knew what I needed him for. It was always the same thing. He found things, or found things out. He knew how to dig and to find information no one else could find. After a ten-year stint in the Marine Corps as an enlisted man, he got his private investigator's license. He did that for a couple of years, then worked as an investigator for the Baltimore District Attorney's Office. He ultimately moved up to chief investigator for that office. He'd somehow gotten sideways with them, just short of his retirement, which made his departure all the more puzzling. He never talked about it. He implied it had to do with race. He was black and the new DA was a white woman who apparently hated him. He did rub some people the wrong way and had a general distrust of authority, but mostly for those who had authority and didn't deserve it.

After his falling-out, he had moved to Washington, D.C., to set up his own private investigation firm. He now worked almost exclusively investigating criminal cases on the defense side and loved making life difficult for district attorneys, U.S. attorneys, and other arrogant government-employed assholes.

"Tinny, I need your help."

"Hold on. Let me get in my car." We could hear him disarming the alarm in his car — his prized black Corvette — opening the door, closing it behind him, then being enveloped in silence. "All right. I'm in a big damn hurry so talk fast."

"The government's already threatening criminal charges against WorldCopter, one of the families will probably hire an attorney who will sue them for infinity dollars, and I got all kinds of questions that need answering. I want you to help me answer them. There's nobody better. I want you to help me dig into everything, starting with the pilot."

"The pilot?"

"The pilot. Collins. You've heard some people on the news talking about what a fabulous pilot he was; war hero. But I've got suspicions I need help with."

"You're going to hang this on the pilot? In the middle of the biggest thunderstorm in the history of Maryland?"

"I'm not trying to hang it on anybody. I'm trying to keep from getting hung on. I'm chasing every fact down every rabbit hole, but I need people who can navigate down rabbit holes that I can't fit in. That's you."

"I'm bigger than you, Nolan, not smaller."

"Yeah. The metaphor broke down. You get the point though."

"What do you want me to check out on this pilot?"

"Everything you can — medical records, fitness reports, his citations, everything. We've got to get them from the Pentagon, from family, wherever we can."

"One Marine to another, Nolan, I can get those records out of the Pentagon. You know I can."

I looked at Justin and Rachel, who were staring at me. I put up my hands. "I don't want you doing anything illegal; this all has to be aboveboard."

"Right. What else?"

"We should probably get together and talk about all the other things. I've got a to-do list that's taken on a life of its own. You've got to help me get some sleep, Tinny."

"All right, Mike, let's do this. But there's

one other thing. I don't think I told you about my new rate sheet."

I just rolled my eyes. I saw this coming. "A new rate sheet? You're killing me."

"No. I wouldn't do that. And the new rates are effective today. I'll fax you a copy of the sheet this afternoon."

"What are your new rates?"

"As of right now, they only apply to complex cases. I'll work the other cases into the new rates as the new cases come in, but unfortunately they're twice what I've charged up until just yesterday."

"Come on, Tinny. Give me a break."

"I'm giving you a break by getting involved in this. This thing has stink all over; you just can't smell it yet. You're too excited about being involved. I'm telling you, this thing's going to be ugly. When you're talking about the president being killed, his family, his wife, an American hero pilot, and a French helicopter company, the currents are going to be so deep and so swift, you'll get drowned in about a millisecond. And I'll be there to pull you out. I may have to triple my rates."

"Just send me the rate sheet. I'll be in touch."

"I'll send you that rate sheet right away. By the way, this pilot, Collins, what's his

125

first name? What's his address?"

"You jumping right on this, Tinny?"

"If you think this guy's got something to do with the accident, somebody else is going to think that too. I'm sure the feds are already digging, but I'll beat them to it. I promise I'll get to something before they do. Something they might not even look for."

"His name is Chuck Collins. His address is in Woodbridge, Virginia."

"Charles? Okay. What's his wife's name?"

"Melissa. What difference does this make? You leave her out of this."

"Not a chance, friend, not a chance. See ya." And with that, his cell phone went dead.

I looked at Rachel and Justin, who were both still staring at the speakerphone. "I hope that was the right decision."

Rachel said, "He's never failed us before. It's just sometimes his methods are a little sketchy."

"I've got to make a call," I said. They got the hint and left for their own offices. I dialed Britt's number at his office in Arlington, Virginia.

Britt was a Beltway bandit. His company lived off government contracts, mostly military. He worked for Bachman Aerospace, which was developing a series of light-helicopter UAVs — unmanned aerial vehicles. Drones. His division had developed a helicopter the size of a coffee table that had eight rotor blades, four rotating in one direction, and another four on top of the first four rotating in the opposite direction. Counterrotating blades. No tail rotor necessary. It ran on a small jet engine the size of my forearm and could fly 120 miles per hour after vertical takeoff. It carried all the sensors the Marine Corps wanted: video, infrared, and the newest radar system. Even weapons. The Marine Corps was hot to purchase this amazing little helicopter. Britt was in the middle of the contract proposal and had no time, but when he heard that the call was from me, he immediately picked up the phone. "Nolan! What are you doing?"

"Thanks for taking my call, Jason, I know you're busy."

"Never too busy for a fellow Marine."

I wasn't sure how to approach him. I needed to gather everything I could on Collins, but I didn't want to make Britt think I was taking advantage of our friendship. "How about Marine One?" I said casually.

Britt sighed. "Unbelievable. Absolutely unbelievable. Can't believe they took off in that storm. You got any ideas?"

"Yeah, I got lots of ideas, but I should tell you what I'm doing."

"What?"

"You remember I practice law in Annapolis?"

"Sure. From Marine pilot to parasite on the great American economy, keeping the world safe for felons and child molesters."

"I'll remember that when you get arrested. Because I'm sure you wouldn't want to be represented by some *parasite* attorney."

"True. I'd rather rot in prison than pay a cent to a lawyer. So what are you talking about?"

"I do civil cases too, not just criminal."

"And?"

"I've been hired to represent WorldCopter in the crash of Marine One."

"Are you shitting me? Talk about getting thrown into it."

"Yeah, it's a pretty crazy time. So far it's just a bunch of investigations, but I'm sure the other shoe will drop at some point. It's the kind of case that you always want, until you're in it, then you wonder what happened to your life. Look, I need to ask you about something, but if you don't want to talk to me about it, that's okay. But I have to find some stuff out. Can you help me out?"

"What?"

"Collins."

There was a pregnant pause as Britt suddenly got the point of my call. "I wondered when somebody was going to start asking me about him. I didn't think it'd be you."

"Anybody else asked you about him? Since the accident?"

"No."

"Listen, if you don't want to talk to me, that's cool. A lot of this is going to get real official real fast, but I need to do some quick checking on Collins. What do you think?"

His voice warmed only slightly. "I'm gonna be answering a lot of questions about him anyway."

I picked up my pen and prepared to take silent notes. Witnesses clam up when they hear a keyboard. "So, let's go back to the beginning."

Once Britt got over the idea of talking about Collins, he began gushing information. He spent an hour talking with me. They had been in the same squadron more than once. He had observed Collins up close both as a peer and as a superior officer. Several things he said stuck with me.

After telling me about a near accident Collins had been involved in, which wasn't his fault, he mentioned in passing that Collins read a lot.

I knew a lot of Marines who liked to read, contrary to their general reputation. Some of it was from the "Marine officer reading list," which was started by General Alfred M. Gray when he was the commandant of the Marine Corps. But this sounded different. "Where did he read?"

"What do you mean?"

"How would you know he read a lot?"

"Because I saw him."

"Where?"

"Ready room. Kept books in his chair in the ready room."

"That's odd."

"It was. Lots of guys were interested in politics, what was going on, Rush Limbaugh sort of books. You know."

"But he was different?"

"Yeah. Very."

"What did he read?"

"It was more serious stuff. Hard-core economics books, for one. Some guy from Austria — can't remember his name — and books nobody else had ever heard of that always claimed to have the Secret. I guess I'd say he seemed fascinated by conspiracy theories."

"You mean black helicopters and world-domination conspiracies?"

"Sort of. I don't know. He didn't really talk about them much. He was sort of a loner."

"Did you get a flavor at all? Anything you can remember?"

"It's hard to describe. Most Marines support the government generally. Except for taxes of course" — he laughed — "which they think are mostly just pissed away and should be used to buy more airplanes and ammo. But some people, like Collins, have a deep distrust of the government. I forget what the political party is called, or what that theory is. They don't think there should be any government."

"Anarchists?"

"No, these guys think there should be some police, and military. What —"

"Libertarians?"

"Yeah, that's it. I'm not sure if he was a sort of radical libertarian, but he thought the government was corrupt. Really corrupt. At the highest levels, and would read book after book about it. He'd get smug and sarcastic about it. When something would go wrong, like we had to deploy early — which was most of the time, by the way —"

"Tell me about it."

"Well, he'd say, 'What do you expect?' and have this snotty smile. Always thought there was a wizard somewhere pulling the levers."

I was writing furiously. "Anything else?"

"Not really. Great pilot. Great guy, usually."

"Was he in any organizations or anything?"

"I don't know, not that —"

"Did the FBI interview you when he got the job as CO of HMX-1?"

"Yeah. What a joke."

"You tell them all this?"

"Hell no. Of course not."

"Why not?"

"They didn't ask about what he read. They asked stupid questions: was he a member of an organization whose intention was to overthrow the government of the United States? What a dumb-ass question. I'm sure they get a lot of yes answers to that brilliant question. I wouldn't have been real talkative anyway. I didn't want to kill his chance to get his dream job."

"Well, was he in any weird organizations?"

"I don't think so. He got a lot of magazines and stuff too."

"You're making him sound like a UFO nut."

"No, he wasn't like that. But a similar

mentality. You've seen it. They'll believe anything — at least in that area. They obsess about it, talk to other people who are obsessing, and sort of form an insiders' club. *They've* broken the code. You know the type."

"Any other officers he hung out with who were on the same page with him on this stuff?"

"Not really. He was pretty much on his own. He used to tell us, though, that our oath was to fight 'all enemies foreign *and* domestic.' You know, the oath — 'I' — state your name — 'do solemnly swear or affirm that I will support and defend the Constitution of the United States against all enemies —' "

"Sure."

"Well, he'd see Ted Kennedy or somebody on the TV, and his jaw would clench. He'd say, 'Foreign *and* domestic.' Like Ted Kennedy was a domestic enemy."

"Good pilot though."

"Probably the best in the Corps. It wasn't even close really. Total natural. You know, frankly, if I were the president? I'd want Collins flying my helicopter too. He'd get you there."

"Except this time."

"Well, I'd bet it wasn't his fault. I'd bet

that French helicopter killed him *and* the president."

"That's my client."

"Too bad for you."

Then I asked him the critical question. "So, Britt, help me figure out how this happened, how did the president's helicopter go down?"

"How the hell would I know? You're the one doing the investigation, why you asking me?"

"Just wondered if you had any theories. You think of anything in Collins's personality that could contribute to the crash?"

There was a pause. Britt finally asked, "What are you getting at?"

"Nothing specific."

"He could screw it up just like any of us could, I guess. He wasn't Superman. But if I were going to pick the pilot least likely to screw up flying through a storm, it would be him. Do I think that's what happened? No."

"But could he have caused it? Could he have . . . caused it?"

The light went on. "Are you asking me whether he did it on *purpose?*"

"You yourself said he could get a conspiracy theory in his head. I've got to consider every angle."

"Shit, Nolan! What are you trying to do? You trying to hang this on a fellow Marine? What the hell kind of shaft job is that? Look, I've got to go. Talk to you later." The line went dead.

Senator Blankenship had accomplished much of what he wanted simply by announcing the hearings. As the chairman of the Senate Armed Services Committee, he could force hearings, which he did. He set them for the Caucus Room in the Russell Senate Office Building, not coincidentally the site of the Watergate and Iran-contra hearings. He was furious and was determined to make WorldCopter feel his heat.

Within a week after his initial press conference, subpoenas had flown out of the Capitol to all corners of the country and even overseas. The subpoenas were not effective overseas, but ignoring them would be untenable for WorldCopter. So Jean Claude Martin was one of the several "voluntary" foreign witnesses.

Blankenship had imposed his will on Lisa Romaro, the Senate majority leader, to start the hearings three weeks after the accident, before the dust had even settled. He wanted to get people on the record before they had a chance to construct their revisionist his-

135

tory of Marine One.

Blankenship knew the DOJ was pushing WorldCopter hard, gathering documents and tickling the pearl handles of their criminal accusations; but he wanted to get it all in front of the world and the television cameras to see what WorldCopter said in response to hard questions. He didn't really care if the testimony he wanted jeopardized the investigation of the Justice Department. He was doing this for the country.

As the hearings got under way, Blankenship was pleased that the entire country and much of the rest of the world tuned in. The government had been quiet about the crash so far, and this was the first chance for people to hear about what might have killed President Adams. People gathered around televisions wherever they could to hear pieces of testimony.

Blankenship set the witness list carefully. He called witnesses from the government who had selected WorldCopter as the winner of the helicopter competition to build the next Marine One. They testified in somber tones with obvious disappointment how they had carefully laid out all of the requirements for the helicopter that would be used as Marine One, not the least of which was a proven track record, a history of impeccable safety, and assurances that whoever built the next Marine One would have the proper employees and subcontractors who had Yankee White–level clearances. They explained how they had *relied* on WorldCopter's representation of how quickly they could have the security checks completed and Marine One delivered in time to fulfill the contract.

The senators on the Armed Services Committee had been bipartisan in their attacks on WorldCopter since the crash. Now they were all in the Senate Caucus Room with all the bright lights and energy the journalistic interest could muster. For the first time since any of the committee members could remember, they all felt exactly the same way about what was transpiring in the hearing.

After the procurement witnesses, Pentagon officials marched through the hearing room to describe the process of selecting the competitors for Marine One and then the fly-off, where military test pilots evaluated the competitors. The distinct impression left by all the witnesses, who had been reading from the same government playbook, was that the *other* helicopter was superior to the WorldCopter helicopter (which *called* itself an American helicopter) that had been selected for Marine One. Left unsaid but clear was that forces had been at play other than merit that caused *someone* to choose the WorldCopter offering. This had of course been the drumbeat of the American helicopter company since the decision had been made, and the company used this chance to provide all kinds of back-channel information to senators and witnesses to make WorldCopter look bad.

On the fourth day of the hearings, the World-Copter witnesses were finally called to defend themselves. Even though I'd had a lot of criminal law experience, I didn't have any experience representing witnesses in Senate investigations. William Morton did, but the bad news is that attorneys have limited power in Senate hearings. Far less than in a trial or arbitration. They can only clarify the questions or attempt to deflect some of the impact. No real rules of evidence apply like in a courtroom where you can rely on an agreed set of rules to object to a question as leading or compound, or to complain that it is obvious political grandstanding and not really a question at all. You might be able to make a claim of attorney-client privilege, if appropriate, but essentially you tried to make it come out better in subtle and clever ways. Some resorted to making comical comments, like Brendan Sullivan's famous statement at the Iran-contra hearings when representing Marine lieutenant Colonel Oliver North when he challenged a senator who was ignoring him by saying, "Senator, I am not a potted plant." But that kind of fun was rare, and most attorneys left the hearings frustrated and the witnesses left bloody from senators standing on top of them.

Senator Blankenship, not one to shy from a confrontation on behalf of the United States, called Jean Claude Martin, the president and CEO of WorldCopter, as the first witness from the company. Martin wanted William Morton to defend him, but he asked me to be at the table too. We entered the jammed Caucus Room through the small aisle that wound between the audience, the journalists, and light poles. Jean Claude sat in front of the microphone at the table covered with green felt. Morton sat to his left. I sat to Jean Claude's right.

Jean Claude looked poised and calm. We knew differently. We had spent countless hours preparing him. Half our time had been spent giving him information about the helicopter's construction and the contract with the government that he had either never known or grown unsure about. The other half was spent grilling him and pressing him harder than any senator was likely to have the nerve to duplicate. But there's a big difference between preparing for an inquisition and being in one. His hands were shaking slightly. Jean Claude knew it and kept his hands out of sight until he was able to settle down.

Blankenship began the questioning himself. This was the moment he had been waiting for. He spent the first two hours grilling Jean Claude on the U.S. operations of WorldCopter, trying to show that it was simply a front for WorldCopter France, and that the only *manufacturing* of the helicopter, in reality, occurred in France. Some "assembly" took place in the United States, but by the end of the two hours everyone understood the helicopter was made in France.

Blankenship moved to the next tab in the notebook full of questions that had been prepared by the lawyers on his staff. "From what I understand," he said, his voice booming with the cameras whirring away, "WorldCopter U.S. was established as a joint venture solely to satisfy the 'made in USA' requirements for the Marine One contract. Correct?" He made quotation marks with his bony fingers when saying "made in USA." "In other words, you couldn't even *compete* for the contract — WorldCopter couldn't — without the U.S. subsidiary supposedly doing the manufacturing, right?"

"No, Senator. That's not right." Jean Claude's English was quite good, but the more he spoke, and the hotter it got, the heavier his accent got. "WorldCopter already had a U.S. subsidiary that has handled all American sales of WorldCopter. We have been selling and assembling helicopters in the United States for almost twenty years."

"My mistake, Mr. Martin," Blankenship said with an intentional American pronunciation instead of the French. "I was unclear. I was concentrating on the joint venture part of this little arrangement. WorldCopter had a U.S. subsidiary, but it joined with the Hammer and Blalock Corporation, the major U.S. military contractor, which then agreed to produce one-fifth of the parts for Marine One. Isn't that right?"

"Partially, Senator. We did enter into a joint venture with Hammer Blalock to provide one-fifth of the parts for the helicopter, that's true."

Senator Blankenship was unimpressed. "Well, the point of my question, sir, is that it was that joint venture that allowed you to participate in the bidding process to manufacture Marine One, correct?"

"Well, sir, there was a requirement that at least twenty percent of the parts of the helicopter be actually manufactured inside the United States borders and that did allow us to meet that criteria."

"Then as I understand your answer, it is yes?"

"It is what I said."

"Well, prior, sir, to WorldCopter bidding on the Marine One contract, WorldCopter didn't make *any* parts in the United States, did it?"

"No, sir."

"WorldCopter never utilized a single American worker to make any single part on a single WorldCopter helicopter before you decided to bid on Marine One on the government contract, isn't that right?"

"I'm not sure I would say it that way. We employ three hundred and forty American citizens in our subsidiary in the United States —"

"*Now* you do, but thirty days before this bid was submitted to get the Marine One contract, you had twenty-seven employees in the United States. Correct?"

"I believe that is correct."

"And *thirteen* of them were French,

correct?"

"I don't know the numbers exactly, Senator, but that sounds pretty close."

"Well, only one person who was born in this country was even an officer of World-Copter U.S. Right?"

"I'm not sure, Senator."

"Not sure? Well, I sure am. Here's the list." Blankenship held it up dramatically for the television cameras. "Would you like me to read it to you?"

"I don't think that will be necessary."

Blankenship sat back and stared at the president of WorldCopter. The tension built in the room. "Sir, this whole joint venture is a charade on the American people. It was created to get the government contract. You certainly didn't need to have Hammer and Blalock build parts that were already being built in France, did you?"

"We were enthusiastic to participate with them in the manufacturing of Marine One and to have them help us manufacture Marine One in the United States. Just like Boeing transferred some of the manufacturing to China when it got the contract to build aircraft for Chinese airlines, or General Dynamics allowed Norway to help build the F-16 when it was placing those aircraft with NATO. It's very common, and

I think it's very healthy for both countries involved."

Blankenship looked at Martin as if he were stupid. "Are you comparing the state of the United States aviation industry to that of the Chinese or the Norwegians? The United States already *has* a healthy helicopter industry, don't we? We don't need a European helicopter manufacturer here to 'show us how' or to 'get us going.' Particularly one that's faking the manufacturing just to satisfy the criteria in a contract bid!"

Blankenship smelled an opening. "Sir, at the time that General Dynamics sold F-16s to Norway, Norway certainly didn't have any native fighter industry, did it? And when Boeing agreed to allow China to help build Boeing aircraft, China didn't have much of a native commercial aircraft industry, did it? It's a completely different situation."

Morton interjected, "Senator, I don't think we're here to debate policy or whether it's wise for various countries to share technology with other countries."

Senator Blankenship leaned forward and looked at Morton. "Who invited you to this hearing, sir? I'm here to ask questions of the president of WorldCopter, not some high-priced Washington lawyer who's trying to keep the truth from coming out."

Morton was stunned. "Senator, witnesses have a right to counsel at these hearings as you well know." He paused. "I'm not trying to keep the truth from coming out at all, Senator. I'm trying to keep this witness from becoming a political *tool*."

Blankenship turned beet red. "A tool? You think this is about politics? Sir, this is about killing the president of the United States. This is about a foreign company winning a contract they didn't deserve to win, and then failing to comply with a contract resulting in the death of the president. This is about fraud. You think that's politics?"

Morton was appropriately quiet. Blankenship was aching for a fight.

Blankenship returned his angry gaze to Martin. "Now I want to talk about fraud." He turned the page dramatically in his notebook. "You're aware there have been allegations of fraud in the contracting process for Marine One."

Martin wanted to throw it right back at him, but restrained himself. "I have heard people make reckless accusations."

Blankenship didn't even look up. "What was the bid and accepted price for the entire Marine One contract, sir?"

Martin said, "Six point one billion dollars."

"And by the time the first helicopter was delivered, the price for the contract was what, sir?"

"Twelve point five billion."

"And that was in spite of the fact that the navy asked for zero changes. Right?"

"No, sir, the navy tasked us with nineteen hundred additional requirements that weren't in the original contract."

Blankenship held up a document. "I have a sworn statement from the lead navy contracting officer, sir. Let me read to you what she says: 'This idea that the navy gave them nineteen hundred additional requirements is simply not true. It's a myth, and it's becoming a legend.' " Blankenship paused. "Is she lying?"

Martin snapped back, "They asked us for a helicopter, then because of the post-9/11 requirements said it had to be able to jam incoming missiles, be hardened to some nuclear blasts, and have the same videoconferencing and encrypted communications capabilities as Air Force One. That made it very expensive to essentially redesign the entire helicopter, and those requirements were *not* in the original contract."

Blankenship smiled ironically. "Funny you should mention Air Force One. Each of those 747s cost less than one of these helicopters. Did you know that?"

"That's not the case, Senator."

"Yes, it is! These helicopters cost the U.S. taxpayers four hundred million dollars apiece! That's more than the 747!"

"Yes, well, the 747s were built many years ago —"

"No, sir! That's in today's dollars! I adjusted the price for inflation." Blankenship paused. "It is hard to believe that a helicopter can cost more than a 747, isn't it? You didn't believe it. You can see why we believe there's fraud. When you pay for an Indy car and get a VW, you look into it. At least this committee is certainly going to."

At that point, I knew one of us was going to have to take a spear for WorldCopter. "Senator, excuse me, I'm Mike Nolan —"

"Who, sir, asked you to speak?"

"Well, Senator, no one asked me to speak, but as an attorney I'm rarely *asked* to speak."

The audience chuckled. Blankenship didn't see the humor. "Please remain quiet, Mr. Nolan. Mr. Martin is represented here by competent counsel. Perhaps you can't see him. He's sitting on the other side of Mr. Martin."

Nice. "Actually he's being represented here by both of us, I just haven't spoken before this. I'd be happy to be quiet, Senator, but I need to say one thing first. You say this isn't about politics, yet you ask questions that imply dishonesty, fraud, lack of contractual compliance, and malice on the part of WorldCopter. The cost increases you just alluded to were based on changes requested by the government. And the cost increases were approved. This has been in the papers for years. There is nothing new here. And as to the implication that World-Copter caused this accident, that is remarkable, particularly in light of the fact that no one has any idea what caused this accident. The NTSB hasn't issued its preliminary findings, yet you are ready to lynch World-Copter when they may have done absolutely *nothing* wrong. You will find out, Senator, that the reason the clearances, for example, were not obtained in a timely fashion was because the FBI failed to do the investigation they promised to do. I —"

Blankenship took his large wooden gavel and was about to slam it down to try to shut me up when one of his aides approached him from behind and handed him a piece of paper. He stopped to read it, then looked at me over his reading glasses. The look on his face told me I didn't want to hear what he was about to say. He said nothing until the room was completely silent. He looked away from me toward Jean Claude. "Sir, I've just been handed what is entitled 'Preliminary Assessment' from the NTSB. I am told this is remarkably quick for that investigative body, but they say it isn't a full 'Preliminary Report.' " He paused, looked at the paper again. "It says some things initially, then goes on to say, 'It is our initial assessment that there was no foul play in the crash of Marine One. We are concentrating on the possibility that there was a design or manufacturing defect that caused the crash.' "

I was still standing. I put up my hands up at my sides, palms out in surrender, and sat down.

Blankenship said to Jean Claude, "Sir, let's back way up and talk about how this helicopter was designed and built. Because I have the same concerns as the NTSB."

9

Marcel called me after the hearing and asked me to meet him the next morning at six thirty at the hangar where the wreckage was being stored. He was concerned about Blankenship's announcement on worldwide television.

As I was leaving for the hangar, my wife, Debbie, asked me if I'd seen the headline of the morning's newspaper.

"What does it say?"

She turned it around and held it up to me and read it: " 'WorldCopter in the Crosshairs.' "

"Perfect."

She glanced at the story that she'd already read, looking for a particular sentence: " 'According to sources inside the government, the lead investigator for the NTSB is focusing on a specific cause that she thinks will explain the crash. The sources were unwilling to disclose the cause, but said the things under consideration all pointed to WorldCopter.' "

I put my coffee down. "That is unbelievably irresponsible. Does anyone think it was a coincidence that the NTSB 'Preliminary Assessment,' whatever that is, was released while the president of WorldCopter was on the hot seat of a Senate inquisition? Somebody at the NTSB owed Blankenship bigtime. What total bullshit this is. Who inside the NTSB would talk to him and then the press like that? That *really* pisses me off."

I headed for the hangar, which was on an old army air base. I had been there on occasion when it was still actively operating. It had been closed in one of Congress's base realignments. The NTSB was there twenty-four hours a day, but most of the team were there from 6 AM to 10 PM.

The hangars now stood empty, surrounded by weeds. The NTSB had cleaned up one of the hangars and mowed around it. It was easy to pick it out from the others by its appearance and the activity around it.

I turned into the army base, which now had a guard at the gate again. IIc took my driver's license and turned to check it against his access list. I looked in my rearview mirror and saw a car go by a little too slowly to just be driving by on the country

151

road behind me. The car was unremarkable and I couldn't see the driver, but I thought I'd seen the same car earlier, on the way to the army base from my house. I couldn't imagine who it would be. It had to be either a coincidence or my imagination.

I parked at the side of the hangar in what was once a pilots' parking lot and walked through the side door. The concrete floor was spotless, and portable light stands all over the massive space illuminated the charred, mud-covered wreckage from Marine One that had been trucked to the hangar. The investigators had spread the pieces out on the floor to represent the places where the pieces had been in the helicopter when it was intact.

Each subgroup of the NTSB investigation had its own table: engines, blades, airframe, maintenance, pilots, everyone. Participants such as WorldCopter had their own areas and tables. Some had put up signs so everyone would know where they were. WorldCopter's logo hung from a now defunct fire sprinkler high above their table.

I quickly spotted Marcel, who was also one of the first people in the hangar that morning. He had scrounged a desk and was sitting behind it with innumerable photographs and pieces of metal in front of him.

He was looking at one with a magnifying glass as I approached. "Morning, Marcel."

He looked up over his reading glasses. "Good morning, Mike. I am glad that you came." He jumped up and turned to face the wall behind him. He turned back to me. "Would you like some coffee? We have brought our own coffee machine out here. The coffee that was being made was not too good. Let me get you some."

"Sure." Marcel took a large bowl-like cup out of a stack, poured coffee into it from an impressive coffeemaker, then reached under the desk and pulled out a quart of milk from a cooler and poured some into the coffee. "Thanks," I said as he smiled widely and handed me the cup. "So what you got, Marcel?"

Marcel ripped off his reading glasses and looked around to make sure nobody was listening. He lowered his voice and spoke to me quietly. "As you know, we are here as part of the investigation. To help the NTSB. I am looking at many things and am not making any conclusions. That's their job. I answer questions. But I think I also notice a few things that we have to deal with in the future.

"Come around here." He indicated for me to walk to his side of the desk. "I want to show you these photographs." He picked up one eight-and-a-half-by-eleven, glossy color print and handed it to me. He put his glasses back on, picked up a pen, and began pointing to a portion of the photo.

I couldn't tell what it was. "What are we looking at?"

"It is the inside threads of the main rotor blade that we found lying on the ground."

"Where it attaches to the rotor hub?"

"Exactly. Look closely."

I looked as closely as I could, but nothing jumped out at me.

"Here." He handed me the magnifying glass.

I glanced around the room feeling like I was about to do something improper and placed the photograph flat on the desk where there was good light. Marcel placed his pen where he wanted me to look. I looked carefully, moving the four-inch magnifying glass in and out until it was perfectly focused on the threads that held the main rotor blade to the rotor hub. The threads looked odd, like they weren't as clean or as precise as you would expect them to be. The threads showed slight bending, some discoloration, and a softness that I couldn't really understand. I placed the magnifying glass down and stood up straight. "What am I looking at here, Marcel?"

He almost whispered, "The threads. The threads are bent."

I shook my head indicating my complete lack of understanding. "And?"

"The threads are bent, you can see the force? The stress?"

"Sure. But I would assume they all have that. When the helicopter hits the ground, the blades flex down, putting a huge amount of force on their attachment to the rotor hub. That *should* stress the threads."

"No," he said. "This blade came off in the air. It was not attached when the helicopter hit the ground, remember?"

"Yeah, but we don't know where."

He shook his head as if I didn't understand, which was accurate. He said, "I do not know if this got the right chemical, the right coating. I'm afraid the coating for corrosion did not get put on this blade. If it didn't, and the blade came off in the air because it had corroded, it could explain everything! It landed by the crashed helicopter, yes, true. It would be one of those . . . 'ironies'?"

"That would be an irony. An unpleasant one. You think that's possible?"

Marcel shrugged and put out his chin.

"You see, the blade threads are bent as if it came off going down, away from the helicopter. It probably came off while the helicopter was in the air."

I sat down in the chair Marcel had been sitting in. This case could be over a lot faster than I thought. "You tell the NTSB about this?"

"They haven't focused on the blade yet, they're too busy with other things."

"You gonna tell them?"

"I will answer whatever questions they ask."

"We need to get our own metallurgist to look at this as soon as we can."

"I don't want somebody from World-Copter," Marcel said.

"I know just the guy. Used to be the head of the NTSB metallurgy lab."

"They will probably like that here," he said, glancing at the NTSB people.

"I don't think so. He thinks the people who work in the NTSB lab now are second-stringers. We'll have to play it very carefully."

"What about the tip weights? Any of them recovered yet?"

"No. This same blade is the one missing its end cap and tip weights. They could have come off in the air, which would cause a terrible vibration. The helicopter would come apart. That could make this blade come off in any direction."

"Well, exactly. If they don't find those tip weights, everyone will think that's exactly what happened."

"Yes, they could." I looked at him. "We have to find those tip weights. We have to show they're intact and they didn't cause the accident."

"If the NTSB didn't find them, it will be hard for us to find them."

"We have to. Otherwise this thing is going to land on our heads." I thought about the assembly of the tip weights. The small washers that balanced the rotating blade. "What about the nut that held the tip weights on? How can we prove there even was a nut?"

"Well, you couldn't rotate that blade for even thirty seconds without the nut holding on the tip weights. It would be out of balance immediately. The bolt at the end, where the tip weights go and the nut holds them on is bent. This blade hit something."

"So the nut and the tip weights could have come off when the blade hit whatever it hit."

"Yes, or the bolt could have been bent after they came off and as it fell. And the NTSB has not found any of these parts. If it was near the crash, they would be on the ground, in the mud. They have looked everywhere. They are not there."

"Oh, yes, they are. And we're going to find them."

I worked at my office late that night reviewing the Senate transcript that Morton had e-mailed me. As I paused for a moment and looked at the ceiling to soothe my burning eyes, the phone rang. I recognized Byrd's number. I put him on the speakerphone. "Hey, Tinny."

"Nolan, you came to the right place. Guess what I've got?"

"What?"

"A fine lady at the Pentagon who just happens to have access to all of Collins's personnel records. Turns out she went to Howard with my son. Used to go to his Omega Psi Phi parties, where he, of course, was the life of the party, just like his old man. She said she owed him. And since he wasn't around right now, his old man would just have to do. You believe that shit?"

"Tinny, you didn't ask her to take any federal documents, did you?"

Tinny responded as if he'd been hurt. "That would be wrong. I couldn't ask her to do that."

"You'd better not."

"Right. Just leave these things to me. You do your lawyer shit. You just don't like the dirty work. You probably let your gunnery sergeant take care of all the shitbirds in your squadron, didn't you?"

"What else you got, Tinny?"

"One other thing. This might be big. Got a contact in the Secret Service. Former Marine. May be our secret weapon."

"Why would someone from the Secret Service have any information?"

"This boy is the head of security at Camp David, my friend. He was waiting for the president on the night of the crash."

I sat up straight. "He could be the key to the entire thing."

"Exactly."

"Think he'll talk to us?"

"Let's just say he's unenthusiastic. Seems others in the government don't want anyone to find out who was at that meeting. Which, of course, makes me push all the harder. But he's not very pushable right now. I'll work it."

"What's his name?"

"No can do. He swore me to secrecy. Says he'll go stone-cold know-nothing and lie through his teeth if I even breathe his name to anyone. Especially you."

"He knows about me?'

"Well, I had to tell him why I was calling, didn't I? It's not like some investigator is going to just wonder about all this for his own good. He recognized you from the Senate hearings. Gotta run."

"Keep me posted."

"Oh, yeah."

As I hung up, the phone rang again. I checked the caller ID and saw area code 212. Only Kathryn would be up this late. "Mike Nolan," I said, answering the phone quickly.

After a pause, a deep, smooth voice said, "Mike, this is Tom Hackett."

He was the last person I expected to call me, but if I'd thought about it or been quick enough, it would have made instant sense. He was one of the most famous lawyers in the country, a plaintiffs' attorney from New York. He called himself, or the legal press called him, Mr. Class, as in class actions, not because he *had* class. He filed massive class-action lawsuits against corporations for any number of reasons and settled them for enormous amounts of money, a nice portion of which went to him. He was one of the wealthiest lawyers in the country.

The reason I didn't instantly know the reason for the call was that I had forgotten that he went to law school with the first lady, Mrs. Adams. "What can I do for you?"

"First of all, we've never met. I am an attorney in New York and deal in major cases —"

"Yes, I know who you are."

"Good. Listen, I wanted to tell you that you did a very nice job at the Senate hearings. Very dramatic. You got Blankenship very angry, which was probably why you were there. Nicely done." He paused. "So I understand that you've been retained for this representation, but not by World-Copter, by AII, their insurance company. But they would only be involved if there was going to be a civil lawsuit."

"And where'd you hear that?"

Hackett said, "That doesn't really matter. I have ways of learning lots of things. So am I right?"

"Maybe."

"Does that mean that you're unsure?"

I fought back the anger building inside me. I just didn't need that right then. I hung up.

The phone rang again immediately. I saw the same number. I picked it up again. "What?"

"It's very rude to hang up on a caller."

"It's very rude to call someone you don't know and insult them."

"I was not intending to insult you —"

"Yes, you were. If you have anything worthwhile to say, say it. I'm busy."

"No doubt. Here is what I do have to say, so listen carefully. I am representing the first lady, or former first lady. Mrs. Adams. I also have indications that I will be representing all the others who perished on Marine One against WorldCopter in a civil lawsuit. You have of course heard the NTSB's initial statement that there was no foul play. That means, a fortiori, there was a defective helicopter. And that means your client owes my clients compensation. WorldCopter does not need the publicity a civil trial would bring. I don't think WorldCopter wants me to take the depositions of every employee of their factory where this helicopter was made and show how disastrous their entire operation is. I don't think they need me digging into their security procedures and security files to show that their employees never obtained the security clearances required by the United States government, and I don't think they need me proving that they killed the president, whether intentionally or otherwise. But if I can have your assurance of confidentiality — may I have that assurance?"

"So I take it from your threats that you're

planning on filing a lawsuit?"

"In the face of the information coming out in the Senate investigation and the NTSB statement, I have to prepare for that eventuality, don't I? It would be malpractice not to. I haven't decided yet, but I must confess what I have learned is very disturbing. But the reason for my call is to discuss something of importance to your client and mine. So may I have your assurance of confidentiality?"

"Yes, except for my ability to convey whatever it is you're about to say to my clients."

"Of course. That's the whole point. But you are not free to disclose it to others inside your firm — except perhaps Rachel — or others who might be interested, such as your wife, Debbie . . . or the press."

This guy was really pissing me off. "If you think your little name-dropping game will intimidate me, just save yourself the energy. You don't impress me."

"Please forgive me; I thought that it might generate some camaraderie between the two of us. I feel like I know you quite well already."

"You *don't* know me 'quite well,' nor will you ever. And if you ever do, you'll probably be on your back staring at the sky wondering what the hell just happened. So what is it you have to say?"

"Did I receive your assurance of confidentiality as I outlined it?"

"Yes."

"Very well then. I'm sure you appreciate that I believe, as does my client, that we have a very strong claim against your client."

"I think any rational person would wait until there's a determination of the *cause* of the crash before they even think about filing a lawsuit against somebody. But what I think really doesn't matter. You've probably put all kinds of wrong ideas into your clients' heads. But again, I'm waiting for you to say something that matters. So far I haven't heard it."

Hackett took a deep breath, apparently annoyed. That was just fine with me. If life was just, someday I'd have the chance to hit him in the head with a chair. He said, "I have persuaded the first lady that now actually might be an opportune moment to resolve issues between our clients, not only her, but I believe I could obtain the authority of the widows of all the others on the aircraft to resolve their claims right now, before we expend huge amounts of money in costly discovery, and adverse publicity for your client. And I assure you there will be substantial adverse publicity. But what we have in mind is that we would be willing to resolve all claims, in a confidential settlement that would not be disclosed to anyone, not even the fact of the settlement. If she or I were later asked by the press why we had not filed a lawsuit as we had contemplated, the answer would simply be that there had been discussions between the two sides, and she was satisfied with what they had said. Simple as that. That's all she or I or anyone else related to the case would, or could, ever say. No one would ever know that World-Copter had paid her a settlement."

"Well, I think that the likelihood of that remaining secret is about as likely any other secret held by the U.S. government. You may as well just e-mail it to the *Washington Post.*"

"You underestimate our ability to remain confidential."

"What's your proposal?"

"We are prepared to consider resolving all claims of the first lady as well as the survivors of all others who died aboard Marine One for a sum totaling one billion dollars."

"You're kidding me, right? Are you seriously demanding a billion-dollar settlement with no evidence of liability?"

"I'm trying to save you from seeing that evidence, Mike. Because I promise you that if this case goes forward, I will have evidence that this crash was WorldCopter's fault, and the *NTSB* will find it was WorldCopter's fault. I will have experts that testify not only that it was WorldCopter's fault, but that it was reckless. We will recover punitive damages. Do you really believe that a jury is going to sympathize with a European helicopter manufacturer that killed the president of the United States?"

"I'm not to the point of even trying to evaluate that. I'm trying to figure out what caused the accident. Tell me, what evidence do you have that this is WorldCopter's fault and that they should pay you anything?"

"Mike, that's what I'm trying to save you from." He hesitated, no doubt for effect. "Maybe this is too complex for you. Maybe you're used to automobile accident cases. You should pass this information and offer on to whoever has more experience in these matters. Because if you go forward and this lawsuit is filed, it is going to be World-Copter's worst nightmare."

I'd never encountered anyone like him before. "Is this how you usually begin a case? Threatening and blustering to avoid the merits of the case? So you don't have to do any work?"

There was a notable pause on the other end of the line. "Do you not know my reputation? Do you really believe I'm afraid to go to trial? What I'm afraid of is that people like you will not understand the implications of what is happening and not make the appropriate recommendations to their clients until it is too late. *That's* what I'm afraid of. I'm afraid that you will force me to drag you into the arena, the court-room, and embarrass you and your client. If you don't think I've tried cases, if you don't think I'm capable of trying this case, ask around. Talk to some people who have been practicing law awhile who have tried some big cases. See if they agree." He waited until that sunk in, then said, "Listen very care-fully."

"What?"

"This offer of settlement that I have just outlined to you must remain confidential. If it is leaked to the press in any way, if there is any implication to the press that the first lady is looking for money, I will not only deny it, but I will attribute the offer to you. I will tell the press that contrary to what you are saying, in fact you called *us* and begged us to resolve all potential cases for one billion dollars, and that we of course rejected it out of hand as being premature, but perhaps indicative of the problems World-Copter was facing. We were frankly surprised that WorldCopter was so disturbed by the Senate hearings, and concerned with liability in this case, that they tried to preempt any investigation on our part. Do you understand that?"

"Yes. Very clearly. If confronted by the press, you would lie. That's very good to know. I appreciate knowing up front I'm dealing with a liar."

"Oh, I wouldn't call it a lie. In fact by the time we'd completed our conversation about it, I would have you completely convinced that what I had said was correct. Words and intentions are elusive little things with content pouring in and out of them all of the time. Much of communication is in tone, timing, and technique. I'm sure you're aware of that."

He continued, "There's one other thing. This discussion that we're having, about resolving this case, will stop seven days from now. If WorldCopter does not get back to me with an acceptance of this 'indication of interest' on my part, then there will be *no subsequent offer.* We will go to trial. Do you understand that, Mr. Nolan?"

"I understand it very well."

"Excellent. I will look forward to hearing from you by telephone. And you can find my number in any number of places. I'm sure you're clever and will be able to do that."

"Yes. For example, my caller ID is telling me what it is right now."

"Yes, but predictably, you have jumped to conclusions. You have assumed that I'm calling you from my office. You have assumed that the line, the number you are seeing, is a direct line and not a trunk line from an office building somewhere in New York. You actually have no idea what you're seeing. In fact, if you think about it, you don't even know that I'm Tom Hackett. I could be Billy Samuels, the young man who lives down the street from you. I look forward to hearing from you."

The line went dead.

I stared at the phone. I couldn't believe I'd just had that conversation. It was like a dream. I turned to my computer and drafted an e-mail to WorldCopter and Kathryn. He was right, I didn't know for sure it was Tom Hackett, but the voice sure sounded like the voice I'd heard on numerous televised press conferences about his victories. Plus it's hard to match that kind of articulate arrogance. You can't find that just anywhere. I finished the e-mail and read it over. I decided to call Kathryn in the morning.

Throughout that night and the next morning as I drove back to my office, I couldn't get Hackett's call off my mind. Sometimes the more desperate people's cases are, and the less likely they are to prevail, the more they demand and the quicker they insist on a response. They don't want to get into the facts; they want to play it with the maximum extortion value. They don't want to get into discovery, where we might find out that their case was a pile of shit. They demand money, bang on the table, try to scare the defendants, and try to extract a settlement. It wasn't my decision, but I couldn't imagine this case being resolved this quickly with no theory of what happened, especially for the kind of money that Hackett was talking about. That was crazy money.

I drank deeply from the coffee in my USNA mug and called Kathryn. Her secretary answered, "Ms. Galbraith's office."

"It's Mike Nolan, is Kathryn there?"

"Sure, Mr. Nolan, I'll get her right away."

Kathryn came on, now sounding as if she hadn't slept in three days. I gave her the whole conversation, which she found odd and remarkable. She waited patiently, but finally broke in, "I read your e-mail. Is he out of his mind?"

"Yes. He is. He wants a billion dollars."

"That's just crazy. He represents the families of everyone who was aboard Marine One?"

"He says he will."

"That's just ridiculous. But there's a big problem with that number, Mike."

"What?"

"WorldCopter is only insured for two hundred fifty million dollars."

"That is a problem."

Kathryn thought for a moment, anger building. "Sounds to me like it includes punitive damages too. Agree?"

"Probably. How much is a dead president worth? How much does a former president earn over the remainder of his life? Hard to say. A lot, but nothing like the CEO of Exxon or something. And former presidents don't become CEOs. So it sounds to me like he's including punitives without saying it."

"We can't insure punitive damages, Mike."

"Yeah. I know."

"Well, we have to reject it. I'll call World-Copter. I suppose if they want to kick in seven hundred and fifty million dollars of their own money, that would force us to decide whether to throw in the policy, but this case isn't even worth our policy, unless someone convinces me otherwise. We don't have any evidence of liability at all."

I agreed. "And Jean Claude will never pay anything over the policy, especially now. Everybody would think it was an admission that the helicopter was defective."

"Did Hackett say he'd keep it confidential?"

"Sure, but I don't even take that into consideration. I've lived close enough to Washington for long enough to know that things are only confidential until someone feels 'wronged.' Then suddenly it appears in the *Post*. You want me on the call with World-Copter?"

"No. I don't think it will be very long. They're indignant about all this. They think they're being slandered by the press and everyone else. NTSB's nice little press release didn't help much."

"Just the springboard Hackett needed to make his call." A thought suddenly struck me. "Maybe he has a friend inside the NTSB. It would explain a lot."

"Great. That's all we need. An attorney manipulating a government agency. Well, keep going. Looks like we're going to have a big fat lawsuit on our hands pretty quickly.

Assume WorldCopter is going to reject this unless we call you back. We're in for a real fight on this one, Mike."

"He said this would be his last offer."

"That's what they all say."

10

"Mike," Tracy, my secretary, said from outside my door as I hung up the phone.

"Yeah."

"Rachel just called. The NTSB is going to have a press conference in a few minutes."

"Get her in here," I said as I turned to my computer and went to MSNBC.com. They were carrying the press conference live. Rachel ran in as I clicked on the video feed and the picture opened in a small window on my computer screen.

"Anyone speculating on what this is about?"

"Nothing. No one was expecting it this quickly."

I expanded the video panel on my computer screen. I recognized the lobby of the NTSB building. The NTSB logo was right behind Rose, who was standing in front of a lectern with a bank of microphones. Rachel came around to my side of the desk and leaned against it next to me.

Rose looked up at all the cameras and the faces of all the reporters. She began reading a prepared statement. She told them she would take no questions, this was a preliminary finding, how tirelessly all the professionals who were a part of the investigation had worked, blah, blah, blah. Everybody in the country wanted her to get to the point. Finally she did. She looked up and her eyes narrowed. I wondered if she had written that gesture into her statement. "First of all, let me say that our findings, again, are *preliminary,* and this is particularly true as to the cause of this accident. I want to state clearly what we believe did *not* cause this accident. We have found no evidence of any explosives, projectiles, or other means of bringing this helicopter down by outside forces. This helicopter was not shot down. Second, we, with the FBI and other investigators, have found no evidence of foul play. The president was not assassinated. Third, it is our preliminary belief that the cause of this accident was due to the helicopter losing one of its main rotor blades in the storm." You could hear cameras clicking in the background. "We are not positive about the *cause* of that rotor blade leaving the main rotor hub. But we know it was put on the helicopter two weeks ago. This was a replacement blade. Our current focus is on the missing tip weights which could have caused blade separation. That is all I have."

She closed her notebook and walked away from the lectern without answering any of the questions being screamed at her by the journalists: So, it was WorldCopter's fault? Was it sabotage? How long before your investigation is final? Have you met with World-Copter? What did they say?

She was true to her word and took no questions. When the door closed behind her, the reporters quieted down. I muted the sound on my computer and looked up at Rachel, who was looking down at me. She folded her arms and stared at the screen. "How could they know that?"

"I don't know, maybe they've got some good metallurgy we haven't seen. I'll ask Marcel. They're clearly not telling us everything. They can wait until the final report is issued to really lay it out. That could be another year or two."

"Marcel would have already told us if they'd found something." Rachel stood there, not moving. She looked down at me again. "You buying it?"

"We've always known that blade was a problem. But do I think that caused the accident? No."

"Then why would they say it did?"

"Because they believe it. You ever heard of Occam's razor?"

"No."

"It's named after some philosopher. His idea, the 'razor,' was that the correct answer to a complex problem is usually found in the simplest solution. The more you construct or assume, the more steps or requirements there are to explain it, the less likely it is to be right. All things being equal, the explanation that calls for the fewest assumptions is likely the correct one. Basically, the simplest answer wins."

"Makes sense."

"I don't think it does, but my point is, that's the way the NTSB thinks. If they can come up with a single screw that explains an entire accident, they'll grab on to that theory and hold it forever. You can tell them whatever you want, you can question all their evidence, it won't matter. You won't push them off of that conclusion. And as you know, the government is never wrong."

"That's certainly been my experience."

She stood up and walked toward the door. "Once you start thinking about this accident, you can't stop. I can see why people obsess about the Kennedy assassination."

"Once your brain locks onto the facts, you can't rest until all the pieces fit into a picture. Here's the NTSB giving us their theory, and nobody even knows who the president was going to meet."

Rachel walked out and said on her way, "We going to be able to find answers?"

"I'm sure as hell going to try."

11

A week passed with daily visits to the wreckage in the hangar and talking to potential experts I was considering using. At the end of one particularly long day that started with me in the office before dawn, I invited Debbie to go out to dinner with me at one of the nicer restaurants in Annapolis. We arrived and were waiting to be seated when I saw Hackett on the television. He was holding a press conference. I asked the hostess to give us a minute. We walked into the bar and strained to see the television at the far end.

Several others were watching and the bartender turned up the volume. Hackett was in his conference room with his law firm's name emblazoned in gold lettering on the mahogany wall behind him. The press had been given plenty of notice that the attorney who represented the first lady was holding a press conference. They packed the conference room. Conveniently, the press conference coincided with the evening news. We had missed the first couple of minutes.

Hackett paused as photographers clicked cameras and print reporters made notes. He continued, "Now that the NTSB has stated what the cause of this accident was, and we know that it was WorldCopter's fault, the first lady has reluctantly asked me to pursue the justice and the closure that she thinks the country needs, the justice that is required to defend the honor of President Adams. She wants answers for herself, not just as part of some governmental investigation. She wants *me* to be able to question the WorldCopter employees who put this helicopter together, the ones that put this blade on this helicopter, the ones who installed the tip weights that came off, the ones who caused the death of the president of the United States. Because of that, Mrs. Adams has requested that I file a lawsuit on her behalf against WorldCopter. I did so this afternoon at four thirty PM. Not only has the first lady requested that I file a suit on her behalf, but the wives of all of the men killed on this helicopter, including the two Marine pilots, the Secret Service agents, and the Marine crew chief, have joined in the lawsuit. They were all killed because of a defect in this helicopter. We will also be examining the evidence to determine whether the conduct here was so egregious or malicious, or reckless, that it calls for an award of punitive damages. If it does, we will ask the jury to award a substantial amount of punitive damages against World-Copter for the damage they have caused to these families and to the greater American family. Thank you. I will now take any questions you may have."

I felt my BlackBerry buzz and pulled it out. Debbie frowned at me as I answered it. "Mike Nolan."

It was Rachel. "I've got the lawsuit."

"Where'd you find it?"

"Hackett posted it on his firm's Web site."

"Figures. And?"

"Guess where he filed it?"

"D.C.?"

"Nope."

"District of Maryland. By D.C."

"Nope. Right here in Annapolis."

"What? Why?"

"That's what I was going to ask you."

Rachel told me everything she could about the complaint. "Thanks. I'll get back to you."

I hung up and looked at Debbie. "Hackett

filed his suit right here."

"Why here? I assumed he would file in D.C."

"That's what I've been wondering. But think about it. Who built the courthouse and appointed *both* our judges?"

"President Adams."

"Exactly. Hackett is guaranteed to have a judge who was appointed by his client's husband. And both the federal judges here, as you well know, are both former plaintiff's lawyers."

"Which judge got the case?"

"Betancourt."

"You like her, don't you?"

"I do. I think she's fair, which is all you can really ask for. I don't think he'll get the advantage from this he thinks he will and Norris will be the magistrate. She likes me."

Debbie frowned. "Then why would Hackett file here? I'm sure he researched judges here."

"Maybe he wants me to try the case, and not Brightman. Maybe he thinks I'm an easy mark, and putting it here will tempt AII to let me try it."

"That's pretty cynical. And that wouldn't be his conclusion if he's done his homework."

Whatever reason Hackett chose Annapolis,

I liked it. I would have picked that court-house if given a choice. Maybe Hackett had just made his first mistake. "You know, what probably drove his decision was the rocket docket. All civil cases go to trial in six months. He wants to get to trial before anyone finds out what really happened."

I got in to work the next morning at six AM Rachel appeared in my door virtually buzzing.

"You're here early," I said.

She handed me a big Starbucks and said, "So are you. We need some new bodies."

"No doubt. This thing is going to be a monster. We could probably use ten new people. We can set up several in the back conference room, but let's get two or three in right away. Why don't you get with Tracy and put an ad together for the *Washington Post,* the *National Law Journal, American Lawyer,* Monster.com, whatever. I want to get someone in here ASAP. And I think we need to aim high. This is a big-profile case that a lot of people are going to want to work on. I've got to call Byrd."

I got Byrd on his cell phone. "Tinny, Nolan."

"What the hell you want now?"

"He filed in Annapolis."

"Hey, I've got stuff on Collins that's pretty damn interesting. But I didn't hear from you on my rate sheet, and it turns out there was a typo. I need to send you my updated rate sheet."

"You're shameless."

"I'm unashamedly and openly trying to accumulate enough money to retire in the Ca rib be an and lay on the beach all day. Guilty as charged. And you're going to help me."

"Come see me so we can talk about all this."

"Will do."

Rachel had called the legal journals and the newspapers and had put the advertisements on their Web sites for staff associates. We were already receiving calls. She was lining up interviews at night because we couldn't even take a breath during the day.

Tinny came to see me on Wednesday morning, when I was to meet with all of our newly retained experts to go back out to the scene. I asked him to come at a different time, but he said he didn't have a different time. He showed up at my office at six thirty knowing that the experts wouldn't get there until eight. He banged loudly on the front door. I went to my window overlooking the bay and looked straight down at our doorstep. Tinny looked up at me. I gave him a wave and walked down to the front. I stepped onto the porch and shook his hand. "Morning, Marine. How the hell are you?"

"I'm doing fine. How the hell are you?"

"I was just going to grab a cappuccino."

"You know, we really should meet in your office; I've got some stuff to show you."

"We can just talk. You can show me whatever you've got when we get back. Experts won't be here till eight."

Byrd looked uneasy. "I prefer working in the shadows," he said, trying to make a joke.

I stopped walking. "You spooked about something?"

He smiled. "Me? Never. Just that somebody's already on this stuff. Or maybe they're on me. You think Hackett knows you use me?"

"What are you talking about?" I asked, studying his face. Byrd didn't scare, so the fact he mentioned it gave me real concern.

"Inside," he said.

As soon as we stepped inside and closed the door, he said, "You know I got a sixth sense. Well, somebody knows I'm around in this case."

We walked back to the coffee room where I had watched the news of Marine One's crash. "I just made a fresh pot."

We sat at the cheap table in the middle of the room. "So you think it might be Hackett?"

"Yesterday, right after you called, I saw a guy. Weird. Maybe Hackett doesn't have good investigators. He just tells his guys to follow the other side and let them lead you to the evidence. Don't know."

"It'd be like him. So we'll be careful. Right?"

"Like always." Byrd sipped his coffee. "But how do we know it's him? Could be anybody. I talked to my boy in the Secret Service too. He said he was cool, but maybe they didn't like me doing that. . . ." He thought about that for a moment, then asked, "Anybody else you know who has a stake in this?"

"If it isn't a defective helicopter, then there's someone who cares a lot."

"Who?"

I shook my head. "No idea. Don't even have a theory. If you could find out why Adams was in such a big damned hurry to get to Camp David, we might have an idea. Short of that, no. So, have you found anything interesting?"

His eyes brightened. "I've got some access. We can take further advantage of it."

Tinny picked up his battered briefcase and folded over the large flap. "First thing I've got . . ." He pulled out two files and handed them to me. They were fairly thick, well organized, clearly photocopies of something, and unlabeled.

"What's this?"

Byrd leaned close to me. "These, my friend, are the personnel records of your hero. Mr. Colonel Charles Collins."

My eyes opened wide. "You got Collins's personnel file?"

"Mm-hm."

"How'd you do that?" I could tell he wasn't going to answer, at least not directly. I felt like I was in the middle of a drug deal. "Did you read them?"

"Yeah."

"Anything?"

"He's been a lot of places and done a lot of things. He's got enough medals for three men, his fitness reports are pegged in the top one percent. He's just a star, plain and simple."

"That's it? No issues? Just pure starhood? Nothing you think you need to follow up on?"

"Nope. Not really. I did get a real good history. I made a summary of that here." He handed me a single sheet of paper. "This is all his commands, his dates of Service, his commanding officers, his awards and medals, and some other stuff you might want to have. I want to follow up with the guys in his most recent squadron. I think you've already talked to one of them."

"Yeah. I did."

"Can I start with him?" Byrd finished his coffee and waited for my answer.

I already knew I was going to be stepping on some friends. "Yeah. Go ahead. Britt's a good place to start. I wouldn't spend a lot of time with him, but get names and numbers from him if he'll give them to you. Keep me posted and don't do anything illegal. Or stupid."

"Wouldn't think of it."

I tossed my paper cup in the green trash can.

Byrd was about to stand up when he stopped himself. "There's one other thing, I almost forgot. You're not going to believe this."

"What?"

"Collins had a nice house, very nice."

"And?"

"I'm not saying there's some funny-money business going on here. Some guys are smart in real estate. We've all seen those Marines who buy a house wherever they're stationed and after twenty years own ten houses. That's fine. But I checked out the house."

"Meaning?" I said with growing interest. I stared at Byrd's face, which had the hint of humor of someone who knew an inside joke.

"Meaning I don't think our boy was getting any."

"What do you mean?"

"You know, with the wife."

"What are you talking about? And how could you possibly know that?"

"I'm talking about exactly what you think I'm talking about. And I have my ways of knowing."

I leaned over the table. "Are you saying he wasn't sleeping with his wife?"

"The man had his own bedroom."

I frowned. "I assume they have a guest room. What makes you think he was sleeping in it?"

"Oh, he was sleeping there all right. I promise you. Not only was he sleeping there, he was living in that other room. His computer was set up there, his clothes were in the closet, and his pictures were on the wall. That was his room, dude. I'm telling you. They were living apart in the same house."

"That's bizarre. What do you make of that?"

"Don't know. But I'm sure going to find out. He was leading some kind of double life. You imagine walking into the ready room and having one of the other pilots say, 'How was your night, dude?' and him saying, 'I don't know, I was sleeping in my own room.' Not going to happen. He'd rather die. Just like I would. Course I would never be in another room, but that's the difference between me and him. At least one of the differences. I'll track it down. Maybe he's a cross-dresser. Maybe he's gay. I don't know, but there's something there and I'm going to find out what it is."

"What could it have to do with the accident?"

Byrd, who was turning away, turned back and looked at me. "You of all people to ask me that. You know accidents, Mike. It's never one thing. It's always a series of things, and you never see the links until the 'Aha!' moment." Byrd chuckled. "Can you imagine if I find a picture of the president's pilot dressed as a woman? And not at a Halloween party? Holy hell. And I know where his personal photos are on the Internet. He used one of those photo-storage Web sites. I think I'll take a look at them today."

"You can't just go look at his photos."

"They're on the Internet. Fair game."

Byrd left and I went up to my office. In just a few weeks, he'd obtained records from the Pentagon that he wasn't supposed to have and knew more about Collins's family life than probably anybody else. That was a little unsettling. I didn't have quite the same constraints a prosecutor would in obtaining evidence illegally. I could even use some illegally obtained evidence, depending on the circumstances. But I had to tread carefully.

12

At eight o'clock sharp, the experts I had invited were waiting in the boardroom. Dolores had ordered muffins and coffee. I introduced them to each other, at least those who didn't already know the others, and gave them a quick summary of where we were in our preparation. They had all read the NTSB's preliminary report, had followed the case closely in the media, and were anxious to get started.

Rachel had been working furiously since before I'd sat down with Tinny. On the large whiteboard at the end of the room, she had outlined the NTSB's preliminary findings, other possible theories, the investigation we had conducted to date, and areas we needed to cover. Her handwriting was meticulous, and the board looked like it had been printed out of a massive computer and stapled to the wall. We all stared at the writing as we sat down.

Wayne Bradley, an extremely bright former chairman of the NTSB's metallurgic lab, was also as big as the proverbial house. A humorous but intense man, he was considered the most brilliant aviation metallurgist in the country. Retired from the NTSB, he was now sixty-seven. He liked to get out in the field, to dig in the ground, to touch the metal. He was phenomenal. I had used him in cases before and was glad to have him aboard. Some people were concerned that his huge size would turn off a jury when he testified, but I never found juries to be that shallow. If you give credible testimony, the rest doesn't matter.

To his left, farther away from the whiteboard where Rachel stood, was Holly Folk. Her background was as different from Bradley's as her petite figure was from his massive one. She had gone to Purdue University in their aviation program because "that's where Amelia Earhart had gone." Not only did she obtain her commercial pilot's license while in college, she graduated with a degree in aeronautical engineering. She got a job flying for a commuter airline, transferred to the big airlines, and got laid off when they declared bankruptcy. She hadn't really liked airline flying anyway and had gone back into the marketplace by devoting herself to investigating airplane accidents. She had obtained her master's degree in engineering and had attended the aviation-accident-safety school at the University of Southern California. She had gone to work for the NTSB and had achieved investigator-in-charge status of several major investigations. But she quickly realized her income would forever be limited by two initials, *GS,* and to get ahead in life she needed to go into the private sector. She had been in demand ever since and was the first person I called when I had an accident case. Every case that she had helped me on, we had won. She looked like an engineer but had a wonderful if quirky sense of humor. We could never figure out what triggered it. She routinely thought things were funny that we didn't.

I saw her look at Bradley's plate while she picked at the five pieces of fruit on her plate and drank the strong coffee.

The third expert in the room, Karl Will, our accident reconstructionist, sat motionless drinking his coffee. He and Bradley had worked together numerous times. Bradley never tired of asking, "Karl Will *what?*" Karl never thought it was funny, not the first time, and *not* the hundredth. He was one of those lean, sober Arizona types. He looked like he'd been cooked in the sun for ten years. His skin was permanently brown, and even though he wasn't wearing a hat, you just knew that he usually did.

I stood at the whiteboard waiting for everyone's attention. Bradley finished his second muffin and leaned back in his chair to turn toward me. "All right, Mike, what do you have?"

I said, "Morning, everybody. We're glad you were able to make it. We're going to talk for about an hour, then we're all going out to the crash site. The NTSB has released it. Rachel and I have been back a couple of times, but we want to get you all out there today. The weather's good. The ground should be dry and firm, and we shouldn't have any trouble."

Rachel passed a handful of CDs to Karl Will, who passed them to the other experts. I said, "These are copies of all of the photos that have been accumulated so far, both the photos the NTSB has given us on a separate CD, and the photos that we took at the scene and at the hangar in Maryland as part of our investigation. I also put together a DVD" — Rachel handed another stack of Diamond Boxes to Karl — "that are the digital videotapes that Rachel took at the scene. There is some footage at the hangar as well, but most is from the scene at the day of the accident."

"Did you give all this to the NTSB?"

"No. They didn't ask for it. We weren't the official representatives of WorldCopter, we were just there to assist WorldCopter. These tapes belong to me, or WorldCopter, or maybe even its insurance company. I don't know, but the NTSB doesn't have them."

"Good," Holly said.

I walked them through the entire investigation as we knew it, including the criticisms we had of the NTSB's preliminary findings. Everybody had criticisms of the preliminary findings, particularly those who had previously worked for the NTSB.

Bradley said, "This is a political nightmare for the NTSB. Nothing they can do will ever survive the scrutiny that it's going to get after that report is issued. This is going to be like the Warren Commission on stilts. I'm sure the conspiracy theories are already flying —"

"They are," I said.

"Figures. The NTSB has got to be dreading publishing their final report. I'm frankly surprised they came up with a preliminary. They probably just did it so everybody would know the president wasn't murdered."

"But we don't know that," I said.

"True enough," Holly said. "This report says there is no evidence of foul play, but that means with missiles, bombs, something that would blow up and leave a residue. There's nothing to say there wasn't foul play on the aircraft itself. If you stab somebody, there won't be any evidence in a body that's burned down to the bone. You might find the blade, but not if it was thrown off the helicopter before it crashed. Do you have confidence they've found every piece of the wreckage that's relevant? Because I sure don't."

I looked over at her to see if she was just speculating or if she had suspicions. "You really think the president was murdered?"

"No. I'm just starting with a blank slate. Whatever the NTSB says is irrelevant. I don't trust their methods, their people, or their politics. If they gather some evidence that's useful, I'll use it. Anything they *say,* or conclude, I'll ignore. We've got to do our own investigation here, Mike. Our own metallurgy, our own analysis, our own fire analysis, our own explosives and foul-play analysis. We need former FBI investigators, we need explosive experts, and we need forensic chemists and forensic pathologists. We've got to ramp this way up, Mike, and I mean right now. I think we've got to beat the NTSB to a final conclusion. They'll probably take two years to get there. We need to get there in six months. That's what I'm saying."

Bradley and Karl nodded. I walked up to the front of the conference room and stood by Rachel. "As you know, and as Holly just implied, timing is critical here. It's not the NTSB we're racing. We're also going to be racing the court. You all know the case was filed here in Annapolis? Well, this court-house is new. It doesn't have that many cases. Most federal cases in Maryland are filed in Baltimore or Greenbelt. The local court decided to increase its docket by creating a 'rocket docket.' You get to trial two or three times faster than in other federal courts. Some courts around the country had done that for patent cases, but this is the first one that has done it for all civil cases. They have a mandatory rule — every civil case *will* go to trial in six months. And if you're not ready, too bad."

They all stared at each other, surprised and concerned. Will said, "How can we prepare the most important investigation in the country in six months?"

"By putting everything else we're doing on the back burner, that's how. It's going to be crazy, but we have no choice. Hackett thought this through very carefully. He can just give the photographs and the NTSB's preliminary report to his experts, show them the blade with the missing tip weights, and they'll testify that this was WorldCopter's fault. We've got to solve this case before he gets to do that."

Bradley took an audible deep breath. "Can we even get our hands on the metal?"

"Some of it. They've left much of the wreckage in the hangar for the participants to continue to work with, but no one else. So if we can get you in as WorldCopter's people, we can get to the wreckage. But not otherwise, and we won't get to do any destructive testing, I promise you.

"This room will be our war room. You can use it for any purpose in this case. We will be having all-expert meetings every two weeks, whether you like it or not. And I know that's not usually the way it's done, but I don't care about preserving walls between experts or attorney work product. We need to share ideas, and brainstorm, to solve this thing. If you need anything at all, let me know and we'll get it for you. If you need manpower, I'll get it. If you need exemplars of parts from a similar helicopter, I'll get them for you. Anything. No stone left unturned, and no reasonable request denied. This is all-out. And we're working against the clock."

Bradley nodded, satisfied for now. "Let's go see the crash site, Mike," he insisted as he pressed down on the table and forced himself to his feet.

It was eerie being back at the site of the accident. The scene had been released by the NTSB, but FBI agents were still guarding everything for a mile around. They were clearly not pleased to be in the middle of nowhere, but they also knew that when a president died, a lot of things happened.

We hiked to the crash site as quickly as we could as a group, which meant mostly waiting for Bradley. He brought an assistant to walk with him to help him along the packed dirt to the site. The handful of FBI agents who had the thankless duty of patrolling the center of the crash site saw us coming. One ducked under the police tape and approached us. "Can I help you?"

I always love it when government officials who know exactly who you are and just spoke to someone about you pretend that they've never heard of you. "Didn't you get a call from your friends up the hill that we were coming?"

"Yeah. I knew you were coming."

"We're just here to look around. We're here on behalf of WorldCopter to begin our own investigation."

The FBI agent said coldly, "I thought the NTSB already came out with their conclusions."

"Preliminary conclusions. Meaning they could change."

The FBI agent looked me in the eye with some pity. "Meaning also, then, I suppose they might not change."

"True enough."

We ducked under the yellow tape and walked into the center of the crash site. Our investigators set down their bags, took out their expensive digital cameras, GPS receivers, and laptops. Bradley had his assistant set up a camp table and put his laptop and microscope on top of it. He then pulled out a camp stool and lowered his weight onto it slowly. He tilted his Indiana Jones fedora back and said, "Tip weights. NTSB is saying basically the tip weights may have come off or been out of balance, caused the blade to vibrate and pull out of its seating. Interesting theory, but unprovable as of now."

We all looked at him, but I said, "Why?"

"They didn't find any tip weights. They aren't on the blade, and they weren't on the ground."

Holly added, "They assume they came off before the crash. Somewhere in the turbulence. They think they're scattered all over the countryside and won't ever be found."

Rachel said, "They used metal detectors all around here. They didn't find any of them."

Bradley shook his head and rolled his eyes. "Metal detectors can give a false sense of confidence. If you really want to find something, like on the beach, something specific, you had better sift the sand, not hope your wand passes over it just right."

"They can't sift the entire countryside."

"We have to work backwards my friend, duplicate what the NTSB undoubtedly did, but perhaps we'll find what they didn't. We have to determine the flight of that blade under various possible scenarios and find the scenario that would allow the tip weights to come out to cause that blade to vibrate off the masthead. Then we calculate the possible speeds of the blade, which should be upwards of six hundred twenty-five knots, and determine the maximum throw distance of those tip weights coming cleanly off the blade at its maximum speed of rotation, which should give us a theoretical radius within which we should find the tip weights."

Bradley turned to the table and turned on his laptop. He placed a case on top of the table next to his laptop and opened it. Inside was a Nikon digital SLR camera with several lenses, mostly macro. He looked at the sky to see the likelihood of direct sunlight, which he preferred when photographing metal. A large cloud was passing over the sun but was unlikely to last.

Rachel asked him, "How could we ever find little washers within a mile or two radius of a particular spot if we can't find them with a metal detector?"

"With determination, diligence, and luck."

Rachel looked around and considered the likelihood of finding a couple of washers in several square miles of woods. "Doesn't sound very likely to me."

"Nor me. But if we use our brains, perhaps we'll think of something they didn't."

"Like what?"

Bradley breathed deeply. "Well, for example, the NTSB is convinced the blade came off a mile or two away from here and just landed next to the helicopter in one of those weird things that happens in many accidents."

I was listening to every word and stopped fiddling with my camera to make sure I heard him.

He continued, "That is probably right, as I see it. I don't think the blade came off right here, on the way down. But it is an assumption. You see how an early assumption can lead you astray? Anyway, the *additional* assumption is that the tip weights came off before the blade came off and therefore are 'out there' somewhere, miles from here."

I jumped in, "Well, if their tip-weight theory is true, wouldn't that make sense?"

"Make sense? Sure. It would make sense. But does it make it *true?* A certainty? Not at all. Physics determines what happens, not theories. Tip weights can stick, they can fracture and loosen those outside of them and come off later, all kinds of possibilities. What I think, ladies and gentlemen, is that the answers lie in this cathedral." Bradley waved his arm around over his head toward the canopy of trees that surrounded the accident scene. "The answers, and perhaps even the tip weights, are right here."

We stayed at the site until dark. We climbed out of the ravine on the now solid and easy-to-follow dirt road and headed home, only to eat, sleep, rise, and head to the office again before dawn.

One night on my way home later that week,

Byrd called. "Hey. What's up?"

"Been pushy on our reluctant witness. You know the one."

"Good. He ready to meet?"

"He wants to go the other way. Suddenly he has no idea who I am. Won't even return my calls."

"That's not good."

"Not. But get this. Tonight I got a visit. Not a call, a visit. I was on the throne, so my wife, Cherie, answered the door. I always tell her not to, but she does anyway. She's human. I come into the family room and there's a guy in my house by the door. Not really a threat, distinguished-looking, older. Like the IRS or something. I ask him who the hell he is and what he's doing in my house. He stares at me and says that he wants a meeting with you."

"Me?"

"You."

"Why didn't he call? . . . Who is he?"

"Exactly what I wanted to know."

"What did he say?"

"He said he wanted to meet with you, and he wanted me to set it up."

"So who is he?"

"You're not going to believe it. Head of security for the State Department."

"The State Department?"

"Yep."

"What does he want to talk to me about?"

"Wouldn't say."

"Well, shit, Tinny. What do you make of this?"

"I thought it was a joke. Another one of Hackett's head fakes. I checked him out. He's legit."

"So now what?"

"So now you tell me whether you want to meet with him. But I've got to say, I didn't feel like we had a lot of choice here. We're going to hear what he has to say no matter what."

I looked out my window, down the dark street. "Set it up."

We met the next night. It was to be at my office at 10 PM. Byrd arrived at nine thirty. "Michael," Byrd said, extending his hand.

"Tinny. How are you doing?"

"Good. So here we are."

"Yeah. To quote Dustin Hoffman, 'Is it "safe"?' "

Byrd smiled. "Good flick. I don't know if it's safe. We're dealing with the government, and they aren't going to do anything too stupid. But here we are at ten o'clock at night meeting someone from the State Department in Annapolis. Can't say I've done that before."

"Why the late hour?"

"Don't know for sure. I expect they want to be able to deny they ever met you if this goes south."

"If what goes south?"

"Well, we're about to find out," he said, looking over my shoulder at the phone as it lit and rang. "Here we go."

I turned and answered it.

A man said, "We're out front. Please let us in."

"It's open. Come on up to the second floor."

The line went dead.

We heard the door below open and two men walk up the stairs. I went to the door of my office, from which I could see the top of the steps. "Over here," I said.

They walked into my office. The first man extended his hand to Tinny. "Mr. Byrd, good to see you again."

"Likewise. This is Mike Nolan."

The man turned toward me. "Thank you for coming. I'm Chris Thompson."

I shook his hand. "And who is this?" I said, watching the other man approach.

"This is my associate Joe Galvin." Thompson was about my size but at least ten years older. Dark hair, cut short with gray throughout, and definitely in shape. He had dark eyes and an intense look. He said, "Thanks for meeting with us. I know this is a little out of the ordinary, but so are the circumstances. May we sit down?"

"Of course." I indicated the two seats in front of my desk. Byrd sat on the arm of the couch slightly behind them. Galvin didn't like that at all, but couldn't do anything about it.

Thompson said, "First, before I go on, I want to ask you both for your personal guarantees of confidentiality. May I have your assurance?"

"Why should I?" I asked.

"Because what I have to say to you is for your own good, and frankly for the good of the country. If you cannot keep the contents of our conversation confidential, then I cannot say what I need to say to you."

"Why would that concern me?"

"Because you need to hear it."

"Okay. For now."

Thompson looked at me sharply. "I need your assurance that you will keep it confidential forever."

I looked at Byrd. "Okay. Unless I don't like the way it's going; then I'll stop listening and we'll be done."

Thompson looked at Tinny. "And you,

Mr. Byrd?"

"Sure."

"Do you have any recording devices on you?"

"No."

"You wouldn't mind if Joe checked, would you?"

"Yes, I'd mind."

"Well, I insist."

Joe checked Tinny for a tape recorder.

Thompson said, "Let me get right to the point —"

"Before you do," I said, "who are you?"

"I work for the State Department. My boss reports directly to the secretary. We're in INR."

"Sorry?"

"Bureau of Intelligence and Research."

"Intelligence?"

"Yes. For the State Department."

"Didn't know there was such a thing."

"Few do. My role is really more about security."

"So what can I do for you?"

"Very simple." Thompson looked at Byrd, then back at me. "You've been talking to a certain Secret Service agent. He seems to have a soft spot for other former Marines." He looked directly at Byrd. "I'm a former Marine too. Grunt. Retired, twenty years as a lieutenant Colonel. I saw a lot. Spent a lot of time floating around with MEUs. So I get the idea of camaraderie between former Marines."

"Go on."

"Well, this Secret Service agent overstepped his bounds. He has been considering talking to Mr. Byrd and may have mentioned a document he isn't even supposed to have. It was a breach of protocol and security for him to keep a copy. It is a State Department document."

"So? And what is the document?"

"You have asked Mr. Byrd to continue to push on this agent, and I suspect you intend to try use him or his 'document' in trial, if your case comes to that. You need to assure me that you won't ask this witness about what he has or saw, and you won't try to dig any deeper about it."

"Are you serious?" I said, outraged. "What he knows could be the key to the entire accident."

"It isn't. That's the point," Thompson said. "The meeting at Camp David had nothing to do with the accident. The helicopter went down because of faulty balancing of the blade and the tip weights."

I stared at him, barely able to contain my annoyance. "Are you telling me the NTSB knows who was at the meeting and the document that Secret Service agent has?"

"Of course they do."

"Why wasn't that part of their press conference?"

"Because it has nothing to do with the accident, and if someone discusses it and the contents get out, it will cause an international incident."

"How would it cause an international incident?"

"You need to stop pursuing this agent."

"I can't do that."

"You have to."

"No, I don't."

"If you pursue it, we will make it very difficult for you."

"Now the threats."

"These aren't threats. If you push, we will push back."

I glanced at Tinny, who was silent. "I'll just subpoena the agent to trial."

"No, you won't. And if you did, it wouldn't matter. He no longer has a copy of that document. He was kind enough to give it to me. Any testimony he might have would be hearsay and not admissible, I'm told. So any such efforts on your part would be futile. And Mr. Byrd here," Thompson said, looking at Byrd, "gave the agent his word that he would never tell you what the agent's name was. We all know at least one thing: Mr. Byrd is good for his word. Right, Mr. Byrd?"

I stood up. "Thanks for coming, but I'm going to keep going just like I have been. I need to find the truth."

"No, you don't. Even if you find out, it won't help you. Lay off. For your own good."

"What the hell is that supposed to mean?"

Thompson lowered his voice to almost a whisper and stood to look me right in the eye. "Meaning you have no idea what you're dealing with here. You're out of your league. Just let it go. Leave the Camp David angle out of it. It's a dead end."

"I'll be the judge of that."

"No, you won't. I am, and I'm telling you to lay off."

"Or what?"

"Or nothing. I wouldn't threaten you. That would be . . . wrong. But the secretary of state is very concerned about the others who were at that meeting. They would be very unhappy if the fact or the purpose of the meeting ever came out." Thompson looked around my office in silence. His sidekick stood up with him as if they were about to leave. Thompson said, "There are

very many people who have the same interest — that you never find out or disclose
anything about that meeting. If you continue
what you and" — Thompson turned —
"Mr. Byrd are doing, they may take steps to
stop you. I have no control over them or
what they do. I don't know what they might
do, I'm just looking out for your interests."
Thompson opened the door to my office.
"Look, this is a product-liability case. Don't
be a hero. Settle it. Make it go away. Don't
embarrass yourself and your client."

"So you would help these 'people' out by
directing them to me, but of course you
would never do anything yourself."

"I don't have to direct anyone to you.
Everyone in the country knows who you
are. Your name is everywhere. I might only
tell certain people that you are intent on
disclosing the content of this certain meeting. Just know that many of the people who
would be angered by what you are doing
are outside our government, and many
would have diplomatic immunity. They
couldn't even be charged with a crime."

"I think you need to leave."

"Not quite yet." Thompson put his hands
in his pockets. "I know you and Byrd like to
play the Marine-brotherhood angle. Well,
Mr. Nolan, if you continue to press this,

this will come back to bite you. You see, I've read your Marine Corps *file.* And you know what's in there." He waited for a reaction. "If you don't do as I've asked, certain people will learn about what happened in Iraq. And," he said, watching the anger rise in my eyes, "I suspect you wouldn't want that to happen."

"There's nothing in my file."

Thompson smiled. "That's what you wish were true. Even though most of it is gone, the copy of the file at Headquarters Marine Corps tells the whole story, Mr. Nolan. And you definitely don't want that out. It would jeopardize everything you've built. You'd be thrown out of the Marine Reserves. And your ability to practice law would be in trouble, wouldn't it? You see, I've seen your application for membership in the Maryland bar too. And it is notably silent about what happened in Iraq."

"It wasn't called —"

"I'm sure you'd have a chance to explain it. But you might just lose your license and never be able to practice law again. So think about it."

"I may just go right to the press and tell them about your threats. About everything that has happened tonight."

"No, you won't, because then *I'll* tell them

everything you don't want out. And when I got here, I asked you if you had a recording device. But you never asked me. If I did have a recording device, and if I felt like it, I could have all these digital sounds duplicated and rearranged to have you say anything I want. So don't press it."

"I don't scare easily."

"I don't expect you to be scared, Mike, I expect you to be smart." Thompson smiled and walked out of the office.

I said nothing as I heard them walk down the wooden steps of my building and close the outside door behind them. I walked over to my office window and watched them as they disappeared down the street. "Well, that was disturbing."

Byrd stood next to me at the window. When they were out of sight, he turned. "So what happened in Iraq?"

"Nothing."

"Really? Nothing?"

"Drop it."

Byrd stood silently.

I said, "What document is he talking about?"

"That's my question too. Now they've gone and made me curious."

13

When you get sued in federal court, you have to file an answer denying the claims made against you. In Annapolis, when you file it, you quickly learn that you have stepped onto the six-month conveyor belt that will take you to trial no matter how much you thrash or complain. It's like a melodrama where the heroine is tied to the moving belt in a sawmill heading toward the large, spinning blade.

Since most court filings are now electronic, things happen in hours, or minutes. Fifteen minutes after I filed our answer, we received a notice by e-mail from the court for the Early Neutral Evaluation conference to be held that same week. The purpose of the ENE before the magistrate was to see if the case could quickly be settled, or if it would go to trial. We had drawn the magistrate I knew best, Barbara Norris. She was competent, did not aspire to greater office

— unlike many magistrates — and didn't inject her personality into the case. She just tried to do what was right, get the case resolved if she could, and if not, help the parties get to trial quickly. You couldn't ask for anyone better.

The day for the conference came. Rachel and I got there early, but not earlier than the press. It looked like a rehearsal for the trial they suspected was coming. Satellite vans were everywhere, cables and cameras running back and forth, and an amazing amount of activity for a hearing they wouldn't be invited to. ENEs are generally held in the magistrate's office, not in the courtroom.

After we made our way into the court-house, we were ushered into the magistrate's courtroom. Margaret, Norris's clerk, closed the doors behind us, keeping the press outside in the hall. As Rachel and I entered, we saw that Hackett and his entourage were already there. Hackett was standing with his back to the judge's bench, looking at us as we walked in. Waiting for us. When he saw me, he said nothing and did nothing. He just stood there holding his briefcase in front of him with both hands. His feet were spread slightly apart, and I was suddenly aware of his size. He had to be at least six feet four and had graying blond hair that he combed back. To his right was another partner that I recognized from Hackett's firm's Web site. Gregory Bass — pronounced like the fish, not the guitar. Bass was about forty with a closely buzzed haircut. He was known in all the articles I had read as Hackett's "bulldog." Their word. He didn't try cases, he just chopped up the other side in motions, depositions, and generally being as tough as he could get away with.

On Hackett's left was an attractive woman, medium height and attentive. Probably a paralegal. I didn't recognize her. The first lady was of course not there, nor was any representative of WorldCopter. This was a meeting for attorneys only.

I looked at Hackett, looked at Bass, looked at his paralegal, and glanced over their shoulders to the judge's law clerk, whom I saw looking from the door in the corner.

Since Hackett hadn't said anything to me, I returned the favor. I saw Margaret heading to the door out of the courtroom that led to the magistrate's chambers — Norris's office — and said, "I think we're all here, Margaret."

She nodded as she continued through the door, sparing me the remark that was undoubtedly on her tongue, that she had already figured that out and it accounted for her heading to the door. I, of course, knew that too, but wanted, in a childish way, to show Hackett that I knew the magistrate's clerk.

I pointed Rachel to a row of seats in the back of the courtroom. We sat down and took out copies of the filings that we had delivered to the court the week before. They were fairly innocuous, committed us to nothing, and left all roads open to us. It gave us something to do.

Hackett stood there and looked at us. After he realized I wasn't going to say anything to him, he seemed just slightly flustered. He turned around and walked through the swinging door between the gallery and the counsel tables in the courtroom, then placed his briefcase on the top of the table. He sat down in one of the counsel seats, and Bass followed suit. The woman went with them, but stood at the far end of the table looking through a notebook.

Margaret came back through the door and said, "Please come into the chambers." Hackett and his two acolytes went immediately into the chambers and the door closed behind them. Rachel and I got up from our seats, walked to the door, opened it, and entered. Magistrate Norris recognized me immediately and said, "Good morning, Mike, nice to see you again." She then turned to Hackett and said, "And you must be Mr. Hackett."

While Annapolis is the capital of Maryland, it is still a small town. The attorneys all know each other, and those of us who try cases regularly know all the judges and they all know us. Our reputations are already established, good or bad. This magistrate would almost qualify as a friend, not that we got together socially, but we saw eye to eye on most things, and she knew I didn't take ridiculous positions.

She motioned for us to all sit down on the couches and chairs placed around the coffee table in the corner of her office. It was the largest magistrate office in the small federal courthouse because she was the senior magistrate judge. Three of the walls were lined with law books, and the other wall had two colorful paintings.

The magistrate smiled at Rachel, who had appeared before her about five times. Hackett noticed and was irritated again. Norris led us through the conference professionally and quickly. We discussed what needed to be done, what discovery we anticipated, what motions might come, the primary issues in the case, and the usual civil concerns. But after fifteen minutes of the usual, with the attorneys only responding to the magistrate's questions, she said to Hackett, "One of the reasons we hold these conferences is to assess the likelihood of settlement. What are your thoughts?"

Hackett almost smiled. "My thoughts are simple. We made a time-sensitive demand, and they rejected it. I told them there would be no other offer, and I meant it. So in short, the case will not settle. We are preparing for trial."

Norris was surprised. She asked Hackett and his group to leave so she could speak to Rachel and me alone. After the door closed behind Hackett and the chambers were quiet, she said to me, "Mr. Nolan, have you seen the press? Have you seen how many people there are standing outside this courthouse this morning? This case is going to be a circus. You know that?"

"That's exactly what Hackett wants."

She didn't respond. She took a sip of coffee from the mug on the table in front of her. "I think Mr. Hackett is right. This case is going to trial."

I waited.

"Mr. Nolan, do you have any settlement authority to even begin discussions?"

"No, I don't, Your Honor. AII and World-Copter rejected his offer out of hand and told him so. There have been no further discussions because he says not to bother. I knew you'd ask and I tried to get some authority, but we really don't know what caused the accident yet. Hackett has filed prematurely. He's in a big hurry."

"The United States government has determined what the cause is, even if it's preliminary, the first lady has asked for compensation, and WorldCopter, the company that killed the president, is stonewalling. That's what he's going to sell. You understand that?"

"Yes, ma'am, I do. We can only do so much and at a certain pace. The NTSB's findings are flawed, and we're working on the cause. I think they may have it completely wrong. I just can't prove it yet."

"What was his demand?"

"One billion dollars."

She couldn't hide her surprise. "For seven wrongful death cases? Even if one of them is the president. I guess it depends on how much you project a retired president would make, but I would think these cases altogether can't be worth more than one hundred or one hundred fifty million dollars." She frowned. "It's amazing how many cases resolve when you force them to go to trial. And I mean force. Motions for continuing trials are denied. Judge Baxter denied one last week even though one of the attorneys had a death in the family. He put in the order that it was sad, but the attorney wasn't the lead attorney and the death wasn't from her *immediate* family." Norris smiled. "So these dates are written in stone. And I expect Judge Betancourt will have no interest in dragging this out. A circus is bad enough. A circus that goes on too long is much worse. You do understand that?"

"Yes, ma'am," I said.

The magistrate stood up and walked toward the door. "I will now speak with Mr. Hackett and see if I can encourage him to approach you with a new settlement demand. I don't expect him to. I do not think this trial will benefit the country or heal the wound that is currently bleeding. But I believe he thinks the fact the wound is open and hurting is better for him. I will try to dissuade him of that notion." She looked up as she put her hand on the door before we went out into the courtroom. "Mr. Nolan, if you think that you can find the cause of the accident that differs from the NTSB's preliminary conclusion, I'd suggest you find it very quickly. If this case goes to trial, it is going to be the biggest case in the history of our civil court system. Don't let that happen."

The next morning at six thirty I met Tinny at the Blue Mug, a coffee shop I knew by the waterfront. I went with some trepidation — he said he was bringing a "friend." I didn't know what to make of that. Byrd scared me. He dug stuff up and found people that I had no idea where they'd come from or how he'd done it. But he had saved my ass several times. This time, much to my surprise, he brought someone I had already spoken to: Jason Britt. They were waiting for me when I arrived. I shook Tinny's hand and then Britt's as I said to him, "What the hell are you doing here?"

I looked at Tinny, who was controlling a smile. He said, "Let's get some coffee. I had to leave at an ungodly hour to get here."

"I thought you didn't want to meet in public."

"Nah, we're early. It's cool."

We ordered and sat at the table in the front that looked through the windowpanes over the water. Byrd said, "So I asked Britt here what you talked about and he told me. You left a lot of things unasked, Nolan. As usual. So I started over. He told me some things that I think you ought to hear. Some more things about your boy Collins."

I looked at Britt, who looked a little bit uncomfortable but also excited. It's funny how some people respond to being a witness in a big case. A lot of people run the other way. They want nothing to do with testifying. Others respond in exactly the opposite way. Suddenly they're the center of attention. Suddenly everybody hangs on every word. Everybody wants to know what they think. They'll be called in a trial and be on world television. Some people love that. It's a problem because it can affect their testimony. It can make them bend the truth or embellish it, so that they are more interesting, or in demand, or, worse, more notorious. Some witnesses even imagine themselves being so popular and in demand that after "this is all over," as they all say, they'll write a book about it. They actually believe that they will have an audience for a book that they will write about what they know. They're almost certainly wrong about that, but they believe it in their hearts. So when a witness suddenly grows interested in testifying voluntarily and wants to let you know things that they remember differently from what they had told you at the initial interview, I'm always wary. But I knew Britt wasn't going to make things up. He'd buff a fact here or there to make it look a little better or different in his story, but he wouldn't make it up.

I said to Britt, "He threaten you? Bribe you? How did he get you into this? You about hung up on me last time."

Britt smiled. "No, he just started asking me a bunch of questions, one Marine to another. He was looking at something, I'm not sure what, maybe like his CV or something. He knew a lot about Collins already and just started asking me if I knew anything about when Collins was here, and when Collins was there."

I nodded. "So he stimulated some memories?"

"Not so much a memory as something that I heard."

"What'd you hear?"

Britt sat forward and leaned on the iron table with his elbows so he could not be overheard. Not that anyone else was around; we were the first people there. "Well, Mr. Byrd here asked me if I knew anything about Collins's Purple Heart. I had forgotten he had a Purple Heart."

"Is that from Desert One?" I asked.

"No. That's the thing. He wasn't wounded

226

in Desert One. This was from the time he was the executive officer of a forty-six squadron in Iraq. During the siege of Fallujah."

I didn't even know Collins had a Purple Heart from Falluja. I was all ears. "What happened?"

"Well, you know how there's sometimes the official version, and then there's the other version?"

"Sure."

"Well, the official version is that Captain America was flying forty-sixes under fire evacuating wounded Marines. Took a severely wounded Marine out of a combat zone and while flying away took an AK-47 round right in the jaw. Bleeding like a stuck pig, he continued to fly, got his wounded Marine to the aid station, where he checked him in and was admitted himself, then later was flown to Germany for surgery."

"And what's the real story?"

"The real story is that the week before he got shot, he had braced up a Marine captain for flying through a prohibited zone to get a wounded Marine back to the base in time to save his life. If he'd gone around, the guy probably would have died. That didn't matter to Collins. The standing order was what mattered. You didn't fly through the prohibited zone no matter what. It endangered one of his precious thirty-year-old helicopters.

"All the other pilots in the squadron thought Collins was out of his mind. The captain's helicopter took a few rounds, but nobody got hurt. Collins went postal, but the other pilots in the squadron thought Collins should put the guy in for a medal. Collins refused. Said he was lucky not to be brought up on charges for violating the standing order. So, get this, the *ground* troops, the battalion from where the guy was rescued, *they* put the captain up for a medal.

"Then, the very next week, Collins himself is flying through the prohibited zone. No call for medevac, he's just tooling around flying through the zone like John Wayne 'cause he feels like it. And he gets shot in the face and his crew chief gets shot in the leg. Collins flies himself to the medical evacuation and puts himself in for a Purple Heart and for an Air Medal. The Air Medal didn't go anywhere 'cause everybody knew what had happened, but he got the Purple Heart because he was 'wounded in action.'

"He went to Germany for facial surgery, where they did a partial jaw replacement with a titanium jawbone. He got sent back to his squadron while it was still in Iraq. So behind his back everybody started calling him T-Jaw. His officers were not impressed, and they thought he was a complete self-promoting jerk. From what I understand, that kind of conduct was pretty typical."

I was stunned. I had never heard this story. Talk like this got around in the Marine Corps. "How is it I've never heard this before?"

Britt shrugged. "Probably people were a little wary of passing it on. It could have torpedoed his career. Marines love bravery, they love real men. They love taking one in the chest for the Corps. But what they *hate*, as you well know, is a self-serving, self-promoting asshole who is only looking out for his own career." Britt took a deep drink from his coffee. "People didn't know for sure what had happened. Nobody was really there except for a couple of people. It was virtually impossible to sort it out. But I heard it. Always in the superhushed 'promise not to tell anybody' kind of talk. But I heard it from a couple of sources. I don't know if it's true, but that's what I heard."

"How did the people who were checking out his background for his job flying Marine One — how did *they* not hear about this?"

"They may have, they may have given him the chance to answer it. Maybe he had a good explanation, maybe he said that the rumor was started by other Marine pilots who were envious, who thought he'd gotten promoted too quickly above others. Maybe he wasn't outside the flight area and someone just tacked that onto the story to bang him for the way he treated that captain. Don't know. Lots of possibilities. You know how that can start. Someone thinks you're bypassing them in the promotion ranks? It's not unheard of that they'll start a false rumor."

"So which is it? Was it a false rumor or did that happen? Is T-Jaw a fraud?"

Britt shrugged. "I don't know, I'm just telling you what I heard."

I looked at Byrd, who was staring at Britt. I asked him, "What do you think, Tinny?"

"Beats the hell out of me. I just thought you should hear what the man had to say. But I tell you what. The more I learn about this guy, the more cracks I see in the marble statue."

I stood up and Britt followed me to his feet. "Thanks for coming down. You didn't have to come all this way."

"No, I had to meet with a subcontractor based here. It's no problem."

He walked to his car and drove off as Byrd and I sat back down. The sky was a bright blue with golden morning sunlight illuminating the city. We could hear the lanyards of the moored sailboats two blocks away slapping against their masts as they rocked with the incoming tide.

"Tinny, I think we have to keep digging."

"I'm deeper than you know."

"One thing continues to haunt me here."

"What's that?"

"Why the hell was the president going to Camp David?"

Byrd nodded as he tossed his cup away. He zipped up his leather valise and said, "You know I'm already on that. That's one of the things that's a little bit deeper. I haven't hit the wood of the buried chest yet, but my shovel's getting close to the lid."

"How do you know there is a chest, how do you know there's a lid at all? How do you know it wasn't just some poker game with a bunch of school buddies?"

"Or strippers."

"Oh, right. The president was risking his life to fly to a stag party. Come on."

"Something big was happening. I'm talking to that other Marine. Boy from the Secret Service."

"The one our friend from State told us to lay off of."

"The same."

"You're not laying off, I take it."

Byrd frowned in disgust. "You want me to?"

"No. But Thompson seemed pretty damned serious and stayed real vague about the consequences."

"Said he'd tell people. So what?"

"Well, the implication is those other people might try to stop us."

"They can just kiss my ass. I'm not stopping for anyone."

I smiled. "So what did he say?"

"Turns out he was at Camp David that night."

"You said that. Waiting for President Adams."

"Yep."

"And?"

"That's all we know. He won't talk. Our Mr. Thompson has visited him. Told him to shut his mouth. National security."

"So that's it?"

"I'll keep pushing him. But there's no telling if he's going to come around. Thompson is pulling a lot of strings and talking to a lot of people. We need to watch out for him." Byrd rubbed his finger on the table. "I asked him about this mystery document." Tinny paused. "I saw it in his eyes, Michael. I think he still has it, or a copy. Whatever it is. I've got a feeling about him. Not only does he know a lot, I think he's dying to tell us. But there are forces out there, Michael, forces." Tinny looked at his watch. "I gotta go. Catch you later." He looked around for any unusual movement and headed toward his car.

14

Hackett had waited around a day after the ENE for the required meeting of the attorneys in the case to discuss the case schedule. It is mandatory and must be in person. *Somehow* the press had received a copy of his letter requesting the meeting at my office. They were waiting for me when I returned from my meeting with Byrd. Microphones and reporters everywhere. I waved them off, pushed through the ranks, and closed the door behind me. Dolores was concerned. Several of the reporters had simply walked into the office, sat in the chairs, and waited for me. At some point Berberian had come out and told them to leave, that if I wanted to invite them in to discuss the case, I would do so, but unless they were clients, it was time for them to go. So they waited on the steps.

Dolores had set up the boardroom for the conference and cleaned out all the materials

I had been working on with the experts. I waited, and after arriving fashionably late in a limousine, Hackett and his entourage made their way through the press slowly, answering a few questions over his shoulder. Dolores showed him to the conference room. He came in, greeted us, and sat down. He and his associates took off their coats, made themselves comfortable, and grabbed coffee and muffins. Rachel was there as well as Justin, our disheveled paralegal. I had drafted a proposed scheduling order that I wanted Hackett to look at. I pulled it out of my briefcase and passed it around the table. "Here's the scheduling order that I would propose. As you know, this court is on the fast —"

Hackett handed the scheduling order back to me. "I don't think those dates will work."

"You haven't even looked at them."

"I have prepared an order that I think is in final form and I would like for you to sign it."

My face began to turn red as I glanced at Rachel, who was trying to convince me not to say what she knew I wanted to say. I took his order and looked at it. It had the most aggressive discovery schedule I had ever seen. It had all the depositions and document discovery completed within four months. This was faster than even the District Court of Maryland contemplated in its rocket-docket standard scheduling order.

"I don't know," I said, looking at Hackett. "This is awfully ambitious. It seems to contemplate that we won't have any discovery disputes and we can get this all done."

"Oh. We won't have any discovery disputes, I'm sure. I believe in turning over everything, I'm sure you do as well. I think after we take depositions, this case will be ready to go. My experts are ready to testify in trial tomorrow. I see no reason to delay."

No doubt his experts were ready to testify tomorrow since all they were going to do was recite the NTSB's preliminary opinion. I had to disprove that theory and needed time to do that.

I handed the order back to him. "Can't do it."

Hackett sat down and leaned heavily on the table as if he were dealing with a dunce or a child. "Mr. Nolan. Do you refuse to cooperate in discovery?"

I sat down across from him and leaned on the table directly toward him. "No. I don't refuse to cooperate. What I refuse to do is capitulate. If you want discovery, then do it.

If you want it done fast, then do it fast."

Hackett shook his head. "As you wish. Your client's employ*ees* are the ones who will be deposed. And I love France." He reached over in front of his associate and placed his hand on the table, palm up. His associate placed a pile of documents in his hand, which Hackett retrieved. Hackett handed them to me.

"Here you go, *Mike,*" he said, emphasizing *Mike* like it was a disease. He took a deep breath and shrugged his shoulders dramatically. "As you know, discovery may commence *immediately* after the Early Neutral Evaluation conference. We just had that conference." He pointed to the documents. "Here are thirty-five deposition notices of the witnesses I want to depose beginning next Thursday in Paris. I will see you there."

It was exactly what I had expected him to do. It was the biggest grandstanding move available to him. Hackett looked for a reaction from me.

"No problem, *Tom.*" I looked at the pile of notices quickly. "This of course exceeds the number of depositions allowed under the rules, but I'll be happy to stipulate that you can do this. I had actually expected to begin the depositions in Paris on Monday, but you don't have them starting until

Thursday." I looked at Rachel. "We can cancel our hotel reservations for those extra days, once we get done here." I turned back to Hackett. "We'll see you there. And by the way" — Rachel handed me our documents — "here is the deposition notice for the first lady and the other widows. I've set them for here, in my office, for the week after we get back from Paris. But if you want to do them in your D.C. office, just let me know. We're happy to accommodate you."

At ten o'clock that night I sat back, took off my tie, and drank a large bottle of water. I hadn't eaten since ten in the morning and I was about to pass out. I had a jar of Planters peanuts in my drawer that I reached for as Rachel walked into my office.

She sat down heavily and smiled. "What a day."

"Remarkable. You ready to go tomorrow? BWI nonstop to Paris. We've got to get our witnesses prepared. I thought he'd give us a couple of weeks. We've got to double track, with me preparing the executives, and you preparing the manufacturing workers."

Rachel chuckled, slid down in the leather chair, put her head on the back of the chair, and looked at the ceiling. "Figures."

"What?" I said as I poured some peanuts

into my hand and tossed them into my mouth.

"Do you know what date today is?"

"No, what?"

"It's my birthday. My thirty-fifth freaking birthday."

"Wow. Sorry. Can't believe I missed that. Happy birthday — want some nuts?" I offered her the jar.

"Very funny. But you know what else?" She sat up.

"What?"

"I told you that I didn't want to get married again. I didn't want to make the same backbreaking mistake I made when I married that asshole — he who shall remain nameless."

"And?"

"Well, I was lying. I do want to get married again. Or at least become a mother before I'm eighty. And since I think after this it goes thirty-six, thirty-seven, eighty, I'm basically done. My womb is going to shrivel up like a raisin. The only thing I'll ever give birth to is another raisin."

"Oh, please. Thirty-five isn't that old."

"Yes, it is. Maybe I don't want to get married, I don't know, maybe I don't even want to be a mother. What I hate is not being in control." She looked down with an ironic smile on her face. She looked at me. "This Friday was going to be my first date in a year. And I'm going to miss it." She didn't sound that disappointed. "He's probably not worth it anyway. It's just Freddy."

I frowned. "Freddy, the dentist?"

"Yes. The dentist. The balding dentist."

"Jeez, you *must* be desperate."

"You're a real encouragement, Mike. I can't tell you how much I appreciate it."

"You can't marry *him*. You're gorgeous. He's . . . Freddy."

Rachel stood up. "All right, I'll send him an e-mail and tell him our big date is off. I think he wanted to go look at coin shops or something anyway. I think he collects nickels. Buffalo nickels. What an incredibly interesting guy." She looked at me as she stood by the door. "Are we going to be up all night? Do we have the materials we need to fly to Paris to begin preparing for these depositions tomorrow? Are we out of our minds? Are you sure you don't want to go before the magistrate and beg for mercy?"

"Nope. Legal jujitsu. Take his energy and throw him over on his back. I expect to be up all night myself. Debbie doesn't even know I'm going yet. This'll go over well. I'll get your ticket. Assume we're leaving on the eight thirty AM flight. We can drive together, but we'll need to leave at about four o'clock. I'll call you at home as soon as I get the info."

I picked up Rachel, drove to BWI, and we boarded our American Airlines flight to Paris. Rachel had called Justin and had him load the documents we had so far onto CDs, which she had brought with her. We spent the entire flight reviewing the documents on our laptops plugged directly into the seats and prepared questions that we anticipated Hackett asking.

We checked into our hotel on the Left Bank, got a bad night's sleep, and went to World-Copter headquarters the next morning by taxi. We spent the next five days preparing each witness for the questions that might come up. Each day we had lunch in the World-Copter conference room where we were preparing the witnesses. The food was outstanding, and each night we would have dinner with one of the WorldCopter officers. Marcel was still in the United States investigating the accident, as were most of the investigation team. But most of those who were actually involved in building Marine One were still in Paris.

One night we were free and Rachel insisted on eating at a fancy restaurant, called

241

George. I agreed as I was happy to eat somewhere other than the restaurant we had eaten at each night with the WorldCopter officers.

The restaurant sat atop the Georges Pompidou Center, a combination museum, display area, multicultural center, and concert center. Rachel had reserved an outdoor table for us overlooking Notre Dame. European techno pop music pounded in the background.

Rachel took a sip from her wine and asked, "How do you think the preparation is going?"

"I think we're on track. Hackett's going to be surprised. I think they'll stand up pretty tall."

She pushed her hair back. "Don't you feel like our time would be better spent out in the woods looking for tip weights? We're just playing defense here."

"Our entire expert team's going to be out at the scene all week. They'll be tearing it apart while Hackett is here listening to himself talk."

"Won't his experts be doing the same thing?"

"I doubt it. The fewer new facts they have, the better. They want to just roll into court, say, 'Tip weights,' and wait while Hackett rings us up for a few hundred million. Plus, I've asked our new guy, Brandon —"

"Braden."

". . . to start preparing a summary judgment motion to dismiss punitive damages while we're gone. We'll get the rough transcripts electronically, incorporate the testimony into our motion, and serve it on Hackett the day he flies home. He'll say it's too early in the case, but let's put him on his heels a little bit. He's the one who's in a big hurry."

"I called the dentist before we left our hotel."

"Tonight? Really? What for?"

Rachel smiled and shook her head. "I just wanted to give him the details of why I missed our date. He said it figures. It's par for the course for him to be drilling the teeth of angry patients while I run off to Paris. Then he said he always figured I was out of his league anyway. He never thought he had much of a shot. He knew I'd come up with some reason not to go out with him."

I frowned. "That doesn't even make sense. He thinks you made this whole thing up so you wouldn't have to go out with him? So what, you persuaded Hackett to notice a bunch of depositions just so you could avoid a date with him?"

"I don't think he's quite that linear in his thinking, more like he knew events would conspire to make sure that I didn't go out with him."

"So when you said yes that was just a cruel joke of fate."

"Something like that. I don't think he's really my type."

"Don't worry, it'll happen. The right guy's out there."

Rachel looked up at me with a sharp glance. "I don't think so."

"Well, what are you looking for? What kind of guy is the right one?"

Our waitress brought our food and set the hot plates down in front of us. "Enjoy," she said as she turned away.

"There are good men out there. All my friends are married to them. They've been married for ten years. They have kids. They're happy. They're working or not working. It doesn't matter. They're happy."

We finished our meal in relative quiet, listening to the pounding, now annoying, music through the ultra-high-quality speakers hidden somewhere. I paid the shockingly large bill and stood. "We'd better get back to the hotel. You know who we meet with tomorrow."

"Jean Claude Martin. *El presidente.*"

"Wouldn't it be *la président?*"

"*Le.*"

"All I know is he's really not very happy. After that debacle at the Senate hearings, all he wants is to answer more questions from some American attorney. You sure we did the right thing by letting Hackett go at him this early in the case?"

"Hackett won't have our documents until the deposition. He'll do way less damage now than in six months when he's a lot smarter about WorldCopter. We've got to let him do this, and then start turning this case back on him."

15

Jean Claude Martin gave us all the time we wanted. But first he had to "express himself." He simply could not understand how in the American judicial system it was possible for Hackett to hand me several pieces of paper and show up the following week with a court reporter and videographer to take his deposition. None of this was allowed in France. It was clearly intended to harass him and WorldCopter.

I agreed. I told him that was exactly the purpose of the depositions. And the harder we fought and more we made of it, the more we were playing into Hackett's publicity-seeking hands. The more annoyed we got, the happier he was going to be. I told President Martin that since Hackett gave us virtually no notice, and we hadn't much time to prepare, Hackett would have to be satisfied with the answers he got. He only got to do this once.

From the top down, WorldCopter had *zero* faith in the American justice system. They all reminded me that the reading of the Michael Jackson verdict was on live television throughout France. Not because they expected great justice, but because it was like watching a circus. And there was absolutely no doubt in their minds, and I mean *no* doubt, that Michael Jackson would get off.

I think American juries get it right 90-plus percent of the time. I had no such confidence in other judicial systems, especially those that let judges decide everything, like the French system. I had seen enough tyrannical American judges to doubt whether tyrannical French judges or tyrannical British judges would somehow be remarkably fair and come up with the right result. I trusted juries. Sure, they could get it wrong, so could I, so could WorldCopter, so could a French judge. We all can get it wrong. But in federal court, where we were in this case, you had to get a unanimous jury. In my experience, a unanimous jury rarely got things just flat wrong.

Once we calmed Jean Claude down, the preparation went well. Toward the end of the discussion, after reviewing the corporate structure and the government contract for the building of Marine One, President Martin sat back and looked at the ceiling, then down at me. "Will I be required to testify at trial?"

"Probably. Hackett will try to use this videotaped deposition against you, but if you're there in person, with nothing to hide, it's much to our strength. I would like you to testify about the contract and World-Copter's entry into the American military market by a bid for Marine One. I definitely plan on calling you."

The next day President Martin was the first witness. Even though Martin spoke English as well as I did, we asked for an interpreter. He needed his own language to express himself properly. It also makes for a record, through the videotape, of exactly what was said in French. Also present at the deposition were Kathryn; the WorldCopter America general counsel, Tripp; Rachel; Hackett, and two people from his office; plus the court reporter; the videographer; and the translator; as well as a second translator hired by WorldCopter to check on the translator hired by Hackett.

Jean Claude did brilliantly. Hackett pressed him about the contract, the security, all the things he had been banging his drum to the press about, even the dramatic completion of the three Marine One helicopters ahead of time and under bud get. Hackett tried to find weaknesses or create them, but he couldn't touch Jean Claude. Watching Hackett during the deposition was interesting. He clearly had not expected us to produce the president at all, let alone the week he was noticed, let alone the first day. Hackett seemed slightly dazed. He had brought Bass and the paralegal with him overnight in his private Gulfstream jet, and they all looked bleary-eyed.

We let Hackett go all day. We let him ask wide-ranging questions on multiple topics. He didn't advance his case at all. He learned some unpleasant facts, and that World-Copter was not going to roll over and write him a huge check.

As the week progressed, the rest of the World-Copter witnesses did almost as well. They were ready in spite of the short preparation time. They knew the accident, knew the helicopter, they knew how it had been built, they knew the documents, and they knew the contract. Hackett didn't really know any of it. He was just there to beat up on World-Copter witnesses and intimidate them, and failed, not that he would agree with that assessment. He was unburdened by self-doubt.

At the conclusion of each deposition, as

we sat in various restaurants on the outskirts of Paris with the WorldCopter officers, their confidence grew. They realized that Hackett was swinging wildly and missing. They realized that he was not much of a threat at this stage because he didn't know as much as he thought he did. The conclusion began to form that his early aggressive stance had been a huge miscalculation.

I reminded them that the NTSB still believed it was WorldCopter's fault, his experts would so testify, and a jury was likely to believe Hackett. All we had done was to blunt his first attack. To win the case we had to find the real cause, or WorldCopter was going down just like Marine One.

Kathryn shared our cab to de Gaulle airport. She was invigorated. She wanted a meeting as soon as possible with all our experts, all the attorneys, criminal *and* civil, and WorldCopter's employees involved in the investigation. Kathryn wanted to walk through the case soup to nuts and come up with a global to-do list. I called Marcel on my BlackBerry from the cab; he thought we should have the meeting at WorldCopter headquarters outside Washington, in the hangar where the Marine One helicopters were assembled.

We flew back to the States overnight and met the next morning after we had cleaned up. The hangar was deathly quiet. World-Copter had been forbidden from touching any of the Marine One helicopters until the Justice Department's investigation was concluded. I walked around the assembly and inspection area with Marcel, Kathryn, and Rachel looking at the spotless facility. We were acutely aware that in ordinary circumstances we could never be there. No one was allowed near the helicopters, let alone the assembly and repair facility, without the required Yankee White security clearance. But the day after Marine One crashed, all those at WorldCopter had had their clearances canceled, and every helicopter was immediately suspect.

We walked by one of the undelivered Marine One helicopters, which sat in the middle of the hangar in perfect condition surrounded by a Plexiglas security wall. It had completed its assembly and inspection and was due to be delivered the day Marine One crashed. It sat untouched behind the Plexiglas wall ever since. I wondered if we could learn anything from that helicopter, but nothing occurred to me. Since the accident, all maintenance had been transferred to the Marine Corps at Quantico, Virginia, and Andrews Air Force Base. And it wasn't coming back to WorldCopter until, according to the Pentagon, they were "cleared" by the Justice Department.

That wasn't likely to happen anytime soon. After Justice demanded documents and unlimited access, and after I'd thrown a little tantrum, WorldCopter had essentially agreed to whatever they wanted. We told them we were ready to provide all documents they wanted — they were entitled to have them anyway by contract. Once again, our cooperation seemed to throw them off a little bit. We told Justice we would get the documents to them in sixty days, and they had accepted that. They had also said that they would wait to interview individuals until after they had received all the documents requested in their subpoena and after they had reviewed the depositions Hackett took. That was fine with us. It gave us additional time to prepare.

The consensus of the group was that Justice was waiting for the final NTSB report. That could take two years or longer, long after the trial. Until then, Justice was focused on clearances and people building Marine One without them.

All our experts were there when we arrived. After the usual greetings and some ambitious coffee consumption to hit the jet lag, we got down to business. Kathryn had asked for the meeting, but I was as anxious as she was to see where everyone was. I wanted to brainstorm theories and find out what the hell happened to Marine One. Pretty simple concept, but nothing about the theories in this case was simple. The World-Copter investigators wanted to blame the pilot, our pilot expert wanted to blame the weather, and Wayne Bradley wanted to blame the NTSB, his former employer, for trying to hang it on WorldCopter without enough evidence.

I asked Bradley to set up his computer with a projector and pull up the wreckage photos. He explained what he saw in the bent metal, the forces necessary to bend the charred remains of the helicopter. He brought up the next slide. "Look at this!" It was a close-up, a macro photo of some piece of metal. I couldn't tell what it was. "These are the threads in the nut of the blade that separated. It is interesting, but not good enough." He said to Marcel, "We need to get this nut into a scanning electron microscope." Marcel nodded and made a note.

Bradley looked at everyone else. "Second, we've *got* to find those tip weights. I don't think they are far away. If my theory is correct, then those tip weights are somewhere near the accident scene. If they came out on impact with the ground, then they're nearby. We've got to find them; we've got to get them."

Kathryn contemplated for a moment. She leaned forward on her elbows and pushed her hair back from her face. "Mike, maybe I'm missing something. How does finding the tip weights help us?"

I looked at Bradley, who waited for me to answer. "NTSB says — implies, really — that the tip weights came off and started the crash sequence. So the tip weights from that blade can't be at the crash site. They'd have to be miles away, if they got thrown off. So if they *are* there, right where the helicopter hit, then they came off when it hit the ground and couldn't have caused the crash. If we find them there, we can prove that. That right, Karl?"

Karl Will nodded. He cleared his throat. "It's a question of sequence, Kathryn. If you jump off a train early, you can't be on it when it gets to the station."

Kathryn nodded. "But the NTSB didn't find any tip weights. They've got to be turning over every rock."

Will nodded again. "They are. And so are

we. If we went out to the scene fifty years from now, I guarantee you we'd find part of Marine One. When these kinds of things happen, you can't ever find everything. We have to try to find what they didn't."

"If your theory is right," she noted.

"Exactly," Will said.

Kathryn glanced around at everyone. "Well, if it wasn't the tip weights, if that didn't cause the accident, what did? What's our theory?" She looked at Holly. "You're the piloting expert, right?"

"Yes."

"What do you think?"

Holly was on the spot. "I'm not really sure. We've got an incredibly talented pilot, but he sounds like he hated the president. I flew the simulator like Mike here did and didn't really learn very much. He flew very well. The FDR and CVR don't help us that much either. So at this point, I'd say he was unprofessional, but I don't see any hard evidence of pilot error."

Kathryn frowned. "What does his professionalism have to do with it? Why do we keep talking about that?"

Holly looked at me to see if she was to say what she and I had been talking about. "Well, if the pilot hates him enough, maybe he does something . . . to stop the presidency. Not saying that happened, but we have to consider it. There have been other examples. EgyptAir, SilkAir, others. The pilots almost certainly committed suicide and took hundreds with them. I don't see that here, not for sure, but it could be homicide. Something we have to think about."

Kathryn was speechless. "Is that what you think actually happened?"

"I'm just saying I don't rule anything out until there's proof it's wrong."

Kathryn looked at me. "What else hasn't been ruled out?"

"Well, there's some talk of hydraulic failure, but I'm not buying that. I'm just not seeing it based on the way this helicopter was flying. The idea that he was shot down or otherwise had an impact with another airplane or anything else, like a bird, I think that's a nonstarter. I don't buy it. I'm with Holly. I don't trust Collins. And why did the flight data recorder suddenly quit? Did he pull the circuit breaker? It's near the hydraulic pump, which he may have thought was failing, but maybe he pulled that circuit breaker too. Maybe he was trying to make it look like an accident. And why was President Adams in such a big damn hurry? Why did he want to get to a meeting at Camp

David in the middle of a thunderstorm? And why fly? The Secret Service wanted him to drive, but he refused. *Why?* I think if we can answer that question, we may make a lot more progress."

Kathryn shook her head. "How will that tell us what happened to the helicopter? I don't want to get distracted by political considerations. Unless you're saying someone didn't want him to get there — someone not on that flight — that would mean somebody attacked the helicopter and the NTSB and FBI have clearly said there's no evidence of that. So don't waste your time with that. The answer is in the metal and the wreckage."

"I agree, Kathryn. But if we find out why he was going there, it certainly won't hurt. I just like knowing everything about an accident.

"Anyway, we need to get these folks into the hangar and finish their examination of the wreckage."

Marcel shifted. "Yes, one thing that the NTSB told me while you were in Paris."

"What?"

"They are going to finish the wreckage access, close access, as they are ready to finalize the group reports."

The entire group was alarmed.

"What does that mean?" Tripp asked.

Marcel replied, but looked at Bradley for confirmation. "It means the reports from the groups: engine group, airframe group, operations group and the like are done. They are finished and are preparing their reports to submit to the NTSB so they can put them in their final report."

This was all wrong. Way too fast. "Did you think the groups were done?"

"No," Marcel said.

"Who says the groups are done then?" I pressed.

"Rose."

We all stared at each other. The NTSB was cutting off the investigation. They had their conclusion so they were making sure nothing was going to challenge it.

Tripp was still confused. "Why is that bad?"

I replied, "Because we'll be cut off from access to the wreckage, and no one will be involved in whatever happens between now and the issuance of their final report. They'll be behind a wall of silence for the rest of their investigation."

"But why?'

"Well, the benign scenario would be because they really think they are done. But the other possibility, the malignant scenario, is because they want to cut us off. They want to make sure we're in the dark."

Kathryn was beside herself. "If they stop looking and jump to a conclusion, this thing will make the debate over the Kennedy assassination look like child's play. It's like the Warren Commission stopping halfway through because they're sure they know what happened."

Rachel said, "Some people think that's *exactly* what happened."

Bradley stood with some difficulty. "But they haven't closed the doors yet. I say we get out to their hangar right now."

16

I should have gone home after spending the entire day at the wreckage hangar, but I hadn't been to my office in ten days. I called Debbie and told her I'd be home after stopping in at the office. I hurried to the second floor of our building and turned on the lights of my office. I could tell by the lights down the hall that a couple of other people were working too. I put my laptop back in its cradle and turned it on while I thumbed through the piles of documents, letters, legal pleadings, magazines, and other papers Tracy had placed on my desk. I was about halfway done when I suddenly realized someone was standing in my door. It was Braden, one of the new contract attorneys. Very good guy. We had received probably two hundred résumés after we put out our ads. Braden's was one of the best and he was clearly the best in the interview. He had graduated from Columbia Law School, something we didn't see often in Annapolis, and had worked at two large defense firms in New York City. He said he was tired of New York and wanted to find a place where he could settle down and raise a family someday. He was the best I had seen. A little too eager sometimes, but overall just trying to please. "Hey, what's up? You're here late," I said.

"Sorry. I didn't want to disturb you, but I heard you knocking around. How was the trip?"

"Good. Come on in. Have a seat. I'm just going through some correspondence. What are you doing here?"

"Working on the memo Rachel asked for on *forum non conveniens*."

"Yeah, that's pretty hopeless. Not sure we'd even really try to transfer this case to another place if we could, but you may as well finish it."

"Yeah, will do."

I looked at him more closely. "Rachel's impressed with your work. Your memos are quite good."

"Thanks, I appreciate it." He paused. "Oh." He reached into his pocket and pulled out a piece of paper. "Weirdest thing. I was using the copy machine last night and I walked by your office. It was late, like eleven thirty. I heard your phone ring, and then it stopped. Then it rang again and stopped. Someone wanted to talk to you but didn't want to leave a voice mail. It rang again so I answered it."

"Who was it?"

"I don't know." He handed me the piece of paper. "Here's the number."

I took it and looked at it. It was a Washington, D.C., area code.

Braden continued, "It was some guy asking if I'm Mike Nolan. I told him I wasn't and he told me to have you call him. I asked him who he was, and he said it wasn't any of my business. He just said that you needed to call him, personally, and that he 'knew all the answers.' I said, 'What answers?' And he said why Marine One crashed. And then he hangs up. That's it."

I stared at the number, then at Braden. "What do you make of it? What did he sound like?"

"I have no idea what to make of this. What are the chances he knows something? I don't know. I suppose in the no-stone-left-unturned approach somebody ought to call him. He might be a crackpot. He sounded like an older guy, maybe fifties."

"Black or white?"

"Not sure, but sounded white to me."

"Okay, thanks. I'll give him a call tomorrow. Maybe."

Braden began to leave, then remembered, "Oh, and he said to call him at night, he works during the day and that isn't a work number."

"It's not during the day now. No time like the present." I picked up the phone and dialed the number.

Braden returned to his office as the number began to ring. I had the speakerphone on and listened as I continued to sort through the piles on my desk. It rang four times, then five, but no answering machine picked up. It probably rang eight times before somebody picked it up. My eyes darted to the phone to note the connection. I picked up the handset and listened. Nobody said anything. "Hello?"

"Who's this?" a gruff voice asked.

"I'm Mike Nolan. You called me."

"Where you calling from?"

"My office. My associate said you have something to talk to me about. What is it?"

"I've got information that will break your case wide-open."

"What's your name?"

"No way. No names, no numbers, no addresses."

"And why is that?"

"Because I value my life, that's why."

"Meaning?"

"I'm not saying anything until I know I'm safe and we have certain arrangements."

"What arrangements?"

"You're going to hire me a lawyer. A fancy lawyer from Washington. His name is Frank Flannery. I got his name out of a newspaper report of a big case I heard about. He doesn't know me. You're going to hire him for me. If you don't, you'll never hear a word of what I know. I'm gonna call him in forty-eight hours and tell him that I'm the one that he's been hired to represent. After that, all communication will go through him. I'll tell him the things I want you to know, and he'll tell them to you."

"Why are you doing this? What do you want?"

"You'll have to compensate me. You have to make this way worth my while."

"We don't pay witnesses."

"Fine. Don't. I'm going to call Frank in two days."

The line went dead. I stared at the phone. I'd never had a call like that. I'd never had a witness call who claimed to have earth-shattering information and demand money while remaining anonymous. I've had lots of witnesses ask for money. It's right about when they realize you *need* their testimony that they suddenly smell a market and try to sell. But you can't buy. Against ethics and taints their testimony. They usually pout, then you serve them with a subpoena, which changes things pretty quickly.

I couldn't decide whether to just slough him off as a nut or to at least get some idea of what this guy was talking about. I turned around to my computer and drafted an e-mail to Kathryn.

Kathryn was intrigued by what this might mean and much to my surprise authorized retaining Flannery to represent him. I called Flannery, introduced myself, and told him the story. He thought it was odd but agreed to talk to the guy when he called. So we would wait to see what came of that.

The time had arrived though for me to take the depositions of the widows, and in particular the first lady. She was the lead plaintiff, the lead name on the lawsuit, now of course the *former* first lady, but everyone in the media seemed to want to call her the first widow. She had moved out of the White House when Cunningham had moved in to take over as president and was now living in a penthouse apartment at the Watergate.

She didn't make many public appearances now, but when she did, she was appropriately mournful and quiet. A sympathetic figure, she was loved by the public. But the public wasn't seeing inside her lawsuit, *Adams et al. v. WorldCopter.* They weren't in the room when her attorney yelled at the WorldCopter employees to get them to say things he could use against them in trial. She was able to maintain her pose of wounded innocent as her hired rottweiler tried to tear up witnesses on her behalf.

I wanted Rachel to take the depositions of several of the widows. She had taken numerous depositions in the past, but these would be important and it would be good for her and good for the case. When I told her that I wanted her to take four of the eight depositions, including that of Mrs. Collins, she was excited. I told her I wouldn't even be there, and that she would run them. She prepared an outline, which I reviewed, and it was perfect. But what had my focus was the first lady.

The notices I had given Hackett asked the widows to bring all kinds of personal documents with them. Their husbands' income statements, files, letters, medical records, anything they had that pertained to their husbands. They would be annoyed by that and would balk. I wanted to get that whole process under way immediately.

The day before those depositions were to start, I got a call from Karl Will. He had been thinking about the accident and wanted to go back out to the scene. He said he wanted to just sit there. He said I should bring a stool or chair, and that we were going to sit there, in the middle of where the helicopter crashed, and let the crash scene talk to us. He and I agreed on many things, but certainly on this. You couldn't go to an accident scene too many times. You would see things differently every time. You might notice how certain flight paths — or crash paths, more accurately — to the site that were theoretically possible under some theories are actually impossible. A certain hill was too high, or the ravine too steep. Things would be struck by airplane parts or rotor blades that you hadn't seen before. Unless it was in a flat desert, the accident scene spoke to you eloquently. Every time.

The location of the fire road was now listed as one of my personal destinations in my Volvo navigation system. I punched it and headed to the scene. I turned off onto the fire road and was stopped at the same place we had been stopped on the morning of our first visit by an FBI agent.

When I got to the scene, Karl was already there. He was in the dead center of the crash site sitting on a blue canvas camp stool, the kind that folded up into a handled walking stick. He was drinking coffee from a large metal travel mug. He had watched me walk all the way in to the site. Will said, "Where's your chair?"

"In the car."

"Go get it. I told you to bring it."

I shook my head. "I can stand, it's okay."

"You can only look around after you've sat. You have to feel it."

I went back to the car and pulled out my lawn chair, the same one that I always carried to my kids' soccer games. I unfolded it and sat next to him. "Anything you wanted to bring up? Or are we just going to sit here quietly?"

"Either way," he said, drinking slowly. "You've got to hear the helicopter straining, fighting to stay aloft, falling down through the storm, the rain, and finally the trees. If we'd been here, could we have heard the tree branches break or would the noise from the helicopter have been too loud? Which parts of it could we have heard? If we had a huge spotlight pointed up to the sky from this point, what would we have seen? Was it on fire as it fell through the darkness? I want to hear you think while you look at where this happened. I want to hear what you really believe. I've heard you hinting about all kinds of shit, but based on everything you know, as a Marine, as a pilot, as an attorney, as someone who's looked into all the pieces of this accident that we have so far, I want to hear what you think happened."

I wasn't sure how much to say. When his deposition was taken in this case, everything that he reviewed or relied on would be admissible, including conversations with me.

I looked at the ashes around us, the charred leaves, branches, and grass. The little pieces of metal and plastic that had burned and dripped leaving patterns like disturbed spiderwebs lying in the dirt. I said, "A couple of things just continue to bother me. First, I don't think that there's any way in hell that rotor blade came off in midair and then just happened to land next to all the wreckage. I think that's certainly possible under the laws of physics, but if you bring statistics and probability into it, I think it becomes so unlikely as to be considered impossible. But I've also learned that catastrophic accidents are sometimes caused by the ridiculously unlikely."

"Go on."

"I find the fact that the flight data recorder stopped before the crash suspicious. I find the fact that he *maybe* had a hydraulic light suspicious. I find the conversation between the pilot and the president suspicious. I find the meeting the president was going to that we know nothing about *really* suspicious."

Karl nodded and finished his coffee. He tossed the cup into an open backpack. "And what about here? What do you see here?"

"I don't know. I don't understand this scene. It just doesn't make sense to me at all." I kicked at the ashes at my feet. "It does feel strange sitting here, where a helicopter crashed killing seven people. Feels like we're desecrating it, sitting here and drinking coffee." Karl didn't respond. I got up and walked around the wreckage site while Karl watched me move uneasily through the silence. I looked down at a pile of ash that had been raked into an area to clear it from something else. The pile was simply charred burned matter, which looked like burned foliage. Something caught my eye. "Check this out," I said. He came over from his stool and peered down. It was American currency. Bills folded in half, charred on the top so it just looked like a random piece of charred paper. But you could just make out a corner of the paper and tell that it was a bill. I picked them up. I turned them over, and on the bottom were four clean $100 bills, which were underneath the charred bill on top of it. "How about that?" I said, and handed Karl the charred bills. I glanced down to the now clean spot on the ground where the bills had been lying and noticed something metal. I bent down and picked up a heavy brass key. It was one of those brass hotel keys that were more common before most hotels went to electronic access. But it was different. It was flat on the top and flat on the bottom with three groves that would be inserted into the door. It looked to me as if the key was brass but electronic as well. I wasn't really sure, but I did notice the name of the hotel. I handed it to Karl. "The Virginian." He took it, examined it, turned it over, and pondered.

I asked, "Why didn't the NTSB find this?"

He glanced at me. "You ever been to a wreckage site where you didn't find something they missed?"

"No. But I've never been to the crash site of a president's helicopter either."

"That just makes it less likely they'd miss something. Doesn't guarantee it. Just looked like ashes. Think the investigators missed anything in the Kennedy investigation in

Dallas?" Karl looked at it one last time and handed it to me. "We'd better give it to them."

"I don't work for the NTSB. I'm here to protect my *client*. The NTSB has already issued a preliminary finding that hammers my client. Why should I help them?"

"Because this is their accident."

"They've released the scene."

"Mike, do you really think that if somebody comes here and finds something relevant, they don't need to turn it over to the NTSB?"

"I don't know. I guess I just don't want to give this to them. It's not a piece of the helicopter."

I slipped the key into my pocket. "I'll give it to them after a friend checks it out. Who on this helicopter had a key to the ritziest hotel in Washington, D.C.? A five-star hotel. They all *lived* in Washington. Why would they need a hotel room?"

I thought about who was on the helicopter. Three crew, Adams, two Secret Service agents, and the White House director of operations. Would Collins have a key like this? Was he seeing someone? Having an affair? Who else? Tinny would find out.

Will wasn't that interested in the human side. He wanted to know about the helicopter. "Well, let's do some other looking while we're out here. I didn't come out here to find a hotel key. Maybe we'll find something else just as interesting that I won't want to give to the NTSB."

He wandered toward the hill as I stood in the middle of the impact point. I looked like a bird-watcher looking up in the trees. It was completely quiet but there was a notable absence of birds. I couldn't hear anything except the occasional breeze that passed through the treetops. I watched one particularly beautiful oak sway far above the ground. It had to be seventy-five feet tall. As I watched it move, I noticed a divot out of the top. I focused my binoculars and could see that several large branches in the top of the tree were hanging, clearly broken. I didn't have quite the right angle and took a few steps closer. I looked at the impact spot and then those trees around it. I called to Karl. "Hey." He turned. "Take a look at this."

He wandered over, stepping around a few still muddy spots. "What?"

I handed him the binoculars and pointed to the top of the oak tree. "Look at the branches up there. Those are fairly substantial. They've been knocked to the side."

He took the binoculars and studied the

branches. "Any other branches like this around here?"

"Not that I've seen."

"Could it be something else?"

"Don't think so."

"Could a piece of the helicopter fall and hit that branch? Like the blade that might have come off?"

"I don't think so. That would have broken it downward. This is broken to the side."

"So you think that's it? The first point of impact with anything touching the ground?"

"I think so. But look at the direction of the break."

He focused the binoculars and leaned forward as if the extra couple of inches would make the difference.

I said, "They're broken left to right. See that?"

"Yes."

"WorldCopters are different. When you're sitting in the cockpit of the helicopter and look up at the blades, they're coming around clockwise. Over your head, as you look up, from left to right. American helicopters go the other way. If you're an American investigator who hasn't looked at French helicopters much before — or Russian for that matter, they go the same way as the French — you might forget that. So if you look at those branches, they are broken in the direction you'd expect from an American helicopter. But for a French helicopter crashing down through the trees, it's all wrong."

He continued to look up, considering what it meant. "So this is the opposite of what you'd expect *if* you knew the direction of rotation of Marine One's rotors."

"Right."

"Meaning . . ."

I took the binoculars and put them in the case. "Meaning Marine One was upside down when it came through the trees."

"Holy shit. Then it sure wasn't an autorotation that hit too hard. They were out of control long before they came close to the ground."

17

The phone rang twice and he picked it up and answered with a tired voice, "Frank Flannery."

"Mike Nolan."

"I've been expecting your call."

"So I guess I need to hear what this guy has to say."

Flannery replied, "Not that easy. He refuses to meet with anyone."

"So what do we do? How am I supposed to talk to him?"

Flannery paused. "He's concerned about his safety. He thinks if he talks to you, his life will be in danger."

"Yeah, he told me that. But I don't get it. How would his life be in danger?"

"He says has evidence that will break this case wide-open. And he thinks you need to talk to him. If someone else, the wrong person, learns this information, it could have serious consequences."

"I'm not following this at all. But I am ready to talk to him."

"Like I said, it's not that easy."

"Look, at least give me a category of what he's talking about."

"No. He wants to be compensated for his time, and to be relocated."

That surprised me. "Relocated? Some kind of civil witness-protection program?"

"I think that's exactly what he has in mind. But obviously he's not working with the government, so it won't apply."

"It might if he is talking about activity that's criminal."

"I don't really know about that. He won't talk to the government."

"Why? If his information is so important, he could tell anybody."

"He thinks you would be particularly interested in it because it would be to the benefit of your client."

"How so?"

"I'm not at liberty to say."

"Shit, Frank, this is ridiculous." I thought for a second. "What does he mean compensated for his time?"

"He says this will cause him to lose his job. He'll have to move out of the area. He wants to be compensated for that loss."

"For a lost job? How much we talking

about here?"

"All he's told me is that it will be significant."

"Whatever that means. How do I know he knows anything at all? How do I know this isn't some random guy pitching a scam?"

"He said you'd ask that. He said you can't know now, but you will once you hear his information."

"I'm going to have to think about it. You looked into the ethics of this?"

"I'm just representing him to protect his identity. I have not been retained to look into the ethical implications for you."

"I'll get back to you."

I hung up and called Braden to my office. I glanced at the clock and again reminded myself to go *home.* Just one more thing. Braden arrived and sat on the couch with a pad of paper ready for whatever new assignment I was about to give him. "I talked to the attorney representing that witness."

"Who?"

"The guy who called. The message you took."

"Right. What did he say?"

"The guy wants money. He wants to be compensated for his 'lost income' because he has to move. Wants us to relocate him. He says his life will be in danger once he tells us his information."

Braden stared at me. "Life in danger? How?"

"Who knows. Take a look at the ethical rules of compensating witnesses other than just witness fees and travel expenses. I don't think you can, but the feds do it all the time. In a criminal case the government pays a guy, gives him witness protection, relocates him to Des Moines, and pays him forever. They probably set them up with new wives for all I know. Why can't you compensate a witness in a civil trial? I don't know. Take a look and let me know."

"Will do."

That Friday, Tinny Byrd showed up at my office uninvited. He didn't need an invitation, but he didn't usually just drop by. But he also didn't really trust any form of communication. He eavesdropped on people's cell phones all the time, even though it was illegal. I always told him never to do it in my cases because we couldn't collect evidence illegally. He assured me he would *never* do it in one of my cases. He also didn't trust e-mail. He pretty much believed that anything that was converted into zeros and ones and transmitted where somebody else could catch it or duplicate it was a really bad idea. He was an old-school investigator who liked to stop by and hand you a manila envelope with a grin on his face. He loved seeing your face when he handed you something new, something that might be exciting. He almost always waited for you to open the envelope. He said it made him feel like Santa Claus.

Dolores called me and said he was downstairs. He didn't even know I'd be there. I went down and got him and walked him up to my office. We sat down and chatted for quite a while about nothing in particular. Sports, law, criminal cases, the shop talk of attorneys and investigators. He sat holding an envelope but was in no hurry either to give it to me or to leave.

Braden came in. "Sorry, I didn't know you were with anybody."

"No, this is Tinny Byrd. He's the investigator I've told you about."

Tinny stood and shook Braden's hand and studied his face. "Nice to meet you, Braden."

"Nice to meet you, Mr. Byrd." Braden turned to me and said, "I'll come back later."

"Since you're here, what do you have?"

"I finished that memo you have on —" Braden paused, looking at Tinny. "The phone call."

"Right. Thanks, I'll come talk to you about it later. Thanks."

Tinny sat back down in the chair opposite me, and Braden went back to his office.

Byrd looked confused. "Where did he come from? I've never met him before."

"New guy. I needed some help."

"He all right?"

"Yeah, I think he's tired. He's been up late nights working. He works his butt off. He's here all hours of the day. What do you have?"

Byrd closed the door and sat back down. He leaned forward and handed me the envelope and began to speak quietly. "The meeting. You wanted to know who A3 was going to see at Camp David."

I was stunned. "You found out who was at Camp David?"

"No, not yet, not about that exactly. But I'm getting him to talk about other things. Trying to lubricate the communications between us. By the way, he thinks all this stuff about WorldCopter is bullshit. He thinks something bad happened. Something real bad."

"Like an assassination?"

"I don't know if he'd go that far. He's not involved in any of the investigations. He just has a feeling."

"That's real helpful. Maybe I can call him as a witness and he can testify about his feelings."

"Don't be a smart-ass," Byrd said. "I may get something out of him, maybe something we can use. I don't know. He's tough, but he knows what was going on at Camp David, and I can tell just as sure as shit he thinks whatever it was that was going on is related to the crash. Too much of a coincidence."

"So what was going on?"

"Won't say. But it was huge. He just shakes his head. Says he may have to go to his grave with this. And he doesn't think the NTSB is even looking in the right place. He doesn't trust them."

"How do we get him to talk about it?"

"I'm working it, Michael, I'm working it." Byrd reached into his pocket. "Oh, I almost forgot." He handed me the key from The Virginian. "Interesting key."

"What'd you find out?"

"That is one stuck-up, stiff-assed place, that's what. They cater to the big shots of the world and all the politicos. And their mistresses, of course. They wouldn't tell me shit."

"Well, thanks —"

"I didn't say I didn't find anything out. You doubt me?"

"What you got?"

"I found one lady who was willing to help."

"You always do."

"Pretty much. Anyway, I gave her the names of everyone on the helicopter. None of them had a room there in the last month."

"What about the key?"

"Interesting. Not for a room."

"What was it for?"

"You know how they have small, secret conference rooms in some hotels? You don't even know they're there? Rooms that don't even have numbers? It was one of those."

"Could they tell when?"

"Yeah. The key was coded for the night before the accident."

"To a hidden conference room?"

"Yep."

"Who was it registered to?"

"John Smith."

"Oh, right. And how was it paid for?"

"Cash."

I stood up and began pacing around the room. "What do you make of it?"

"I asked her if there were any bigwigs staying there that night."

"What did she say?"

"Always. Every night. Assortment of international big shots."

"Does she know who used the room?"

"No idea."

"We need to get a complete guest list."

Byrd shook his head. "She can't get it for me. It's encrypted on their system."

"Fine. I'll subpoena it."

Byrd frowned. "Not sure I'd do that, Michael. People would notice."

"So?"

"There's more. She didn't know who used the room, but she said one of the maids is Chinese. Taiwanese, actually, and walked by the room when the door was open. She heard someone talking inside in perfect Taiwanese. Big shot. Like he owned the place. Talking to a couple of other Taiwanese. Ordering them around. She couldn't tell what it was all about, but no doubt they were Taiwanese. There were a couple of Westerners in the room too. Americans she thought, but couldn't be sure. She thought it was strange that he was talking loudly in Taiwanese when the Americans couldn't understand him. But it was just for a second."

"Taiwanese? What would they have to do with the president?"

"That's your job. I just find out what happened. You're the one who's supposed to make sense of it all."

Taiwan threw me. I couldn't imagine what that would have to do with the crash. "I don't know, Tinny. Adams was always making a big deal about his Chinese policy, although I couldn't really tell you what he meant by that. I thought it was the usual political bullshit, lots of air and posturing. Maybe he had something going on. I'll have to think about that." I turned, then thought to ask again, "The night before the crash? You sure? Is she sure?"

"Yep."

"We'll keep digging."

Tinny frowned. "I don't know, man. There's stuff out there. A lot of anxiety. Something. I don't know who's working this, but there's more out there than just the government."

"So what? I'll subpoena the guest list from the hotel for that night. I've got to get to the bottom of this, Tinny. Our client's neck is in a noose."

"Let me give it another shot my way. Let me try."

"We've got to get something solid, Tinny. Something admissible. We're so close to breaking this open. Call your Secret Service guy again too. Tell him to *talk* to me."

18

I hadn't spoken to Marcel in a couple of weeks so I wasn't expecting his call at 6 AM. He sounded far less confident than usual. When we had been in Paris for the depositions of the WorldCopter officers and workers, they had of course checked on and produced the documents that showed when the blade was balanced against the Golden Blade. We already knew the blade that was lying in the wreckage at the crash site had been added to the helicopter after its date of manufacture. The previous one had developed a crack and had been replaced ten days before the accident. It had been balanced against the Golden Blade one week before that. Marcel had gone back into the records to check on exactly what tip weights were used and the origin of those tip weights. Theoretically, a shipment of tip weights might have been defective. We doubted it, but we wanted to run that to ground. He said he had found the records of the tip weights that were added to blades in that time period. They were ordinary, and from the usual supplier. The shipment had arrived the week before being added to the blade, but that was normal. WorldCopter used just-in-time supply, which saved money and lessened the need for ware houses full of parts, as items arrived just as they were needed.

Marcel was concerned because they couldn't find any records of exactly which weights were added to the blade that made it to the president's helicopter. No documents specifically showed it. Maybe if we found tip weights at the scene, we could show they fit in the right time frame, but proving the numbers of the weights that were actually installed was proving impossible.

His voice quivered with anger. I asked him the obvious question, whether a blade might be so perfectly matched to the Golden Blade that it didn't need tip weights. He reminded me that it was designed to have them. It was built two to three ounces light at the tip just so you could adjust it. They didn't try to make a perfect blade. He did admit though that it was *possible* a blade could match the Golden Blade without any additional weight, but we both knew that was just wishful thinking, trying to explain away missing documents.

I said, "So we know for sure the blade had tip weights, and they're missing, and now we can't find the records of which tip weights were on that blade."

"That is it exactly."

"Well, shit, Marcel."

"Yes. My feelings are the same. Shit."

I walked over to tell Rachel about this wonderful new development and ran into Braden in the hallway. He handed me his updated memo on paying the mystery witness. As I walked in Rachel's office, she was working at her computer typing in her staccato manner and looked up, then returned her gaze to the screen. I sat in the chair across from her desk, and handed her Braden's memo. "You seen this?"

"Yeah. He gave it to me last night."

"What do you think?"

"I didn't check his research, but there aren't many cases dealing with it."

I read over his memo. "Basically says it's probably over the line. You can make an argument, but it's probably a loser. You could get charged with unethical conduct and lose your law license." I looked at Rachel, who seemed uninterested. "What do you think?"

"I think the whole thing is crazy. We shouldn't even call the guy back. It's probably a scam anyway."

"Don't we owe it to our client to find out what this is about?"

"If you're going across an ethical line, you're going without me."

"I'm not going across any line. With you or without you. But what if WorldCopter wants to pay him? They're not admitted to practice law in Maryland."

"Doesn't that sound a little too cute?"

"Maybe. Let's at least see if we can find out what the guy knows."

The next morning as I was shaving I heard my BlackBerry buzzing on my dresser. I checked the incoming number and closed the bathroom door behind me. "Tinny, what the hell are you doing calling me at five thirty in the morning?"

"You gotta come to D.C. this morning. No doubt about it. You've got to come to D.C. right now."

"Why?" I turned the water off in the sink and listened carefully, trying not to speak too loudly and wake Debbie.

"My friend, the one I told you about that

I can't tell you about, that works for a certain outfit that you know about, has some documents he wants us to have."

Byrd was being remarkably evasive. It occurred to me for the first time he was afraid that somebody was listening to our conversation. Easy enough to do. "I got all kinds of meetings this morning. People coming from out of town. You sure?"

"Come. I'll leave my cell on." Byrd hung up.

"Dammit," I said as I hung up. I'd have to call Rachel and ask her to meet with Holly alone, at least for a while. Byrd *never* asked me to come to D.C. I left messages for everybody at the office as I drove toward D.C. As I merged onto the beltway to head into the city and slowed to a crawl, I called Byrd on my cell phone. "Byrd. Where are you? I'm on the beltway. I'll be there in about eight hours at this pace."

"You know that place that we met that one time where you felt really out of place?"

Boy did I. "Yeah."

"Be there at eight o'clock."

He was referring to a café in the Northeast section of D.C. called Mercedes' Grill, named after Mercedes Benson, a legendary, larger-than-life woman who owned the grill. It was a popular hangout for D.C. politicians, police, and others in what they liked to call the second society. The first society of course were all the white people who worked on Capitol Hill, at the Supreme Court, and at all the federal agencies, almost all white, who comprised the decision makers in the federal government and who lived in Virginia and Maryland. The real Washington, the second society, were those who lived in and ran the city: the mayor, the city council, the police, the fire department, and local religious and civic leaders. Notably they were all black. It was like two cities. One on top of the other. White on top of black. The white part of the city didn't realize it, the black part of the city did. And those who knew that and understood it hung out at Mercedes' Grill. I had felt out of place the last time I had been there because white people simply didn't go there. Everyone there, from the owners to the workers to the customers, was black. So when I went in, everybody wondered why somebody from the first city had come to the grill of the second city. They fairly quickly realized that I wasn't actually part of the first city. I wasn't a congressman or a staffer or a judge, or anybody in the federal government who longed to be higher in the federal government. I was just the white guy with Tinny Byrd. Pretty soon that was just fine and nobody stared at me. But I still felt awkward. I was going to get another chance this morning. Byrd liked to meet me, or anybody else, there because usually those who wanted to give him any kind of difficulty were white.

I saw Byrd sitting in a booth in the back facing the entrance. He waved at me. I nodded to him and walked back to his booth. I was the only white person in the entire establishment. "Tinny, how you doing?" I said, shaking his hand.

"Sit down, Michael. Coffee?" He gestured to the waitress, who came over with a pot of coffee and poured a cup for me in a heavy porcelain mug.

I thanked her and said to Byrd, "What's this about?"

He was eating a large breakfast of fried eggs and potatoes. "You want something to eat? You know all this bullshit of cholesterol coming from eggs is just a conspiracy by the anti-egg people." He chuckled.

"If you believe Collins, everything's a conspiracy, right?"

He said, "Before I left your office last time, one of your other new attorneys, Lynn Carpenter, told me about Collins's reading list. He sounds like Mel Gibson in that movie with his eyes taped open."

"I don't think he was quite at that level. I don't want anything to eat. I had breakfast before I left."

"Good coffee though, huh? Best coffee in D.C. My opinion."

"No doubt. So why did you make me drive all the way into the dreaded District?"

The waitress delivered Tinny's side of bacon. He had clearly done this before as he had a specific approach to each egg and each piece of toast. Buttered a certain way, placed underneath the egg. "You remember our good Marine friend?"

"The one you been talking to?"

He nodded. "Well, I told you he said that he had some information about the meeting at Camp David. He said there was a document that would, as he put it, 'tell the tale about why the president was heading to Camp David that night'."

"What —"

Tinny put up his hand. "I've been beating on him to get it ever since. Absolutely refused. Wouldn't even hint at the content. So I told him to go back and *read* it again with understanding. Just read it and give me a call. Just tell me that it had *nothing* to do with this investigation and couldn't *possibly* have anything to do with the crash of

Marine One. If he did that, and told me that" — Byrd sat back with his hands out palms up — "that'd be good enough for me."

He leaned forward across his plate of eggs. "But I knew that wouldn't be the case. If it's that important, how could he say it had nothing to do with the crash? Unless he just went all NTSB on us and blamed World-Copter. But he's smarter than that. More honest. More suspicious." Byrd took three bites without saying a word.

I waited impatiently for him to continue. I didn't want to spoil the pace of the story, but this sounded ominous.

Byrd continued, "So this morning, this morning at five AM, he called me. Woke my ass up out of a deep sleep, a very pleasant, very warm deep sleep. I was pissed. I figured my mother had died or something. So I started screaming at the phone and it turned out it was our guy —"

"What's his name, Tinny?"

He went right on as if I hadn't made a sound. "When I finally realize it's him, I ask him whether he's going to tell me that his document had nothing to do with the investigation. He goes icy cold quiet on me, and then he said, 'It may, but I still can't give it to you.' You believe that shit?

"So I'm about to threaten him and he says he can't even talk about that document. But that he has something else for us. I say, 'Talk to me.' He says I'm to meet him in a McDonald's restaurant in the southwest part of the city. So I called you, than went to meet him. He sits down and hands me this folder." Byrd slid it across the table to me. "Go ahead."

I picked it up, but didn't open it. "So that document he can't talk about isn't in here."

"No."

"Damn, Tinny. How does he even have it? He's a Secret Service guy." Plus that Chris Thompson asshole said he didn't have it any more.

"Well, he said he was supposed to get it ready. That's all he'll say. It was his job to get it ready, and guard it. Everybody else was coming to Camp David, but he was already there. Others arrived before the president. But when they heard about the crash, everybody just left. He was still there with this document. Maybe I made a copy and Thompson doesn't know. Hell, I don't know really, it drives me crazy. He wouldn't give me the damn document, at least not yet — I'm not done with him. But he did give me some other stuff that's pretty damn interesting. Look."

I opened the envelope and looked at the contents. They were black-and-white photographs of people standing around. I looked up at Byrd. "What's all this?"

"The White House has numerous security cameras."

"I sure hope so."

"These are photographs from the security videos from the ballroom in the White House where there was a reception for the Japanese prime minister."

"And?"

"Well, one thing that I didn't know is that the commanding officer of HMX-1 is sometimes invited to these receptions. So you can see our boy, Colonel Collins, in these photographs."

"Okay, and?"

"Look at them. Can you think of a reason why the first lady and Collins would be whispering to each other. 'Cause I sure can't."

"Where do you see that?"

"Look on photographs three through seven. It shows them doing just a lot more than a casual greeting. She's talking to him and he's talking back. Now what would they have to talk about?"

That was a really good question. Could just have been casual conversation. Could be that they struck up something of a friendship on various flights. "Could be she's just friendly."

"You don't think Collins was playing around with the first lady, do you?"

"Hard to say. Nothing surprises me anymore. I've seen people do all kinds of stupid things. She's attractive, he's attractive, and the president was an ass. Who knows."

"Even if they were, you saying that would make Collins want to kill the president? Why? He's going to do what? Divorce his wife and marry the first lady? Never happen."

"No, hell, no. I'm not saying that."

Byrd moved forward and said in almost a whisper, "I'm just saying these are interesting photographs. You're the one with the big brain, you figure out what this is. You figure out why they're whispering in each other's ear and touching. I know why I whisper in a woman's ear, and I know why I accidentally brush against her ass."

"That's just impossible. No way."

Byrd sat forward and looked at me hard. "Maybe that's why he's sleeping in the other room. Maybe Melissa Collins is the only other person who knew about this."

"That's impossible," I said, staring at the photos, running through them again and again. They were all from one party. People were mingling around punch bowls and sandwich trays. Waiters and waitresses were scattered throughout carrying trays of hors d'oeuvres. But in six of the eight photographs, there was Colonel Collins standing right next to the first lady, and either she was whispering to him or he was whispering to her. I thought maybe it was because they were close to a source of music or noise. But none of the other people standing near them seemed to be having the same problem.

"When were these pictures taken?"

"Three months before the accident."

I put them back in the envelope. "I can keep these?"

"You can *keep* them, but not use them. You can't show them to anybody or ask anybody about them. But you may use them to lead you to other evidence, if you get my drift."

"He's got to testify, Tinny. And bring his document."

"Won't happen."

"Then WorldCopter may go up in flames and he may be responsible."

"He said that was your problem, not his."

"What's his name?"

Byrd looked at me intensely. "No, you

don't. No way am I turning him over. You'll subpoena him to trial. I know you will. Or you'll try and depose him and force him to lie under oath, which you know he won't do. No way."

"Then maybe I'll subpoena your ass and ask you to testify to his name under oath."

Byrd laughed. "Yeah, but I'd be happy to lie under oath. I got no problem with that, and you know it. And I'm like a journalist. I don't give up my sources."

"Even journalists can be forced to give up their sources in federal court."

"Not this journalist."

"So what do I do?"

Byrd looked around the restaurant and then back at me. "We've got to find out who else was at Camp David that night. Then we'll know why."

19

We drove to Hackett's office early in the morning so we could get set up for the deposition. His Washington offices were spectacular, just like his offices in New York, Los Angeles, and San Francisco. He had a paneled, corner office at each location, surrounded by those of numerous associates who ran his cases day to day. He had no partners. That would require sharing his profits.

He'd fly in on his Gulfstream and set up shop for a day or two at each office each month, but his primary office, his home base, was still in New York. Since the crash of Marine One he'd spent most of his time in Washington. He had increased his staff, hired a couple of additional attorneys, and taken on a well-known woman to handle the PR. Her job description must have been to get him on the front page every week. She issued written statements from him on everything. Every time the NTSB said anything, every time WorldCopter said anything, every time a document was filed with the court, every time there was a hearing, the press always got his opinion in a faxed, professionally prepared statement, which was usually quoted word for word.

Knowing all that, I should have anticipated what Hackett did next. When we arrived at his office and were ushered into the gorgeous conference room, sitting around the table and against the walls were at least ten reporters with their note pads ready and "gotcha" looks on their faces.

I tried not to say anything right away. I shook Hackett's powerful hand, as did Rachel, then the hands of the other three attorneys who sat by him. Rachel and I sat down and put down our heavy litigation bags. After we exchanged superficial pleasantries, I asked Hackett, "Who invited the press?"

"Well, obviously since you didn't, and we're the only two parties coming to this deposition, I must have. Did you really think someone else might have?"

"I just like to confirm things. I thought maybe they had offices here."

Hackett smiled. "The press calls me all the time, just as I'm sure they call you. Unlike you, I answer them because I have nothing to hide. They asked me what was happening next in the case, and I told them about this deposition. They asked if they could come, and I said of course. Depositions are open to the public. So unless you obtain an order from the court before the start time of this deposition — ten minutes according to my watch — they'll be here. You set this deposition for nine o'clock. Mrs. Collins is here, the court reporter is here, and I'm here. So we're ready to begin. If you find the presence of the press and the scrutiny of your case intolerable and want to try to exclude them, you will have missed your chance to take Mrs. Collins's deposition and you won't get another. Now, are you ready to begin?"

Hackett loved gamesmanship. I wasn't going to let him or his scheming distract me. I sat down, opened my notebook, looked at the court reporter, and said, "Swear the witness." I looked at Melissa Collins carefully for the first time. She was surprisingly attractive. I had met Chuck Collins and found him rather ordinary-looking, in a Marine sort of way. He was in excellent shape with short hair and sharp features, and he was always tan from his noontime runs. But I didn't think anyone would call him handsome, although Tinny had. I had always carried around a stereo type that attractive people married other attractive people. I found it unusual when an average-looking person married someone attractive. This seemed to be one of those exceptions. Melissa Collins was beautiful. Especially for a woman of her age, maybe thirty-five. She was tall and slender and at least the same height as Collins. She had steel blue eyes and looked directly at me with infinite curiosity and clarity. It was quite an amazing look. She was obviously strong, and composed.

Many attorneys begin by asking witnesses if they understand they've been sworn to tell the truth, and other silly questions that are essentially throat-clearing, but I had abandoned that long ago. I went right at the hard questions from the beginning, then asked follow-up questions as I went along. I just asked whatever question came to my mind and only looked at my outline later to make sure I had covered everything.

She had clearly been prepared for the usual approach. I started in by asking if she was the wife of the pilot of Marine One, which she of course quickly acknowledged. I then asked, "Did you ever consider divorcing Colonel Collins?"

Hackett came out of his chair. He accused me of harassing the witness, of trying to intimidate her, of inappropriate questions, whatever he could come up with. I looked at her again and said, "Your attorney has objected, but he did not instruct you not to answer, which was wise on his part because that is inappropriate in a federal case. Did you ever consider divorcing Colonel Collins?"

"No," she said softly and firmly. She was annoyed by my question but wasn't going to show it.

I went back and started at the beginning of her relationship with Collins, how they had met, where they had been married, the various places they had been stationed, his time in the Marine Corps, how difficult the separation was, and how absolutely wonderful their relationship was before he was killed. "Did you and your husband ever sleep in separate bedrooms?"

This time Hackett came unhinged. He accused me of invading the privacy of her relationship with her husband, which of course I responded to by pointing out that she had made a claim for loss of consortium — the loss of sexual satisfaction from her marriage — and that as I understood it, she wanted WorldCopter to pay her for that loss.

I had to determine what that loss was. Hackett acknowledged that and said that I was entitled to inquire, but the questions had to be appropriate. The question was of course appropriate. He just hated it. After our debate Hackett stood up. "We're going to take a break. I want to speak to my client about this."

Being obstreperous is common among attorneys. It was what they did. And they got away with it because, if you brought a motion to stop it, the judge would always say, now now, you young children get along, go back and try it again. There just aren't enough judges around who will spank an attorney for behaving badly.

Hackett probably wanted to ask her why in the hell I was asking about her and her husband sleeping in separate rooms, and if there was something he should know. Clearly she hadn't told him about their marital problems. He'd find out soon enough. It wouldn't make any difference in his demands or anything else about the way he'd approach the case, but he'd find out. And he'd be a little annoyed. But I wasn't there just to point out things to him that he didn't know, I was there to find answers that would change the case. If a woman came into a courtroom crying about the death of

305

her loving husband, and it turned out they hadn't slept together in five years and she'd filed for divorce while sleeping with someone else, that was an entirely different case.

She returned. Hackett sat down beside her. "She's ready to answer."

"Do you remember the question?"

"Yes."

"And what's your answer?"

"Our relationship was fine. We slept together in the same bed, every night."

I looked her in the eye and saw nothing but hardness. So she was willing to lie. Either that or Tinny Byrd had gone to the wrong house. So how do you prove that a woman hadn't been sleeping with her husband? Who else is going to testify about that when she's lying and he's dead?

"You're still living at the same house where you lived on the day of the accident?"

"Yes."

"And have you changed anything, have you rearranged any furniture, moved anything from one closet to another, anything like that?"

"I've cleaned up a little bit."

"Have you moved your husband's things? Have you taken his books, clothes, personal effects, and moved them from one room to another?"

Hackett sat up and leaned his elbows on the table. "What is the possible relevance of this, counselor?"

I ignored him. "You can answer the question."

"No. I've left everything where it is. I'm not able to do that yet."

I looked at Hackett. "I'd like you to instruct your client to keep everything as it is. I will be preparing a formal demand to enter her premises and inspect the house, and I will have it personally served on you today. We'll be doing that inspection" — I glanced at my watch — "in ten days."

"There's no reason to inspect her house. This is just to annoy her," Hackett said, annoyed himself.

I turned to Rachel and whispered in her ear, "E-mail Braden to prepare a demand to inspect her house." She nodded and pulled out her BlackBerry.

I continued, "And if you were sleeping in the same room, when was the last time you had sex with your husband prior to the accident?"

Hackett slapped his hand on the table. "This is ridiculous. You don't need to ask these questions."

"Are you making a demand for loss of consortium?"

"Of course. It's part of the standard wrongful-death case."

"Then I am entitled to find out the nature of the relationship."

He sat back and huffed, but said nothing else.

"Your answer?"

"The night before."

"Are you sure?"

"Yes."

"And before that night, when was the last time you had sex with your husband?"

"I don't know. A couple of days."

"On the average, how often did you have sex with your husband?"

"It varied. He was gone a lot."

"When he was home."

"I don't know. Maybe three times a week, maybe twice."

Now that I had her feeling uncomfortable and realizing that this was very real, and that this testimony could be used in trial if it came to that, she was much more reserved than she had been when we entered the room.

"Did you understand what I and your attorney were talking about? That we're going to ask that you allow us into your house to inspect it, look at it, videotape it, and have a better understanding of your living relationships with your husband, where he spent his time and the like, you understand that?"

She shook her head. "I don't understand why you would need to do that to me."

"What I need from you now, ma'am, is an assurance that you will not change anything materially inside your house that might help us understand your relationship with your husband. Do you give us your word on record that you will not change it any?"

Hackett put his hand in front of her on the table so she wouldn't answer. "She's not here to make promises. She's here to answer questions."

I continued to look at her and said, "I have asked her a question, whether she's willing to give me that assurance. If not" — I turned my head to Hackett — "I will simply ask the court to impose an order that nothing be changed or modified. We can do it either way."

Hackett said, "She won't change anything materially."

"I appreciate that you're willing to give me your assurance. But unfortunately you don't live there."

I looked at her again. "Will you give me yours?"

"Yes, there's nothing to change, of course."

"Fine. Let's go on with some of the other questions then." I spent the rest of the day asking the questions that you have to ask in a wrongful-death case. It's difficult to probe into a person's life and ask questions that he or she has never been asked by anybody, not even their parents. It's difficult to ask how someone values the death of a spouse. What did her husband mean to her? How different is her life? She told us of the dreams that they had together, the life they had planned after his retirement from the Marine Corps, the mountain home he planned to build in North Carolina, how difficult it had been not to be able to have children. They had grown to love the in de pen dent life that they lived, the ability to travel at the drop of a hat. Her ability to go visit him in the places he was stationed, in Japan, in Europe, in ports in the Mediterranean. She had traveled the world and had enjoyed her life. And that had all been snatched from her. She cried, she took breaks, she showed that she cared and that she was vulnerable.

And I wasn't buying it. Ever since she had told me that she and her husband had slept in the same room, I wasn't buying it. It was just fabrication to support the first lie. If it was as she said, how could their lives not be completely intertwined in a wonderful relationship? She was just giving me the answers she had to give. It all sounded too good and sweet.

I ended the day after she was tired and wanted to quit, and after I had implied that we were going to go on for three days. "Your husband was quite the reader."

"Yes."

"I know that you provided copies to us of the books in his den, or rather in your house."

"Yes."

"He left margin notes in nearly every book he read."

"True. He was always writing in the margins."

"He said what he thought about things in the margins, about the author, or the topic, or something else entirely."

"I didn't really read his notes."

"It would be strange for him to say things he didn't mean in those notes, wouldn't you agree?"

"I'm sure he meant every word. He was never one to say something he didn't mean. It was one of his pet peeves, when other people would say things to please others, or to be better regarded."

"Did he have any particular interest in the

international policies of President Adams? And Asia, in particular?"

I walked to my car in the parking garage in the basement of Hackett's building. I thought the deposition had gone reasonably well and checked my BlackBerry for messages. I had an e-mail from Frank Flannery. He was ready to meet. I said to Rachel, "You want to go meet the mystery witness?"

She looked at her watch. "It's almost six. But I guess so, yeah."

I pulled out of the garage and headed directly for Flannery's office. We parked in the cramped garage underneath his office building on M Street and took the elevator up to the lobby, then to his law office. The office of the well-known firm was stately. People were leaving, and the receptionist was shutting down her computer when we arrived. We told her we were there to see Flannery. She asked us to wait and he would be with us shortly.

Flannery came up and I stood to greet him. I introduced myself and Rachel, and he escorted us into a glassed-in conference room next to the reception area. He closed the miniblinds to block the view into the conference room from the reception area and told us how the meeting would proceed.

Just a meeting, the witness would say whatever he wanted. After the meeting we would all figure out what we were going to do.

The door from the back of the conference room opened and the witness walked in. He wasn't at all what I expected. He was dressed poorly, had a bad haircut, and obviously did not eat well or exercise. He wasn't exactly fat, but he was lumpy. He had the hands of a workingman, and the eyes of someone who could anger quickly, particularly when intoxicated, which I guessed was often. He sat next to Flannery across the table from us.

"Good evening, I'm Mike Nolan and this is Rachel Long."

The man sat silently and stared at us. His attorney responded, "He would love to tell you his name, but we are not to that point yet. The purpose of this meeting of course is to discuss whether or not you're interested in the information that he has, and whether you are willing to meet his terms to obtain that information." Flannery paused as he searched for exactly the right words. "I am taking no position on the appropriateness of his demands. He has asked me to put this meeting together, to protect his identity, and to make sure he crosses no boundaries.

I have done that, and he is here. You may ask him questions, to which he will respond as he deems appropriate."

I wasn't sure where to start. An uneasy tension was in the room. "You have some information about the accident that you think we might want to know. I believe that's why you called me."

"Yeah. I called. I have information that will blow the case wide-open."

"In what direction?"

"In all directions. Case over."

" 'Case over' meaning what exactly?"

"I can't go into it until we decide whether you're going to meet my terms."

"I'm not even going to consider your terms until we find out what information you have, at least in general. Do you know why this helicopter crashed?"

"I know what happened to the helicopter before it flew. And it will end the case."

"How? How did you gain access to this knowledge?"

"I was there."

"Meaning what?" I watched him as he considered how to answer.

"I'm not going to say. You might figure out who I am." He sat back in the leather chair. He looked uncomfortable.

"If I don't know how you got your information, let alone what it is, how can I recommend that you get paid?"

"You have to tell me that you're willing. You have to give me your word. Then I'll tell you."

"Will it be admissible? Can I get it into evidence at trial?"

"I don't know anything about that."

"And what if your information is all crap and you don't know anything?"

"You want this or not?"

"I don't know. What kind of compensation are you looking for?"

"Hundred thousand dollars, cash. No questions asked. Tell you what, you bring that cash to this attorney here, leave it with him, I'll tell you what I know. You don't like it, you take the money back. Otherwise, I take the money and disappear. You'll be able to get more based on what I tell you. You can go ask other people questions. You think about it."

The man stood up and walked through the door from which he had come. I looked at his attorney as I closed my notebook, not having written anything. "This is real sketchy."

Flannery was uninterested in a discussion. "I'll be here when you call."

As I pulled out of the garage, Rachel said,

"Are you buying that?"

"I don't know. I really don't. I'm going to tell WorldCopter about it and see what they think. I want you to take another look at Braden's memo. Check the cases and ethics opinions of the state bar. See how close to the line this is. And check one other thing. What if the client does the paying and not the attorney? They're not bound by our ethical obligations. What if we can't control them?"

"Can't?"

"Or don't."

The next morning my cell phone rang as I was dressing. New York number. I answered quietly, "Mike Nolan."

"What were you thinking?" a female voice demanded.

It sent an awakening jolt of adrenaline through me. It was Kathryn. "What do you mean?"

"You let the *press* sit in on Melissa Collins's deposition? Have you seen the headlines? Let me read from the front page of this morning's *New York Post,* which I was just privileged to pick up. 'WorldCopter Lawyer Grills Marine One Pilot's Widow on Sex Life.' Did you do that?"

"I wouldn't put it like that, but basically,

yeah. Of course. Just like *you* did when you were practicing. Those questions are routine."

"You don't grill a widow about her sex life in front of a roomful of reporters!"

"I didn't anticipate him inviting them, but it wouldn't have made any difference. I could have adjourned the depo and gotten a protective order, which probably would have been denied, and that would have been worse. 'WorldCopter Tries to Grill Widow in Secret.' And then I would have asked the same questions anyway."

"The protective order may have been granted. It would have cut down on the circus. We have to get a protective order for the other depos now. Hackett's whole idea is manipulation, winning in the press. It has nothing to do with the facts."

"I know that, and *you* know that. But we've got to be willing to take some lumps to prepare this case. Otherwise you can just write him a check."

She paused, obviously frustrated. "Just try to see these things coming so we can talk about it before it happens. All right? I don't like talking about bad things unless I anticipated them and prepared for them."

"Fair enough." I'd been working with

Kathryn for years. I'd never heard her raise her voice. Hackett was really starting to piss me off. Trial was now sixty days off, and I had thirty days to finish my discovery, come up with my theory, get my expert reports together, and otherwise look like a genius. This thing was going to trial whether I was ready or not.

As I drafted an e-mail on my BlackBerry to Rachel about a protective order, I saw a new e-mail from Tripp at WorldCopter. The light bluish white screen glowed in the dark as Debbie slept. Tripp had read my e-mail report on the secret witness and wanted to meet with him immediately. If this guy was going to lead us to evidence, Tripp wanted to get on it right away.

I told Tripp where Flannery's office was and he said he was on his way. I called Flannery after Tripp, and he said he could have the witness there at 9 AM. I had a couple of minutes to talk to Tripp before we went into the conference room. I sent Rachel an e-mail asking for anything she had found about Braden's memo.

We went to the same conference room as the day before, and Flannery went through the familiar routine of lowering the shades. The witness walked in right on cue. He was wearing the same clothes he had been wearing the night before, and his hands were still dirty.

Tripp didn't want to hear about his clothes or hands or what he might do for a living. He knew the man had information that could exonerate WorldCopter. After the introductions, Tripp jumped right in. "What is it that you know that would be so valuable to us?"

The guy shook his head. "I'm not going to go into it until I get paid."

"Let's say that we can arrange for you to be paid. Can you tell me the kind of information that you have?"

"If I tell you what I know, I'll lose my job, I won't be able to hang around here anymore. I want you to move me to a different place and find me a job. I'm not afraid they're going to like kill me or anything, but I'm going to have to get out of here. I want to go to Montana and set up my own tire store. I'll need at least a hundred and fifty thousand dollars, and moving expenses. Probably another thirty or so. So a hundred and eighty grand."

I said, "We could just subpoena you. And last time you said a hundred thousand. What changed?"

"No, you can't. You'll never find me. You

319

don't know my name or where I work, and
—"

"You sure about that?"

"Yeah, I'm sure. There's no way you could. So I won't be there when you come looking for me. And I've been thinking about everything I will need to do. One fifty is the minimum."

Tripp said, "Let's agree in principle —"

"Can I talk to you for a second?" I said, indicating the door.

Tripp stopped, looked at me, and said begrudgingly, "Sure."

We got up and walked into Flannery's deserted lobby. I looked around and saw that we were alone. I said in a loud whisper, "We don't know anything about this guy. We can't pay him. It will taint the whole case. If this gets out — and I assume *everything* will get out at some point in this case — we'll be crucified. I say we shut this guy down. Challenge him to testify about the truth, or shut the hell up with this cloak-and-dagger bullshit."

Tripp's face turned red. "Mike, we may miss a chance to blow this case wide-open if we don't take this guy up on his offer. What's a hundred fifty grand in the big scheme of things?"

"It's not the money, it's the principle."

"What principle? Helping a witness who has critical information not to have his life ruined for bringing the information out? We'll tell the jury what we paid and why. They'll understand."

"No, they won't. And it's probably unethical. I could be disbarred."

"So what? You can get rebarred. We'll bring you in-house to work for us until you're cleared again."

I stood back and looked around. He started to turn. I grabbed him arm. "David, I'm advising you not to do this. Let's walk away. It smells."

"I can't. I've got to find out at least what he knows. Come on." Tripp turned and hurried back into the conference room.

Before we even sat down again he said to the witness, "What kind of information do you have that would make it worth that much money?"

The man leaned forward and looked Tripp squarely in the eye. "Are you saying you can do this? That you will?"

"I don't know. I'm saying I might. Depends on the kind of information you have. You've got to let me know why it would be worth our while."

The man spoke softly but openly, "But if I convince you that it's worth it, you're willing to do this?"

I leaned over to speak to Tripp, but he was already responding, "Yes."

The man nodded eagerly and sat back. "Smart man. What I've got are maintenance records."

Tripp waved his hand at him dismissively. "We've already got all the maintenance records. We've been through them with a fine-tooth comb."

"You don't have *these* maintenance records."

"What are you talking about?"

"Maintenance records on the rotor blade the day before the accident."

Tripp swallowed, not believing what he'd just heard. "You have maintenance records on the blade right before the accident? Where'd you get them?"

"Never mind. I'll give you copies, hard copies that you can then pursue. There are maintenance guys' names on them, and it shows what they did to the rotor blade."

"What did they do?"

"You'll have to wait to see. You wire the money to this law firm — I forget what they call it —"

"Our client trust account," Flannery said.

"Right, the trust account. Then I will have him fax to you and send hard copies overnight of the five pages of maintenance records."

"How do we know you have any?"

The man pulled a folded piece of paper out of his Windbreaker pocket, unfolded it, and passed it across the table. I immediately recognized it as a standard Marine Corps maintenance form. It was a copy of a sheet noting vibration in the helicopter three days before the accident. He said, "Bet you've never seen this."

We both examined it and looked at each other. We hadn't. Tripp asked, "Is this one of the five pages?"

"Yup. The juicy stuff though is on the other four pages."

"May I keep this?"

"Yup, and I want the money in this account within forty-eight hours. Can you do that?"

I couldn't just sit there. This just didn't make sense. "Let me make sure I understand. You give us an example of a maintenance record that we've not seen, you tell us there are others that have critical information on them, but you won't tell us what that information is, and we're just supposed to wire a buttload of money to you?"

"Yes, sir."

I shook my head. "It's up to my client,

but I'm telling you this, I won't recommend that he do this unless you tell me right now what the content of those records is. We can't use it without you or without the records. Maybe we can find the Marine who did the work, but it sure gives us some motivation to comply with your request if you tell us what they did. Otherwise, I'm not sure why we would do it."

The man thought about my request. He had been playing with a paper clip the entire time he was speaking. This nervous habit seemed out of line for somebody who was so sure and steady. After an interminable pause, he replied, "It's about the tip weights, they had an incident with that blade. It was worked on the day before the accident. I'll prove it to you."

Tripp was about to wet his pants. "Give me the account number."

"Give me your e-mail address and I'll get it to you," Flannery said.

Tripp stood. "We'll wire the money tomorrow."

20

Never did I think bringing a motion for a protective order would work against us. The next day was the date set for the first lady's deposition. I was up most of the night and early in the morning doing the final preparation. I was driving to Hackett's office with Rachel when they announced on NPR that Hackett was holding a press conference to disclose "dramatic new developments" in the case against WorldCopter. He was undoubtedly holding the press conference in the very office where the deposition was about to take place, the one subject to the newly issued protective order excluding everyone except parties to the lawsuit and their attorneys. Journalists from all over the world were probably standing in the reception area of his law firm where he had placed a lectern on which to mount all the microphones. NPR switched live to the press conference, and Hackett's unmistakable voice came through our radio.

Hackett said, "Thank you for coming so early this morning. I'm sorry to get you out of your normal routine, but this development was so remarkable to me that I wanted to let you know as soon as I had heard of it. First of all, for purposes of background, the first lady's deposition is set for this morning at nine o'clock. I would like for you to be able to see it, to hear the questions asked and answers given as with Mrs. Collins, but WorldCopter is apparently unwilling to let others see the kinds of questions they ask the widows in this case. They have asked the court to keep the press, and the public, out of the deposition so I will be unable to let you attend the deposition. For that I apologize, but it is out of my hands. I believe in full disclosure, but I am not in control of WorldCopter or their tactics.

"But my reason for talking to you this morning is something that happened last night. I received a phone call from a gentleman with whom I've spoken before. He had approached me with evidence that he said would solve the case for all of us. I, of course, rejected it immediately as an obvious scam. Yet, apparently yesterday, attorneys for WorldCopter and the vice president and general counsel of WorldCopter himself agreed to pay this man one hundred fifty thousand dollars for forged Marine Corps maintenance records. They were apparently so eager for good news in this case that they walked into a con. He apparently had access to some blank Marine Corps maintenance sheets, made up some fake records, and sold them to WorldCopter." Hackett paused, looking at the journalists. "I am shocked and saddened that World-Copter would resort to such desperate tactics to avoid liability in the case where their helicopter is responsible for the death of the president of the United States and six others."

Several reporters began yelling questions. Hackett said, "I'll have time for a few questions at the end. But there's another thing; not only is it bad judgment to try and buy a witness, to buy testimony that is favorable to your case, but it's *unethical.* The attorney involved here, Mr. Mike Nolan of Annapolis, Maryland, the attorney in charge of the defense of WorldCopter, violated the ethical rules of the state of Maryland.

"Because of that, we will be filing a motion for sanctions against WorldCopter and Mr. Nolan, and a motion to disqualify Mr. Nolan as counsel for WorldCopter due to his unethical conduct. We're frankly surprised by these developments as Mr. Nolan was not known to violate the ethical rules, at least not to this extent, prior to this time. So as I said, we will be moving to disqualify him and for sanctions against him and World-Copter. The motion is already prepared and will be filed later today. I do want you to know as members of the press, though, that this will in no way delay the trial that is currently scheduled for sixty days from today. We are going to trial because we need to have our day in court. The first lady has waited long enough for justice, and justice delayed is justice denied."

The journalists were in disbelief and hurled questions at Hackett.

"I'm sorry, I just noticed the time. I must go prepare the first lady for her deposition with the same Mr. Nolan. I don't know what he has in mind, but we certainly need to discuss what he might try to do at this deposition. Again, I'm sorry that you cannot attend because WorldCopter did not want you to be there. I therefore regrettably don't really have time for the questions I know you have and that I expected to be able to answer. I need to go back to my office. But Mr. Nolan will be here shortly to conduct the deposition. There is no protective order from the court that says you can't ask *him* questions. And you're welcome to stay here in the lobby of my office until the deposition starts. Thank you."

Rachel muttered, "You've got to be shitting me."

"Don't worry about it. He's overplayed his hand this time."

Rachel sat up and turned toward me. "How, exactly? Didn't Tripp offer to pay this liar? And that doesn't make us look bad?"

"He offered all right. Sort of. But this isn't as simple as Hackett thinks."

"Well, help me understand then. 'Cause it looks pretty simple to me."

"You'll hear it when I tell the press."

We entered the District of Columbia at a snail's pace with the rest of the traffic coming in from Maryland. We arrived at Hackett's building, parked in the garage, and came up in the elevator. By the time I got to Hackett's office, the journalists had not only not left, they had increased in number. Those who hadn't been invited to the press conference had heard that the deposition was about to occur and immediately went to the office. The reception area was jammed, and they were all waiting for me.

As I opened the door and walked in with Rachel, they began firing questions. Did you pay a witness to testify against the first lady? Can you go to jail for ethics charges? Do you think WorldCopter will keep you on the case after this ethical breach? Will the judge hold you in contempt? Will she put you in jail? Have you been charged with ethics violations before? Why doesn't WorldCopter admit it was their fault and settle the case? Are you going to ask the first lady about her sex life with the president? Why did you ask the judge to keep us out of the deposition? Are you trying to hide something?

I put my hand up, smiled, and asked if they could please excuse me so I could get through to the conference room. Two refused to move from the door to the conference room unless I answered some questions. I turned to the journalists. "I don't believe in trying a case in the press."

They were not to be deterred. My statement just encouraged them. I turned, put my briefcase down, and moved to the podium that Hackett had so recently vacated after his press conference. "All right, I'll answer a couple of questions, but I don't have much time."

I stood behind the microphones, which they had notably not taken off the podium. "Yes," I said, pointing to a female journalist in the front.

"What do you have to say about the charges of Tom Hackett that you tried to pay a witness to testify to false information? Did you meet with a witness who wanted to be paid?"

I waited for the group to become completely quiet. "Mr. Hackett seems to have gotten some bad information. A few days ago I did receive a phone call from a gentleman who refused to identify himself and said he had conclusive proof that the accident was not WorldCopter's fault. This was obviously of interest, but he said he wanted to be paid for his testimony. I met with him and his attorney to evaluate him, and then met with him a second time to hear him out and find out what his terms were. It became clear to me that his request would be impossible. However, I obtained from him a sample of the evidence he said he could produce. It was a single-page maintenance record.

"We did not tell him no, and we left him with the impression that we were going to meet his demands. But of course we weren't, and we didn't. Since I had met him before and could describe him, the second time we met, I had my private investigator post some of his coworkers at every conceivable exit from the building in which we met.

We had him followed. We know where he lives, and what he drives.

"But most important, I gave to my investigator my copy of the bogus maintenance record this gentleman had given to me. As I suspected, since it was that shiny kind of copying paper, there was a good fingerprint on it. The Washington, D.C., police were happy to trace this print for us as it would lead to the identity of someone trying to defraud those involved in a very important civil case.

"The man claiming to have records is a convicted criminal from New York. He is known to associate with a certain William Watters."

The journalist was stunned. She couldn't not ask the question. "Who is William Watters?"

"I believe he is a private investigator who has worked with many New York attorneys in the past. Check him out."

Someone yelled, "Including Tom Hackett?"

"Ask him."

"So you didn't pay the witness?"

"Of course not."

"What about the deposition? Why did you ask the court to close the depositions to the press?"

"Well, since Mr. Hackett is so familiar with Maryland State Bar ethics opinions, he should also be aware of the bar opinion where a plaintiff's attorney from Baltimore was disbarred for repeatedly trying his cases in the press. Several of the type of statements Mr. Hackett insists on making to you are prohibited by the Maryland Code of Professional Responsibility. You can't make public statements that are intended to bias prospective jurors. That's what seems to be happening, at least if journalists are any indication of public perception. So because it is unfair to my clients to try this case in the press, I asked the court for the chance to have this case tried in a courtroom, where it belongs. You may not like that, which I understand, but that's what the court thought was the right result as well. Now if you'll excuse me . . ."

I headed toward the conference room. As we entered, Rachel said quietly, "Do you think we should have told them about Tinny?"

"I just told them we had an investigator."

"Everyone knows who you use."

I shut the door behind me. The court reporter and the videographer were in place for the deposition. Hackett was there, the Secret Service was there, and the first lady sat across the table from the point where I entered. It was the first time I'd ever seen her in person. She was beautiful. She was elegant and composed and would make the best imaginable witness.

"Good morning. Everyone ready? I'm sure we all want to get out of here as soon as we can."

Hackett stood and reached across the table to shake my hand. "Good morning, Mr. Nolan," he said, trying not to smile.

I shook his hand.

He said, "Do you expect to continue on this case now that you'll be facing ethical charges?"

I stared at him. "I guess you didn't hear what I just said to the press. Why don't you ask me that question again after you've had a chance to hear it."

He looked confused. "What did you say?"

I took off my coat, put it on the back of my chair, and was about to sit down when the first lady rose. She smiled at me and held out her hand. "Good morning, Mr. Nolan. I'm Rebecca Adams."

I smiled at her as I shook her hand gently. She had soft hands but a firm handshake. I noticed her thin fingers. I was surprised that while she had probably had a manicure, she wore no nail polish, nothing fancy. "Yes, ma'am. I know who you are. It's very nice to meet you. I'm sorry we have to meet under these circumstances."

"So am I."

She sat back down. She was wearing an expensive dark green suit with a cream-colored silk blouse. She was taller than I had expected. She was probably five-eight. I don't know what I'd expected, probably five-five or so. Her light brown hair was pulled back in a fashionable style, and she looked poised and ready to go.

I pulled out the binders that Rachel had prepared, glanced at my outline, turned to the court reporter, and said, "Please swear the witness." The first lady turned toward the court reporter, raised her hand, swore to tell the truth, and turned back to face me.

The first couple of hours of questioning were boring and tedious, by design. I asked her about her background, education, employment, and her work as the first lady. Then about President Adams. I got to hear his whole life's story from childhood to being elected president. In a wrongful-death case, the value of the case is based to a great extent on the earning power of the person who died. Needless to say, a former president has massive earning power, even though few actually take full advantage of it. Aggressively pursuing money is thought to be unseemly for a former president.

The longer he stayed in politics though, the lower his lifetime earnings would be. So if he was likely to get reelected — a point worthy of debate — his earnings would substantially decrease. Only after leaving the presidency would his earnings have dramatically gone up. She might make a claim for book royalties, similar to the $8 million advance that Bill Clinton got for his memoirs, or the $100,000 a pop speaking engagements that Gerald Ford was paid for years. Former presidents could make even more if they served on corporate boards or as advisers to corporations, but most thought that was beneath them. They had lifetime pay at the same salary they earned as president, so anything earned on top of that was simply bonus money. They also had lifetime Secret Service protection and office staff. We tediously covered all that and much more in the deposition.

As we approached lunch, I decided to ask her about the photographs, indirectly. She said she went to all the White House receptions, it was part of her job as first lady. She spoke with everyone, whoever was nearby. She tried to concentrate on the guests of honor, their spouses, assistants, and staff, but talked to numerous people throughout the evening. She liked to circulate and keep the reception flowing and energetic.

"Did you ever have the opportunity to have conversations with Colonel Collins?" I detected a slight hesitation in the first lady's eyes, a sense of danger. Hackett was alerted and stared at me suspiciously. He stopped taking notes.

"Perhaps on occasion, I don't really remember."

"Well, on December seventeenth, there was a reception for the prime minister of Japan. Do you recall that?"

"Yes."

"At that reception, at the White House, you spent a good deal of time speaking with Colonel Collins, did you not?"

"I don't really remember that."

"Do you recall what you were wearing?"

"No, I really don't. My wardrobe is selected by my assistant."

"Well, regardless of who selected it, do you recall what you were wearing?"

"No, I said I didn't."

Hackett put up his hand. "What is the possible relevance of what she was wearing to a reception three months before the accident?"

"You can answer the question."

"I did."

"Was the reception loud?"

"Loud?"

"Yes, was there loud music or anything else that would make it difficult to hear others?"

"Not that I recall. I don't recall there being any music at all."

"Can you explain then how it is that you were whispering in the ear of Colonel Collins on several occasions during that reception?"

She looked shocked. "I don't remember that being the case. Where'd you hear that?"

"Do you deny it?"

"Deny what?"

"Whispering in Collins's ear during the reception for the prime minister of Japan on December seventeenth."

"I don't remember doing that and I don't know why I would. *Denial* is a very rigid word. I would like to deny it, but I don't really recall the events at all."

"Did you have any kind of personal relationship with Colonel Collins?"

Hackett yelled, "This is outrageous! What is the meaning of this?"

"The implications are not as dramatic as you imply, it's a simple question. Did she

338

have any relationship of any kind, even as a fellow coin collector, with Colonel Collins." I looked back at her. "Did you?"

"I knew him, as I flew on Marine One many times. When we were in various locations, we would occasionally find ourselves near each other and would converse, but nothing substantial."

"Did Colonel Collins ever express to you any dislike for the president?"

"No. Absolutely not."

"Are you aware that he purchased a substantial life insurance policy sixty days before his death?"

"No, I was not."

"Did you speak with the president on the night of the accident, before he climbed aboard Marine One?"

"Yes, of course." She shifted uncomfortably in her chair.

Hackett interrupted, "Is this a good time to stop? It's twelve fifteen and we need to grab lunch if we're going to go beyond the morning."

Without looking at him I answered, "We're definitely going to go beyond the morning, and, no, this isn't a good place to stop."

I asked the first lady, "You were aware when you spoke with the president that there was a major storm outside, correct?"

"I believe that storm had been going on for a few hours at that point."

"Did the president tell you why he needed to go to Camp David that night?"

"He said he had an important meeting."

I paused and waited for her to look at me. "With whom?"

"I don't know. He didn't say."

"Did you ask?"

"Yes. I was always asking questions."

"What did he tell you?"

"He told me it was highly confidential and he couldn't go into it."

"Have you since determined why he was going to Camp David that evening?"

She looked at Hackett. He said, "Other than what your counsel may have told you."

She looked back at me. "No, nothing other than what my attorney has told me."

"Did you ask President Adams why it was so important to get there so quickly that he was willing to fly in that storm?"

"Yes, I did. I thought it was unwise to fly."

"What did he say?"

"He said it was the most important meeting of his presidency."

I paused and looked at the others in the room, including the Secret Service agents, who were completely expressionless. "Did he tell you what he meant by that?"

"No."

"Do you know now?"

She hesitated. "No."

21

I should have noticed that one of Hackett's associates was frantically e-mailing on his BlackBerry during the entire deposition. I actually did notice, but assumed he was taking notes. I was quickly dissuaded of that idea. Several members of the media that had waited in the lobby during the entire procedure pounced on me and asked, "Did you actually ask the first lady if she was having an affair with the pilot of Marine One? Is that WorldCopter's theory? Do you have any basis for that? Can the first lady sue you for slander?"

I smiled, waved at the press, and walked into the elevator to go down to my car. Several members of the press joined Rachel and me in the elevator, which was particularly awkward and uncomfortable since I didn't say anything. They peppered me with questions throughout the descent. I should have known Hackett would try something like that. He had insisted that the language of the order be extremely specific about how the press was excluded from the deposition in which the room was taken or from any access to the transcript after the deposition. I had expected the testimony to come out somehow. In a case like this, in something this politically volatile, everything will come out. It's just a fact. But I had expected Hackett, or more likely one of his associates, to slip a transcript of the deposition to a reporter, then claim to have no idea how the reporter had gotten it. But with this he had slipped. The press corps, or some of them, had obviously received e-mails from inside the deposition room.

I waited for one of the journalists to step away from the door of my car, then I got in and drove away. As soon as my BlackBerry had reception, my phone rang. It was Kathryn.

"You asked the first lady if she was sleeping with Collins?" Kathryn asked, surprised.

"Where'd you hear that?"

"It's all over the Internet. Some reporter posted a story about it, and every news site in the world picked up on it. So did you?"

"No, I didn't. Hackett's associate was e-mailing the press during the depo. I asked her if she had any particular kind of relationship with Collins, but that's all. Kathryn, I've got photos of her whispering in his ear at a reception. Several photos. They don't know I have them, but I've got to find out if there's anything to it."

"I want to have a meeting. I want Mark Brightman there, and Morton, Tripp, everyone. I want to meet at WorldCopter."

"Brightman?"

"The only way London would let me keep you on as the lead was to have Brightman basically shadow the whole case from New York. He's got everything I've got and knows as much as I do. We want to bring his thinking into the circle."

Great. "Let me know when you want to meet. And, Kathryn, don't let this depo stuff get to you. Hackett's going to try this case in the press and twist it as hard as he can."

"It just really makes me crazy, Mike. And the meeting is already on for tomorrow morning."

"Okay. See you then." We hung up.

I turned to Rachel, who had been quiet. She said, "Why didn't you tell me you were setting Hackett up with that mystery witness?"

"I wasn't sure how it was going to play out. If Tinny hadn't gotten that print run by his cop buddy in D.C., we wouldn't have had anything. And I think maybe you didn't really trust me. You thought I might actually pay a witness a hundred fifty grand to testify. Never going to happen."

Tripp met me at the reception desk at World-Copter's headquarters and escorted me to the conference room near his office. The corporate offices were fairly nice, but the conference room was third-class; it could have passed for a government conference room. A cheap table stood in the middle with metal chairs, with styrofoam cups for the bad-flavored coffee brewing in the corner. I poured myself a cup and said hello. Brightman and Morton were both there already, as were the others. I wasn't sure how to deal with Brightman, so I did what I usually do — went right at it. I walked around the table and shook his hand. "I don't believe we've ever actually met. Maybe once at a conference, but I'm Mike Nolan."

"Hi, Mike. Mark Brightman. I'd recognize you anywhere. You've been on TV a lot."

"More than I'd like," I said, trying to keep it casual.

Kathryn took control of the meeting. "Mike, I got a call from London, and the press over there is crucifying us. All the questions to Mrs. Collins, and the first lady. Looks bad."

"We've got to ask, and we've done our best to keep it confidential. That's all we can do. We can't really worry about what the press thinks. We've got to build our defense and get ready for trial, which is coming down on us like a train."

"Tell me about the photographs you mentioned."

"She's standing right next to Collins at a reception where he had no business being, and at which she had no business talking to him. It's an odd photo that just shows them in what appears to be a very confidential conversation. And it looks like his hand is on her . . . lower back — best case. I just wanted her to explain to me why she was talking to him in that way."

"And what did you hope to gain from that?"

"This is discovery. I look into everything. I don't assume I know what anything means in particular. I have gotten the most remarkable testimony in my career by asking questions that everybody thought shouldn't be asked because they were obvious or stupid. Sometimes they do turn out to be stupid questions. But sometimes, just sometimes, people will be honest or caught off guard and tell you things that you never would have discovered otherwise. So, yes, sometimes I do ask questions that are a little bit uncomfortable. We've got to prove what really happened, wherever that takes us."

"Well *tell* me. I'm all ears. What did happen?"

The room was remarkably silent. I spoke slowly but deliberately. "One theory that comes from the evidence, at least arguably, is that Collins crashed the helicopter on purpose. To kill the president. It may be that he hated him and saw the storm as an opportunity to take him out."

Kathryn shook her head slowly. "Prove it."

"I've got every book in Collins's library. He had a lot of fringe ideas. And a lot of side notes about President Adams. I don't have the smoking gun, some note that says he hated Adams, but just listen to the cockpit voice recorder. He wouldn't even talk to him."

She wasn't persuaded. "That's all you've got?"

"Collins bought a life insurance policy two months before the accident. A big one. Million dollars. And he wasn't sleeping with his wife — still not sure what that was about — but I think he was fed up. I don't know. But just maybe he was fed up enough to slam Marine One into the ravine in the middle of the storm. And maybe whatever was going on at Camp David was the last straw.

"I think the flight data recorder circuit breaker was pulled before the final descent on purpose. He wanted everyone to think he had hydraulic problems. Maybe he was trying to fake a hydraulic failure to cover the accident, and then rolled the helicopter over on its back and crashed in the middle of the night." I took a sip of the cooling coffee.

Kathryn said, "That's going to be hard to prove without more. Do you personally think that's what happened?"

Good question. I sure doubted it, but enough evidence suggested at least keeping it as open as a possibility. "Personally? I don't know. I've seen enough in this business to not be too quick to rule anything out. Could the pilot of Marine One kill the president? Sure, if he thought the president was a big enough threat to the country. People think that kind of thing all the time. But I still think the real explanation lies somewhere else. I think it has more to do with who was at Camp David that night."

Kathryn was growing frustrated. "You have any proof of who was at Camp David, any rumor, anything?"

"Byrd knows a guy who has that answer. I'm working it. But Byrd won't even tell me the guy's name. It's a Secret Service guy who is in charge of security at Camp David."

She looked encouraged. "Get his name. Byrd knows?"

I nodded.

"Get him to tell you the name. Set up his deposition. Let's develop this." She looked at the other attorneys, who nodded enthusiastically.

"He won't testify."

"Why not?"

"Refuses to even acknowledge any of it."

"Not so much that he wouldn't meet with you, I take it."

"He didn't meet with me. He met with Tinny."

"So how are you going to prove any of this?"

"We still have thirty more days of discovery."

"Right, so *how* are you going to do it?"

"I don't know."

Kathryn looked over at Brightman. He picked up on the hint. "You've got to force it, Mike. This is life-or-death for World-Copter." He glanced at Tripp, who was staring at me.

"I know, Mark. I'm on it. I can't force it yet."

"You think Byrd will tell you even if the Secret Service guy doesn't want him to?"

"Honestly?" I asked, looking around the table. "I don't know."

"Thirty days and you don't know. And have you thought about what you're going to do if you can't prove this? Do your investigators have a theory yet other than what the NTSB has said?"

"No. That rotor blade did come off, but that could have happened when the helicopter rolled inverted too. They're not designed to fly upside down. I'm just not buying the NTSB's theory."

Tripp asked, "And why not? Where is the flaw?"

"They don't have the tip weights. They have no idea when those tip weights came off."

"But doesn't that make it *more* likely they came off before the crash sequence started? Otherwise, they'd be nearby."

"I don't know. I don't think their failure to find them really proves much of anything. I think they've just jumped on that because the tip weights weren't there and that blade separated. That blade could have hit something on the way down and knocked the tip weights loose. Really, I think we're left with two possibilities. Either that the blade came off in flight, or the pilot did it on purpose. Fortunately, the plaintiff has the burden of proof."

Brightman stood up. "Do you have any *doubt* that Hackett is going to have an expert sit there on the stand and testify in somber tones about how this accident was caused by the failure to properly balance the rotor blade, and that the tip weights became unattached causing vibrations and resulting in the ultimate crash of the helicopter?"

"No. I don't have any doubt that he'll get an expert to say that. He can't cite the NTSB report of course because the conclusion is inadmissible. But he'll say it. No doubt. He'll say it. But our experts are the best experts in the country. And if they say it didn't happen that way, it's not at all a sure thing that Hackett will prevail."

Kathryn nodded toward Morton. "What about the Justice Department and congressional investigations?"

"Pretty much status quo. Since we gave them the ware house full of documents, they've gone quiet while they go through them and look for damaging information.

The Senate hearings have adjourned — most of the drama is over, and the grind of one witness after another pretty much emptied the room."

"Anything at all from any of that we can use to defend ourselves?"

"Just the materials I already gave to Mike. We can show the delay was the FBI's fault, but that's really only relevant to punitive damages. So, as to the cause of the crash? No, not really."

Kathryn thought for a moment while everyone waited in silence. The frustration of each person in the room was slightly different but palpable. She finally spoke. "Why does Hackett want you involved?"

"I've wondered about that. Like maybe he filed in Annapolis so I'd be sure to be involved. It seems to me that he has two equally attractive theories if he wounds me before trial. First, I go into trial with a national reputation of being unethical, or stupid, and he has the upper hand, or second, you or WorldCopter decide they don't want me on the case anymore and I get tossed. Then Mr. Brightman, or somebody else, rides in to save the day and defend WorldCopter, not having been involved in discovery, not having spent every waking hour dealing with this case for the last six months, and again he thinks he has the upper hand. For him it works either way. Plus, if I may be allowed an editorial comment, he may not have the greatest respect for Mr. Brightman's abilities either."

Kathryn said, "I think his whole strategy ever since he filed the lawsuit in Annapolis has been to get you deep into the case, through almost all of the discovery, and then start trying to cut your legs out from under you. He uses the press, false witnesses, personal confrontation, and probably a lot of other things we aren't yet aware of. He wanted me — this is really probably more about me than you — but he wanted me to remove you from the case to stop the barrage of bad press. But you know what, Mike?" She actually waited for me to answer.

I shook my head.

She continued, "He missed. You saw the fake witness coming, his deposition stories and leaks make us look aggressive, but not necessarily wrong, and otherwise we're matching up with him. Yesterday, frankly, I asked for this meeting with the idea of asking Mark to take over the lead of this case." She looked at him and he returned her look with barely concealed annoyance, knowing now where she was going. "But I think you're exactly the right guy to try this case. You've got the right experience, the right mentality, the helicopter knowledge, the *trial* experience, and the local knowledge. He may not fully realize how clever you are in trial. You're at your best when the fur is flying.

"We're going to put Mark's name on the caption. He'll stay up on things in case you get hit by a bus, but this is your case. You're going to try it. And based on their settlement demands, this case is going to get tried."

Kathryn walked back around to the other side of the table and picked up her now cool cup of coffee. "But you've *got* to find out what really happened. You've got to start *pushing* people. You've got to tell Byrd to put all his other cases on hold and work overtime. I want him working eighteen hours a day turning over rocks. I want him banging on that Secret Service agent to testify, or if he won't, then give us his name. I want our experts up all night, every night, running experiments, running aerodynamic analyses, figuring out what in the hell happened here. This helicopter did not fail just because it threw its tip weights. Something else happened. Maybe it was Collins. I'm not convinced, but it could be. Something happened and we need to find out what. And we need to *prove* who was going to be at that meeting and why. If you spring that in trial, all kinds of possibilities open up. You've got to find the proof. You've got to dig, and you've got to make it happen."

"That's what I'm trying to do."

Kathryn looked around at everybody else in the room. "Everybody okay with this?"

Brightman said, "You're taking a big risk, Kathryn. No offense to Mike, but his credibility may be at risk. All these deposition issues, and the bogus witness. We think the public gets it, but they may not. If he walks into that courtroom with no credibility, if the jurors think he is unethical, attempting to buy witnesses, and accusing the first lady of an affair, they won't cut him any slack at all. I think that's a risk for WorldCopter."

"I agree, but I think the opposite is equally likely. They may know — if they're paying attention — that Hackett is a bad guy, and Mike is fully aware of the traps that are being thrown in front of him. They'll identify with him and hate Hackett. Very possible. If there is any issue left by the time we get to trial, if we ask the right questions in voir dire, we'll be able to disarm it. Do you agree, Mike?"

"Maybe not all of it, but I think we'll get

a jury that will give us a fair hearing. That's all we can ask for."

Brightman said, "And facts, Mike. You need some *facts* to convince the jury that you're right. Not just theories."

22

I dialed Tinny. He answered his cell phone on the second ring. After some preliminary conversation where I told him of the meeting and we insulted each other and challenged each other's heritage, I asked, "You got anything new for me? We're in the last strokes of discovery and trial is right around the corner."

"Yeah, one thing, but what was the meeting about?"

"Case isn't going to settle."

"Never figured it would. Hackett wants this to go to trial and grandstand. It's his biggest moment on the world stage."

"No doubt. But the point of this is that Kathryn told me to tell you to clear your time. She wants you dedicating your time exclusively to this case. Same for all of our experts. It's balls-to-the-wall time, Tinny. And you've got to help me get to this Secret Service guy and prove who was going to be at Camp David. Everything may turn on that meeting and the timing."

"You're killing me. I can't just quit working on all my cases. I've got thirty or forty things I'm working on. I can't just tell them to sit there while I do this."

"You have to."

"Man, I don't know. I can clear a lot of it. There might still be a couple I'm going to have to do things on, but I'm with you. I've got to rent a damned car too."

"What happened to your Vette?"

"Some asshole covered it in paint."

"Construction?"

"No. I mean covered it. I was at Mercedes' eating breakfast. I come back out to my car and somebody has poured gallons of black paint all over it. Windshield, everywhere."

I felt a chill. "Who did it?"

"No idea, or I'd be over at his place right now helping him check in to the ER."

"You think it's related to our case?"

"No idea. Could be. It's a message from somebody."

"You been messing with anyone's wife?"

"Naw, man. I don't do that."

"Then what do you think?"

"Could be our case. Could be one of our State Department friend's boys. Or maybe

Hackett knows who I am and had one of his goons hit me for pissing all over their little scam with the bogus witness. Hard to say."

"I don't like it," I said. "They may be talking to me."

"Pretty indirect if they are."

"Call me tonight so we can go over some things."

"Catch you later —"

"Wait, you said there was one thing you wanted to tell me about."

"Yeah, there's somebody in Annapolis who is talking about you."

"No doubt."

"On a cell phone. I'm working on it, and I probably shouldn't tell you anything 'cause this is premature. I'm tracking it down, but somebody is having a lot of conversations with somebody else from New York. At least it's a 212 area code. But you're the subject. Hard to know exactly what they're talking about, 'cause they're assuming somebody's listening. They talk in shorthand or code that I can't quite get. But somebody wants things to go badly for you."

"Male or female?" I asked, my mind racing.

"Male, probably white."

"What do you make of it? Could it be a

journalist?"

"I don't know, I can just tell that there's something going on, where you're the subject, and they're trying to hide something."

"I don't follow you."

"That's all I got right now. One other thing. I . . . you know I ain't afraid of nobody. Well, one of those cases I got to keep an eye on is about an Asian gang member here in D.C. He's headed for trial on murder charges, and it's ugly. But the last couple of weeks I've noticed an Asian guy now and then. Has a sort of sophisticated look. Doesn't look like a gang guy to me. Could be the head cheese, but they never show themselves. This guy is different. I've seen him maybe twice, maybe three times. Don't know what to make of it, but I got to keep an eye out. Lots going on, Michael."

"See him around your car?"

"No."

"You've seen him like . . . he's following you?"

"Can't say. I see somebody I'm not looking for more than once in a couple of weeks in D.C.? I figure something's up. I have no idea who this guy is. Could be an IRS agent for all I know. I'm just telling you what's going on."

"You think he's one of Hackett's investigators?"

"Possible, but I doubt it. But watch yourself. Lots of things going on that we don't know about, Michael. And for what it's worth, I'm getting a feeling Collins had nothing to do with this accident."

"Feeling? What the hell am I supposed to do with that?"

"Don't know. Just a feeling I have. You ever feel a shadow?"

"I don't know. I guess you feel a coolness that wasn't there before."

"Just like that."

"Shit, Tinny."

"I got to go. Hey, by the way, you had any e-mail issues?"

"Meaning what?"

"I don't know. This phone conversation with somebody in Annapolis, they mentioned e-mail. I don't know what he's talking about, but I just wanted you to be aware that there may be something out there. Maybe someone is going to spam your server, I really don't know. Just beware. Call me in the morning." He hung up.

I didn't like the idea of somebody spamming our server or crashing our e-mail server or worse yet slipping some worm or virus into our system. That would be a disaster. I called Ralph, our outside IT guy. He answered his cell on the first ring. "Hey, Ralph, Mike Nolan."

"Hey. What can I do for you?"

"How secure do you feel we are? Could someone cram a virus or worm or something into our system and ruin our databases and the like?"

"Anything's possible. If there's somebody out there malicious and smart enough. They can ruin pretty much any computer system, particularly those that aren't hardened against attack, which yours isn't."

"Set us up. I want to make sure no one can sabotage us."

"I can start doing some things. I'll check out the whole system."

"This morning. I want you over there within an hour."

"I've got stuff backed up to two weeks from now."

"Within an hour or I'm gonna get somebody else. I've got to get this done, this is not negotiable."

"Mike, come on."

"I'm serious as a heart attack. You've got to be there in an hour or I'm going to get Dolores on the phone and get the next best guy. I don't have any time to mess with this. If somebody is going to attack our computer system, if I don't stop them now, when I know there may be something coming —"

"All right, all right, I'm on my way. I'm going to forward all the hate e-mails I get from other clients to you."

"Please do. See you there."

When I walked in and closed the door behind me, Dolores was startled. "Good morning, or rather afternoon, Mr. Nolan. You don't look so good, did you get some lunch?"

"Actually I didn't. Would you mind having the deli deliver a turkey sandwich for me? Whole wheat."

"No problem, sir. Anything else?"

"No. Messages?"

"There were two or three reporters sitting here in our waiting area all morning. I finally told them that you weren't coming back all day and they took off."

"Where'd you hear that?"

"I made it up. I was tired of looking at them."

"Well done."

"Thank you."

"Is Ralph here?"

"Yes, sir, he's back in the server room."

"Thanks." I left my briefcase and jacket behind her at the reception area and walked to the back of the office. I went into the computer room, which was across from the coffee room, and found Ralph sitting on a folding chair with his laptop in his lap and a cable hooking him up to our server. He seemed to be running two or three software scanners at the same time. I looked at his screen and had no idea what he was doing.

"Hey."

"Hi, Mike, how's it going?" he said without looking at me.

"Good. So can you upgrade our security?"

"Sure, but something's going on here."

"Meaning?" I asked, still staring at his baffling screen.

"Look at this."

It meant nothing to me. It could have been a finger painting. "I have no idea what I'm looking at."

He pointed to the lower-left corner of the screen. "This is a graphic representation of your e-mail and Internet traffic. It's sort of like looking at a galaxy in the distance through the Hubble telescope, where they look at certain invisible light ranges and make them visible?"

"Not sure what that means. What you got?"

"Well, this area right over here should be symmetrical." He took his mechanical pencil from his pocket and pointed. "See this thing right here, this little dent?"

"Yeah. What of it?"

"It's a tunnel."

"A tunnel? To what?"

"Well, every server, yours included, has a system set up to channel access to and from the Internet, control access to e-mail accounts, etc. This line over here represents the symmetry that should be on the screen, but there's this one section that's missing, like a piece that has been chipped away. Or actually a better way to look at it is sort of what it is. It's like you have a country with borders set up, and somebody has built a tunnel underneath the border. It allows people and things to go in and out through the tunnel without being noticed. They don't cross the border, they don't go through the firewall or the virus scan or the other security software."

"What does it mean?"

"Somebody who really knows what they're doing has access to your server and has built a tunnel."

"Can you tell what it's been used for?"

"Not really. It's like a real tunnel. Things go through it coming in, and things go through it going out. And unless the things are actually in the tunnel when you're looking, you won't be able to trace them. But . . ." He raised his hand and pointed his finger toward the ceiling as if he had one piece of information that was much more significant. "Sometimes there are wires through the tunnel, just like in a real tunnel. They have to sometimes have air and light, and they need wires or things that you can follow. This one has a wire. It may be traceable."

Ralph worked on the keyboard for some time, then turned toward me with the laptop still perched on his knees. "It's a tunnel, like I said. Somebody has attached a stairway from your e-mail to the tunnel." He could see my puzzlement.

"What it does" — he thought — "what it does is take every e-mail that you send or receive and duplicates it and sends it through the tunnel."

"So I don't get them?"

"No, you get them. What you'd see is just what you'd always see. But somebody else sees it too."

"Somebody else is reading my e-mail?"

"At the very least."

"Who the hell is doing this?"

"Impossible to say."

"How? Would they have to get into the firm physically? Has someone broken into the firm?"

"No, they wouldn't have to be here physically. I said it's *like* a wire. It isn't a physical wire. Every computer is easily identifiable on a net, and they identified yours, and that's the one that is being used. I can tell you that this is from outside the firm."

"Shit, Ralph. Can you fix it?"

"Sure." He started typing away on his computer.

"Are there any others? Would this be like an individual's e-mail site or log-in address?"

"Yeah, it is individual, but I checked all the others. Yours is the only one that has this."

"Does it have access to my computer? Can it get in and see my outlines and my Word documents and the like?"

"Only if you send them as attachments in e-mail."

"How sophisticated is this? Is this hard to do?"

"Top one percent of computer geeks might know how to do this."

I jammed my hands in my back pocket and started pacing back and forth in the room. I stared at his screen for a minute or two, considering. I said, "Tell you what. I've got another idea. Just leave it like it is."

23

It had been a long day. Too much going on. I was the only one left at the firm, except of course Rachel and Braden, who were always there. My eyes felt like sandpaper, and I found myself taking deep breaths for no particular reason. As I got up to leave and shut down my computer, my phone rang. It was a D.C. area code, but it wasn't Tinny. I answered it.

"Evening, Mike. You're working late."

"Who is this?"

"Thompson."

"My good friend from State. What do you want?"

"I'm just outside. Why don't you come down and talk to me here."

"Why should I?"

"Because I'm a suspicious type, and sometimes I don't like places that are fixed, like offices. Sometimes I like to be outside."

"You can be outside by yourself. You don't

need me."

"I need to talk to you. Actually . . . you need to talk to me. I'm in the gray sedan." He hung up.

Well, shit. That's all I needed. I grabbed my suit coat, closed my briefcase, turned out my office lights, and headed downstairs. I checked my watch. Ten thirty PM. What did this asshole want? He was nothing but trouble. He was probably the one who had screwed with my computer system.

I closed the front door of my office building behind me and looked for a gray, government sedan. I didn't see one. It suddenly hit me that I had been lured out of my building at a predictable time with no one else around. I stepped off the porch and walked to my car. I unlocked it and put my briefcase on the floor behind my seat. I closed the door and looked again. I saw a car parked on the side street down the block. The headlights flashed briefly. So I was supposed to walk over to him in the dark. Not a chance. I leaned against the driver's door of my car and shook my head. I motioned for him to come to me. Nothing happened. I waited. Still nothing. Fine. I opened my driver's door to get in and was about to leave when the door of the sedan opened. Thompson got out. I could see he wasn't alone. Probably the same guy who came with him before.

Thompson passed under a streetlight as he approached me. He was wearing dark clothes and a leather bomber jacket. He had his hands in his pockets. I waited. He walked around to my side of the car. "Don't trust me?"

"No. I don't trust anybody, and that would include you."

"I'm here for your own benefit."

"Just like last time?"

"Yes. Just like last time. You may not agree, but if you had done what I suggested, you wouldn't be stirring up the things you are stirring up."

"What exactly am I stirring up?"

He glanced around. "You have a recording device?"

"No. You?"

"No."

"So what do you want?"

"You have done what I told you not to do. Your investigator continued to talk to my acquaintance in the Secret Service. I warned you."

"I have to protect my client's interests. I have to defend the case."

"No, you don't. If you were smart, you would have listened to me." He turned toward me. "And stayed the hell away from the Secret Service, and your digging about Camp David. All you've done is stir up a hornet's nest, and you can't even see the hornets. They're all around you. And now you can't get them back into the nest."

"What the hell are you talking about?"

"I told you I'd have to tell the people involved that you were digging. I told them. They didn't appreciate it. That's all I know. And then you kept digging, and I told them that. Now they really don't appreciate it, and frankly, there's nothing I can do about it."

"So you set them on me?"

"I didn't do anything. I told you how to avoid this problem, and you ignored me. I told you I would tell them, and I did. When you put a stick in the eye of some people, they don't say thank-you, they put a stick in *your* eye. Simple as that. Especially when it has nothing to do with the accident. If you had just done your job, if you had left Camp David out of this, you'd still be the big attorney with the biggest case in the country. But no. You had to keep going. You had to send Byrd back."

"We follow the truth —"

"Save it. I don't care about what you think you were doing. I'm just here to tell you that you've put a noose around your own neck and it's tightening. I can't do anything about it. And the closer you get to trial, to putting on any evidence, the tighter that noose is going to be."

I shook my head. "This is unbelievable. My government comes to tell me that things are out of its control and I need to watch out?"

"Basically, yes. Your government is telling you that you dicked it up, Mike. You were forewarned and laughed it off. That was your choice."

"Who's so concerned? That's the least you can tell me."

"No, I can't. That's the whole point. I can't even hint at it."

"You talking about violence? You think they'd come after me?"

"No idea. All I know is that the people I told you would be upset, are."

"I've got to find out what happened. The public deserves to know. So does my client."

"You just don't get it, do you? Camp David had nothing to do with it! You're banging on the wrong door, and the people behind that door are sick of it! You can tell the public anything you want! But you should have stayed away from this, like I told you. Now I don't know what will happen." He stepped toward his car. "You probably won't hear from me again. I've got nothing else to say. I tried to stop all this, but now I can't. You're on your own." He walked away.

I called to him. "Let me ask you something."

He stopped and turned.

"You working with Hackett?"

Thompson smiled and walked back toward me. "At least you're thinking. He would benefit the most, wouldn't he?"

I nodded.

"But no. I've never spoken to him and don't plan to. He is formidable, I have to admit, but he's the least of your worries at this point."

"One other thing."

"What?"

"You tapping my e-mail?"

Thompson frowned. "That would be illegal."

"Are you?"

"No." He walked away and said over his shoulder, "You do have problems, don't you?" He got back to his car, climbed in, started it, and drove away slowly.

I opened my car door and climbed in. I locked my door and dialed Tinny. I got his voice mail. I hung up.

Two days later we had a hearing in front of Judge Betancourt. It had been on calendar for eight weeks. It was my motion to dismiss Hackett's claims for punitive damages. Making a settlement demand was one thing. Demanding punitive damages to *punish* the defendant made things much more difficult and risky for a defendant. This case had punitive damages written all over it. Everybody in the country was mad at World-Copter for "killing" the president. The Justice Department was investigating "fraud" in how WorldCopter had obtained the contract.

I felt like we had effectively deflected those claims in our court filings. Hackett's assertions didn't seem to have the heat they initially had when Senator Blankenship went on television the day of the accident and started throwing around accusations. The truth is usually less dramatic.

We did have one lingering problem, and it might allow the plaintiffs to get through my motion to dismiss punitive damages. It came down to the tip weights. Hackett was zeroed in on that issue. I would be too if I were him. The NTSB hadn't given any indication that there was any other cause.

The entire country had become obsessed with the washerlike pieces of metal, and it was an easy theory to explain. Hackett would get an expert to say that was the cause, and that was good enough.

Our *problem* was the documentation about the tip weights was sketchy. For cases throughout the country, companies had got hammered by juries or judges for destroying documents. Such as a case from a computer-memory company that supposedly had held a "shred" day for damaging documents, to others who failed to set documents aside that were relevant to a lawsuit. The juries had awarded punitive damages. And here we were with a dead president, a foreign helicopter, and documents that could not trace specific tip weights to the specific blade on Marine One. You could have the same kind of problem with the chain of custody of a critical piece of criminal evidence. If you can't prove where that piece of evidence had been from the time it was collected at the scene of the crime until the trial, you would be accused of manipulating the evidence.

For the tip weights, we had the purchase order from a Taiwanese company that manufactured them according to the specifications created by WorldCopter. We had the delivery receipt, and the storage records. The tip weights were individually numbered, and when one was placed on a blade, the entry went into the manufacturing logs, and into the documents that went with the blade as it got shipped. The shipping documents showed which numbers had been on the blade that was found by Marine One, but somehow, no records at WorldCopter headquarters confirmed that those were the tip weights that had been placed on the blade when it was balanced. That made it possible for Hackett to say we didn't know which weights were on which blade.

The tip weight bin was protected and in a secure location. The weights were placed on the blade for balancing by authorized personnel. WorldCopter had no doubt that the integrity of the tip weight system was intact, but what they couldn't prove was that somebody hadn't put a couple of extra tip weights in the bin that were not built to specification or had the quality-assurance check at the same level as every other piece of equipment that went on Marine One. The engineering tolerances allowed for materials on Marine One were substantially less than for a general WorldCopter helicopter.

But we couldn't prove that the tip weights

on this blade satisfied this specification. We could argue by implication, but we sure couldn't prove it. And Hackett said it was a hole big enough for him to drive his punitive-damages truck through. I think the truck he had in mind was a Brink's truck, but it was his analogy. Hence my motion to get rid of the threat of punitive damages. At the very least, we would find out what he had up his sleeve.

The hearing before Judge Betancourt was set for 9 AM. As usual, the journalists and television crews beat us there by hours. We hadn't had a hearing or been in front of the judge for over eight weeks, so the press was happy to have another reason to reconvene the circus.

I walked into the courthouse and into the courtroom on the first floor on the right. It was the largest courtroom of the new courthouse and was perfect, as Judge Betancourt saw it, for this "important" trial.

Hackett and his minions were already there. He had set up his papers at the appropriate table, the one closest to the jury box, and was seated with his legs crossed, turned toward the door, watching me come in. For reasons that I couldn't understand, we were the only ones in the courtroom.

Hackett looked smug and said, "Morning,

378

Rachel."

"Morning," she said.

I walked up through the bar, let the gate swing behind me, and placed my briefcase on the table opposite him. He turned in his chair and followed me with his eyes. I said quietly to Rachel, "Go check the tentative."

She nodded and walked back to the entry-way of the courtroom and examined the document pinned to the corkboard. It listed all the motions being heard that day by the judge, and her tentative ruling on each one. Rachel returned, looking surprised. She leaned over and said in a whisper, "Tentative is to grant."

I was as surprised as she was. I never thought Betancourt would have the nerve to dismiss the punitive-damages claim. Hackett seemed unusually sanguine for that tentative. And he didn't seem prepared for the hearing.

The court clerk entered the courtroom followed by the court reporter and the bailiff. They took their positions, and the bailiff suddenly said, "All rise."

We stood as I continued to look around in wonderment as the journalists were not swarming into the courtroom. The bailiff announced the judge, who took her seat, and asked the clerk to call the calendar.

"Number one on calendar, *Adams et al. v. WorldCopter,* case number C334232."

The judge looked at us with her reading glasses on her nose and began, "Mr. Nolan —"

She was immediately interrupted by the doors being opened from the back and the two men guarding the doors walking into the courtroom. They were followed by other men in dark suits, then ultimately by the first lady, Mrs. Adams. She walked down the aisle with grace and an insistent presence. No one said a word. I immediately knew that the Secret Service had been there since two hours before the hearing. They had checked out the entire courtroom, every seat, every piece of equipment, and had kept the courtroom cleared except for the attorneys and the court personnel until the first lady entered. They had been waiting outside where she would arrive in a place that was unobtrusive. They had others watching the door to make sure that people didn't enter the courtroom and had spoken with all the journalists, who knew not to go inside.

She walked toward the small gate that kept the audience separate from the attorneys and the clients, pushed the gate aside, and walked over and sat down next to Hackett.

He nodded at her and she smiled back at him. The Secret Service sat beside her, behind her, and in the corners of the courtroom. Then, and only then, did the journalists and other members of the public file in and fill the courtroom as the judge looked on.

Judge Betancourt continued, "Mr. Nolan, it's your motion. Do you have anything to add?"

I stood. "No, Your Honor. We will submit on the tentative."

She looked up from the papers over her reading glasses, surprised. "Are you sure?"

"Yes, Your Honor."

She turned from me. "Mr. Hackett? Do you have anything to add?"

Hackett stood slowly, dramatically. "I think the Court fully understands the implications of eliminating punitive damages in this case when WorldCopter has defrauded the government, lied about its clearances, hid documents about what caused this helicopter to crash, and put parts on the helicopter contrary to the contract, which calls for a verified numbering and precise record of every part. They have violated the direct orders of the United States government and have now killed the head of that same government. With respect,

Your Honor, if any case ever called for punitive damages, it is this one." Hackett sat. The former first lady sat quietly.

"Very well," the judge said. "The motion is denied. The tentative is confirmed. I must add for the record that this was not a close question. There is sufficient evidence based on the information developed so far in this case to allow punitive damages to continue and be presented to the jury at trial. Of course if there is insufficient evidence to support that charge in trial, I will reconsider my ruling. But for now, punitive damages stay in the case and the motion is denied. Mr. Hackett, will you prepare the order?"

"Happy to, Your Honor."

The judge gaveled the hearing to a close and walked off the bench. The journalists began asking questions. The Secret Service hustled them out and made an aisle clear for Mrs. Adams to pass through to her limousine, which waited to whisk her back to Washington.

I tried not to show what I was thinking. I looked at Rachel, who immediately became defensive. She said in a low, intense voice, "It said *granted.* The tentative was to grant."

"No, it didn't. She just confirmed her tentative, and it was to *deny.* I didn't even get a chance to *argue.*" I looked at the back of the courtroom and saw Bass, Hackett's hatchet man. "Let's go look."

We exited at the end of the audience and stopped to look at the list of tentatives. I found our motion. "Tentative — Denied." I pointed to it to Rachel.

"I'm telling you, it said granted."

I looked around, then put down my briefcase. I removed the thumbtack and took down the entire sheet. I examined it. It all looked correct, but I noticed two holes in the document where the thumbtack had gone through. The paper had been taken down and put back up. "That son of a bitch."

I turned back into the courtroom and found Bass. "Hey, Bass."

He turned and walked back to me, surprised I was still there, and happy to see me angry. "Yes, Mike?"

"You play some little game with the tentative this morning?"

He feigned confusion. "What do you mean?"

"Like substituting a page in the ruling list changing the tentative for our hearing?"

"Wow," Bass said. "Mr. Hackett said you could be paranoid, but *I* gave you the benefit of the doubt. Guess I can't do that anymore." He turned and walked back to the front of the courtroom to Hackett, who stood by the table where he had been sitting.

We left the courtroom and walked down the front steps. Rachel said, "It wouldn't have made any difference. She said it wasn't a close question."

"Probably not. But I would have liked to try. They're showing their colors a little too obviously. Imagine what they're doing that we can't see if they're willing to change an official court document hanging on the wall of the courtroom. These are bad people, Rachel."

"No doubt about it. Maybe we need to be a little paranoid."

"Especially now that someone's reading our mail."

"What?"

We got into my car. "Do you have a home e-mail account?"

"Yeah, Gmail."

"Make another one. With only numbers as your address. Random numbers. I'll continue sending you regular stuff at work and you the same. But anything that's really critical? Send it from your home computer on that numbered Gmail account. I'll set up a new account. I'll give you a number on a piece of paper which will be the Gmail address. Send whatever matters to that account.

"Get a new cell phone too. Different provider, new number, and keep it in the bottom of your purse. Never let anybody else even see it. You will only call *me* on it, and when I want to talk to you, I'm going to call you on it. So keep it on even when you're at home. I will still call you on your other cell phone and home number and office number, but when I really want to talk to you, I'll call you on your new cell. I'm going to get one myself. Two people are going to have the number. You and Tinny. Maybe Debbie too."

"I'll get one on the way back to the office."

"Try to use text messages. No names, no numbers to call, nothing like that."

She looked concerned. "Do you think somebody's tapping our phones? And listening to cell phones?"

"I don't know. We've got to think defensively."

Rachel went silent as her mind raced.

I dropped her off at her place so she could pick up her car. On the way back to the office I stopped by a kiosk at the local mall to buy a new cell phone. I felt as if I were buying drugs. I kept looking around to make

385

sure nobody could see me doing it. The idea of somebody breaking into our e-mail server and stealing every e-mail sent to me was chilling. Based on what Thompson said I assumed it was Hackett, or one of his bag-men — not that I could really believe Thompson. It was probably Bass. He was an aggressive lawyer and had a reputation for leaning over the ethical lines, but this was criminal.

I got in my car and called Byrd. I again got his voice mail, this time immediately, as if his phone was off. I left a message.

24

The next day Rachel hurried into my office, her face dark. She pointed to my computer. "Turn on the D.C. news channel."

I went to their Web site and called up the streaming video. The image of the female newscaster quickly filled the screen. Over her shoulder, superimposed on the screen, was a picture of Tinny Byrd. The reporter said, "Repeating our breaking story, the body has been found of the missing private investigator, Tinny Byrd. He had been reported missing by his wife late yesterday. His cell phone had been found in the possession of a homeless man near Union Station. His body has now been found, or I should say his remains. This is a grisly find by the Washington police and was unexpected. They had reports of unusual activity at a ware house down by the Navy Yard, and when they investigated it, they found human remains in the corner of the dirt lot by the ware house. The ware house was guarded by two Doberman pinschers that had displaced some of the remains. The remains had been ground up in a meat grinder and tossed over the fence into the warehouse lot. It is thought that it was the intention of whoever murdered Mr. Byrd that the dogs would consume the remains, leaving no evidence. The dogs were not interested though, and when the owner came to the warehouse early this morning, he called the police. DNA evidence has confirmed that the remains are those of Mr. Byrd. It is unknown if his murder is linked to the work he was doing on one of his cases. He was working on several cases according to his wife, including a couple that involved notorious drug dealers in Washington, and also the investigation of Marine One for the attorney representing World-Copter, the European manufacturer of the helicopter. The investigation into this brutal murder is ongoing." The reporter went on to another story and I turned off the television. I looked at Rachel, who looked ashen. She turned and ran out of the room.

I felt as sick to my stomach as she looked. Poor damned Tinny. My palms began to sweat as I tried to imagine what had happened. I knew there was no point. I'd never be able to know, and all it did was fill my head with unbearable images and thoughts. I wanted to go get one of my shotguns and find whoever had done this to him. He was my friend.

I sat down heavily in my chair, loosened my tie, put my head back, and closed my eyes.

I started getting paranoid. I worked on the case outside of the office when I had to do anything that really mattered. While at work, I did what everyone thought I should do, and after work I did the really critical things that I left at home.

Late one afternoon, I told Dolores I was running over to Starbucks to get a Frappuccino. While there, I called Wayne Bradley, Karl Will, and Rachel on my new cell. I told them I wanted them to come over to my house that night, and not to send me anything to my work e-mail account. All were puzzled, but agreed.

They arrived together just as Debbie and I were finishing dinner. We went into my den, which was built into what was the music room in the old house when we'd bought it. It was nearly as big as our family room.

Bradley looked uncomfortable. "What's

with the new cell number?"

"I'm starting to see shadows. You guys heard about Byrd?"

They nodded. Will asked, "You think that has anything to do with this case?"

"Don't know. I'm sure going to assume so though. Which makes me crazy, just so you know. And I've had a couple of visits from the INR, State Department security."

"Huh?" Bradley asked, confused. "What would they have to do with Byrd?"

"Probably nothing. But they went to his house and then came to my office to meet with us. And basically threatened us. Lay off the Secret Service witness."

"What do they have to do with the Secret Service?"

"Yeah, good question. Don't know. Must have been some international thing. Other countries involved, diplomacy, something. And they *really* don't want it to come out. And there was some document that the guy had that he was thinking of giving to Byrd. The security guys have it now, whatever it was."

Will was considering the implications. "You're not saying *they* had anything to do with Byrd . . ."

"I really doubt it."

"I mean the news said he was investigating all kinds of cases. Drug cases, bad stuff . . ."

"He was. I don't know who did it. Maybe somebody else knew he was getting close to something."

"Like Hackett," Rachel said.

Bradley nearly choked. "You're not saying he'd do that, are you?"

"No. I'm not."

Rachel continued to let her imagination go. "Maybe the first lady called the State Department. I mean, who knows?"

"I don't trust anyone. And I mean no one. You've all got to be incredibly careful. Don't let anyone get close to you that you don't know. Check you car for bombs —"

"Are you serious? How are we supposed to do that?"

"I don't really know. I shouldn't have said that. I'm not really checking . . . just use caution."

"That's why we're meeting here?" Bradley said, looking around the den.

"Yes, and somebody's reading my mail. My e-mail."

"What?" he said, leaning back on the leather couch. "Seriously?"

"Somebody has set up a tunnel through my server so all my e-mails are forwarded. Very sophisticated."

"I've never heard of such a thing."

"Me neither. So whatever you get from me at work, phone, e-mail, whatever, won't mean shit. Only when we're here, or on my new cell."

Will breathed deeply without saying anything. He started looking around the room. "If they're smart enough to tap your e-mail, what makes you think they haven't bugged your house?"

"I had it scanned."

"What about your office?"

"I don't want to tip anyone off. Maybe when we get close to trial. When I figure out how to use it all to my advantage."

Will said quietly, "Shit, Mike. Somebody really doesn't want you to win this case."

"They may not care about the case. But they may really care if they get exposed. And they see the two as linked, because they are. Problem is they know what happened and we don't."

"So what did you want to talk about?"

I was glad to get to the facts. I could deal with that. Build a case, gather evidence, and get ready for trial. "I want you two to go back out to the site with me. I've been thinking about my last time out there. I've got an idea."

"What is it?"

"I'll tell you later."

"Why later?"

"After your deposition. I want Hackett to hear your opinions and think they're unremarkable."

Bradley said, "That shouldn't be too hard right now."

"If what I'm thinking about has any merit to it, I don't want them to know about it until it's too late."

"Is that kosher?"

"Right now it's just a thought in my head."

"All right. We'll just criticize the report and not give them much of a theory of our defense."

"Exactly. Did you get your animation done, Karl?"

"It's on my computer if you want to see it."

"Absolutely."

Karl had a large Apple laptop. He opened it up and put it on the coffee table in front of Bradley. He called up the file. He said, "I took the animation from WorldCopter based on the flight data recorder and CVR and filled in the blanks. I had a surveyor get us the heights of all the significant trees and got the terrain-contour information from the USGS charts of the area." He started the animation. "If you watch here, I've gotten the bugs out of some of the data." He pointed. "See, right there, the helicopter starts down. We can't tell why from any of the data. So I just had it tumble to the ground and had the blade come off as it broke through the trees —"

"Stop it," I said as the helicopter plunged down through the trees in a frighteningly lifelike animation. "Why there? If the NTSB's theory is right, the blade came off much earlier and just landed there coincidentally."

"I'm not convinced of that," Will said. "If the tip weights failed, or came off, that doesn't mean the blade's going to come completely off. It will just throw the helicopter out of balance and it will come apart. But that doesn't mean necessarily that the blade comes off."

"Well, then why did it?"

"Not sure yet. I think from impact, but we need to go back to the scene, like you said."

I sat on the couch and looked at the stopped animation. "What's your theory, Karl?" I asked. "Why did it go down where it did?"

Will hesitated, then said, "Could be tip weights. I can't rule that out. It fits. But with the pilot's attitude toward the president, and the FDR circuit breaker pulled, could be intentional on the pilot's part too. There's one other possibility."

"What?"

"Maybe the president came up into the cockpit to watch out the front during the storm. Maybe they hit a big pocket or had a bad updraft and the president pitched forward into Collins's lap. He might have pushed the cyclic and the helicopter would have nosed down. Could account for why they were upside down too."

"We don't hear the president on the CVR again though before the crash."

"True, but it might have happened before he even had a chance to say hello. Gets there, they hit big turbulence, and over they go. I don't know."

I nodded and considered. It was possible. "Hard to prove, Karl."

"It's all I've got right now."

"We'll see what happens when we go back out there."

Rachel said to me quietly, "Can I talk to you alone?"

I looked at her face, then said to the others, "Excuse us for a second, will you?"

We walked into my living room and I closed the den door behind me. "What is it?"

"We can't do any real work at the office? How are we supposed to prepare?"

"We do the best we can."

"Mike, we hired our contract attorneys because we need them. We need their help. Braden is the smartest guy I've ever worked with. He does the best work in the office. And Elizabeth is tireless. Are you saying we can't use them? Don't you trust them?"

"We just can't take the chance."

"But that puts us back to where it's just you and me doing all the real work. That's the very thing we were trying to avoid. Maybe whoever did this did it just so we'd all turn on each other. Not trust each other. We should tell them about it and get their help to prepare for trial."

"We can't chance it, Rachel."

"We're not going to get it all done, Mike."

"We'll do the best we can. Trust me on this, Rachel."

25

I felt exposed and Hackett felt invulnerable. I was trying desperately to develop a nonexistent case while looking over my shoulder, yet I had to produce my experts for depositions.

At the conclusion of Bradley's deposition, Hackett tried not to gloat. The court reporter and the rest of the attorneys left the conference room; Hackett and I were standing there with Bradley, who was putting his papers back into his lopsided briefcase. Hackett put the cap back on his expensive fountain pen and put the pen in his shirt pocket. He looked at me. "Mike, help me here. You have refused to settle this case, and I had assumed it was because you had something to say in the defense of World-Copter. But now we're done with the experts." He looked confused. "You don't have *anything*."

I tried to answer a little more quickly then

I would otherwise have so as to look defensive. "They're going to show that the NTSB's conclusions — and your experts — are wrong. They're just speculating."

Hackett shook his head. "Mike. You know if you don't tell the jury a story better than mine, you're going to lose. Mine not only is right, but everybody has heard about it in the newspaper since the NTSB announced it. How in the hell do you expect to win?"

I looked at him somewhat smugly. "Maybe something will break between now and trial. Maybe some witness will come out of the woodwork."

Hackett bit. "A surprise witness? Surely you mean somebody on the witness list then? And we've deposed virtually all of those who have anything to say about anything. Plus, if it was an actual surprise, I don't know how you could anticipate it now." He adjusted his coat. "You're not planning on pulling something, are you, Mike? Because that would be unethical."

"I'm not saying anything. I'm just going to go back to my office."

He said to my back, "I've got your witness list, Mike. I'm going to hold you to it."

Bradley and Will met me at the crash site like we had planned. The FBI agents recognized my car and didn't even ask me to stop. I stopped anyway to tell them who else was coming. I parked and dragged my lawn chair to where the helicopter had hit the ground. I unfolded it and sat in the still morning. A slight chill was in the air as I sipped from my coffee travel mug and looked at the trees. This was just a hunch really, and unlikely to produce much, but I had to know.

I could hear a van approaching over the hill. Wayne Bradley no doubt, with Karl Will.

After a few minutes they appeared at the crest of the ridge and came down to where I was sitting. Bradley was breathing hard. Will said, "I see you took my advice. Brought your chair."

"Of course. Where's yours?"

"Right here." He unfolded his chair and sat next to me.

Bradley said, "We don't have time to sit around in lawn chairs and talk about our grandchildren. This trial is *on* us. We're already on the record as not knowing anything. If we don't come up with something pretty quick, frankly we're going to look silly."

Karl had stopped listening. "So what are we going to look at, Mike?"

We could hear a truck approaching. Bradley asked, "Expecting someone?"

"Yeah. They'll be here in a minute. What I wanted to take a look at is that limb that was broken during the accident." We looked up. "That one," I said, pointing. They both looked up into the gray sky and could just make out the brown branch that was still attached to the tree. "I think we need to go up and look. You and me, Karl. I've got this feeling that branch is trying to tell us a story, and we need to go up there and listen to it."

Will asked, "What are you thinking?"

I looked at the hill as the truck struggled over it behind us.

Will looked at the truck. "Who is this?"

"My tree trimmers. I asked them to bring their cherry-picker truck out here so we could go up and look at that branch. Bring your camera, Karl. If we find anything interesting up there, I want to document every step we take and exactly where everything was."

The truck parked where I showed it to go, lowered its outriggers for stability, and freed the bucket. Will and I climbed in and started up. I wasn't sure the truck's extension arm would take us high enough, nor was I sure what I would do if it did. We passed quickly by the fattest portion of the tree, and I moved us closer to the brown, broken branches. Only one large branch had broken, but numerous smaller branches were attached. It had broken close to the trunk and in the direction that I had suspected. The helicopter's blade had clearly smacked this branch on the way by, and by the direction of the break the helicopter had to have been upside down.

Will pointed at the location of the break. "I thought we'd see a cut or some other blade impact point. This just looks like it was hit. I don't see anything cut at all."

I inched us closer and we could both see where the blade had hit the branch. It had knocked off several small branches and taken the bark off the three-inch-thick branch where it had broken — not been cut, but broken. Violently. Bark held the branch on and kept it from plunging to the ground like the other branches.

"Hit it pretty hard," Will said.

We looked down to where the others were standing, trying to imagine Marine One passing by in the crashing storm.

Will looked around. "So if the blade hit this branch hard enough to do this kind of damage, maybe a tip weight came off here, Mike. Where would it have gone?"

I shook my head as I looked with him.

"No idea. I just wanted to look up here to put my mind at ease. Let's push this thing as far into the tree as we can."

Will looked down. "I think the men who brought the truck are already thinking we're pretty far out from the truck. I don't want to tip over —"

"I'm not going back down until I've seen everything there is to see up here."

Will bent down as we passed under another heavy branch and into the shaded inside of the tree. I drove the basket deeper still inside the tree as the small electric motor worked against the branches. It was darker than I expected. The sun was blocked by the higher branches. My eyes adjusted slowly and I looked at every twig. Karl looked above us for any sign that other branches had been involved but weren't visible from the ground.

Karl said, "I'm not seeing much. You?"

"Not yet." I pushed against the tree. I couldn't force the basket any deeper into the tree. Karl reached up and grabbed the branch directly over our heads, pulled on it to feel its strength, and pulled himself up and out of the basket. "If we're going to do this, we've got to do it right. I've got to get to the trunk. We're still five feet away."

"You'll kill yourself."

"No, I won't. These branches are strong."

He crouched on one branch while holding the other one above his head like a rope. He moved slowly to the trunk and stood up. The broken branch was directly behind and below him. He turned carefully and grabbed the two small healthy sections of the branch that were still attached to the trunk. He felt the twisted, broken turn of the branch and the small, shredded section that kept it from plummeting to the ground. He looked outward to the brown section of the branch and imagined Marine One crashing down next to the tree.

I could see the massive blade hitting the branch and tossing it aside like a plastic straw. I tried to imagine exactly where the end cap and the tip weight would have hit. I could tell Karl was wondering the same thing. He stared for several seconds considering the numerous possibilities. He hugged the trunk and stepped down to the next branch. He looked directly under where the broken branch attached to the trunk, and there it was. Something had hit the trunk and scarred it. "See this?" he asked, pointing.

I nodded.

He moved inward and looked at the mark. The light-colored mark wasn't where something had hit the trunk at all. It was a tool mark. A knife. "Somebody worked something out of the trunk here, Mike. Could have been the NTSB found a piece of metal embedded in the trunk here and worked it out."

My heart was pounding. "Tip weight?"

Karl hesitated, then said, "Could be." He touched the bark and found a small flap next to the blade mark.

"We'd better measure the impact point and mark it on our diagram. Check the depth too. Take a picture. Maybe it will help our reconstruction."

He did, then looked for anything else that could help us. Finally he said, "Let's go back down."

I couldn't. If there was one tip weight, there could be more. They had to have been stuck to the bolt in the end of the blade, or the threads. "We'll get that tip weight from the NTSB."

"No, we won't. They'll never talk about it until the docket is released, which will be years and they may not have found one. Just dug with their knife but came up empty."

"What about the branch itself?"

Karl touched the end of the branch that was still attached, where it had been exposed from the break. Nothing. He dug his finger into the stringy remains of the connection between the still living tree and the brokenness farther out. "Something . . ." He pulled his Leatherman out of the case on his belt and opened the needle-nose pliers. He grabbed the branch above with one hand and reached down with the pliers with the other. He found a hard point and grabbed it.

I leaned over to look, careful to brace myself. I couldn't see anything, and he found it again with the pliers. He pulled on it hard as I grabbed the camera in the bottom of the bucket and began photographing Karl and where he was pulling. It gave. He pulled it up, wrapped his left arm around the branch, and brought it up to look at it. It was a tip weight. Half a tip weight. The circular washer-shaped piece of metal, perhaps an inch and a half across, was broken completely in half. I looked closely at it in the dim light, wondering what had caused it to break. He held it where I could see it clearly and photograph it with and without the flash.

"Tip weight," I said, confirming the obvious.

He climbed back into the bucket and handed the broken tip weight to me. A frown clouded his face. "How does this help us exactly?"

"I'm not sure it does."

"Looks broken to me, Mike. Looks like it failed in fatigue somehow. Too much of a gap between it and the next one. Probably defective. We'll have to tell the NTSB about it, and Hackett."

"In due time."

"You're not going to hide it or something, are you?"

"No." I started moving the basket back out into the sunshine.

"So what's the plan?"

"I'm going to let Bradley look at it, and he can take his time. Discovery is over in our case."

"You've got to let them know about it."

"I said I would."

"Well, it looks to me like the tip weight fractured and the lost weight did what we would expect — it caused uncontrollable vibrations. It caused the crash, Mike."

I pushed the lever on the basket and drove us downward to where Marine One had hit the ground. "Maybe. And maybe not."

26

The trial was upon us. I drove to the courthouse with Rachel, Braden, and Justin, my paralegal. The back of the Volvo was full of boxes of deposition transcripts, motions, attachments, witness outlines, and pleadings, all in clearly marked three-ring binders. I never knew what I would need, so I usually took too much. We walked up to the courthouse from our reserved parking spot. The first lady had to park out front too; there was no underground or secret parking anywhere. The journalists were quite happy about that.

It was a beautiful, sunny day, and fairly warm for Annapolis that time of year. The press had been there all night. The satellite vans were everywhere. Cords and cables ran across the street and through the bushes. Some cameras were set up on tripods, others were on the shoulders of cameramen who walked around looking for something to film. We were an hour early for the motions *in limine,* which were to be heard at 9 AM.

As we grabbed our boxes and began putting them on our luggage carts to wheel them into the courtroom, we were surrounded by the press. Do you have any comments, Mr. Nolan? What is your theory of the case? You say in your expert reports that the NTSB was wrong, but what do you think happened?

They had been doing their homework; they had read all the expert reports that had been filed with the court and had of course published them for all the world to see. They had read the motions *in limine* and had their legal consultants on top of all the issues. They were ready to go. But I wasn't talking. Nor was anybody else. "Thanks for your interest. I can't talk about it. I'll be happy to talk to you after the trial is over."

"You've got to give us something, Nolan. Tell us who your witnesses are going to be. Tell us what you're going to ask the first lady. Are you going to cross-examine her? Do you think you'll win any of your motions *in limine?*"

I smiled and ignored the reporters. The four of us made our way through the throng. The courthouse was brand-new, but unlike many federal and state courtrooms built today, our assigned courtroom actually had windows. Real, live daylight streamed in. Many courtrooms feel like post-op rooms, but this courthouse was designed by an architect who respected the traditional colonial architecture that dominated Annapolis. It was beautiful and inspirational, and new. It made me proud to be a lawyer every time I walked in.

We walked up the aisle and through the small gate and put our materials at the defense table, always the table farthest from the jury box. The windows were on the long wall to the right, and the imposing bench of Judge Betancourt was in the front, with the windows to her left. The clerk was going through the exhibit lists and the premarked exhibits and smiled as we walked in. She glanced at the members of the press who had nearly filled the available seating and were looking for something to do. Many began scribbling, describing no doubt that Rachel had decided to wear a navy blue gabardine pantsuit on the first day of trial rather than a skirt. I didn't care what anybody wore as long as they looked respectful to the court. But I'm sure with Rachel's looks she was going to get a lot of ink about how she dressed and how she behaved as a woman attorney in a massive trial. What a pain. Many of the reporters had already commented on what weaklings we were compared to the irresistible force of Tom Hackett and his army. I saw it as an advantage for us, but the press didn't see it that way.

I wheeled my cart up to the table, unloaded the boxes, lined up exhibit and witness notebooks in order in front, and placed the boxes in the corner with the cart. Rachel did likewise on her side of the table. The table bent around in an L shape, and our notebooks lined their way around the corner. Braden put the remaining exhibit books behind us and took a seat directly behind us in a chair on the inside of the rail. Justin, my paralegal, did likewise. I pulled out my motions *in limine* notebook and began rereading the argument outline that I had prepared for the twenty-three motions *in limine* that we and Hackett had filed. They were motions that attempted to limit the evidence and keep prejudicial or wrong evidence from even coming into play in the trial. I thought that some of them might get granted, but wasn't optimistic we'd get them all. As I continued to study my outline, I could hear the reporters whispering questions behind me. I continued to ignore them as I had the reporters outside.

Suddenly the door opened and Hackett and his entourage walked in like they owned the place. He had a cart, as did each of the other attorneys that were with him. There was Bass, his buzz-cut hatchet man, his stunning female paralegal, and an associate I didn't recognize at all. Hackett walked through the gate, placed his briefcase on the table, and said, "Mr. Nolan."

"Mr. Hackett," I said in response without looking at him. "Mr. Bass."

"Ms. Long," they said.

"Mr. Hackett. Mr. Bass."

I waited for one of the plaintiffs, one of the widows, to come in for the arguments because I had figured Hackett for someone who wanted his client there during the motions *in limine* arguments to elicit sympathy from the judge. Most of the time clients skipped the motions *in limine* because they were usually legal and technical in nature and not something to which the parties could individually contribute. But sometimes they would show up in the hope that the judge would grant their motions out of sympathy.

The judge had considered conducting a lottery for seats to the trial because of the demand from the public. Instead, the court had opted, at least for the first week, to have people line up outside the courthouse for the back five rows. The doors would be open to the general public thirty minutes before court began. By the time I had gone through my outline three times and begun reviewing the motion papers, the bailiff opened the doors of the courtroom to the public. They had gone through security and been thoroughly checked and now were abuzz with excitement. They tried unsuccessfully not to be loud. They could also see that the judge was not on her bench. They thought that gave them freedom to converse loudly, which I suppose it did, but the noise was annoying.

After the public was seated behind the press, the bailiff went up on the other side of the gate and stood between the counsel tables by the lectern. He turned around and said, "If I could have everybody's attention, please."

He waited until the room was completely silent. I continued to work. He went on, "Although court is not in session, the attorneys and other people working on behalf of the parties are preparing for the hearings which are about to take place. I therefore request that you remain quiet during this time. I will ask you to stand when the judge enters and court is about to be in session."

They all nodded, anxious to please, and the room grew silent. The artists there on behalf of the press were sitting front and center. They were drawing Hackett and me and undoubtedly Rachel. Judge Betancourt had made it clear there were to be no television or still cameras. The only images that would be allowed out of the courtroom were artist drawings of the participants and witnesses.

After another twenty minutes had passed and it was ten to nine, the court's clerk came in and took her seat before her computer. She began typing away on her keys and asked for appearances. Hackett and I both got up, walked to the clerk, and handed her our business cards. She knew who we were, who we represented, and why we were there; she just needed to go through her procedures, which I actually appreciated. I liked precision and order in the conduct of a trial. I liked rules that everybody followed and I could count on being applied equally. I told her I was there on behalf of World-Copter SA, the European company, and World-Copter U.S., and she nodded and wrote those names on my card. Hackett did likewise and told her he was there on behalf of all the plaintiffs, whom of course he called "widows." He said, "I'm here on behalf of all of the *widows* of Marine One."

I tried not to roll my eyes and went back to my seat. I could feel the pressure rising in my chest as we approached the commencement of this immense trial and was sure that my heart rate was now over a hundred beats per minute.

Rachel seemed calm and was preparing a chart for me for the jury selection, or voir dire, as it is officially called. Judge Betancourt was a bit unusual, at least for federal courts now, in that she actually allowed the lawyers to conduct some of the questioning of jurors. Most federal judges made you submit written questions, some of which they would ask, then ask the rest on their own. They would give you no room at all in your attempts to load the jury box with people favorable to your client and to eliminate those you believed might be against you. That was of course what we did; it was part of the adversarial process. The idea was that the resulting jury would end up somewhere in the middle and therefore be fair. Judges, thinking themselves unbiased and balanced, often cut the process short, made their own decisions, and ended up with a jury that was in fact biased. I'm sure the judges were less rosy about the role of judges when they were trying cases as lawyers.

The door in the back corner of the courtroom opened and Judge Betancourt came in. She stopped just short of the three steps that led to her seat behind the bench. The bailiff said, "All rise. United States District Court for the Eastern District of Maryland is now in session. The Honorable Patricia Betancourt presiding. Please be seated and come to order."

The judge climbed up to her black leather chair and sat down. She looked smaller then I remembered. She was perhaps five foot three and 115 pounds. She had short-cropped brown hair and reading glasses. I could tell she'd spent extra time on her makeup that morning. I wondered if she actually thought of the reporters, the press, and the artists who would be drawing her that day. It's human nature to try to look good, especially if you think it's for a big audience. This was without a doubt the biggest audience she would ever be in front of in her entire life. Would trying to "look good" affect her decisions? It was disquieting to think of the judge of your case primping for the press.

"Good morning, counsel."

"Good morning, Your Honor," all the attorneys responded, standing.

She had the clerk call the case, then said, "Mr. Hackett, I don't believe you've ever tried a case in front of me."

"No, Your Honor, I've never had the pleasure," he said.

"Usually I do motions *in limine* in chambers, but since this is a case of such note, we will have the motions *in limine* arguments here."

"That's fine, Your Honor, wherever you'd like to do it is fine with me," Hackett said.

"Mr. Nolan, good morning."

"Good morning, Your Honor."

"We have twenty-three motions *in limine* to argue this morning, and I believe you win the prize as you filed thirteen of them. We shall therefore deal with yours first."

"That's fine, Your Honor, how would you like to address them?"

"In order. I don't think we need to stand on formality during this initial proceeding. Why don't you be seated, Mr. Nolan. Mr. Hackett, I will ask you for your comments in addition to whatever you said in your opposition as we proceed through his motions, and then we will address yours. Do you understand?"

We all did and we began. Judge Betancourt was clinical in her rulings on the motions. For each motion she gave us her tentative ruling and explanation and asked for comments from the side that would be unhappy with the ruling. It was extremely efficient. When that party had had his say, her ruling stood, and we went on to the next one. Her rulings were well thought out, precise, and fair. It was a good start. Six of my motions had been granted, and four of Hackett's. None of them gutted the other side's case. The rulings resulted in evidentiary changes that nibbled at the edges of the case, but nothing that went to the heart of anything significant.

After completing the arguments on the motions, Judge Betancourt launched right into her explanation of how she was going to do the jury selection. We hadn't even reached our morning break yet. She had the clerk call the jury room to have the jury panel come in the room immediately after the morning break.

They were all there when we returned. The bailiff had asked three of the observer rows to wait in the hallway during the jury selection process. They would be allowed to return to their seats after the jury was selected and trial had commenced.

After the voir dire panel had been seated, Mrs. Collins entered the courtroom. Nice timing. Everybody knew who she was. Her picture had been in the paper hundreds of times over the last few months. She was always the sympathetic and grieving widow, who was extremely pretty and everyone wanted to meet. She had not granted a single interview since the accident, and the public was starving to hear her voice and find out more about her. As she made her way down the aisle, Hackett feigned surprise as he stood to welcome her. He walked over to open the gate for her, and she sat down gracefully next to him. She looked even prettier and more radiant than during her deposition. She obviously knew how to take care of herself. She wore a nicely fitted suit with a gold Celtic cross around her neck. As she sat, she turned back around toward the gallery and smiled at the prospective jurors. Her smile was perfect for the occasion. It wasn't a smile ingratiating herself to the jury, nor was it a smile of embarrassment. It was an acknowledgment of their presence, a statement of her appreciation of them, and a quick demonstration of humility. I just couldn't imagine it had been rehearsed, but I also couldn't dismiss that as a possibility.

The judge came in, the courtroom was called into session, and jury selection began in earnest. The court had sent out a large number of jury subpoenas to accommodate the necessary jury pool for this case. It was thought that a lot of people would be dismissed for cause, for not being able to be fair in a trial. That was certainly my expectation. A French corporation that "killed the president" was likely to be unpopular. Some would probably want to make speeches about how outraged they were. It was important that the court acknowledged that, but equally disheartening. No one was going to be biased against the first lady or the widow of the pilot; any bias was going to run toward WorldCopter, the evil foreign corporation.

The judge had required everyone in the jury pool fill out a questionnaire. The jurors were identified by number. We had copies of all the questionnaires and had stayed up late the night before going over them. Rachel and I had huddled together in my office to make a list of those we planned to challenge for cause depending on who from the larger group ended up in the actual jury box. You don't know that until the clerk calls out the numbers randomly selected from the larger group.

My final list was given to Braden and Lynn Carpenter, two of our contract attorneys, in the morning so they could compare our thoughts to their own. World-Copter had also insisted we use and at least "include in our decision process." The consultant was sitting in the audience looking like any other observer. If we had time to talk, we'd compare notes, but if not, the consultant would send me a "Must Strike!" list by BlackBerry. It made it a little more challenging, but I refused to have a jury consultant sit at counsel table during voir dire the way some lawyers did. It's the kiss of death with a jury, in my opinion. It was like bringing a psychologist with you on a first date.

Judge Betancourt motioned to the clerk and said, "Call the first twenty-four." Judges selected juries differently, but this judge had decided to bring twenty-four people up, twelve into the box, and twelve outside the box, for initial questioning. This would allow us to question them together and know who was coming next if someone inside the box was stricken. In addition to trying to remove somebody for admitted bias, we were each entitled to three peremptory challenges, where we could strike a juror without any explanation at all. I watched as the clerk called each person by juror number, each of whom was then told exactly where to sit, from seat number one, whose occupant would become juror number one if sworn in, through juror number twelve, and then four alternates. Federal court, of course, has no alternate jurors. The requirement is a minimum of six jurors in a civil trial, with no fewer without a stipulation by all parties. Judge Betancourt had told us she intended to seat twelve because it was going to be a long trial. Fine with me. I'd have preferred fifty. Hackett had to convince *all* of them; he needed a unanimous jury to win in federal court.

The clerk called out the numbers. The twelve in the box were a diverse group of old and young, men and women, black, Hispanic, and white. It was a cross section of America. I liked the looks on their faces. They were intelligent, and ready. One of the concerns, one of the things I was watching for, was eagerness. People *really* wanted to sit on this jury. They would be able to tell their grandchildren about this trial. Some were probably thinking they could cash in on this experience somehow. They'd be interviewed by innumerable television shows like a cat with a new toy. But they wouldn't know they were the toy. They'd get their fifteen minutes of fame, then the interest of the world would turn to the next question or crisis. If you were able to discern who those people were, it would be best to ask them to leave, especially on my side of the case. Because what kind of book would be most likely to sell? One about a defense verdict saying the French company did nothing wrong, or the first trillion-dollar verdict in the first presidential wrongful-death case that found a foreign corporation killed the president?

The judge began the voir dire herself by asking questions that had been agreed upon before the trial by the parties. The prospective jurors were asked whether they knew any of the attorneys. Many knew *of* Hackett, but nobody knew him. They were asked about their knowledge of the case from the press and whether they had formed an opinion based on the press reporting. No, no. No one had, they all assured the judge. They were asked about their understanding of helicopters, the safety of helicopters, the safety of flying, foreign corporations, foreign manufacturing of goods destined for the American military, and their ability to be fair to a foreign corporation. All the usual kinds of questions that any high school student would know to ask when trying to find out whether a juror was biased.

The prospective jurors assured everybody

in the room that they were certainly *not* biased against either party and would absolutely give a fair hearing if allowed to serve. Most of the jurors were nearly gleeful. The press hung on every word, although they knew the jurors only by number. The judge didn't want the press doing background investigations on every juror to try to figure out how they might vote or digging up dirt on them to throw the trial into disarray. They were to be known by numbers only until the conclusion of the trial or they were dismissed from the jury pool.

After the judge completed her preliminary questioning, she looked at Hackett. "Mr. Hackett, you may examine the jury."

27

Hackett began with flare. He would select a juror by number, all of which he had memorized. He followed up gently on several of the questions that had been asked by the judge, then picked one woman, juror number six, the last person in the top row to the left, and asked her questions that were obviously aimed not only at her but at everybody in the jury pool.

He glanced around the entire room, even looking at the remaining jurors sitting in the gallery, to make sure everyone was listening. He wanted them to know that he was going to ask them all essentially the same questions. He began with his voice so low that the room grew even quieter as everyone strained to hear him. "Good morning, ma'am. Thank you for taking the time out of your busy schedule to consider sitting on this jury panel."

She smiled. "I didn't really have much

choice. They sent me a subpoena." This caused a great deal of laughter in the courtroom and broke the tension.

"Well, thank you for being here anyway. I know it's a burden. You've already told the judge that you can be here for the three weeks that this trial is expected to take. Are you willing to pay close attention to the evidence for that entire time?"

"Of course."

"There's going to be some evidence that will be quite gruesome. Pictures of dead bodies, discussion of the manner of death. Are you prepared to listen to that evidence?"

"Well, I don't look forward to it, but, yes, I can hear it and understand it."

"You understand that I am here representing the first lady, or I should say the former first lady, Mrs. Adams. The wife of former president Adams."

"Yes, of course."

"And do you also understand that I, with my colleagues, am also representing the families of the other people who were killed in this incident? Including Mrs. Collins?" He pointed to her. "And Mrs. Rudd, the wife of the copilot?"

"Yes."

"Can you give each of them a fair trial? Because their damages will be different. The president's damages, the value that you will be asked to place on his life, could be enormous. It might be argued by the other side that the damages for a combat-veteran, Marine Corps sergeant who was the crew chief would be less, but can you give him as fair a hearing? Can you give his family as fair a trial as you would give the first lady or former first lady?"

"Oh, yes, of course."

Hackett paced momentarily, forcing everyone's attention back on him. He had noted a distraction, a noise outside that sounded like a commotion or a confrontation. He let that noise die down without being obvious about it. People then returned their attention to him from the windows. He told them he was going to ask for a *lot* of money. He wanted to make sure they didn't have some conscientious objection to awarding piles of money.

He asked a black man with silver-rimmed glasses in the back row, "Can you give World-Copter a fair trial? Because I don't know what evidence they're going to put on." Hackett turned toward me and then back to the jury. "I don't know if they have any evidence, but I just want you to be open-minded if they do produce evidence that you think is relevant. I want you to consider

426

it, even if you're completely persuaded at the conclusion of my case. Can you do that?"

I wanted to throw something at him. After a few more questions it was finally my turn. I asked a few innocuous questions, particularly of those jurors who'd indicated they had family members in law practice or that had worked in law firms. I questioned all the jurors for five minutes or so each and tried to emphasize that this was a complex case, that it would require the testimony of experts in metallurgy, piloting, and mechanical engineering, and that if they had formed a conclusion before they heard all the evidence — before they heard all my experts — they would then have to persuade themselves that they had been wrong. I told them people didn't like to be wrong, and if I had to persuade them that an earlier conclusion they had reached was wrong, it made the entire process unfair for my client. They had to not form that conclusion until the end of the evidence, until the closing arguments were done, and the judge had instructed them on the law. While they were all agreeable instantly to that concept, I knew that none of them would follow it. Jurors usually pick sides at the conclusion of opening arguments, and most stuck to those decisions right through to the jury verdict.

I finished just as the clock moved to noon, and the judge announced our ninety-minute lunch break. Justin had saved a table for our team in the cafeteria on the second floor, where I compared notes with our jury consultant, who'd been sitting in the first row, Rachel, Braden, Justin, the general counsels for both WorldCopters, and of course Kathryn with Mark Brightman, who was sitting in the audience in his expensive suit trying to look indispensable.

As usual, the jury consultant tried to tell me which jurors to challenge, but frankly, I was content with the entire panel. I'd take them just as they were, but of course Hackett wouldn't. He'd try to strike some for cause, then use some of his peremptory challenges, and we'd have new jurors to question. So I made my list of the jurors Hackett was most likely to strike, and the ones I would strike in order if he started. Our jury consultant was unhappy with my list and tried to tell WorldCopter that I was making a mistake, but he was getting a deaf ear from everybody.

When court reconvened at one thirty, the jurors sat in their chairs anxiously, the gallery was in its place, and the attorneys were at the counsel tables. The clerk announced the judge, everybody sat, and the judge asked me if I had any additional questions to ask the jury.

"No, Your Honor."

"Very well then —"

Hackett stood. "Your Honor, if I might. I am informed that my clients are waiting outside, and I'd like the court to wait one moment before we begin our challenges, such as they might be."

The judge nodded. "Hurry it up, Mr. Hackett."

Hackett turned toward the aisle as the back door of the courtroom opened and the first lady and the other five widows walked in. They were quite a sight. The first lady was of course impeccably dressed and looked as if she could be president. She was dignified and confident in her walk, but not such a fast walk as to be disrespectful to President Adams or the court. The other widows followed behind, dressed very differently but all perfectly for who they were. I was ready to bet a lot of money that Hackett had hired a fashion consultant.

They made their way to the front row and sat next to Mrs. Collins, except for the first lady, who made her way through the gate and sat next to Hackett. The Secret Service agents that had accompanied her sat in the front row directly behind her. Nothing like having your client make a grand entrance accompanied by an armed guard just before the conclusion of jury selection.

Hackett nodded to the judge.

"Are you ready to proceed, Mr. Hackett?"

"Yes, Your Honor."

"Mr. Nolan?"

"Yes, Your Honor."

"Mr. Hackett, any challenges for cause?"

"No, Your Honor."

"Mr. Nolan?"

"No, Your Honor."

"Mr. Hackett, your first peremptory."

Hackett stood. "Your Honor, plaintiff accepts the jury as impaneled."

I looked up in complete shock. I turned around to look at the jury consultant, who encouraged me with an immediate clenched face to challenge the first person I had listed on my note pad. I glanced down at the note pad, then over at Rachel, who was frozen. I looked up at the judge. "Your Honor, defendants accept the jury as impaneled."

The judge was surprised but pleased. "Will the jurors in the box please stand and be sworn?"

The jurors looked at each other and smiled with a pleased, surprised look, then stood. The clerk stood up, told them to raise their right hands, recited the oath, which they all repeated, and then they sat down. Several picked up the pads that had been on the floor next to their chairs, took out their pencils, and opened them to begin writing. The judge said to the rest of the jury panel, "Thank you very much for your willingness to sit on this jury. Your Services will not be needed, and you may now return to the jury room."

They left the courtroom quickly, after which additional spectators were allowed to fill their vacant seats. The courtroom was once again full and humming. No one had expected the trial to get under way on its merits at one forty-five on the afternoon of the first day.

Judge Betancourt waited until there was quiet. Her face was so stern she didn't need to say anything to the newcomers. They knew that they were lucky, and that if they weren't quiet, they would be very unlucky very fast. When the room was completely silent, she said, "Mr. Hackett, your opening statement."

28

Hackett stood, adjusted his suit coat and cuff links, and said, "Thank you, Your Honor." He moved to the lectern and began without notes. "Ladies and gentlemen of the jury, as I told you earlier, my name is Tom Hackett." He paused and waited for each juror to look at him. "I'm here on behalf of Mrs. Adams, the former first lady, and the other wives who are now widows of those men killed when Marine One crashed on March seventeeth. I also represent their children. On the other side of this case is WorldCopter, a European consortium that is essentially a French corporation, and its American subsidiary. The evidence will be very clear, ladies and gentlemen. The reason that the president of the United States died, the reason all the men aboard that helicopter were killed, is because of WorldCopter.

"The president was on his way to Camp David for an extremely important meeting.

It was so important that it is classified as top secret and we have not been allowed to learn the reason for that meeting. Even the first lady doesn't know the reason for the meeting." Hackett looked into the jurors' eyes. "But it was so important President Adams chose to take off late at night in the middle of a terrible thunderstorm to fly to Camp David.

"Was it safe for him to take off in the middle of that storm? Not only did he have what was supposed to be the strongest helicopter ever built, but he had perhaps the best pilot who ever flew a helicopter. What for you or me might be dangerous was well within the range of what was reasonable for this helicopter and this pilot.

"But that assumes the helicopter was built properly. The specifications had been approved by the Department of Defense to build the strongest helicopter ever made, one that could handle this storm. It was bought by the Marine Corps to be its primary helicopter for the next twenty years.

"But the evidence will be that this helicopter was *not* built to those specifications." Hackett stared at each juror. "How did this helicopter become Marine One, with all the protection for the president, and have a defect, a flaw, a problem so significant that it would cause the helicopter to crash? How did that *happen?*

"It started back when WorldCopter submitted its bid to be selected to build the next Marine One. The evidence will show how they rigged the game so they would appear to the government to be an American corporation. How this European company entered into a joint venture with an American company to deceive everyone into believing that this could be called an American helicopter, because that was the requirement for building Marine One.

"They won the bid. They got the contract. But the Department of Defense required that those working on the helicopter, those building the parts for Marine One, get appropriate clearances. It was mandatory. No helicopter was to be used for Marine One at all unless everybody involved in the construction of that helicopter had the required clearance. And guess what? They didn't. Of the two hundred and fifty people who touched the parts that went onto this helicopter, forty-seven of them did not have their clearances. Forty-seven. And guess where three of those people worked? They worked in the room with the Golden Blade.

"So what is this Golden Blade?"

Hackett lowered his voice. "In Paris,

France, there is a separate room in the factory where these helicopters are built. In that room is a blade that is never touched, and against which all other blades are balanced. They complete the balance of each new blade with small, washerlike pieces of metal — tip weights — that slide onto a bolt and are tightened down with a nut. Once the new blade balances, it is ready to go.

"So what caused Marine One to crash? The tip weights that were put on one of the blades came off. When the tip weights came off, the aircraft began vibrating and shaking and ultimately shook itself to death. The blade ultimately came off and the helicopter plummeted to the ground and burst into flames.

"Why did the tip weights come off? Because the three men who work in the room with the Golden Blade, the three men who put the tip weights on the blade that came off of Marine One, were three of the forty-seven that didn't have their clearance. But there must be records you might say. *Surely* there are records showing the balancing of this blade and that it matched the Golden Blade.

"There have to be. Right? If you're going to balance a blade that will be on Marine One, you're careful about the records, right?

Wrong. We went to France and I asked to see the records that show the balancing process for the blade that was found on the ground next to Marine One where it crashed. I wanted to know the serial numbers on those tip weights. But the records are gone. And WorldCopter has no answer. They don't know if the records ever existed, if the record keeping was sloppy, if the records have been lost, or if somebody destroyed them after the crash of Marine One. WorldCopter is unable to answer that question. Isn't that curious?

"Ladies and gentlemen, the evidence will be that the brave men who were aboard that helicopter didn't die from the crash. They died from the burns. Imagine the suffering, imagine the pain of knowing that your helicopter is going down. One of the blades came through the fuel tank and covered the occupants with burning fuel. As the helicopter plummeted to the ground, the president and the other occupants were burning to death.

"The helicopter then slammed into the ground, destroying some of the evidence, but not so much that we couldn't figure out what happened. So you can know exactly what did happen, I'm going to play the cockpit voice recording after the helicopter took off from Washington, flew towards Maryland, and crashed. Unfortunately, the recording stops just before the impact. But I think you can feel, you can hear in the pilot's voice, that something was going wrong. It's the last recording we have of Colonel Collins. Let's listen." Hackett crossed to the digital recorder sitting on his counsel table with a court microphone bent down toward its small speaker and hit play. The room filled with Collins's voice as everyone sat mesmerized. It was the first time anyone had heard the recording played outside the NTSB room. This had been one of my motions, to preclude the playing of the tape. Too emotionally charged. My motion had been rejected after Judge Betancourt heard the tape herself.

After the CVR recording was finished, Hackett turned off the recorder and continued quietly, "Ladies and gentlemen of the jury, this is pretty simple. WorldCopter did not do background checks on its employees, and they didn't have the clearances that they were required to have in order to build Marine One. Yet, they assured the Department of Defense that they were in compliance. Then when building the rotor blade that killed the president and all aboard his helicopter, they can't even tell you that it was balanced, what tip weights were put on, how much weight was put on, or the serial numbers for those tip weights. Whatever they did, they did wrong. The tip weights came off. That is their fault, plainly. So what do they say? They can't tell you because they've lost the records, or they never existed, or they've been destroyed."

Hackett paced. "There is more to this than simple negligence on the part of World-Copter. We have reckless disregard for the safety of others, particularly the president of the United States and his crew on Marine One. It might even be more than reckless. There could be malice here. We may even find intentional conduct. We'll have to see how this evidence comes in, but you listen carefully." He paused, glancing up and down the rows. "You listen to what these witnesses say. You wait and see who shows up to tell us what happened from World-Copter."

Hackett took a deep breath. "At the end of this trial, I'm going to ask you to award a substantial amount of damages to my clients. And by damages, I mean money. It's the only thing we have that we can force World-Copter to do. We can't bring back President Adams and put him back in charge of this country. We can't bring back my clients' husbands and fathers or take the pain of the fire away. But we can ask you to compensate them for the loss that WorldCopter has caused. There will be a lot of evidence over the economic value of these cases, as well as the losses suffered through their loss of consortium — sexual relations — the loss of care and comfort, the loss of society. Losing the relationship. These cases have enormous value. I will be asking you for damages in excess of one billion dollars." Several jurors frowned at the number. "So listen for the evidence which will support that, which you will see very clearly. Thank you very much for your attention, ladies and gentlemen. I will speak to you again at the conclusion of the evidence, in my closing argument, and I'll tell you what you need to do to award my clients what they're entitled to in your verdict."

Hackett sat down and the first lady put her hand on top of his hand in gratitude. It was very touching.

At that moment the judge looked at me and said, "Mr. Nolan, your opening."

29

"Thank you, your Honor," I said as I stood and crossed to the lectern. I opened the notebook that contained the outline for my opening statement and looked at the jury. I expected many had already picked sides.

"Good afternoon, ladies and gentlemen. Again, my name is Mike Nolan, and I am here with Rachel Long," I said, indicating. "We represent WorldCopter." I paused and scanned their faces again. No movement.

"Mr. Hackett made a very compelling opening statement. I expect it generated sympathy in you and persuaded you that what he said is exactly right. It may be. But rather than evaluating the case based on sympathy for the families, which we all share, or feeling the loss of our president, which we all feel, let's focus on the *facts* of what happened in the accident, on what we know. Mr. Hackett said this accident was caused by WorldCopter. That it was the fault of WorldCopter. Was it? Think about what he said and how much he talked about the actual facts. The investigation. What experts are going to say. Who is it that has said that this is WorldCopter's fault? What evidence points to WorldCopter? Essentially, Mr. Hackett points to the fact that several of the workers, including those who worked on balancing the blades and installing the tip weights, did not have the Yankee White security clearance required to work on the presidential helicopter. That is true. And whose fault is that? His implication is that WorldCopter intentionally dodged the security-clearance process so they could hire workers determined to sabotage the president's helicopter. Why didn't he just say that? He tries to impugn the character of the people who worked hard on this helicopter, without explaining how those clearances had anything to do with the balancing of the blade. True, the documentation is not as precise as it should have been. World-Copter acknowledges that and the evidence will support what Mr. Hackett says. So if you want to award a judgment against them based on poor record keeping, then I can stop now. But I'd rather explore with you what facts Mr. Hackett will put on that will support his theory, and what other things you may conclude based on those facts."

I turned the page of my notes and looked up at them. They were listening but skeptical. "There are four other possible causes of this accident I want you to keep in mind. First, the helicopter crashed in the middle of one of the worst thunderstorms we have ever seen. Marine One was flying right through the middle of that storm. It was in what is called a cell. A cell is the part that reflects on radar and shows tremendous turbulence, hail, rain, and the like. It is the real thunderstorm. Could it be that the helicopter simply came apart due to the huge forces inside a thunderstorm? I want you to hold that in mind as a possible cause of this accident.

"A second possibility though is one that is difficult to contemplate. You've been watching the first lady, as we all have since she entered the courtroom. She is admired throughout the country and is a person of great dignity. It is appropriate to notice her and give her the respect she's due. Behind her though, directly behind her in this courtroom, sits Mrs. Collins. She was here this morning during the voir dire process. She also is entitled to tremendous respect. She's also entitled to your sympathy, outside of your role as a juror. But one of the possible causes of this accident must be mentioned. Her husband, Colonel Collins, was the highly decorated and respected pilot of Marine One. You heard his voice on the cockpit voice recorder that was played for you earlier by Mr. Hackett. But he didn't play the first part of that recording. The part before the helicopter took off from the White House."

I walked over to the console between the counsel tables that had all the electronic equipment on it and pushed play on track two. It played the exchange between Collins and Rudd, the copilot, and the discussion of the president. I watched the faces of the jurors as Collins demonstrated his contempt for the president. They were surprised. "You undoubtedly have heard a lot of information about this crash; the press has covered it extensively. But this is the first time the cockpit voice recorder has been played anywhere outside of the NTSB headquarters. As you can see, there may be more to this story than a loose tip weight. Not only did Colonel Collins hold the president in contempt for his political views, he didn't even give him the formal respect due to the office. For example, it is well-known that President Adams claimed to be the third Adams president, in the same family line with John Adams and John Quincy Adams. But that claim was thought to be fraudulent by Colonel Collins. I will prove to you that he wrote letters to people about what a fraud the president was.

"That's not all. A couple of months before the accident, Colonel Collins took out a new life insurance policy with the Armed Forces Insurance Association for one million dollars. That was ten times the insurance he had before. What would inspire a Colonel who was approaching retirement to suddenly take out a massive life insurance policy that he had no interest in before, even when he was in combat? The Collinses have no children. Coincidence? Maybe. But the other possibility, the more malignant possibility, is that Collins knew what was coming. He anticipated, or even caused, the accident." A loud gasp came from the audience and the jurors. "So do I think that Colonel Collins killed the president and everyone else on board on purpose? That he disagreed with the president's policies so much that he ended it on purpose? Let me give you one additional fact. The evidence will show that the flight data recorder stopped. It stops thirty seconds before impact. In the wreckage we found the panel that has the circuit breakers on the right side of the cockpit by the pilot's knee. The circuit breaker for the flight data recorder was out. Could it have been tripped by an electronic short or other failure? Yes. But you heard the cockpit voice recorder. It was working fine. And there's no indication of other electrical problems. It's possible that he perceived a hydraulic failure and was trying to pull the hydraulic-pump circuit breaker and got the wrong one. It's absolutely possible. But it's also possible that he pulled the circuit breaker for the flight data recorder so that we couldn't know what actually happened. Right after that circuit breaker popped, this aircraft started an immediate descent and crashed into the ground almost inverted. One of the scenarios you're going to have to consider is that Colonel Collins disliked the president and everything he stood for and used this storm as a cover to kill the president. Is that what I think? I don't know, and what I think doesn't matter. The question is, what does the *evidence* show? And *your* job is to determine what happened based on the *evidence.*"

I turned the page. "Mr. Hackett spent a lot of time discussing the people who balanced the blade, making them look like bad people. But did you notice how little time he spent discussing with you the mechanism of the crash? How it happened? The evidence regarding the tip weights, at least as presented by Mr. Hackett, is nonexistent. All he noted was that the tip weights were not on the blade that was found on the ground next to the crash. That could happen in a number of ways. That blade is spinning almost at the speed of sound, and if the end of the blade hits anything, the tip weights will be thrown off. All the experts will agree with that. But Mr. Hackett would have you believe that somehow the tip weights came loose and flew off the end of the blade. On what is that theory based? The tip weights were not found during the investigation. And of course we know they had to be on the blade, because the helicopter never could have taken off if that blade weren't in balance on takeoff. It would have generated such vibrations as to make the helicopter unflyable. And this helicopter had flown for several weeks with this blade on it. There were no vibration problems whatsoever. So we *know* the tip weights were on the blade and that it was in balance when flying to the White House. So what happened? We don't know. The lost blade could have been the cause of the accident, or it could have been an effect of the accident. It could have been that the helicopter was already coming apart because of the horrible storm, and the blade hit another part of the helicopter like the tail boom, and the tip weights were thrown off. We don't know. Mr. Hackett doesn't know, nor do his experts. But because there was an irregularity in the documents, he jams his theory of the crash into that one fact. He wants to imply some kind of sabotage or some kind of inappropriate placement of tip weights. He would have you believe that World-Copter intentionally, or with unbelievably reckless disregard for the safety of the president, caused this accident by misbalancing the tip weights, or by not tightening the nut that held them on.

"Perhaps neither of those three possibilities captures your attention. So if it wasn't the weather, and it wasn't Colonel Collins, and it wasn't the tip weights coming off of the blade, what was it? What caused the accident? There's one other cause, one other way that this helicopter may have been brought down, that is simply hinted at in the evidence that will be presented to you." I looked at the eyes of the jurors, who had started listening more carefully. "You will need to be discerning, and you will need to listen very carefully to the testimony. I'm not saying you can't consider the other three possibilities. Perhaps they are the cause. But there's one additional possibility that you're going to have to consider. Rather than tell you what it is now, I will simply ask that you pay very close attention to the evidence all the way through to the end. And at the conclusion of this trial, I will ask you whether you saw that fourth cause. The fourth possibility. Perhaps the real reason that this helicopter crashed.

"That will require that you not decide yet what you're going to do. And not decide after Mr. Hackett's evidence is complete. And not decide midway through my presentation of evidence. It means you'll have to wait till Mr. Hackett and I have an opportunity to stand back up here and tell you what we think the evidence has shown. Then you can make up your mind and go into the jury room and do what's right. Just know this. Mr. Hackett may be wrong, or I may be wrong. Or we both may be wrong. It's up to *you* to decide what happened. And that will require you to pay very close attention to the evidence and listen very carefully to the witnesses. Thank you for your attention, and I look forward to speaking with you at the conclusion of this trial."

As I made my way back to the table, I saw

Rachel, who looked stunned and somewhat horrified.

I heard the judge say behind me, "Mr. Hackett, call your first witness."

I sat down and took a deep but silent breath. Rachel put a Post-it note in front of me: *What is this fourth theory?*

I wrote, *Don't know yet,* and handed it back to her.

Hackett stood and said, "Your Honor, plaintiffs call Mrs. Adams, the first lady."

The first lady walked to the witness box, took the oath, and sat. She considered crossing her legs but realized there really wasn't room. She sat slightly forward. The jury was mesmerized, and the audience was absolutely silent. I could hear the scratching of the chalk on the paper of the two artists sitting in the front row.

Hackett began his questioning with the usual background information, college — graduate school for him, law school for her — marriage, his political career. Then Hackett asked, "What was your relationship like when he was the president? Did he ignore you?"

She smiled. It was the first time I had seen her really smile in person. She had a warm, engaging smile. "No, he included me in almost everything. I sat in on meetings with heads of state, I talked to him about foreign affairs and domestic issues. We were a team, sort of. I mean, I didn't have any real say, or authority, but he cared about what I thought. I think he respected my judgment and liked to have someone as a sounding board who wouldn't call the *Washington Post* the next day."

The gallery chuckled. Hackett was smooth. Mrs. Adams was comfortable, relaxed, articulate, and trustworthy. He continued, "You were in the White House the night the president died, were you not?"

"Yes." Her face looked suddenly downcast.

"Do you remember the evening?"

"Of course."

"Do you know what the president was doing before he got aboard the helicopter that ultimately crashed?"

"He was with me."

Hackett hesitated as if he didn't know the answer to the next question, as if there were some danger in his asking it. "What were the two of you doing?"

The First Lady gave a wan smile. "We had dinner together. He had been working late, and we didn't begin eating till after eight o'clock."

"Where did you eat?"

"In our private quarters."

"Do you remember what you had? It's not important, I was just wondering whether you remembered."

"Actually I do. I love fish and eat it as often as I can. Jim really doesn't . . . didn't like fish much, but he read somewhere that eating fish at least once a week made a difference in something or other. So he ate a fish dinner with me at least once a week. And this was that dinner."

"So the evening he died, he was eating fish at home with you. But then he got up and headed to a meeting."

"Yes. He said he had to go out to Camp David, just for one night. He was to come back Friday evening."

"Do you remember the weather?"

"It was a terrible storm. The wind was throwing the rain against the windows to where it made that loud clicking kind of sound, almost like hail, but it's just rain hitting glass hard. I'm sure you've heard it."

"Have you ever been to Camp David, Mrs. Adams?"

"Of course. Many times."

"Have you ever driven there from the White House or been driven there from the White House?"

"Yes."

"How long does it take to get there?"

"It depends. But it's about an hour and a half."

"Did you know that the president was going to fly to Camp David that night in the presidential helicopter?"

"Yes. He told me that."

"Didn't you wonder why he needed to fly when he could be there in an hour and a half by driving?"

"I did. I asked him."

Hackett turned toward the gallery and then back toward Mrs. Adams. "What did he say?"

"He said he had a meeting. He was meeting people there, that it was very important, and that they had a very short window of time."

"Who was he meeting there, Mrs. Adams?"

Everyone waited for her answer.

"I don't know."

"Did you ask?"

"Of course. I wondered who was so important that he had to fly there that night, let alone who was so important or secret he couldn't tell me about it."

"Had you encountered other times when he had meetings and he wouldn't tell you who was attending?"

"Rarely."

"What kinds of meetings were they that he couldn't tell you about them?"

I stood. "Objection. This calls for speculation. How could she know the content of meetings he refused to tell her about?"

The judge nodded. "Sustained."

Hackett said, "Thank you, Your Honor. Let me rephrase. Had you discussed the types of meetings with the president before that he would not allow you to know about?"

"Yes."

"What types of meetings were they?"

"Usually dealing with secret material or very high-level things I never got to learn about."

"And you understand that the government has refused to tell us what the nature of the meeting was or who the attendees were. Is that your understanding as well?"

"Yes. I still don't know."

"But your husband had something important he needed to do on behalf of the government, right?"

"Absolutely. Otherwise he would have stayed home with me."

Hackett said, "No further questions."

I stood up quickly and proceeded to the

lectern. "Mrs. Adams, good afternoon."

"Good afternoon."

"Mrs. Adams, you have no idea why your husband was going to that meeting at Camp David on the night he was killed, correct?"

"That's true. I know it was because of his duties as president, but not beyond that."

"And as to why he had to be there within that short period of time, you don't really know that to be true other than that's what he told you, correct?"

"Yes."

"Do you have some other information that he had to be there that night and that driving would not get him there in time?"

"No, I know that he was a truthful person. And if he told me he had to be there, then he did. So I do know it to be true unless he was lying to me. But that was not his character, Mr. Nolan."

Ouch. "So you believe him, that there was some compelling reason that he needed to be there *that night,* and that driving for one and a half hours to get there instead of flying for thirty minutes would somehow have been detrimental to his objective. Right?"

"That's my understanding."

"Am I right, Mrs. Adams, that you would love to know why your husband was in such a hurry to get to Camp David that night?"

"Yes. I would like to know that."

I decided to take some chances. "And you've asked around the White House, haven't you?"

"Yes, I have."

"You've asked President Adams's chief of staff why the president went to Camp David that night, haven't you?"

"Yes."

I gained confidence. "And you've asked the vice president, who is now the president, haven't you?"

"Yes."

"And they wouldn't tell you, would they?"

"No."

I paused and looked at her hard. "Because they didn't know, did they?"

"That's true. They did said they didn't know."

"Did you accept their answer, that his chief of staff and vice president didn't know why he was going to Camp David?"

"I don't think it is any more likely that they would lie to me than that my husband would lic to me."

"So you accept their statement that they do not know why President Adams was going to Camp David the night he was killed, right?"

"That's right."

"Don't you find that odd, Mrs. Adams?"

"Yes, I do."

"What do you make of that?"

"I don't know what to make of it."

"Others went with the president, including his head of the Secret Service detail that protected him, right?"

"Yes, he was one of the ones who was killed."

"But someone has replaced him as the chief of the president's security detail for the then vice president, now president, Cunningham. That person's name is Larry Hodges. Did you ask him what his predecessor was doing with President Adams going to Camp David that night?"

"I did. He said he didn't know."

"So as you sit here today, Mrs. Adams, no one from the government has or would tell you why President Adams was going to Camp David the night he was killed, correct?"

"That's right."

"Isn't it true, Mrs. Adams, that never in the time that President Adams was president was he out of your sight for twenty-four hours when you did not know what he was doing?"

"I'm sorry, I didn't understand the question."

I nodded. "You knew where your husband was and what he was doing every day that he was president, right?"

"For the most part. Not all the details. Yes."

"Except one. The night he was killed."

"I knew where he was —"

"But not what he was doing."

"That's true."

I turned the page in my outline. "Now, Mrs. Adams, you knew Colonel Collins. Right?"

"I knew who he was. I've ridden in Marine One many times."

"No. I mean personally. You would talk to him when you had the opportunity, right?"

The First Lady frowned and glanced at Hackett. I always liked it when a witness glanced at his or her attorney, because it meant that I had departed from their expected script. I was asking questions they hadn't anticipated.

"Well, no, not really. You asked me some questions in my deposition about it, but, no, I didn't really talk to him."

"You conversed with him at several White House gatherings, or parties, did you not? Where he was invited and wore his Marine dress uniform?"

She frowned again. "I'm sorry, Mr. Nolan,

but I don't know what you're talking about."

I reached over to our counsel table and picked up the brown envelope that was lying next to the notebook at my place. I opened it and pulled out three photographs. I handed one to Hackett and said, "May I approach the witness and give a copy of this photograph to the clerk?"

The judge said, "You may."

I handed a copy to the clerk, who handed it to the judge, and I handed the other copy of the photograph to the first lady. I returned to the lectern. "Mrs. Adams, do you recognize the setting in this photograph?"

"Only when you asked me about it at my deposition —"

Hackett said, "Objection, Your Honor. This photograph is irrelevant. We objected to it when he listed it on his exhibit list —"

"It's relevant to her familiarity with Colonel Collins, Your Honor."

"And *that's* irrelevant," Hackett added. "Mr. Nolan somehow accessed confidential government photographs from the White House security system. He's not entitled to have those photographs and is not entitled to have them here."

Before the judge could respond, I said, "Your Honor, I'm not offering this into evidence. She said she couldn't recall having conversations with Collins. I simply would like to have this marked as next in order and use it to refresh her recollection. I could use a plate of spaghetti to refresh her recollection if it would help."

The judge nodded. "He may use anything to refresh recollection, Mr. Hackett. He has not offered it into evidence, and we will discuss the means of obtaining these photographs and whether or not they should have been produced later. You did not file a motion to preclude these photos, so we will deal with them as they come. You may proceed, Mr. Nolan."

"Thank you, Your Honor. Mrs. Adams, do you recognize this reception?"

"Well the date is stamped in the upper-right-hand corner, so it was December seventeenth, a few months before my husband was killed."

"And if I could direct your attention to the middle of the photograph, I believe that is you standing there in a ball gown. Am I correct?"

"Yes, that's me."

"Would you please tell the jury what you're doing?"

Hackett debated whether to stand up, but didn't. She waited, then said, "I am standing there."

The jury chuckled.

"Is it your belief that the photograph shows you doing nothing but standing there?"

"That's right."

"Mrs. Adams, who is standing next to you, in the direction toward which your head is turned?"

"That is Colonel Collins."

"The pilot of Marine One on the night your husband was killed, right?"

"That's correct."

"From this photograph, Mrs. Adams, it looks like your mouth is perhaps six inches from his ear and your mouth is open as if you are speaking, would you agree?"

"It's a little difficult to say, but it could be."

"And where is Colonel Collins's hand, his left hand?"

She stared at the photograph and then looked up. "It appears to be behind me."

"It is behind you, but on you. Right?"

"I don't know."

"His hand is either in the small of your back or . . . lower. Right?"

Hackett jumped up. "Objection, Your Honor, this is pure speculation."

"Sustained."

"Does that photograph refresh your recollection on whether you've had conversations with Colonel Collins?"

"I don't really remember any. He may have been saying, 'Excuse me.' I don't know. I don't remember talking to him."

"Do you deny that this photograph is authentic?"

"I don't know. I don't know where this photograph came from. I can't tell you whether it's authentic or not."

"Well, on that date was the reception for the prime minister of Japan, do you remember that?"

"Yes. I remember that."

"What were you saying to Colonel Collins?"

"I don't remember saying anything to him."

"Your Honor, may I approach again?" I handed a second picture to the clerk, to Hackett, and to the first lady.

"Mrs. Adams, this is another photograph that I'd like you to look at. It is of a different reception, one for the delegates from NATO. Do you remember that reception?"

"Yes, I do."

"If you look in the left-hand corner, the bottom left, you're standing facing Colonel Collins perhaps eighteen inches apart. Do you see that?"

"Yes."

"Again, it appears that your mouth is open and you were speaking. Were you speaking to Colonel Collins?"

"I don't know. Perhaps . . . What difference does all this make?" She put the photograph down and looked at me. "What exactly is it you are trying to imply, Mr. Nolan?"

"I'm not trying to imply anything, ma'am. I'm simply asking whether you had a conversation or relationship with Colonel Collins."

"What if I did?"

"It would be up to the jury to decide the relevance —"

Hackett had had enough. "Your Honor, this is leading nowhere. Mr. Nolan is fishing and simply trying to assault the first lady through innuendos that have no bearing on anything. These are desperate trial tactics and we need to have it stopped."

"Do you have anything further in this area?" the judge asked me.

"I'll move on, Your Honor."

The judge looked at the clock. "Would this be a good time to break for the day, Mr. Nolan?"

"Yes, Your Honor, that would be fine."

"Very well. Court is adjourned until tomorrow morning at nine o'clock. We will

462

recommence with the cross-examination of Mrs. Adams. I assume you have additional cross-examination, Mr. Nolan?"

"Briefly."

"Very well. Ladies and gentlemen of the jury, you are not to discuss this case amongst yourselves, your family, or read or learn anything else about this case outside of the courtroom. I will instruct you about that every single day, but please keep it in mind. The only facts you learn about this case are right here in this courtroom, and you don't discuss it with anybody until you get into the jury room when you begin your deliberations. Do you understand that?"

They all nodded.

"Court is in recess until tomorrow morning at nine."

We stood as the jury filed out of the courtroom and closed the door behind them. Everyone else began to discuss the case immediately, and some journalists hurried from the courtroom. The rest of us made our way out in an orderly fashion only to encounter the journalists standing outside the courtroom. I waved them off and proceeded to my car.

Kathryn met me halfway to the car. "Let's get together at your conference room. We need to talk."

30

Rachel rode with me on the short drive and we reconvened at my office. Journalists waited there too, but we kept them out of the building. The president of WorldCopter, the general counsel, Kathryn, and Brightman were all there.

Dolores had ordered food. Kathryn said before anybody had a chance to sit down, "Mike, what are you doing with the first lady? I thought you were going to ask her a couple of softball questions, not try and make it look like she was having an affair with Colonel Collins and conspiring to kill her husband. Help me understand what you're doing here."

I drank a Coke deeply. I said, "All I can tell you at this point is that it doesn't have anything to do really with the first lady, and it has everything to do with those photographs."

"What do you mean, it has everything to

do with those photographs? *What* does? What is your point?"

"I'm working on a theory, the fourth theory that I can't really discuss yet. If I even mention it, to anybody, it could completely blow up in my face. So you're going to have to trust me."

"I need to know what it is I'm trusting you *with* before I know if I can trust you."

I pushed back. "I know those questions were odd, and I'm sure the press will chew me up for being mean to the first lady, implying she was having an affair with the pilot or something. I understand all that."

I looked at Justin. "Justin, have you heard from Curtis?" Curtis was the investigator I had hired after Tinny's murder. I told him his job was to find out the name of the Secret Service agent in charge of security at Camp David on the night of the accident. "I haven't heard from him on that Secret Service agent's name. Tell him to pull out all the stops. I've got to have that name." Justin nodded and hurried out of the boardroom.

I continued, "Look, I have sort of a crazy theory I'm developing, and unfortunately we don't have a lot of time. I've got people in the field, the experts are working, and I'm trying to put it together."

Kathryn was exasperated. "Put *what* together? Tell me what you're working on."

"I can't."

"Why not?"

"Seriously, if I even mention it out loud, it will be known. I don't know how exactly, but I just can't."

She wasn't satisfied, but said, "Then at least tell me what else you're going to ask the first lady. Let's discuss the rest tomorrow. Why don't we sit down."

Everyone else in the room sat down, with Rachel right next to me, Braden next to her, Lynn next to him, and everybody else on the other side of the table closer to the door.

As we sat, Brightman asserted himself. "Mike, I thought your opening was fine, but you really left it wide-open about what —"

I looked up with surprise and interrupted, "Is this going to be a critique of my first day of trial? Because I don't really have time for it."

"Well," he said slowly, "you're going to have to take time, because if we don't right this ship while it's under way, it just might roll over completely."

"Kathryn, is this what you want to do every night after trial? I've got witnesses to prepare for, I've got experts to track down.

I've got subpoenas to get out. This isn't a drill."

Kathryn winced slightly. "I did ask him to give us a couple of comments if he thought he could help at all."

"Oh, Lord," I exclaimed.

He just kept right on. "So in your opening you mentioned four theories, but only identified three. What is this fourth theory and how are you going to prove it? Because if you can't, you will —"

"Have you not been reading my e-mails? We don't *have* a fourth theory, we have a theory that may become a fourth theory if things fall into place. But my investigator has been murdered, and my experts are working twenty-four hours a day but aren't there yet. We're developing something, but I can't go into it. And I sure can't tell the jury about —"

"Why?" Brightman demanded. "Why can't you go into it? These are your clients, Mike. They're the ones who have to sign off on what you do. This isn't just your show!"

He was right, but I still didn't know whom I could trust, or who was on a cell phone talking to someone from Hackett's camp. And I sure didn't want to alert anyone that I suspected someone of duplicity. "Because it isn't well developed enough to even outline it."

"So let us help you develop it. We're some fairly smart people here, Mike."

"I'm sorry. I just can't. Soon."

Brightman looked at Kathryn, who was perturbed.

She said, "You're asking a lot, Mike."

"I know. It may be worth —"

Brightman said, "Now, when you began your cross-examination of the first lady —"

"Are you seriously gonna sit there and go over everything that happened today?" I turned to Kathryn. "Look, if you want this guy to try the case, just say the word. I've just had enough of this."

That seemed to hit him. He said loudly, "I know a good trial when I see one. We're not there."

"And a good trial would be what? Admitting that the tip weights caused the accident and that we put the tip weights on, and that the guys that did it didn't have clearances, and we can't prove by documentation what the hell exactly happened in France. Is that a good trial? What would your theory be, Mr. Brightman, whose last airplane trial was ten years ago about a piece-of-shit Piper Cub that ran into a wind sock and you got your *ass* kicked?"

"Mike . . . ," Kathryn said unhappily.

Brightman's eyes narrowed and he tried to remain calm. "You don't need to get personal with this, Mike."

"Sorry," I said, not meaning it. "It's been a stressful day. But I've got to go to my office and get ready for tomorrow."

Kathryn looked concerned, as if she was afraid I was losing it. "Mike," she said calmly, "I asked him to make his comments. Would it be better if I asked him to e-mail them to you later on this evening?"

"Yeah. Sure."

She said, "Mark, why don't you go ahead and type up your notes into an e-mail and send them to Mike so he can consider them for tomorrow. What would be particularly helpful is if you think there are certain directions he should go with the other witnesses that we expect tomorrow. You've read all their depositions, seen all the outlines and notes, you know how this is heading. If you have some thoughts, why don't you give him those in writing rather than us taking up his time right now."

Brightman closed his expensive leather notebook. "Whatever you say, Kathryn."

I stayed in my office for a few minutes, gathered my things, then headed home about seven thirty that night. In front of my house was a car that I immediately recognized: Wayne Bradley. Here we go, I thought. I pulled into the driveway and into the garage, lowered the door, went into the house through the kitchen door, and dropped my briefcase and jacket on the bench by the window. Debbie was in the kitchen doing dishes and came over to me when I walked in. "Well, how did you think it went?" she asked, kissing me.

"Oh, okay I guess. How's the press?"

"Wall-to-wall coverage. They've talked about nothing but the trial all night."

"I wouldn't watch it if I were you."

She smiled. "Some of them think you've got something up your sleeve."

I loosened my tie. "We shall see. Never surrender. Bradley's here. I hope you don't mind."

"No, that's fine."

I went to the front door and opened it. Bradley got out of his car, walked to the den, and sprawled out on the couch.

"Dr. Bradley," I said, following him.

He looked up. "Sorry. I didn't want to — sorry — you said only at home or on your new cell and you didn't answer — what time is it? I'm really tired."

"About eight."

"Oh." He sat up and took a deep breath.

He was then completely awake. "We've got to talk."

"What? New developments? Did you find something?"

He nodded.

I went to my car and got my cell phone out of the glove box. I typed in a text message, *Come,* and sent it. I walked back inside and began making a pot of coffee. This was going to be a long night.

Debbie passed through the kitchen and looked at me quizzically. I said, "May have a big development."

"Good or bad?"

"I'm not sure. Rachel's on her way."

It was normally fifteen minutes from Rachel's place to mine, but she was there in ten. I was in my den with Dr. Bradley trying to get him back to his normal self. He seemed very odd. Almost out of it. Rachel walked right in the front door without knocking and came into the den. She looked like a fireman with an ax ready to cut through a wall. I pulled in another chair from the living room and closed the French doors behind us. We sat in a small triangle with Bradley on the couch.

"Okay. So what do you have?"

Bradley leaned forward and put his elbows on his knees. Pushed his thick glasses back up on his nose and ran his fingers through his dirty hair. "Well, I've given this thing quite a look. SEM, you name it. Compound is correct. Within spec. But it fractured under stress, Mike. Broke." He held out the semicircle half of the tip weight I had dug out of the tree branch.

I stared at it in his hand. "This kills us."

Rachel sat back heavily in her chair and looked at the ceiling. "We've got to give it to them. We can't not let them have it."

I said to Bradley, "So the tip weight was defective and came apart and that caused the vibration leading to the crash of Marine One. Just like the NTSB said. Is that how you see it?"

Dr. Bradley shrugged. "Well, it sure is unusual for something like this to just fracture. But that's what seems to have happened. It's a fairly clean break. That indicates to me that it wasn't properly manufactured and that it was too brittle. You don't realize what kind of stress those tip weights are under, but they're under endless centrifugal force, and if the flat surface of the other tip weights isn't exactly right, it gives it maybe a thousandth of an inch to maneuver. Over time, it will cause a fracture if something is too brittle."

"So that's it?"

Bradley adjusted his glasses, wishing he had something else to say, something positive. "Pretty much. I mean, I can keep studying it. I didn't examine every single molecule in it."

I took a deep breath, closed my eyes, and looked up. I thought for a moment, then sat forward. "Let me see it."

He handed it to me and I brought it as close to my eye as I could. "Do you have a magnifying glass?"

"Always." He pulled a Sherlock Holmes glass out of his pocket and handed it to me.

I maneuvered under the brightest light in the room and examined the tip weight. I could see several numbers that were part of the serial number. "This serial number — or the part you can see — is in the group of unaccounted-for tip weights that might have been in Marine One?"

"Yep."

I continued to study it. I couldn't see anything significant, and the odds of me seeing something that Bradley hadn't found were nil anyway. I gave him back his magnifying glass. Then a thought washed over me like a shower with an electrical current running through it. The fourth theory, the one I had saved for the jury, had just occurred to me. If I could only prove it. "You run any chemical tests on it?"

He frowned. "No. Why would I?"

I nodded. "Do them. Do them all. Don't talk to anyone about any of this until you've done those tests."

He got it. "I'll do it as soon as I can."

"Let me know. . . . If it goes bad, maybe tomorrow I can talk to Kathryn and we can start talking settlement with Hackett before we have to give it to him. Maybe we can settle without him ever knowing about this tip weight." I thought for a moment and knew that would never happen. "We'd have to give it to the NTSB so they could finalize their report anyway, though. It will come out, but maybe we can settle before, I don't know. I'll have to think through this."

"I'm about to keel over, Mike. I've got to get some shut-eye. I'll try and get up at four or five and start on it. I'll sleep at the lab — I've got a cot in my back room — then I'll call you." Bradley rose and walked slowly to the front door with the tip weight in his pocket.

He closed the door behind him silently, almost as an apology.

Rachel looked gutted. "So we're done?"

"No. If that chemical test comes back positive, we may be in business."

31

Bradley's tests weren't likely to amount to much, and if he came up empty, our road led right off a cliff. And I had no indication that Hackett would be interested in settlement even if we were interested. He would smell our desperation. The second day of trial opened with the shadow of disaster deepening all around me.

As the clerk called the courtroom to order, I stood. "Your Honor, I have no further questions of the first lady."

The judge looked surprised, as did Hackett, and the judge said, "Call your next witness, Mr. Hackett."

Hackett said, "Your Honor, we call Mrs. Collins to the stand."

She took the oath and sat in the witness chair. She looked at the jury, then at Hackett, who began his questioning by asking about her, not her husband. She testified just as she had in her deposition, only better. She was the perfect Marine wife, faithful, true, loyal, devoted, and smart. *Semper fidelis.* The jury loved her. They loved everything she stood for, everything she said, and how she said it. I think they all wanted to invite her over to dinner. She went on at length about what a hero her husband was, how much he had sacrificed for the country, how much his injuries hurt him when they were alone, how his titanium jaw was never the same as his real jaw, how his teeth didn't work the way they used to. How he saw himself serving in the Marine Corps until the last possible moment because nothing was greater than serving his country. Hackett had the jury on his side, and they were hanging on every word.

She concluded by saying that although they hadn't had any children, they were happily married and planned on staying married for the rest of their lives. While he hadn't yet begun to look forward to retirement, she had already been thinking about it, the hikes they would take in the mountains, the trip to Europe that he had always promised but they hadn't yet found time or money for, the sailboat trips to the Caribbean that they had considered, even though neither of them knew how to sail, and the mountain condo where they would go skiing every winter in Colorado. The dreams of a married couple looking forward to a little more free time in their lives. Hackett waited until everyone wanted to go with them, then said, "Your witness."

I glanced at the clock. We only had twenty minutes until lunch. I had given Rachel the job of cross-examining Mrs. Collins. I didn't think it would come this early in the trial, but Rachel was ready. She had maybe twenty minutes of questions. Now that it looked like we were cooked, that our theory was wrong, and that the NTSB and Hackett were right, I wasn't sure if we should even ask her any questions. Before I could decide, Rachel stood and decided for me.

"Good morning, Mrs. Collins," Rachel said, her nervousness apparent in her voice, at least to those who knew her well. Rachel was wearing a dark blue pin-striped suit that looked black. She wore heels that made her almost six feet tall.

"Good morning, Ms. Long."

"You paint a picture of your husband, Colonel Collins, that is very complimentary. Well deserved no doubt. But, Mrs. Collins, isn't it true that your husband despised the president?"

A murmur swept through the audience.

Mrs. Collins frowned. "No, not that I'm aware of."

"You heard the recording of the cockpit voice recorder here in this courtroom, did you not?"

"Yes."

"Did you hear the section where the copilot, Lieutenant Colonel Rudd, chastised your husband for ignoring the president, who had spoken directly to him?"

"Yes."

"That wasn't respectful, was it?"

"I think he was distracted preparing the aircraft to take off and probably a little concerned about the weather. He was preoccupied." Mrs. Collins had been well prepared. I saw several of the jurors nod.

Rachel continued, "Well, the copilot sure didn't take it that way, did he?"

"I don't know that I'd say that. I thought he was simply pointing out an oversight of courtesy."

Rachel raised her voice only slightly, still proceeding in her gentle way. "Did you hear the rest of the tape where your husband essentially said the president was a fake? That he wasn't related to John Adams or John Quincy Adams?"

"Yes. I heard that."

"You would agree that your husband was

less than complimentary about the president."

"My husband was a trivia buff. He loved to know details and play games with other people who didn't know those details. That's just something he always did."

"Well, in this case, the details he was knowledgeable about concerned the family history of the president. And he was critical about the way the president represented that history. Correct?"

"Oh, I don't know that I'd agree with that. I didn't hear it that way."

Rachel grew frustrated. "Mrs. Collins, your husband was obsessed with the president and his politics, wasn't he?"

"I wouldn't say that."

"He disagreed with virtually everything President Adams did, right?"

"I don't really know."

"Mrs. Collins, you would agree that your husband was a conservative, even ultraconservative, wouldn't you?"

"It depends how you mean that, but generally I would agree with that." Mrs. Collins shifted uneasily in her witness chair and glanced at Hackett, who was writing, taking notes, and not giving her any visual cues.

I watched her carefully as Rachel tried to

read the witness. "And I think you would agree, perhaps we could even stipulate, that since President Adams ran on a moderate-to-liberal Democrat platform, and proudly called himself a 'modern liberal,' or sometimes a 'progressive,' it's fair to say that your husband disagreed with much of what the president stood for politically, right?"

"Depending on what in particular you're talking about, but, yes."

"Mrs. Collins, your husband had an extensive library, did he not?"

"Yes, he did."

"During the discovery in this case we had every book in his library copied so that we could review the numerous margin notes in his books. Did you know that?"

"Yes."

"And he read those books extensively, did he not? They weren't just for looks, to have a big library."

"Yes. He did."

"Mostly books about politics, international affairs, but also conspiracy theories and some what might be called 'fringe' writing on who was really running the world contrary to what all the rest of us believe. Fair?"

She smiled. "Perhaps."

Rachel went to the counsel table, picked

up an exhibit, and put it on the ELMO, essentially a television camera suspended over a flat, illuminated base that projected whatever was on the base onto numerous screens around the courtroom. It was a modern overhead projector, but much more useful — you could lay a helicopter-gear bearing on it, or your hand, or a pen, or a document, and project it to the courtroom. In this case Rachel pulled out a copy of one of Collins's margin notes. Rachel continued, "Let me show you what's been marked previously as Exhibit 274. It is a copy of a page from a book from your husband's library. The title of the book was *The Real Government.* This is page seventy-one of that book. Do you see the paragraph bracketed is discussing the forces that supposedly control the U.S. government with strings, 'like puppets'? Can you see what your husband has written on the left side of that paragraph?"

"Yes, it says, 'Adams.' "

"It says Adams with an exclamation point, right?"

"Yes."

"That's what your husband thought about Adams. That he was being controlled by forces outside of the United States government, correct?"

"Not that I'm aware of."

"Well, you are aware, are you not —"

Hackett had enough. "Your Honor, this line of questioning is irrelevant. We're wasting the court's time. This is bordering on harassment."

Rachel countered, "I can explain —"

"Approach the bench," Judge Betancourt said, annoyed both with the questions and Hackett's interruption.

Rachel walked to the side of the judge's bench, as did Hackett. I joined them. The court reporter picked up her reporting machine and walked over to where the judge had wheeled her chair on the side of the bench. The reporter pulled a small slide, like a cutting board, out of the side of the judge's bench and placed the reporting keyboard on it. When she nodded to the judge, the judge said, "Ms. Long, where are you going with this line of questioning? What difference does it make?"

"Your Honor, it is my objective to show that it was Collins's opinion of the president's policies that predisposed him to at least consider causing the accident."

Betancourt looked at me. "Are you seriously trying to put on a case that the pilot of Marine One murdered the president?"

Rachel answered, "I want to leave that

open as a possibility for the jury to consider."

"The jury doesn't get to form its own conclusion unless you have evidence, Ms. Long. What *evidence* do you have? How do you tie the president's policies to Collins's actions?"

"Perhaps at the meeting in Camp David the president was about to make a major policy shift."

"Perhaps?" the judge asked. "That's all you have?"

Hackett hunched his large frame over and tried to contain his fury. "Your Honor, I have been over every exhibit Mr. Nolan listed in the pretrial order. There is nothing in there about some new dramatic development. He had notes in the margins of nearly every book he read. It is *meaningless*. Unless Ms. Long tells us *right now* how she intends to prove this, I would request the Court to instruct her to move to a different area of questioning immediately."

The judge looked at Rachel over her reading glasses. "Ms. Long? What is your proffer?"

"I was hopeful of having some evidence that I don't have."

"So you don't have it."

"That's right, Your Honor, not yet."

"Then you will move on to a different area of questioning immediately. Are you nearly done?"

"Yes, Your Honor."

We returned to our positions, and after a moment the judge said, "You may continue, Ms. Long."

"Thank you, Your Honor. Mrs. Collins, you portrayed your husband as happily married to you. Correct?"

She frowned. "I hope so, because we were."

"And the damages you've claimed in this case, that you want WorldCopter to pay you for the loss of your husband, are in part based on the loss of that relationship, right?"

"Yes."

"Mrs. Collins, isn't it true that your husband slept in a different room from you?"

She looked surprised. "How do you know that, Ms. Long?"

"Is it true or not?"

"Yes. It is true."

"In fact your husband essentially lived in a room separate from your bedroom. His clothes, his books, his desk, his computer, they're all in a different room from you."

She looked annoyed. "Yes, that's true."

"In fact, Mrs. Collins, you're husband

484

didn't sleep with you, did he?"

She fidgeted slightly and responded quietly, " 'Sleep with' as in sleeping in the same bed? Or 'sleep with' as in having sexual relations?"

"He didn't sleep in the same bed with you, did he?"

"No."

"No further questions, Your Honor."

Rachel sat down and looked at the clock. It was two minutes until noon. It was a good way to end. The judge picked up her gavel and said, "We will adjourn at this point for lunch and return —"

Hackett stood up and interrupted, "Your Honor. My redirect will take only the two minutes that remain before lunch. May I complete this witness so that she may be excused from the witness stand?"

"Of course, Mr. Hackett, proceed."

Hackett stood up and without any notes said, "Mrs. Collins, had you and your husband stopped having sexual relations?"

She blushed slightly. "No."

"Did you have sex on a regular basis — without too much detail; was it a normal marital relationship?"

"Very normal."

"Well, then, why was he not sleeping in the same room as you, Mrs. Collins?"

She hesitated, then said, "Because he snored."

The gallery laughed out loud.

Hackett nodded and smiled. "Why did he have all his clothes and his computer and his desk in another room?"

"Out of respect for me. I volunteer with Annapolis Hospice, and my sleeping patterns were very irregular. Sometimes I needed to go to bed very early, sometimes I needed to sleep late. He didn't want to disturb me with the clicking of keys on his computer or getting dressed in the morning. So he did it to allow me to rest."

"No further questions," Hackett said.

Rachel jumped back up. "May I, Your Honor? Less than five minutes."

The judge looked at the clock and said, "Make it quick, Ms. Long."

"Thank you, Your Honor." Then to Mrs. Collins: "You slept in separate rooms because he snored?"

"That's right."

"You didn't mention that in your deposition when we asked you about having separate rooms, did you?"

"You didn't ask."

"You knew we wanted to know why you had the arrangement you had, right?"

"I didn't know what you wanted, frankly."

486

"Mrs. Collins, I will represent to you that I have reviewed every page of your husband's medical records. He never mentioned snoring, ever. Are you aware of that?"

"No, but it doesn't surprise me."

"Why is that?"

"I don't think he saw it as a medical problem."

"So the two of you simply accepted that state of affairs?"

"Yes, for now. Then."

"You said you worked for a hospice, right?"

"Yes."

"You mentioned that in your deposition, although not in connection with your husband's separate room. I'd like to show you your volunteer records of Annapolis Hospice. Your Honor, may we have these records marked as next in order?"

Hackett said, "I object, Your Honor. These records were not listed in their exhibit list."

"Impeachment, Your Honor."

"They'll be marked," Betancourt said.

"Mrs. Collins, these records show you hadn't volunteered for Arlington Hospice for more than a year before your husband's death. Correct?"

"I don't know what the records show."

"It's true, isn't it, that you hadn't volunteered there for more than a year before his death?"

"I don't remember."

"Mrs. Collins, you would have the jury believe that the reason you weren't sleeping with your husband was because of a medical condition he never told a doctor about, and out of sensitivity to volunteer work you weren't doing, right?"

"I wouldn't put it like that."

"Nothing further, Your Honor."

Judge Betancourt dismissed us for lunch.

I checked my BlackBerry. Rachel asked, "Any word from Bradley?"

"Nothing. I sent him an e-mail but he didn't respond. I had Tracy call his office too. Didn't respond." I pondered what could possibly have happened to Wayne Bradley as I packed my notes. My thoughts were quickly interrupted by Kathryn, who had come up to counsel table in the middle of the courtroom. Brightman was with her.

Kathryn said, "Mike, let's go back to your office."

"I was just going to grab something over at the cafeteria. I need to prepare for this afternoon's witnesses."

"No, we need to talk about how this is going." She looked around to see if anyone was reading her lips.

Rachel and I headed to our car and then to the office. Kathryn, Brightman, Tripp, even Jeff Turner arrived a few minutes later. Someone had ordered sandwiches, but I was in no mood to eat. I wanted to get back and get ready for our next witnesses. As soon as everyone was in the room, Kathryn closed the door behind Justin. She turned, still standing with her arms folded, and said to me, "Mike, I thought you did okay on the opening statement. You left it a little open as to what our theory was going to be, and based on what I know, that seemed right to me. But now I've watched the first two witnesses, and it isn't working. I don't see the jury identifying with us."

I sat down and leaned back in my chair. "That's what I would expect when their first two witnesses are the most sympathetic witnesses in the world. Look, I know what I'm doing, Kathryn. I just can't change the facts. This case is just getting under way. I can see the stress on your face. I know the press hates us, they think I'm outmatched, you're answering to London, I get it. But you can't panic on me now."

"I am not panicking. But I do want to tweak things a little. Instead of Mark being a passive attorney on the pleadings but not in the courtroom, I've asked him to sit at counsel table during the trial, to take some witnesses, change the feel of things a little."

I couldn't believe my ears. "What?"

"He's been associate counsel since the case was filed. He's just never done anything in court. But he can and I'm asking him to do it now. He has copies of all the expert depositions and has prepared cross-examination outlines of all the plaintiffs' witnesses, including the experts. I'd like him to do those cross-examinations and to also perhaps do the closing arguments, we'll see about that. But I want him involved and I want him at counsel table."

"Do not do this, Kathryn. It's going to look like desperation to the jury, and to the press. It's going to look like you're cutting my legs out from under me."

"I'm propping you *up,* not cutting your legs out from under you. We've got to make some changes here, Mike, because we're going down."

I was so pissed I couldn't even speak for a minute. This was exactly what we shouldn't do. "This isn't coming from you, is it?"

"That doesn't matter."

I stood. "It does to me. Is this from you?"

"I agree with it."

"It's London, isn't it? They're over there on Lime Street watching the legal experts on television and panicking. Did they call you at the end of this morning's session?"

"I talk to them at the end of every session, so, yes, they did call. But this is what we're going to do."

I tossed my pen onto the table. "Whatever you say."

She could tell I was peeved. "Well, do you have a plan, Mike? A plan to get us from here to the end of the trial with something to tell the jury?"

"Our experts are still busting their asses, and you know that. I expected to hear from Wayne Bradley this morning, but he's gone radio silent. I also expected to hear from Curtis, but I haven't yet. He's trying to find the witness Tinny was supposed to give me, but Tinny got murdered. So we're stuck. There's just lot of weird stuff going on right now, Kathryn, and I'm not really sure what's happening."

"Well," Kathryn said, still annoyed, "if you don't start laying this out soon, then Mark will have to take the lead and finish the trial."

I didn't even want to be having the conversation. "I need to go prepare for this afternoon's witnesses."

Kathryn wasn't about to let me sting her. "The next two witnesses are Hackett's experts. Mark will be handling those."

I thought Rachel was going to come out of her skin.

I turned toward Brightman reluctantly. He had a notebook perfectly prepared with outlines for each expert witness. He had his hands folded on top of it. I asked him, "You need anything from me?"

"No, I prepared cross-examinations in case I was called on to do them." I stood up and Rachel followed me.

32

The afternoon dragged on forever. When Brightman sat at the counsel table on the other side of Rachel, a lot of whispering and scratching of pencils came from the journalists. He had never appeared at any proceeding before, although his name was on the pleadings. The legal press wondered whether I was being elbowed out of the way in the middle of trial. They loved the reputation drama that surrounded every major trial. I sat there dutifully taking notes like a cub associate as Hackett put on two expert witnesses that afternoon: his economist, who testified about the president's likely career earnings, and his accident reconstructionist. Hackett was being smart. First build the sympathy with the widows, then show the jury the value, *then* you explain the liability. Easy stuff first. Brightman's cross-examinations were fine. The reconstructionist did as expected and essentially recited the preliminary NTSB report, adopting their conclusions and performing retests or identical analysis where necessary to be able to testify about it. He was polished and left the jury believing everything he said was correct.

We went back to our large conference room at the end of the day. The power had shifted to Brightman. He was fielding all the questions, telling everyone how he was going to handle the next day's witnesses.

I interjected into the discussion, "Kathryn, one thing we might consider is a settlement offer."

She was shocked. "We're at the absolute nadir of our *case;* you think now's the time to approach them?"

I nodded. "We need to get the conversation started."

Brightman shook his head. "I couldn't disagree more. I'd suggest we motor through this. If they want to try to come after us for punitive damages, maybe that would be the time to approach Hackett. Then we'll —"

"No, you don't get it. We found one of the tip weights."

The room want completely silent. "What?" Kathryn stared at me, looking betrayed. "When? When were you going to tell me?"

"Couple of weeks ago. Went up in the tree.

494

There was a tip weight embedded in the branch. Half of a tip weight. It had fractured."

"Meaning it failed and caused the accident?"

Brightman was speechless. "You started this trial knowing there was critical evidence against us . . . and didn't tell the other side or the court? Are you kidding me? Is *that* your fourth theory? It's all our fault and we're screwed?"

Kathryn looked pale. "What are you doing, Mike? This could get you sanctioned. The court could enter judgment against WorldCopter for this alone."

"I thought I'd hear from Bradley. I asked him to run some additional tests on it before we turned it over. Nothing destructive. I just can't get ahold of him. I'm afraid for him, with what happened to Tinny. So I thought we should approach Hackett now, with him thinking we just don't like the evidence. Once he gets wind of this broken tip weight, he'll never settle."

Kathryn slouched in her chair, rested her head against the wall with her eyes closed, and said, "Call Hackett."

I dialed the hotel where Hackett was staying, where he had leased one of the ballrooms as his "war room." It was probably as much square footage as my whole office building. I asked for Hackett's ballroom. One of Hackett's associates picked up the phone.

"Hi, this is Mike Nolan. Is Tom Hackett there please?"

"Mike Nolan?"

"Right."

"Um, yeah. Hold on one second." I heard his hand go over the receiver. Kathryn indicated to me to put it on speakerphone, which I did. Hackett came on the line.

"This is Tom Hackett, is that you, Mike?"

"Good evening, Tom, yes, it is."

There was a pause. "You've got me on the speakerphone. Is there anyone else in the room listening to this?"

"Yes. That's why you're on speakerphone. I want them to hear you."

"Please tell me the name of everybody in the room or this conversation is over."

I rolled my eyes, then went around the room and told him everyone who was there.

He said, "An august group. I am honored. What can I do for you?"

"When you and I last spoke on the telephone, we had discussed settlement. I wondered if you had any interest in further discussions."

"Are you serious?"

"Quite."

"So let me get this right. I made a settlement demand at the outset of this case for one billion dollars. You rejected that and essentially told me I was out of my mind. That's fine. I can live with that. But now, after you've had your head handed to you in jury selection, the first few witnesses, and the experts, you come asking to talk settlement?"

"Look, before we get all the way through this trial and send this case to the jury, we wanted to call and see if you've come to your senses yet and are prepared to discuss settlement."

"*My* senses? I made a settlement demand to you a long time ago, and I am not about to discuss settlement over the phone. But if you and Kathryn come over here right now, we can discuss our positions and see if there is any point in negotiations. But you must be here within fifteen minutes. I have work to do and a case to try."

I glanced at Kathryn, who shrugged, then nodded reluctantly. "We'll be right there."

I drove Kathryn to the hotel. Neither of us said a word. We parked in the hotel parking lot, went in through the lobby, and back to the ballroom, where I had attended numerous bar receptions and balls. A security guard standing at the door recognized us and opened the door. When we walked into the room, I was stunned. It was the most impressive high-tech legal setup I had ever seen. Desks with oversize flatscreen monitors were everywhere. A big-screen TV in the middle in the back — had to be seventy-two inches — had been split into four quadrants to see four networks that were following the trial, including Court TV, CNN, MSNBC, and FOX. They were all giving it essentially twenty-four-hour coverage. Hackett undoubtedly had a PR person feeding the media theories and information all the time. That person was probably sitting in the ballroom as we entered.

A huge white screen on the right side with an ELMO set up was probably used to practice the use of the trial exhibits to make sure they projected well across a large room like the courtroom. A PowerPoint projector sat next to the ELMO and a DVD player. In this mini-court, Hackett and others could practice witness examination and evidence presentation. All his associates and paralegals had their own desks and computers and were busily working. In the middle was a square conference table with six chairs set up around it. We stood there waiting for someone to recognize us. Finally, Greg Bass came over and greeted us. He pointed us to the conference table. We walked to it and stood by it. Presently, Hackett came out from behind a large black curtain or screen that I had not previously noticed but which undoubtedly constituted his office. The aluminum framing had high-quality black curtains that set up a square-walled office that took up an eighth of the ballroom in the corner. Bright lights could be seen shining from behind the curtain. Hackett had his coat off and his tie loosened. He looked more fit than I thought he was. He walked over to the conference table and extended his hand to Kathryn. "Good evening, Ms. Galbraith. I'm glad you could come over."

She shook his hand. "My pleasure."

He turned to me and shook my hand. "Mike, good to see you."

"Evening."

"Please, sit down," he said. "Would you like some coffee or tea?"

Kathryn and I both shook our heads.

"All right, then let's get down to business. You called me about settlement. What do you have in mind?"

Kathryn glanced at me, leaned forward on the table with her hands folded, and said, "We're not stupid. I realize that so far the evidence has not gone our way."

Hackett tried not to smile.

"We think that will change when it's our turn to put on evidence, but even if it doesn't, the value of your cases will not change. I'm prepared to offer you the full policy limits for settling all the cases. Two hundred fifty million dollars."

Hackett shook his head slowly. "That's a quarter of my demand before I filed, before discovery. This accident was your client's fault. That's just as clear as it could be now. The value of the cases hasn't gone *down*. You just heard my economist testify about what President Adams would have earned after his second term. This was not a president who was going to sit around as a former president and play golf or build rocking chairs. If he gave a speech every night, he could earn a million a week!" Hackett leaned forward for emphasis. "He was going to change the way former presidents lived. He was going to contribute to the economy and become a CEO of a major corporation. Kathryn, did you not hear what my economist said? Think Exxon. You know how much the CEO of Exxon made last year?" Hackett continued without hesitating, "Well, I'll tell you. He made three point six in salary, three point nine in bonuses, and twenty-eight in stock awards. That's in *millions,* by the way. That's a total of thirty-five and a half million dollars for one year. You think maybe President Adams wouldn't have done a stinky oil company? How about Wal-Mart then. Thirteen point one million dollars. You think maybe a bank? Citigroup perhaps? Try thirty-three million dollars. Maybe he'd run a hedge fund in New York. Some of those guys pull down five hundred million dollars a year. Maybe something more family-friendly? Mouse Ears, say? Eight million. You want to know what a former president will make? Well, how about Clinton? While his wife was running in the Democratic primaries, she disclosed their tax returns. Seven years, one hundred nine million dollars — and not much of that is from her Senate salary. So that's not too bad. I think you get the idea. Multiply any of those by his remaining work life, and you get the idea of why my settlement demand is going nowhere but up.

"Then you have the great American hero, the Marine pilot of Marine One, who was shot in the jaw in Iraq and came back to fly the president around. You've got your crack attorney here accusing him of being a homosexual or something —"

"I said nothing of the kind."

"Yeah? Well, you sure implied there was something mischievous or unhealthy about their relationship. So on the one hand you've got President Adams, who was going to set a new world record for earnings after leaving the presidency, and you've got the most sympathetic plaintiffs in the history of American civil litigation. So two hundred and fifty million dollars is a *joke,* Kathryn. We'll get six hundred million dollars in economic damages, minimum. Then the jury will double it for general damages, loss of companionship, society, and consortium. That's one point two billion. And then we'll go back and ask them for punitives. My prediction is they'll award twice what they already did, for another two point four billion, a total of three point six billion. I could be wrong. They might use a multiplier of, say, ten, and award twenty-four billion for punitive damages. This jury is just waiting to punish this evil foreign corporation that killed their president. As you both know, under *Campbell vs. State Farm,* the Supreme Court believes the multiplier of actual damages to punitives must be less than ten in order to comply with constitutional due process. Okay. I'll give you six — even though I'm going to ask for more than that from the jury at the end of this trial. Six times three point six is twenty-one point six billion dollars. So you want my demand? My demand to settle this case tonight — for all plaintiffs — twenty *billion* dollars."

Kathryn was stunned. "You're out of your mind."

"Really? Who's been right so far, Kathryn? You could have resolved the case before it got filed. Your policy, a bunch thrown in by WorldCopter — which seems only fair — and it would have been done. But as usual, you weren't thinking big enough. You thought this would be some ten-million-dollar case and didn't take my demand seriously. Fine!" Hackett threw his hands up. "You don't have to. But don't come crying to me now saying I'm being unreasonable. You had your chance."

I was furious. He was toying with us, trying to humiliate us. I felt uncontrollable anger welling up, which if left unchecked would result in my punching him in the face. I looked over his head at the curtain behind him to avoid looking at his smug expression.

Kathryn replied, "This conversation is over. What you've demanded is insane. I don't see the point in even offering the policy to you. So even if we could —"

"We're done. Here." He grabbed a piece

of paper and wrote *$20 billion* on it. "Give this to your insured. To WorldCopter. Tell them this is my demand." He gave it to me. "You are obligated under the ethical code, Mr. Nolan, to convey this offer to your clients. To WorldCopter. It will be open an unpredictably short time, and I will withdraw it when I feel like it. Since you said the conversation is over, Kathryn, I will take you at your word. Good night."

He walked back to his curtained office.

Kathryn and I left and headed back to my office in a silence even deeper than that which had enveloped us on our way to the meeting. As I pulled into my parking spot in front of my building, my secret cell phone buzzed in the glove box. I reached across Kathryn's skirt and opened it. I pulled out the phone and looked at the screen on the front, which said new text message. I opened the phone and read, *May have found something. WB.*

When I headed home that night, I texted Bradley from my phone and asked him for clarification, which was not forthcoming. I then called him, trying to figure out where he was and what he was doing, and again, no response. That made me wonder if he had been kidnapped and his cell phone was now being used to torment me. Tinny Byrd killed, Wayne Bradley kidnapped. Not likely. But it was hard to get to sleep.

I spent most of that night wondering what Bradley had found and where he was. If I had thought about other things, I might have seen coming what happened the next morning. I'd have wondered why Hackett had insisted on our coming over to his "office." I assumed it was to impress us.

When I got to the office at six thirty the next morning, Dolores was there and handed me *USA Today* and the *Baltimore Sun.* Both had nearly identical headlines: WORLDCOPTER BEGGING FOR MERCY?

Hackett had undoubtedly notified his PR hack, who almost certainly called a reporter or two and told them to station themselves somewhere in the hotel lobby or outside the hotel. They saw Kathryn and me approach and were left to speculate on why the two of us would be at Hackett's office at ten o'clock at night in between two important trial days. The only conceivable reason would be to discuss settlement. Which, of course, was true. I could just hear the conversation with the PR hack and the journalists. Be where? In front of the hotel. Why? Interesting people will arrive. What people? You'll see. Why are they coming? To testify? They're part of the trial. To discuss the trial? At ten o'clock at night? To *settle?* No comment.

WorldCopter had gone ballistic when Kathryn had told them that they could settle the case by chipping in a mere $19.75 billion dollars to WorldCopter's insurance-policy limits of $250 million. Wednesday of that week was perhaps the worst day. Hackett had completed his case and he rested. Nothing had gone wrong, we hadn't really dented any of his witnesses or experts, nor had we challenged his theory, at least during his case. The media was proclaiming victory all the way around and wondering why we didn't just pay Hackett whatever he was asking for. Of course they didn't know what he was asking for, and if they had, they would have been horrified, or at least I hope they would have. And Bradley was nowhere to be found.

That night though, things turned. The usual weary group was in our conference room when I received an e-mail on my BlackBerry. It was the word that I had told Bradley to e-mail me when I needed to go outside and check my cell phone in my car.

I excused myself as if I were going to the bathroom, walked down the stairs, and out to my car. I sat down in the passenger seat and opened the glove box. I took out the phone and read the text message: *Call me ASAP. WB.* I dialed his cell phone and waited for him to pick up. I could tell by the background noise that he was driving when he answered. Before he even greeted me, he said, "Mike. You're not going to believe this. Are you at the office?"

"I'm sitting in my car. Where the hell have you been?"

"I'll tell you all about it. Can you meet me at my lab?"

"Sure, I guess. What do you have?"

"I've got to show you. I'm heading there now. When can you get there?"

"I don't know, maybe forty-five minutes."

"See you then."

"Oh, one other thing. You've got to call WorldCopter. You know that other Marine One, the helicopter they have in their hangar out there, the one behind that Plexiglas wall?"

"What about it?"

"You gotta get me in there. Tonight. With tools. Get whatever permission you need. Get Marcel, get whoever you need. Have them meet us out there. And don't tell anybody else. Nobody. I mean nobody."

"I'll see what I can do. I've got to sneak out of here somehow. See you at your lab."

I hung up and grabbed some paper out of the glove compartment. I wrote notes to Marcel and Rachel: *Meet me at the World-Copter hangar at 10:00 PM. No questions. Do not let anyone follow you.* I went back inside and back to the conference room. I said to Brightman, "So you're going to start with our meteorologist tomorrow morning, just laying the groundwork on the severity of the storm and the like?"

"Yes. I'd guess that's the safest way to begin. We need to warm the jury up to the idea of listening to what we have to say. The meteorologist has nothing controversial, so I think we'll start with him."

"Got it. Look, I told Wayne Bradley to be here tomorrow morning at nine o'clock, so I think I'll stay back and prepare him. We can put him on second?"

Brightman hesitated. "Maybe. We haven't really talked about who was going to take him. I was kind of assuming I would."

"I think I need to take him."

"I thought he'd gone quiet on us."

"I finally reached him. He'll be ready. I just want to prepare him, and then we'll have him ready to go in the afternoon."

Brightman had his arms folded and tapped his lips with his finger as if he were thinking. I knew what he was really thinking: how does he break it to me that I'm not going to do anything for the rest of the trial? I was going to let him think that as long as he wanted. As long as I had time to do what I needed to do. I asked Brightman to put a list of order of witnesses on the board so we could all agree how we were going to present the case. Everyone's eyes turned to the whiteboard, and I slipped the notes to Rachel and Marcel. They both read the notes and glanced at me with quizzical looks. I nodded, confirming I meant what I said.

I told Brightman that since he was prepared for the morning and I wouldn't be needed till the afternoon, I was going to catch up on some sleep and excused myself.

I headed toward my house, then turned sharply and floored my Volvo to head toward Bradley's lab.

33

I raced through the darkness trying to imagine what Bradley had found and why he needed to meet with me at his lab. His lab was halfway to Washington from Annapolis, in Bowie, Maryland, about a half hour away. We could go on to the World-Copter plant from there no problem.

It was a little hard to find, but I typed the address into my GPS so I wouldn't miss the turn, an unmarked road that led deep into the woods. I found the turn and kept my bright lights on as I hurried down the dark pavement. It was about a mile from the main road to his lab. It looked unusually bright as I approached the end of the road. My cell phone rang, and I picked it up.

It was Bradley. He sounded panicked. "Where are you?"

"I'm on the road to your —"

"Stop! Don't go down the road!" The tone of his voice was alarming.

I hit the brakes. "Why not?"

"My lab is on fire! The flames are fifty feet high. I'm heading back toward the main road. They may be there, Mike. There may be somebody waiting for us there!"

I felt a quick jolt of adrenaline. "On fire? What happened?"

"I don't know. I was driving down —"

"Is that you driving away?"

"Yes. Stop, that's me right in front of you."

He stopped his Honda Pilot right next to me. I opened my window. "What started the fire?"

"Not what, who. They're after us, Mike. They're onto us. I was staying away, trying to use other labs or make due. But I had to go back to get something. They know we're going to blow this thing sky-high, and they're trying to stop us." He looked in his rearview mirror and around in the darkness.

"We don't know what happened. Maybe somebody left the coffeepot on."

"No, Mike. We don't leave coffeepots on. It's the safest lab in the country. Somebody thinks wc found something and burned the place down. Either to burn the evidence or to warn us. Or to get me."

I listened to the engines of our idling cars and looked at the glow at the end of the road. "They know the critical evidence is the tip weight. You still have it?"

Bradley nodded, with his mouth open.

"They wouldn't know that. But they would know it is made of bronze, or some other type of metal that's not likely to burn in a fire. It would make it through a fire, right?"

"Depending on how hot the fire is, but generally."

"That means they're talking to us. They don't want to kill us — we're too obvious, too much in the public eye. They just want us to shut up and let this case take its course, us losing and them fading into the shadows."

"You think it's the other attorney?"

"Hackett? He's sinister enough, but I don't know if he'd go that low. Can you show me at WorldCopter what you found?"

Bradley nodded, regaining his composure. "It would have been better here, but I have a portable in the back here." He indicated the back of his pilot.

"Let's go. Stay right behind me. If you see anything suspicious, flash your brights."

I pulled up in front of the WorldCopter facility and stopped quickly. I was sure we hadn't been followed; of course, I'd thought that before, every day, and now realized I was probably wrong. Rachel and Marcel were waiting in the parking lot. Bradley pulled up right behind me. He got out of his pilot. He looked disheveled, with his cuffed khakis hanging up on top of old brown leather boots that were two-thirds unlaced, and a large Hawaiian shirt overhanging his portliness. His reading glasses dangled around his neck, and his hair was everywhere.

"So what do you have, Wayne?"

Marcel and Rachel greeted him, but Bradley was all business. He pointed to the back of his pilot. He opened up the back hatch, and there was what could only be described as a traveling lab. The backseats had either been taken out or laid really flat, and he seemed to have built out the back with snugly fitting cabinets and padded toolboxes. At the very back was what appeared to be a flat bottom; but he reached down, pulled on an invisible handle, and a table came up to his waist level. He reached over to the left, opened a door to one of his fixed cabinets, and pulled out a leather bag, or pouch, the kind of pouch you might expect to hold coins in the eighteenth century. He reached to the right side of the Pilot, which was still running, and pulled up the extension arm of a halogen desk light, which now sat directly over the table in front of him, illuminating the black felt surface. He opened the drawstring of the leather bag and dumped out the contents. It was the tip weight, but it had been further dismantled. I tried to control the panic rising in my chest.

"Shit, Wayne. You've destroyed it! We'll never get this thing into evidence."

"Bear with me here, Mike."

"Marcel, Rachel, this is one of the tip weights from Marine One. Marcel, see this serial number here. We can only see four of the six numbers, but they're the last four, and these are among the numbers of one of the tip weights that are missing from your list of known tip weights. We found it embedded in a tree at the accident scene."

Marcel leaned over, lifted the shattered disk up to his eyes, and examined the tip weight carefully. "How long have you had this? Why wasn't I told?"

Bradley nodded. "We weren't sure what it meant. Look at this." Everyone huddled under the upraised rear hatch of his Pilot with the bright halogen light shining on the tip weight of Marine One. Bradley pulled down a large magnifying glass that was attached to a boom from the ceiling of the pilot. He pulled it down and held up the tip weight, now brilliantly illuminated behind the lens. He took a small metal instrument like a dentist's pick, although straight, and pointed to a section of the tip weight. "See this?"

We all squinted and looked hard. I thought I saw what he was pointing at. He continued, "See this?" Bradley waited for recognition to hit us. A small window was cut half the depth into the tip weight, showing a small wire.

I was suddenly thunderstruck by the implications. "Bradley, is that what I think it is?"

He smiled and nodded. "It is. I tested it."

I closed my eyes in disbelief. "Are you *shitting* me?"

"I shit you not."

I put my hands to my head as my thoughts raced to help me understand what I was looking at. "What does this mean? What do we do with this?"

Bradley put the pieces back in the leather pouch, placed it in his pocket, turned off the halogen light, put the magnifying glass back up where it belonged, stowed the shelf, and said, "You need to get me in to see the helicopter sitting behind that Plexiglas wall inside. If my theory is right, we can confirm it right now."

I wasn't following him. "How?"

"This tip weight didn't end up on Marine One by accident. There have to be more just like it. Probably many."

Bradley turned toward Marcel. "Have you looked into this helicopter?"

Marcel said, "In what regard?"

"Any of the blades replaced in the last three months?"

"I don't know. Probably. They replace blades all the time. The slightest nick and they replace a blade on Marine One."

Bradley nodded. "What I'm thinking may be true even if it was more than three months. But if less than three months, I think we could be almost sure. You've got to get us in there, Marcel. We've got to get access to that helicopter, and I need to take the end cap off of the blade that's been put on most recently."

"They'll never let us touch it. It's a Marine One helicopter. We don't have clearances."

I shook my head. "Make it happen, Marcel. Call Jean Claude if you have to."

Marcel shrugged and threw out his chin. "Let us try."

We closed the Pilot, walked into World-Copter headquarters, and persuaded the guard to let us go back to the hangar area.

Then we were confronted with the Plexiglas wall and a humorless guard. Marcel pleaded with him and begged for access to the helicopter. Not a chance. Marcel got the head of the Marine One maintenance program out of bed and begged for access. No. To allow anyone to even touch the helicopter without a Yankee White clearance would ground it forever unless they completely dismantled it and reassembled it. No way. Marcel wasn't giving up.

He continued up the chain of command, to the president of WorldCopter U.S. He was persuaded, but said it wasn't his call. He said we needed to get a hold of Jean Claude. Jean Claude was staying in a private home that had been rented in the hills of Annapolis for $10,000 a week. The mansion was owned by some mysterious businessman who had some indirect relationship to a shipping line that no one seemed to know the name of. Jean Claude's phone was off. Marcel grew more frustrated. He called everyone he knew, including Jean Claude's personal secretary in France. She was sound asleep when he called and was annoyed when he awoke her. When he explained the importance of what he was doing, she happily agreed to contact Jean Claude and seemed to have some other secret number for him. We waited and stared at the brightly lit Marine One helicopter sitting behind the Plexiglas wall, hoping against hope that we'd be able to test Bradley's theory.

Marcel's phone rang. He spoke in French and seemed pleased. He handed his phone to the head of security, who stood as he listened to the president of WorldCopter SA tell him to allow access to this group even though it would mean losing the use of this helicopter as Marine One. The guard threw the bolt electronically and pulled the heavy Plexiglas door toward him. We walked inside the restricted area, very aware of the intense lights and scrutiny that were on us. The security guard had called one of the other security guards, who had brought a video camera and was filming everything we did. Fine with me.

Bradley quickly grabbed a ladder and pulled it over to the helicopter. He turned to Marcel. "Which blade was put on more recently?"

Marcel said, "I will check. Do you want to take off the end cap?"

"The end cap and the tip weights."

"I'll check the maintenance records and bring the tools."

Marcel disappeared toward the back of

the hangar, reviewed the maintenance records, and came back with two hand tools. "The blue blade was replaced forty days before the crash." Marcel looked at the rotor hub, saw the blue marking on one of the blades, and put the ladder underneath the end of it. He labored up the ladder and removed the Allen screws that held on the end cap. He pulled it off, handed it down to me. I set it on the floor, well out of the way. I looked up and saw the tip weights properly placed with a large nut holding them onto a bolt. Marcel loosened the nut, pulled it off, and removed the four tip weights that had been attached to the blade when it had been balanced in France. Marcel handed the tip weights to Bradley and climbed down from the ladder. Marcel asked, "Is that all we need?"

"That's it," Bradley said excitedly. "Let's go back to my car."

We exited the sterile environments of the hangared Marine One and waved to the security guards as we hurried outside to the pilot. Bradley set up his portable lab and put a small block of metal on the tray. He put the tip weight on top of it and picked up a chisel and a hammer.

Marcel was horrified. "You're not going to destroy it, are you?"

"I'm going to break it open." Bradley raised his hammer and cracked the chisel into the tip weight, breaking it in half.

I got no sleep that night. And contrary to what I had told Brightman, I wasn't going to go meet Bradley the next morning. He was coming to my house. I still couldn't take the chance that the office was bugged and that Hackett would know what I was doing before I pulled the trigger. Bradley had agreed to stay at the first hotel he encountered, pay cash, and come to my house for breakfast at eight o'clock the following morning. He was to keep the tip weights in his possession at all times, including inside the hotel room. He was not to leave them in his car, and he was to have a separate bag for the tip weights taken from the Marine One at the WorldCopter hangar.

I was up banging out a new outline on my computer before the sun even hinted at the horizon. I stayed there while Debbie prepared breakfast for the kids, got them ready for school, and they left.

He arrived at eight. I let him in, brought him to the den, and got him a cup of coffee. He looked confident and rested. I felt confident and unrested. We walked through his testimony. He understood. He was ready to go. One pocket held the tip weight from the crashed Marine One, the other pocket held the tip weights from the intact Marine One.

I heard the front door open, which was a surprise because Debbie always came in through the back after she parked her car. I glanced out through the den's French doors and saw Debbie. She looked concerned. I excused myself.

"What's up?" I asked.

Debbie looked at the front door and put her car keys in her purse. "There's a woman standing in front of our house who said she needs to see you."

I rolled my eyes. "Reporter."

"She looks very unsure of herself, very much out of her element. She kept looking around."

I walked toward the front door. "What does she look like?"

"Black, pretty; early fifties."

I looked out the thin window next to the front door. I saw the woman Debbie had described. I'd never seen her before. I checked my watch. It was nine fifteen. The trial was back under way, any journalists would be there. "I'll see what this is about. Did you talk to her?"

"She said she needed to talk to Mike

Nolan. I told her I was your wife, and she said she could only talk to you."

"Come with me."

We walked out of the front of our house and went to the woman on the sidewalk. She looked uneasy as I approached her. "Hi, I'm Mike Nolan. My wife says you need to see me."

She nodded. She handed me an envelope. I looked into her eyes, but she wouldn't look at me.

"What is this?" I took the envelope and saw that my name was written on the outside, in what was probably a man's handwriting.

"He said to give this to you."

"Who did?"

"My husband."

I looked at Debbie, but neither of us had any idea what this woman was talking about. "Who's your husband?"

"Tinny."

I felt a shot of fear. "You're Tinny Byrd's wife?"

"Yes."

Debbie glanced at me and reached to her. "Won't you please come in?"

Mrs. Byrd nodded her head.

As Debbie walked next to her, she asked, "What's your first name?"

"Cherie."

We went into the house and I signaled to Bradley that it would be a minute. He continued to study some documents that he had spread on his lap. We took Cherie Byrd to the kitchen, where she sat at our table. Debbie poured her a cup of coffee, which she took gladly. I asked her, "Did you drive from D.C. this morning?"

"Yes."

"How'd you find where I lived?"

"Tinny had your address on that envelope. I just used MapQuest."

"Thanks for coming. What made you want to come find me?"

"Tinny was mur—"

"I know. I'm so sorry. It's so . . . horrible. Police have any leads?"

"Nothing. He was working on a lot of cases. It could be anything." She clutched her purse to her chest, then looked into my eyes for the first time. "It could have been this case. I always told him something like this was going to happen. He wouldn't listen to me. He just kept doing it, living his life, thinking he was bulletproof and smarter than everybody —"

"I'm really sorry. He was a good friend of mine. I can't believe I never met you."

"I know. He spoke of you."

"So why did you come see me?"

She nodded her head and relaxed slightly. "I've been going through his things. One of them was our wall safe. He kept it in his closet, and I never went into it. I didn't even know what was in it. I'd forgotten the combination to it because I'd only done it once when he put it in. But I remembered he wrote the combination on the bottom of the drawer of my dresser with a black-ink pen so if I ever needed to get into that safe, all I ever needed to do was turn over my drawers. That's what he said, just turn over your drawers and you can get it. So I remembered that and found the combination and opened that wall safe yesterday. There were all kinds of things in there that I don't have any idea what they were. Some things I did know and didn't want to know. Like a gun and some bullets and some cash money. Then I found this envelope. He had a yellow sticky on it that looked pretty new. The sticky said — hold on, I've brought it with me." She reached into her purse and pulled out a folded yellow sticky. She tried to unfold it, but the adhesion was too strong. I looked at it and read, "If anything happens to me, give this to Mike Nolan."

The envelope that I held had my name and address on it. It was a letter-size, not thick. I asked, "Did you open this?"

She shook her head. "No. He told me to bring it to you and I have. It's out of my hands and into yours. So I think I'll go now."

"Wait one minute. I want you to be here when I open it."

She was hesitant, but said nothing.

I broke the seal of the Scotch tape on the back flap and opened the envelope. I pulled out a piece of paper and a key. On the piece of paper was written, *If you're reading this, something has happened to me. I can't tell you what, 'cause I don't know. I also can't tell you if it was related to this case. I hope not. And I hope I didn't make a fool of myself, but I told you I'd take care of you so I'm going to.* Then in large block letters he had written, *J. Mark Grosvenor.* Underneath was a home address, cell phone number, home telephone number, and pager. Taped to the bottom of the page was a key. I pulled the key off and looked at it. I wasn't sure what it was. I held it up. "Do you recognize this?"

Cherie took her reading glasses out of her purse and examined the key. "Well, I do. It's a key for a safety-deposit box at our bank."

"Is this from your safety-deposit box?"

She shook her head. "No, ours is a different number."

"You think this is another safety-deposit box at your bank?"

"Looks like it to me."

I looked at my watch and considered the implications of putting Bradley on the witness stand with no preparation. If anyone could do it, it was him. "Take me there. Now. We don't have any time to lose."

I stood up, put the key in my pocket, and said to Debbie, "Would you watch Wayne? Don't let him out of your sight, except for the bathroom. Seriously. Literally. Do *not* let him out of your sight. If anybody comes to the door looking for me or him, or anybody else, nobody's home. I'll call you on your cell phone, otherwise don't talk to *anybody.* Don't answer the house phone. Understand?" She looked alarmed at my intensity.

"I understand, but explain this to me."

"Later." I turned to Cherie. "Let's go. I'll drive."

As I started my car, I pulled out my cell phone from my glove box and texted Rachel, who was sitting next to Brightman in trial. She was probably pulling her hair out. I told her to call me at her first break and I headed off to D.C.

It was an awkward drive. I was actually

surprised I'd never met Tinny's wife. Tinny talked about her in glowing terms all the time, yet I'd never met her. I didn't know how to even start a conversation with her. I finally thanked her again for going out of her way to track me down and give me something that she didn't know was significant. But she knew her husband well enough to know that if he thought it important enough to put in a safe and ask her to do it after his death, it was important enough for her to actually do it. She related that it had actually done her good to get out of the house and get out of D.C. to see the rest of the world. She hadn't been outside the District in almost two years. Tinny was always going outside the District in his Corvette, jetting here and there in airplanes, but she preferred to stay home in their small house. I asked her to tell me about their life together, the fun they'd had together. She relaxed and told me stories of their courtship and marriage, their early days when he was work-obsessed and she was repeatedly pregnant. They'd been in love for thirty years, and she still was. When he was killed, her life had been gutted and she would never be the same.

As we drove along, I continued to look at the cars around me. I noticed one that had been behind me the entire way. A fairly new Dodge Caravan. It had stayed fairly far back most of the time. But once it had come close enough for me to get a look at the driver. I had seen young Asian men drive all sorts of cars, but never a Dodge Caravan.

By the time we got to D.C. and headed toward the Northeast section, near Mercedes' Grill, I had almost forgotten about the trial. That was refreshing. As we turned down Tennessee Avenue, she said, "The bank is up there on the right."

We turned into the parking lot, found a spot, and walked into the bank. I followed her straight to the back left corner of the lobby, where they had a light wooden wall with a glass door that separated the safety-deposit boxes from the rest of the bank. She pressed a buzzer next to the door. A young black man appeared on the other side of the glass, recognized her, and smiled. He pressed a button on his side of the glass that released the door, and he pulled it open. We stepped through. "Hello, Ronald," she said, shaking his hand gently. "This is my friend Mike Nolan."

Ronald said, "Hello, Mrs. Byrd. I'm glad to see you. I'm really sorry about Tinny." His face clouded as he shook my hand as an afterthought. "I just can't believe it. I'm so sorry."

She nodded and fought back a tear. "Thank you. Would you give us a hand? I'm here to open a safety-deposit box."

"Yours and Tinny's? I wondered when you were going to come for it."

"No. Another one. Show him the key, Mike."

I handed Ronald the key, which he examined.

"Sure, let me check it. Was it listed under Tinny's name?"

"I don't know. I assume so."

He returned with the signature card in his hand. "It's in Tinny's name and yours." Ronald looked embarrassed. "But we've got a problem. The only signature on the card is Tinny's. To give you access I have to have the owner's signature."

I couldn't believe my ears. I said, "He gave me the key to this box and told me to retrieve something. I'm in the middle of a trial, and it may be evidence. Don't you recognize me?"

Ronald looked at me and suddenly realized who I was. "You're the attorney in the trial about the president's helicopter."

"Exactly. And Tinny was my investigator. He'd found something critically important, was killed, and left a note for his wife —" I pulled it out of my pocket. "Here's the note he left for her to give me in case he died. He wants me to have access to that box."

Ronald read it and returned Tinny's note to me. "That's amazing. There must be something really important in there, but I'm sorry, I can't let you into the box. The bank has rules. I can't change them."

I felt that old nemesis of mine, that white anger that I sometimes had to fight, raging up inside me. I had to pause for a moment. "Ronald, this is not the time to be a bureaucratic hero and screw me with rules. Let us into that safety-deposit box."

I had miscalculated. He felt the power that came from being able to deny an angry person his strongest desire. "I can't, Mr. Nolan. Sorry."

"You'd better get the manager."

Ronald said, "It won't make any difference. He's the one that told me never to change these rules. But worse, he's out."

I detected just a slight bit of joy in Ronald. It was total bullshit and I was not going to be deterred. "Is there anyone here senior to you, Ronald?"

"Assistant manager. Debra Hastings. She's over there."

I looked around, saw Debra, went back to the glass door, buzzed the button I'd seen him buzz, and slammed it open. I marched across to Debra's desk and interrupted a conversation she was having that was undoubtedly extremely important, probably somebody opening a new checking account. "Ms. Hastings. As the assistant manager, I need your help with a safety-deposit box immediately. This is an emergency. Ronald asked me to get you."

She looked at me like I was a lunatic. "I'm with a customer, sir, you'll have to wait —"

"No, I'm not waiting for anything. Get up, come with me right now to the safety-deposit-box area. I must insist."

"Sir, are you threatening me?"

"No. I am not. I am begging you."

She looked at this customer sitting in a chair that was right next to me who was trying to inch away from me and said, "Will you excuse me for just a minute, I'll be right back."

"No problem. Take your time," the customer said.

Debra got up and followed me to the safety-deposit-box area. She put her access card in front of the reader, and the glass door opened away from us. We walked in. Debra walked over to where Ronald and Cherie were silently standing. Debra was about forty-five, thin, and homely. I said to her, "My name is Mike Nolan. I'm an attorney involved in the trial over the crash of the president's helicopter. Do you recognize me?"

She looked at me with shock on her face. "Yes, I do."

"I had a private investigator working for me, Mr. Tinny Byrd. You may have heard they found his remains. He'd been murdered and thrown to the dogs. Do you remember that?"

"Yes, I do. That was —"

"This is his wife. She found a note in her home safe from Tinny to me that instructed her to bring me a key to the safety-deposit box right over there in your bank. I have that key and asked for access. That access has been denied by my good friend Ronald here. Would you please tell him to give me, or you can authorize it yourself, access to that box with that key that was given to me by the owner of that box?"

She nodded with immediate understanding. "That should be no problem. Do you have the signature card, Ronald?"

He handed it to her and she looked at it. "Only Mr. Byrd's signature is on the card. So he would have to be the one to sign for the box."

I tried to slow down and take a breath.

"Right. He's dead. I just told you that. So is it your belief that no one left on the face of the earth can now open that box?"

She smiled as she understood the implications of my question, but also recognized the simple solution. "Oh, no. It's no problem. His wife can access the account."

I relaxed. "There we go."

Debra continued, "All we need is the death certificate and the documents appointing you executrix of his estate."

I looked at Cherie. She said, "I don't have copies of those on me."

Debra understood. "That's no problem. You and Mr. Nolan can just go get it, and when you get back, then you can have access to the box."

I tried not to scream. "I don't have time for her to go retrieve a copy of the death certificate. I want you to open the box *now*."

"I can't do that."

I wanted to break something, but then a thought occurred to me. I looked at Ronald. "You said the box was in the name of both Mr. and Mrs. Byrd. Right?"

"Yes, sir. But she never signed the signature card."

"But the other owner can add her signature to the account, to the box signature card, at any time, right?"

"That's true."

"Then give it to her now, let her sign it now in your presence."

Ronald shook his head. "Can't do that. The signature has to be notarized."

"Is there a notary in the bank?"

"Yes, Rikki Carlson is a notary."

"Which window?"

"The first —"

I headed to the glass door, pressed the buzzer, and ripped it open and jogged over to the first window. A customer was talking to Rikki. I took her CLOSED sign, and slammed it down in front of him. "This window is closed. Rikki, please come with me and bring your notary kit."

"Sir, I don't know you."

"Debra, the assistant manager, and Ronald, the gentleman at the safety-deposit-box area have asked you to notarize the signature of one of the box owners. It is critically important and you will be right back."

The customer was pissed. "This is ridiculous. Who do you think you are —"

I reached into my pocket, pulled out my wallet, pulled out a $50 bill, and slammed it down in front of him. "Here. Is your two minutes worth fifty bucks? Take it."

Rikki shrugged, turned behind her, grabbed her purse, and followed me to the safety-deposit-box area. Ronald buzzed her through when he saw her coming, and I followed her quickly. We went through the process, the charade, the ridiculousness of her notarizing Cherie's signature on a signature card so she could turn around and sign a piece of paper authorizing herself to have access to her box. We finally stepped into the safe, used our key and Ronald's, and pulled out the long, medium-size box. Ronald said, "Would you like to step into the booth to open it?"

"Yes," I said.

Cherie and I stepped inside the booth, a small wooden structure like a study carrel that had walls that went up about seven feet. We closed the door behind us, turned on the small fluorescent light, and opened the top of the long box. As I lifted it up, I could see two envelopes in the box. I opened the first one with some trepidation. As I laid the contents on the desktop, I just stared at it with my heart pounding. I leafed through the pages to see what they were, then laid them down flat and ironed out the creases gently with my fingers.

Cherie was baffled. "It looks like some kind of government document. What is it?"

"It changes everything." I opened the second manila envelope and pulled out the several pages that were inside. I turned them around so they were right side up and stared at them. "That son of a bitch."

"What is it?" Cherie asked.

"The who, and the why."

I picked up the document and yelled, "Ronald! You got a scanner?"

34

I dropped off Cherie at her house and told her I would have her car sent to her later that day. I headed back to Annapolis way faster than I should have, trying hard not to kill myself.

I had left my new cell phone out on the seat next to me as I was driving and picked it up immediately when it rang. I recognized Rachel's new number. "How's it going?"

"If you like a mediocre attorney questioning a dull expert, you'd feel right at home."

"Good. I want everybody lulled to sleep because this whole trial is about to blow up."

"Blow up in a good or bad way?"

"I hope a good way, but all I know is that I've got the explosives. Let's see if I can control it."

I could hear the excitement in her voice. "When does it start?"

"Right after lunch. I've got to get Kathryn

to let me take over."

"What do you want me to do?"

"Get two subpoenas ready. One I want you to serve tonight is on J. Mark Grosvenor."

"Who's he?"

"The Secret Service agent at Camp David. Tinny's source."

"Holy shit. How did you get that information?"

"Tinny's wife showed up on my doorstep this morning. I can't go into it right now, just know that you need to get ahold of Justin and have him prepare a subpoena for Grosvenor. He lives in Maryland so he's under the court's jurisdiction. I want you to drive over and serve him at his house tonight."

"Okay. You heading back?"

"Yeah."

"Who's the other subpoena for?"

"You'll see. You won't have to go very — Shit! An accident!" I exclaimed. I dropped the phone as I slammed on the brakes and tried to keep from hitting the car in front of me, which was skidding to a stop. I could feel the pulsing antilock brakes, then I realized it wasn't an accident at all. The Dodge Caravan right in front of me had just slammed on his brakes. I could see the driver's face in his side mirror watching me. We were in the fast lane, and a concrete barrier was to my left with no shoulder. I looked right to see if I could go around, but a car was stopping at the same rate I was stopping. The driver was wearing a ski mask. *Shit.* I could see a sedan behind me closing quickly. I was about to be trapped between three cars on the freeway.

They wanted what I had just gotten. They had waited until they were sure I had it and were going to get it, whatever the cost. Because they knew, and I knew they knew, that if I got these documents to court, they'd be exposed. I had scanned the documents onto a flash drive on my key chain; maybe if I gave them the hard copies, they'd let me go . . . no, they wouldn't. Not if they were ready to risk this kind of open attack.

I suddenly became my other self. My Marine, kill-or-be-killed self. Adrenaline flooded my system; everything I was seeing rushed into my mind all at once. I had to decide what to do in a half second — in only a few feet I would hit the minivan in front of me. The nose of the car stopping to my right was just slightly behind the front of my Volvo. He was stopping faster than I was, assuming I'd stop and not hit the car in front of me. I braked harder and he did too. I suddenly took my foot off the brake and slammed the accelerator to the floor while I threw the steering wheel to the right to miss the minivan. My passenger door caught the car to my right on his front left fender and pushed him to his right. He started to lose control and began spinning clockwise. I turned back to the left and stayed in the lane next to the fast lane. I shot by the minivan, which was still braking hard.

I kept the accelerator on the floor and tried to avoid the cars that I was closing on at an increasing rate. I glanced at the speedometer as it passed through fifty, sixty, and seventy. I kept it floored. The minivan was coming after me, and the white sedan was right behind him. The car that had been to my right had spun completely around. I watched as he stopped, but only to be hit head-on by a Lincoln Navigator that couldn't go around him. I couldn't hear the impact, but I could see the glass flying. Good. I hoped the son of a bitch swallowed his mask and choked to death.

I looked back down and saw I was passing through a hundred miles per hour. I saw an exit approaching and knew exactly where I was. I had fished every creek wider than eighteen inches in Maryland. I knew the countryside like the back of my hand. I wasn't sure I'd be safer off the freeway, but I thought I knew just the place — and just the bridge — to lose whoever was following me. I wished I had put one of my handguns under the seat the way I had thought about hundreds of times, especially after Tinny had been killed. But of course that would have been *illegal*. And I had convinced myself I was being paranoid.

I looked to my right and turned sharply across the other two lanes and exited the freeway on the fly. I continued to accelerate recklessly down the off-ramp. As I got to the bottom, I slammed on the brakes and turned west onto a two-lane highway. I saw the other two cars racing down the off-ramp behind me as I pulled away from them. I checked the engine temperature, which was increasing.

After a mile I saw the road rising in front of me. The bridge. The small, arched bridge made of brick allowed a railroad track to pass underneath the road. It was an active track, but I didn't see trains on it often. I glanced down the track in both directions and didn't see any trains.

As I got to the front of the bridge, I slammed on the brakes. I started a turn to the right off the road as I crested the bridge and headed down the other side. I knew I was betting on my soccer-mom Volvo, which I had never wanted in the first place. The reviews I had read before buying it were screaming at me — made for driving *to* the woods, not *through* them. The four-wheel drive did exactly what I had hoped though as I turned sharply and dangerously off the road, down through the grass, and up steeply to the railroad tracks. I didn't know the width of the tracks or whether it was even possible to drive on the rails. I didn't even try. I forced the right wheels across the first rail and toward the right, but not all the way to it the other side. I straddled the left rail and accelerated, shocked by the jarring from the railroad ties. I suddenly saw dirt kick up in front of me.

I looked in my rearview mirror and saw the sedan stopped on the bridge with two men firing at me. I was at least three hundred yards away. They had no real chance of hitting me, even with a rifle. But they might get lucky. I slouched down a little and pressed harder on the accelerator. The minivan tried the same turn I had tried. He started into the grass but the top-heavy Caravan just kept rolling. It rolled onto its side and slid down the hill into a mushy shoulder below. The two men in the sedan climbed back in and learned from what they had seen. They took the descending turn gently and slowly and successfully climbed up onto the tracks. *Damn* it.

I accelerated to seventy, straining the limits of my suspension, which was clattering and protesting. I watched for the water I knew was ahead as the sedan fell farther behind me. As I saw the first indication of water, I waited for the clearing I knew would be nearby. I saw it coming and slowed slightly. As I approached the dirt road that led away from the tracks, I turned hard left, jumped off the tracks, and flew down the embankment onto the dirt road into the woods.

Still intact, I tore through the woods on the rutted dirt road looking ahead for the right turn that would take me to a place I had once fished. It was memorable because it was the worst place I'd ever fished. Brackish water, no fish, and impossible to get to. But I had remembered it. And I had remembered that at this time of the year the water would be low and you could even drive across it in an emergency.

Just as I got to the other dirt road, I saw the sedan come down from the tracks and onto the dirt road. I had almost a mile on them now. I drove down to the end of the road, came to the T intersection, and turned hard right. Five hundred yards later I came out of the trees and onto a beachlike area of sand and loose gravel. I could feel the wheels bite and distribute the pull needed to keep me going. The water was lower than I had expected. No more than fifteen feet across and maybe eight inches deep. Fast or slow into the water? I had no idea. I just kept going, probably twenty miles an hour by then. The wheels sunk slightly as I approached the creek. I didn't even hesitate. This was my gamble. If I got stuck, it was going to be ugly. No one was around, probably wouldn't be for weeks.

The Volvo hit the creek and arches of water rose up on either side of the hood. The car made a sickening move to the side that told me I had just hydroplaned on the top of the water. The wheels settled into the water, straining to find something to grab, and hit the mucky creek bottom. One wheel would find a rock or solid piece of ground and push me forward, then another. Momentum alone was almost enough to carry me across, which made me think the sedan behind me might even make it.

I kept going and came out of the creek on the other side. I climbed up the shallow bank and away from the creek. The road on the other side was mushy, unused, and overgrown with tall grass, which didn't slow me down much. It would sure make it easy to figure out which way I had gone though. The Military Highway, as it was known, was less than a half mile ahead at the end of the dirt road and would take me straight to Annapolis.

I made the half mile in a half minute and climbed up onto the highway. No cars in sight in either direction. I stopped and got out as steam surrounded the car from the water on the hot engine and transmission. I strained to see the creek behind me and thought I could see the top of the sedan where the creek would be. It didn't seem to be moving.

I turned toward Annapolis and wondered if more of them were waiting there for me.

I went to my office, got out of my car carefully, looked around, and headed in. The Volvo had a huge dent in the passenger door, with mud and grass stains all around. The car looked as if it had been picked up in a tornado and thrown back down.

I waited to see anything out of the ordinary, but saw nothing. I went inside and Dolores directed me to the conference room, where everyone had gathered for lunch.

"Hi, everyone, sorry I'm late. I got side-tracked." I tossed the envelope to Justin. "Make five copies of each of the documents in there."

He was surprised by the look on my face and hurried out of the room, saying nothing.

I said, "Well, Wayne Bradley is ready to testify. He'll basically say what he said in his deposition."

They all returned to their sandwiches and outlines. "I've got to make a quick phone call. I'll be right back."

I stepped out of the conference room and into my office and sent a text message to Kathryn, who was sitting in the conference room. I told her to come to my office, to say she was going to the bathroom, and to invite no one else, under any circumstances. I waited. About three minutes later Kathryn walked into my office and closed the door.

"What is this about?"

"Hi, Kathryn," I said slowly. "How are you?" I looked at her like I was out of my mind and pointed at the ceiling and all around as if there could be a listening device somewhere.

She frowned and shook her head but

didn't say anything.

I tightened my tie and tucked in my shirt as I put materials into my briefcase. "Kathryn, I need to put on Wayne Bradley next." I was nodding vigorously as my tone was passive.

She sat on the couch in my office rather heavily and put her arms back on the cushions. "Brightman's doing all the experts."

"I was hoping that since we're going to lose anyway" — I shook my head, indicating I didn't really believe that anymore — "you'd let me just put on a couple of witnesses." I wrote on a pad of paper and handed it to her.

She responded, "Maybe."

Then she read the paper, which said Bradley could explain the tip weight. Her eyes grew and she looked up at me quickly. I nodded and held my finger to my lips. She looked at the paper again and mouthed to me, "Seriously?"

I nodded. "So what do you think? I've had Braden prepare the outline, so we're ready to go."

"You know we're getting creamed, don't you?"

"Yeah. I know. We'll just wait for the judgment, and then we'll take it up on appeal and try and settle for some reasonable amount."

"That's pretty much what I was thinking too," she said, trying not to be too hopeful.

We returned to the conference room and Kathryn now had color in her face. Rachel looked at us suspiciously and I gave her a dirty look. She continued preparing some notes. Kathryn said to Brightman, "Mark, I told Mike that he could put on Wayne Bradley next."

Brightman sat back in his chair, looking offended. "I thought I was doing all the experts."

"That was the plan, but what difference does it really make at this point? He's prepared Bradley all morning, and Braden has done the outline."

She glanced at Braden, who looked up and smiled.

Brightman replied, "Do I have any say in this? I think consistency of trial counsel at this point would be —"

"I've decided. I want him to put on Wayne Bradley this afternoon."

"Well, I'm on the record then as opposing this idea. Do you want me to be in the courtroom?"

"Sure, you can sit next to him, between him and Rachel."

"Well, I disagree with this, but I'll do whatever you say, Kathryn — as long as WorldCopter agrees with this."

Tripp nodded, although he was confused at Kathryn's motivations. He had given up.

I wolfed down half a turkey sandwich. As I finished, I said to Braden, "You've been working pretty hard. You should come to court and see Bradley testify."

"Wouldn't miss it," he agreed.

"I'm going to go get set up. I'll see you over there." I headed for court and called Debbie. "Can you take Bradley to the courtroom now? Walk him all the way in. Don't let anybody come near him."

"Will do. So that's my new job. Personal escort Service."

"That sounds wrong somehow."

"Yes, it does. How about personal security detail?"

"There you go, see you there."

I dialed Marcel's number and he picked up immediately. "Marcel, you got that info for me on the tip weights?"

"Yes."

"What's the answer?"

"Just as you thought."

"Can you prove it?"

"Yes, I can."

"Any doubt?"

"No. None."

"Bring it."

"I will be there in a few minutes."

I got to court before all the other attorneys, including Hackett and his minions. Court was to reconvene at one thirty, and I arrived just after one. People were beginning to tire of the routine, only coming in at the last minute instead of being there eagerly awaiting the next event. Brightman must really have put them to sleep. Some of the journalists sitting outside writing on note pads and typing on computers were surprised to see me.

I sat at the lead counsel position at the table, and a few minutes later Rachel joined me. I asked Rachel quietly without looking at her, "Did you bring it?"

"Yes."

"You gonna serve it?"

"With pleasure."

"Should be an interesting afternoon."

"To say the least. I can't wait to see what you've got."

"Well, if this ends up somehow with me in jail for contempt of court, just claim that you didn't know anything about any of this."

"It would be true."

"Keep it that way. Enjoy the show."

The door creaked open behind us and Hackett came in. "Speaking of the literal devil," I said to Rachel under my breath.

"You think he sees it coming?"

"Not a chance."

She smiled and reached into her briefcase to pull out a manila envelope. She put it next to her at the counsel table.

Hackett sat down, glanced at me with some surprise on his face, and said nothing. His other associates returned, as did the gallery. The courtroom filled, and just as the clerk was ready to bring the judge in, Debbie walked in with Wayne Bradley. She looked beautiful and triumphant. She had never helped me in any case or at any trial before, and I think was surprised that I had asked her to watch over the most important witness in the case; the most important witness in my life. She was wearing a navy blue business suit that I didn't even remember she owned, with a V-neck, cream-colored blouse. She walked right up to me, opened the gate, and held it open as Bradley walked through. Brightman came in and sat with us at the table.

Others filed in and filled the courtroom in anticipation of the afternoon session. The clerk retrieved the jury from the hallway. The jurors retook their seats and the judge took the bench. She looked at Bradley, then looked at Debbie, sitting in a chair behind me. "Your next witness, Mr. Nolan."

I looked over at Hackett, who looked bored and smug. "Your Honor, the defense calls Mr. Wayne Bradley."

I turned the pages in my notebook to the outline that Braden had prepared for me, turned past it, and looked at the outline I'd spent almost all night preparing.

Bradley made his way to the witness stand, took the oath, and sat with his battered briefcase on his lap. He looked his usual disheveled self, but had at least put on a wrinkled navy blue sport coat out of respect for the court. I walked him through his qualifications, his prior experience as a testifying expert in metallurgy or materials science, the number of aircraft accidents he'd been involved in investigating, and spent a good deal of time on his prior job as a chairman of the NTSB metallurgical lab.

I watched the jury as he went through his qualifications. They had already decided this case, but they were interested in what someone of his qualifications had to say about the accident and certainly wanted to hear what, if anything, WorldCopter had to say about the accident. If we had another story to tell, it had better begin now or we would lose them forever. I led Bradley through the initial part of his testimony as if the last ten days had never happened. He talked about Hackett's experts, how they had jumped to conclusions based on insufficient evidence, how assigning blame to the tip weights was Convenient, but unsupportable. It was impossible to know whether the absence of tip weights on the blade that had been found by the wreckage was the *cause* of the accident or a *result* of the accident. When blades start slamming into the side of a broken helicopter in the air, the blades can come apart, they can shred, and they can certainly knock the end cap off and jettison tip weights. So it was premature to form a conclusion that the tip weights caused the crash without finding the tip weights. And, he noted, the plaintiffs' experts had never found nor seen the tip weights from the blade of Marine One. I glanced down at the yellow note pad in front of Hackett. He was doodling, drawing a bunny or an odd dog. I asked Bradley, "The testimony you've just given to the jury, is that the same testimony that you gave at your deposition that Mr. Hackett here took?"

"Yes, he asked me basically the same questions and I gave him the same answers."

"When you filed your expert report and gave your deposition at Mr. Hackett's request, were your opinions final at that time?"

"Yes."

I turned the page. "Has anything occurred since you gave your deposition to cause you to reconsider your opinions?"

"Yes."

Hackett's head snapped up and his pen dropped to the pad.

I asked Bradley, "What has happened?"

"I just couldn't accept that the federal government couldn't find the tip weights. I worked for the NTSB for many years. Head of their metallurgy lab. You would think they'd find everything. Every single blade of grass that matters. Well, in my experience, since we're human, that isn't possible. They miss things. Sometimes important things. So I asked if we could go back out there again in the hope of finding something. We all — all the experts working with you on this — were in agreement we should never stop looking."

"Hadn't the NTSB already exhausted the hunt for tip weights?"

"Well, they had put a lot of manpower and time into it, but we had no knowledge of whether they have found any of them because they've closed their investigation to outsiders, even to the members of the investigation, like WorldCopter."

"Did you find anything?"

"Yes. We did."

Hackett shot to his feet. He had a choice. He now knew that I had something he didn't know about. He had to make a choice, to rush up to the court for a sidebar conference so that the jury would not hear any of the discussion, or to go for the fatal blow, and shut the witness down right in front of the jury. Hackett said, "Your Honor, this witness is about to testify about information that was not in his report or part of his deposition. He may not do so. He's only allowed to testify about his final opinions as they were prepared and exchanged with the other side. Anything else he 'found' is irrelevant."

I replied, "Your Honor, what he found is not only relevant, it is critical to know what happened to Marine One. Mr. Hackett has based his entire case on the idea that the tip weights came off the helicopter. I don't know why he would be concerned about what, if anything, has been recently found at the accident site."

The judge responded, "I don't see any

harm in learning what he has found. You may continue."

"Dr. Bradley, what have you found?"

"While at the scene recently, Karl Will and you went up in a cherry picker — one of those trucks tree trimmers use — to get a close look at a broken branch high up in one of the trees. Well, he found a tip weight embedded in the broken branch and an indentation in the trunk where another tip weight had been but was no longer. I have examined it and I believe it is one of the tip weights from Marine One."

The courtroom sucked in its breath. Hackett started turning an odd reddish color. He jumped up again, "Your Honor, this is out of order. He is not allowed to do any further testing or prepare any testimony after his deposition. I'm being blindsided here, Your Honor."

The judge now wanted to hear what the evidence was. "Your objection is noted. Continue, Mr. Nolan."

"Dr. Bradley, how do you know it was the tip weight from Marine One?"

"Well, first, because it was found in a tree at the accident site of Marine One. It is unlikely to find a helicopter tip weight in any given tree, I think. But most significantly, because two-thirds of the serial number are on the piece that I found. It matches one of the numbers in the gap of weights that can't be accounted for. In other words, all the other tip weights are accounted for within the company, but these that would have been on Marine One are not accounted for by documents, and this matches one of those missing numbers."

"What kind of shape was the tip weight in?"

Bradley leaned back and extended his legs as he slipped his hand into his pocket. "I have it right here."

Almost as one, the jury leaned forward in their box to see what he was going to pull out. Bradley had the leather pouch, opened the drawstring, and dumped the tip weight out in his hand. "Here is the tip weight from Marine One. It's about an inch and a half across, at least in its full size, but we have only about three-quarters of an inch of it. About half of the tip weight."

Hackett wasn't sure whether to challenge him or to rejoice. A broken tip weight, a fractured tip weight, could prove his entire case.

I continued, "Dr. Bradley, what did you conclude from this fractured tip weight?"

"After I examined it preliminarily, I concluded that this tip weight fractured in flight, came off of the blade from Marine One, and caused the blade to go out of balance. And while I'm not an accident reconstructionist, it is virtually certain that out-of-balance condition on that blade caused the helicopter to go into massive vibrations, which resulted in its throwing the blade off of the helicopter and the helicopter ultimately rolling over and crashing."

Hackett smiled and shook his head. I had proved his case.

"Since your preliminary conclusions after finding this tip weight, have you had an opportunity to conduct further examination?"

Hackett didn't like where this was going. He stood. "Your Honor, I was under the impression that Dr. Bradley had just found this tip weight. We're now led to understand that he's had time to conduct additional investigation and examination? Mr. Nolan informed me of none of this. This is critical evidence to the case which he has kept in his possession, examined and tested with his expert, and told me nothing about it. This is unethical. I request the opportunity to take this witness on voir dire to determine exactly how long he's had this tip weight, what kind of tests he's done, and what his new opinions are before they're disclosed to the jury." Hackett raised his voice, "This is an ambush, Your Honor."

The jury was attentive. Some thought this was great sport, others seemed confused that although the evidence I had presented seemed to confirm Hackett's theory, he was outraged.

The judge looked at me over her reading glasses. "Why have you not informed Mr. Hackett of these developments prior to your calling of this witness, Mr. Nolan? You're aware of the ongoing obligations under the federal rules."

I looked over at Rachel, who opened the manila envelope lying in front of her and pulled out a document and kept it facedown on the table. "I am very aware of my obligations, Your Honor. But I couldn't possibly notify even those in my own firm of this development."

The judge frowned. "I'd like to know the answer to this question, but perhaps it would be more prudent to dismiss the jury for this —"

Hackett was hot. "No, Your Honor, let's hear it now. I want to hear Mr. Nolan explain how he's collecting evidence after the closing of discovery to bring it in here and try and hijack this trial. He's obviously violated his ethical and legal obligations, so let's hear why." He looked at me smugly.

I looked at the judge, waiting to see if she wanted to do this outside the presence of the jury, but she seemed to want to get it over with. I said, "Your Honor, every significant step I've taken for the last few months I've had to take in secrecy. Mr. Hackett planted a spy in my office and that person forwarded every e-mail and document of significance directly to him."

The judge deeply regretted not dismissing the jury when she thought it was prudent to do so, but it was too late now. "Mr. Nolan. Surely you are speaking hyperbolically."

The jury stared at me, stunned.

I shook my head. "I am not, Your Honor. Mine is a small law firm. But we were hired to do this case. I needed some additional help and hired several contract attorneys, one of whom turns out to be a plant from Mr. Hackett." I nodded at Rachel, who pushed her seat back quickly, grabbed the piece of paper in front of her, turned around, walked back to the barrier between the counsel table and the gallery, and slapped Braden in the chest with the subpoena that had his name on it. I turned and pointed at him. "Braden Randall, or Jonathan Dercks, which is his real name, is a former employee of Mr. Hackett, who he encouraged to come work for me. He is responsible for hacking into my computer system, sending all my e-mails to Hackett, sending research memos and litigation plans, and setting me up for all these supposed ethical allegations Mr. Hackett keeps stumbling on.

"The document that Ms. Long just gave to Braden is a subpoena to testify at this trial. Your Honor, I request at this point that we excuse Dr. Bradley for a moment and call to the stand Braden Randall to confirm to the court everything that I've just said, and to show the court, and Mr. Hackett, why I didn't inform him of Dr. Bradley's discovery in a more timely manner, and that I was completely justified in handling it exactly as I have."

The journalists were scribbling furiously on their pads, and the artists turned their sketch sheets toward Braden, who sat frozen in the first row between Kathryn and Tripp.

The judge had seen enough. "We're going to recess this trial right now. The jury is dismissed. Everybody else stay where you arc." The clerk stood and pointed to the jurors, who knew it was time for them to file out of the courtroom, which they did with regret. They wanted to stay and see the fireworks.

When the clerk closed the door and nodded to the judge, she said, "The Court is in recess. Everyone is free to go, but I need to talk to counsel during this break." No one moved. Braden looked at the subpoena that had dropped to the floor after Rachel had slammed it into his chest. He was beet red and sweating. He hadn't said a word, nor had he looked at anyone.

The judge took off her reading glasses and tossed them aside. "Mr. Nolan —"

The court reporter looked up. "Is this on the record, Your Honor?"

"It most certainly is." Then the judge turned to me. "Mr. Nolan. What are you doing subpoenaing your own associate to testify in a trial? What is going on here?"

"Your Honor, there has been subterfuge and fraud by Mr. Braden Randall on behalf of Mr. Hackett. I suggest that we put Mr. Randall on the stand and ask him about it. Hence the subpoena."

"Mr. Hackett?" the judge asked, looking at him.

Hackett had regained his composure. "Your Honor, Mr. Nolan is obviously delusional. His case is lost. This is a desperate attempt to take the jury's attention off the facts. I would ask that the court ignore this side show. Let's complete Dr. Bradley's testimony and submit this case to the jury to let them decide what happened. Frankly, all we've determined so far today is that Mr. Nolan's own expert has confirmed my theory, that a tip weight that was improperly mounted fractured and caused this helicopter to crash. I'm surprised that Mr. Nolan hasn't just stipulated to a judgment at this point. Why we need to inquire into Mr. Randall's secret motives, I can only imagine. But I can tell you that it's not relevant to this case."

Damn he was good. "Your Honor, I simply ask that you allow me to examine Mr. Randall for fifteen minutes, then you determine whether this is relevant to the conduct of this case or not. Mr. Hackett has objected to Dr. Bradley's testimony. You asked why I hadn't disclosed certain information to counsel prior to now, and this is why."

The judge was unhappy the case had taken this turn, but she knew she had to sort it out. "Take the stand, Mr. Randall."

Braden stood up and inched down the row, trying not to step on the others. His face was white. He walked slowly to the stand, turned, and faced the gallery as the journalists in the front row quickly and confidently drew their new favorite. After taking the oath, he sat in the witness stand and adjusted the microphone. Rachel handed me the exhibits for his examination.

The clerk said to him, "Please state your full name and spell your last name for the record."

He did.

I said, "Good afternoon, Mr. Randall."

"Good afternoon, Mr. Nolan."

"You just took the oath before this court, which carries with it the penalties of perjury for making a knowing misstatement, do you understand that?"

"Yes, sir."

"Yet when the clerk asked you to state your name, *after* you took the oath, what you told her was false. Correct?"

"That's my name."

"That's the name that you go by. But that's not the name on your birth certificate. Is it?"

"No, sir."

There was a hum behind me as I continued, "Your actual name is Jonathan Dercks, correct?"

He looked surprised. "Yes, sir, that's my given name."

"Yet when you applied to me for a job, you lied to me and told me your name was what you just told the clerk, correct?"

"Yes, I've had some problems with my old girlfriend, who has been stalking me. I have gone by —"

"What's her name?"

"I'd really rather not say."

"You now have testified under oath that the reason that you lied to me was because you'd been stalked by a female. What is her name?"

"Ah, I don't remember."

"You don't remember? How is that possible, that you don't remember the name of a former girlfriend who is stalking you?"

"There is . . . I am just sort of flustered right now."

"You have never obtained a restraining order against this female in any court in this country, have you?"

"No."

"Never applied for one, have you?"

"No."

"Your Honor, I'd like to mark as the exhibit next in order the résumé that was submitted to me by Mr. Dercks when he applied for a position with my firm."

I walked to the front and handed him a copy of the résumé. "It says here you graduated from Columbia Law School. That's correct, isn't it?"

"Yes, it is."

"But your name on your diploma is Dercks, not Randall, right?"

"Yes."

"And you list here all the places that you have been previously employed in the practice of law, right?"

"Yes."

"They're accurate?"

"Yes."

"It's accurate but it's incomplete, right?"

Braden glanced down again at the paper. "I'm not sure what you're getting at."

"Well, you failed to list Mr. Hackett's law firm as your place of employment for over two years. And therefore the résumé that you gave me when you asked me for a job is incomplete, right?"

"Would you ask that again?"

I shook my head. "Did you or did you not work for Mr. Hackett's law firm for over two years?"

"Yes."

Several people behind me gasped audibly. "Why did you leave that information off your résumé, Mr. Randall?"

"I don't really know. I certainly didn't intend to. It was prepared by a professional headhunter that I had used before. They must have forgotten to put that on. I don't know."

I stared at him in disbelief. "So the fact that you worked for my *opponent* on the very case you were applying to me about, it's your claim that was left off your résumé by a *headhunter?*"

"Yes, I think so."

"That's a remarkable coincidence. Don't you agree?"

"It's unfortunate."

"Sir, you are the one who handed me your résumé. I did not receive it from a headhunter."

"I don't recall if I did or not."

"You knew I wouldn't hire you to work for me if I'd known you worked for my opponent for two years, right?"

"I don't really know what you would have done."

I approached Braden, handed him a document, and handed a copy of it to Hackett. "Let me show you what's been marked as our next exhibit in order. It's an article about a case that Mr. Hackett's law firm won three years after you had left his employ. Do you see this?"

"Yes."

"Coincidentally, you worked at the law firm on the other side of Mr. Hackett in *that* case too. You did work there then, didn't you? It's on your résumé."

"Yes, I did."

"And you were helping Mr. Hackett at

567

that time and in fact you sent him confidential and privileged information about the case, didn't you?"

Braden swallowed. "No," he said quietly.

"Well, surely when at *that* law firm you told them of your prior employment with Mr. Hackett's firm, right? Because that's the place where you went to work immediately after leaving Mr. Hackett's employ."

"I'm sure I did."

"Well, that's very interesting. Because I called the chairman of recruiting of that firm on the way over here this afternoon and asked him about you — under your old name of course — and he remembered you very well. He was sad to see you go. When I asked him whether you had been —"

Hackett stood up. "This is hearsay and we are running very far afield, Your Honor. This is a complete waste of the court's time. I move that we suspend this interrogation and continue with something more fruitful. This case is not about résumé peccadilloes." Hackett sat back down.

The judge wasn't having any of it. "Mr. Hackett, do you not understand the implications of this inquiry? Let me cut to the chase. Did this young man work for your law firm?"

"It's possible, Your Honor. But frankly I don't remember. I'm sorry to say I go through a lot of associates, some of whom I remember and some of whom I don't. Obviously he didn't stick, and where he went after that, I have no idea."

"Overruled. You may continue."

"So, Mr. Dercks, I have a copy of the résumé that you submitted to that firm. Please let me show it to you." I advanced and gave him a copy of the faxed résumé, as well as a copy to Hackett. I turned again to Braden.

"Do you see it?"

"Yes, I do."

"Is this the résumé you submitted to their firm?"

"I'm not sure."

"Well, I'll represent to you that it's the one that's in their file that they claim you submitted to them, and I'll bring them down here to say so if it's important."

"It's probably mine."

"Do you note how Mr. Hackett's firm is absent from this résumé?"

"Yes, I see that."

"Headhunter?"

"I'm not sure. I quit referring to it at some point. It must have been because it was a plaintiff's firm."

"So now it's because you were afraid they

might not hire you if they knew you had worked for Mr. Hackett's firm, is that right?"

"Right."

"Well, I will also represent to you, sir, that I checked when that case was filed. The one that came down with that big judgment for Mr. Hackett's client when you were working for the other side. It was filed two months before you went to work for them. Are you aware of that?"

"No. I wasn't aware of that."

"So that's a surprise to you? You're learning here for the first time that the biggest case that firm had ever lost was the one against the firm you used to work for? That's your testimony?"

"Yes."

"Well, sir, I decided to check on the next firm that you worked at. And I got a copy of your résumé from them. And once again, you didn't tell them that you'd worked for Mr. Hackett's firm. Does that surprise you?"

"I guess not."

"And surprisingly again, that firm lost a big case to Mr. Hackett's law firm, and sure enough, they appeared in that lawsuit three months before you went to work there. Were you aware of that?"

"No."

"Sir, do you understand you're under oath? And that if you knowingly make a false statement you can be punished under the penalties of perjury and put in prison?"

"Yes, sir."

I lowered my voice and slowed down. "Sir, isn't it true that after you left Mr. Hackett's employ you got hired by the firms representing Hackett's opponents, and they all lost their cases to Mr. Hackett?"

"I don't know what you're talking about."

"He gave you a cut of those cases, didn't he? You got part of the money."

'No."

"Do you deny helping Mr. Hackett win those cases against those firms that you worked for?"

"I do."

I turned toward Rachel, who was carefully watching, and I nodded to her. She knew what I wanted her to do and typed an e-mail message onto her BlackBerry and hit send. If things had gone according to plan, Ralph was standing out in the hallway with Justin, who would receive that e-mail message on his BlackBerry. I turned to Braden again and paused. "You're quite good with computers, aren't you?"

"Oh, I don't know. Nothing special."

"Even though your résumé that you sent

to me says you majored in history, isn't it true, sir, that your undergraduate major was actually computer science?"

Braden stared, without answering. I continued, "Because I have your transcript. An official copy. You see an employer is entitled to get that. So I got it. Actually Mr. Byrd got it for me and left it for me. You know him. You met him. My investigator who was murdered. Well, he didn't like you. He was suspicious and checked you out. Your transcript says that your major was computer science. Do you deny it?"

"No, I don't."

"Yet on the résumé that you submitted to me, it says you majored in history and it makes no mention of computer science. Right?"

"I don't like computers anymore, and I didn't want to get pigeonholed into doing intellectual-property litigation. When firms would see that I was a computer-science major, they would want me to do technical cases."

"So that's why you lied to me about that, because of my flourishing intellectual-property practice. Is that your testimony?"

He smiled, appreciating the irony even in his desperate condition. "No."

"No, because I don't have an intellectual-property practice, and you know that. Right?"

"Yes, it was just habit by then."

I heard the door open behind me and I saw Braden's face. I could tell by the look on his face that it was Ralph, my IT expert, and he was carrying Braden's laptop. I continued, "Sir, in fact you're so good at computers that you know how to create a tunnel through a server, correct?"

"I'm not sure what you mean."

"You know how to prepare a tunnel which takes all incoming and outgoing e-mail traffic, Web access, and even internal e-mail traffic within a firm like mine and copies it and transmits those copies to a destination e-mail address. You know how to do that, don't you?"

"No, I don't."

"Sir, are you familiar with the federal wiretap laws?"

"Vaguely."

"Are you aware that it's a felony to put an illegal bugging device in someone's office?"

He shrugged but was beginning to perspire slightly. "I would assume so."

I turned to Ralph and nodded to him. He tossed me a small device, which I caught, then I turned back to Braden. "Sir, this is a bug that was found underneath the desk in my office. You put it there, didn't you?"

"No. I didn't."

"I asked Ralph to bring in your laptop, sir. He is the one who discovered the tunnel through our server that was copying every e-mail sent to or from my law firm and forwarding it to an e-mail address which appears to be a random number. And he's prepared to open up your laptop right here and show us how you did it. Isn't it true, Mr. Dercks, that you are the one who put the bug in my office and sent all my e-mails, memos, even voice mails which are captured by our e-mail system, to your real boss, Tom Hackett?"

Braden looked at Hackett, which was a dead giveaway. Everyone in the courtroom saw it. He hesitated, then said to everyone's surprise. "I would like to invoke my Fifth Amendment privileges at this point."

I looked surprised. "Fifth Amendment privilege? Are you saying that you're afraid that testimony that you might now give here could be used *against* you in court in a criminal action where you would be the defendant?"

"I really think it would be best for me not to answer any more questions. I would like to assert my Fifth Amendment privilege."

I nodded and looked at the judge. "Your

Honor, I don't have any further questions."

She looked at Hackett. "Any questions, Mr. Hackett?"

He stood up, having renewed his self-confidence. "I don't have any questions of this young man, Your Honor. I have no idea what this is about. He's asserting things that are patently untrue. I have never received anything from him regarding Mr. Nolan's trial preparation or trial strategy. If he is sending e-mails and bugging people's offices, he certainly isn't sending it to me. I don't know how this is even relevant to this case." His voice was confident as was his demeanor, but something in his tone, something in his voice, betrayed fear.

The judge responded, "Mr. Hackett, if you don't see the relevance, you're not tracking what's going on here. Mr. Nolan, you may recall Dr. Bradley and continue with your examination of him. We will evaluate whether there is need for a mistrial, or a deposition of Dr. Bradley after his testimony once it is concluded. As for now, we're going to keep right on going. We're going to take a five-minute break and then return with Dr. Bradley's testimony."

35

The journalists spent the five-minute break, which of course turned into ten, screaming into their cell phones from every imaginable point on the property of the courthouse. Braden had left the courthouse as soon as his testimony was over, and most people expected him to head directly to Madagascar or Chad or Tibet. The reporters seemed not quite sure if they bought my entire story, but I had clearly gotten close enough to cause my own associate to take the Fifth Amendment. That was something you didn't see every day. Something about Braden Randall was fishy and possibly evil, which the journalists would now begin to look into. They were torn between whether to begin that inquiry or to sit in the courtroom and listen to Wayne Bradley, who promised to be even more explosive. If I took the risk of holding back on telling the other side about critical evidence in the case, let alone the Secret Service, the FBI, and the NTSB, in the hope of forcing Braden to blow up on the witness stand, it must be really good evidence. We were about to find out.

The jury looked around the courtroom somewhat disappointed they hadn't been there for the fireworks. They could tell something had happened, but they couldn't tell what. All they knew is that I was picking up right where I had left off.

Judge Betancourt called Dr. Bradley back to the stand.

He resumed his seat, adjusted the microphone, and placed the two leather bags in front of it. Hackett immediately noticed there were two bags and not one.

I began again. "Sir, when we left off, we were discussing your finding of the tip weight from Marine One. Do you remember that?"

"Yes, I do. It's right here."

"Is that, which we'll have marked as the court's next exhibit in order, a tip weight from Marine One?"

"Yes, it is."

The court clerk said, "658."

I looked at the judge. "I'd offer Exhibit 658 into evidence, Your Honor."

"Any objections?" the judge asked Hackett.

"I have more objections then I have time to list, Your Honor. This is completely outrageous. He's been sitting on this evidence —"

"Overruled. Exhibit 658 will be received as evidence."

"Now you said before our break that the tip weight had fractured. Is that right?"

"Yes. Right in half, like a doughnut had been cut in half across the hole with a large knife, leaving two semicircles."

"Now, Dr. Bradley. Since finding that tip weight have you formed an opinion as to why that tip weight fractured?"

"Yes. Initially I thought it had fractured from metal fatigue. I thought it had been improperly manufactured."

"And what did you do when you learned that information?"

"I came to your house and showed it to you. You said that we would simply have to tell the court whatever we find, regardless of how it impacts the case."

Hackett shook his head and threw his pen down. "This is self-serving hearsay. This is ridiculous."

"Overruled. Continue."

I said to the judge, "Thank you, Your Honor." Then to Bradley: "But since then your opinion has changed?"

"Yes, it has. I noticed a very small hole on the inside portion of the broken tip weight, on the fracture surface. Barely larger than a human hair. I was puzzled. So I x-rayed the tip weight, and while the X-ray didn't show very much, it showed me a shadow on the internal portion of the tip weight. I had no idea what that was about, so I machined off the top of the tip weight over the shadow, and I found this." He held it up so I could see it, then so the judge could see it, then so the jury could see it. But it was so small no one could tell what he was looking at.

"May I approach?" I asked the judge.

I went to the witness stand and took the tip weight from Bradley, returned to the podium, and placed the tip weight faceup on the ELMO. I zoomed the television camera down to it and turned on the screen so that everybody in the courtroom could see it. I went to maximum zoom so that the entire screen was filled with the area in the small tip weight that had been drilled out. People strained to see what they were looking at.

"Dr. Bradley, what is this?"

"It's a microchip."

"What is it for?"

"It should be for nothing. Tip weights are supposed to be simply metal. They're there for their weight. They're there to balance the rotor blade. It would be like taking one of the little balance weights off the wheel of your car tire and finding a microchip embedded inside of it. That would be just as mysterious as this."

"Did you pull out the drawings of these tip weights from the materials provided from WorldCopter?"

"I did."

"And the tip-weight drawings call for an internal microchip?"

"They did not."

"Sir, what did you do, if anything, to confirm that this tip weight came through WorldCopter?"

"I went out to WorldCopter headquarters and obtained access to the other Marine One helicopter that was there for maintenance. It hasn't been touched since the day of this accident when all the Marine One helicopters were grounded. I climbed up to the newest blade, removed the end cap, took off the tip weights, and examined them."

"What did you find?"

"I x-rayed the four tip weights from that blade and saw the same shadow. I ground down the face of one of the tip weights and exposed the chip, the path of this wire through the angled hole, and then the fiber that runs across the diameter."

"May I see that?" I approached and took the tip weight. I returned to the ELMO, laid the tip weight on the ELMO, zoomed in the television camera, and everybody in the room could see exactly what had happened. After I let everyone stare at it for a time, I said, "Your Honor, I move this into evidence as next in order."

"Any objections?"

"Yes —"

"Overruled."

"So all the tip weights have these chips?"

"I doubt that. I suspect only the most recent blades have the chip."

"So on the accident tip weight. Why is the microchip there?"

Bradley pushed his hair back with his hands. "That's what I was trying to figure out. It made no sense to me at all, but I realized the chip was connected to that hole that I found. I did a chemical test on the edge of the tip weight checking for one particular chemical."

"What chemical?"

"Well, it's PETN. Pentaerythritol tetranitrate."

"And was it positive? Did your test find the chemical you were testing for?"

"Yes. It was positive."

I paused and looked at the jury. They were hanging on every word but not yet understanding. "Dr. Bradley, tell the jury what is significant about your positive finding on that test."

He nodded. "It is the chemical that is almost universally present in detonation cord. Explosives."

The jury sat back startled. The journalists were talking audibly to each other. The judge said, "Quiet, please."

"Dr. Bradley. What is your opinion of what happened to this tip weight?"

"The microchip is actually a microscopic RFID, a Radio-Frequency Identification Device. You see those in shipping and tracking of goods all the time. They're very common. Some of them are passive, some active. This is a miniaturized device just like one of those, and it's passive. No power source required. The radio frequency that stimulates it provides enough power for it to emanate a single short signal, which in this case is set not to respond and identify, but rather to trigger the very, very thin detonation cord embedded in this tip weight. It's very ingenious. The entire thing weighs less than the weight of a human hair. It wouldn't change the weight of the tip weight in any measurable degree."

It was so quiet I could hear Dr. Bradley's knee rubbing up against the front of the witness box as he undoubtedly bounced his knee up and down as he testified. "What would happen if it worked?"

"The explosion it would create would be so small that if we duplicated it here in the courtroom, we would probably not even hear it, we wouldn't notice any change, and we wouldn't hear or see anything, but what it would do is cripple the tip weight's metal integrity. When under loads, like on a spinning rotor blade, it would ultimately fracture right along the line of the detonation fiber. This tip weight was fractured because of a microscopic explosive device."

The jury was stunned.

I asked Bradley, "Let me just be clear. What was the cause of Marine One falling out of the sky?"

"Fractured tip weight, which separated and threw the blade out of balance. That caused uncontrollable vibration and that blade separating from the aircraft. The helicopter broke up and crashed to the ground."

"And what is the cause of the tip weight failing?"

"A radio-triggered detonation cord built inside the tip weight."

"How would it be triggered?"

"All it would take is a common radio transmitter at that discrete frequency."

"Where would they have done it?"

"They could have been driving by the White House, or in a park in D.C. Marine One takes different routes every time, but usually goes out over the Potomac when heading northwest. Lots of places to park with a small transmitter. No one would notice at all. Could be anywhere. That helicopter is going to come down after the transmission, it's only a matter of when."

"What about the dummy Marine One? You know whenever Marine One is airborne, there's always a decoy Marine One, or two, or three, flying nearby. What if that helicopter had flown over the radio transmission?"

"We'd have to check and see if one of these RFID tip weights was on it. If it was, then it would have gone down. As it was, they got lucky and the real Marine One flew over whoever was transmitting the radio frequency to set off the RFID det cord."

"I have no further questions, Your Honor."

The judge seemed shocked by the developments. She looked at Hackett. "Seeing the lateness of the hour, Mr. Hackett, and the surprise of the testimony, I would assume that you would like to break now and begin your cross-examination in the morning."

Hackett stood eagerly. "I'm not sure I'm going to have any questions, for two reasons. First, the proper discovery and evidence disclosure did not occur, and I do not have enough information to cross-examine him. I have no idea if he's making this up. But since he has testified under oath, and Mr. Nolan has adopted his testimony, I think what he's proved is not only that World-Copter caused the accident — they're the ones responsible for the integrity of the tip weights — but I think he's now proved that WorldCopter *murdered* the president. I will be asking this court for a directed verdict on liability and a request that we proceed in this trial only on damages, including punitive damages."

The judge nodded in complete understanding. "We will discuss that in the morning. Court is in recess."

That evening everybody was coming completely unhinged. WorldCopter, including Tripp, including Jean Claude himself, were furious at me for now having proved that WorldCopter murdered the president. They didn't want to hear that I wasn't done, that they needed to wait until the next day before they sent out the lynch mob.

Kathryn was completely baffled and asked me if that was what everyone had been waiting for, for me to prove that it was World-Copter's fault? I told her to concentrate on the tip weight and not on WorldCopter and said we had found the cause of the accident. But she didn't want to hear that because the cause of the accident fell right on our heads. She didn't want to wait until the next day either. The press was absolutely apoplectic. They had so many things to write about and so many angles to pursue at once that they didn't know where to start. The entire case was flying apart, and little pieces of it were hitting all kinds of things like the hail on Marine One on the night of the accident. Senator Blankenship demanded new hearings on how the NTSB failed to find this tip weight — assuming it was legitimate — and how their investigation could be so flawed. The Department of Justice was considering an action for destruction of evidence by Wayne Bradley and me for finding a critical piece of a federal investigation and not notifying them before conducting "destructive testing." The NTSB demanded the tip weights, which of course we couldn't give them because they were now admitted into evidence at a federal trial. The commanding officer of HMX-1, who had only recently begun flying the Marine One helicopters again, grounded all of them until all of the tip weights could be inspected and x-rayed.

The public cried out through every available means that the president had been murdered, that now it clearly wasn't an accident. And if he'd been murdered, why would a helicopter company want to do that? The conspiracy theories began afresh.

I didn't want anything to do with any of that. So rather than have Rachel serve the subpoena on Grosvenor by herself, I went with her.

We drove to his house in Bethesda, Maryland. As far as I could tell, no one was following us, and no one had any idea where we were going or why, and he sure didn't know we were coming.

Rachel was overflowing. "What an absolutely amazing day. I've never seen anything like that."

"Neither have I. Probably because there's never been anything like that. But the explosions aren't done."

"So what do we have for tomorrow?"

"I think it's better that you not know."

"Why would that be?"

"I just have this feeling that we're not out of the woods, and if this guy that we're going to talk to tonight doesn't show up, I am absolutely dead and I'd rather have you not go down with me. I want to preserve at least a little of your own personal deniability. Of course I could end up in a meat grinder."

She turned to me in the seat suddenly. "Do you really think somebody had Tinny Byrd murdered?"

"Well, somebody sure did. But what you mean is, somebody related to this case."

"Yes. Hackett."

"Or the government."

"What? Why in the world would the government have him killed?"

"They wouldn't. There's no way. People talk about 'the government' like it's a monolith. But all it takes is one lunatic in the government and bad things can happen."

"You think they had something to do with it?"

"No, I'm just telling you I'm not assuming anything. The fewer people that know what I'm up to, the better off everybody's going to be, including me."

The GPS in my Volvo led us right to his front door. The lights were on, but no car was in the driveway. Rachel said, "How do you even know he's going to be here? What if he's out of town?"

"If he's out of town, we're cooked. But he's not."

"How do you know?"

"Because Tinny has a brother."

The two-story brick house of Georgian design was on a beautiful tree-lined street in Bethesda. We looked up and down the street and saw no activity at all. "Let's go talk to him."

We walked to the front door and rang the bell. I stood back so Rachel was alone in front of the door. I heard some activity in the house. Then I saw the peephole go dark. He was looking at Rachel and asked, "Who's there?"

She said, "It's Rachel Long. I'm here with Mike Nolan. We'd like to talk to you for a minute."

"What about?" he yelled through the closed steel door.

"We're friends of Tinny Byrd's. And Mike's a fellow Marine."

The door opened and Mark Grosvenor gestured us to come into his foyer. We shook hands and introduced ourselves. He said, "Really bad deal about Tinny. I can't imagine who would do that to him."

I said, "I can't believe it. He was a smart

guy, I don't know how somebody snuck up on him like that."

Grosvenor shook his head. "Actually that's pretty easy, but still it surprised me."

I reached into my suit pocket and pulled out an envelope with my firm's letterhead on the return address. "Here, this is for you."

He took it into his hands, which was all I needed. Now he was served. "What's this?"

"It's a subpoena to testify in trial tomorrow."

He looked at me like he wanted to kill me. "You son of a bitch. You used Tinny to get into my house and then serve me with a subpoena?"

"Sorry, I had to get it to you. I really need you to testify tomorrow morning at our trial in Annapolis."

"You're him? You look different on television."

"Yeah. That's what they all say. I need you there first thing at nine o'clock. You're our next witness."

"What in the hell do you need me to testify about?"

"Those photos you gave Tinny. You saw them. I put them into the trial. I have to authenticate them. You're the only one that can do that."

"I could lose my job if they find out I'm the one who gave him those photos. And how did you find out it was me? Tinny swore he'd never tell anybody. *Damn* it." Grosvenor put his hands on his hips and turned away. He turned back. "You can't force me to testify. All you can do is get the court to find me in contempt for failing to comply with your stupid subpoena."

He was completely right, but I didn't want him to have much confidence in that idea. "You don't want to do that, because I will file such a motion and I'll move to continue the trial until you are compelled to testify. I will put your name everywhere. I'll tell them exactly what you had and where it came from, and I'll tell them that I came here and asked you to authenticate it and you refused to stand behind what you had done. It will make you look so dishonest in so many directions that you'll lose your job *and* credibility. At least if you testify, it will look like you tried to do the right thing, to get the facts out."

"I can't. I've got duty tomorrow."

"That doesn't matter and you know it. Tell them you've been subpoenaed to the first lady's trial and you have to go testify. They've got backups."

He stared at me and Rachel with eyes so

intense I was actually concerned he was going to assault me. He was a lot bigger than I was. "Just photos?" he finally said.

"Mostly. I'll have to ask you a few other questions too."

He looked into my eyes as if he could read what was in my head. "Nothing about what Tinny and I talked about?"

"I can't really give you any guarantees. A lot has happened in the last twenty-four hours."

36

Grosvenor was there even before I got there at eight o'clock. The turmoil during the night had turned the court-watching news cycle into a twenty-four-hour breathless reality show. Everything was analyzed from every conceivable direction. There were calls to halt the trial, arrest Wayne Bradley, disbar me, disbar Hackett, sequester the jury, and indict WorldCopter; everything was on the public table. When I arrived, Grosvenor was sitting on the bench outside the courtroom. People were asking him who he was. He refused to identify himself to anyone and sat quietly in a dark suit with his legs crossed looking pissed. I didn't acknowledge him in any way. I walked by him and into the courtroom. Wayne Bradley was sitting in the front looking over his notes, and the gallery was filling from the daily line that began hours before trial commenced and snaked through the hall and down the front steps.

By the time the jury filed into the jury box and the gallery was full, the tension was higher than it had been since the first day of trial. Judge Betancourt took the bench, sat in her chair, and swiveled quickly toward Hackett. She glanced at the jury and the rest of the people in the courtroom and said, "Good morning. Mr. Hackett, did you want to cross-examine Dr. Bradley?"

Hackett stood and looked around the courtroom, then at the judge, and said, "No, Your Honor. All he's done is prove my punitive-damages case."

She nodded at him with a slightly annoyed look and looked to me. "You may call your next witness, Mr. Nolan."

"Your Honor, I'd like to call Marcel Remy."

Marcel stood up from the front row and walked to the witness stand. He raised his hand, took the oath, and sat down. Marcel explained his role as the chief accident investigator for WorldCopter. He described his work on the investigation of the crash of Marine One, his work with the NTSB, and told the jury of the investigation hangar, the layout of the wreckage, and the testing that had been conducted.

He then confirmed what Bradley had said,

that the partial serial number on the tip weight Bradley had found almost certainly came from Marine One. I asked him several questions about the tip weights, the design of the tip weights, the drawings, and then I asked him the questions that were the reasons I had brought him on first.

"Marcel, are the tip weights x-rayed when they're received by WorldCopter?"

"No, of course not."

"Why is that?"

"They're not complex, they're just weights, pieces of metal. They're like washers. There is nothing to see."

"Does WorldCopter check them against the specifications to make sure they're the right size and weights?"

"Of course. They're measured and weighed."

"Does WorldCopter make the tip weights?"

"No."

I paused, making sure everyone was listening carefully. I waited for complete silence. I then asked quietly, "Who makes the tip weights, Marcel?"

"Chang Manufacturing."

"Where is Chang located?"

"In China. Well, not China exactly, the Republic of China. Or Taiwan. Whatever it is called."

"So not the *People's* Republic of China, but the island, Taiwan."

"Yes. Exactly."

I looked at Hackett. "Your witness."

Hackett stood, looking puzzled. "I don't have any questions for this witness, Your Honor. He simply confirmed that these tip weights were installed by WorldCopter."

The judge said to Marcel, "You may step down. Call your next witness, Mr. Nolan."

I said loudly, "Your Honor, WorldCopter would like to call at this time Mr. J. Mark Grosvenor."

Hackett looked at the witness list, then at me. He looked at the witness list again, then stood. "Your Honor, Mr. Grosvenor is not on the witness list."

"Is that right, Mr. Nolan?" the judge asked.

"Yes, Your Honor. I was unaware of Mr. Grosvenor until yesterday morning. I personally served him with a subpoena last night at his home in Bethesda. He's in the hallway."

Hackett wasn't going to relent. "Your Honor, I don't really care if he's in the hallway. What I care about is that he's not on the witness list. I have not had any opportunity to do any discovery against this witness, and I'm not prepared to cross-examine him. If this is a new witness with important information, I should be allowed to take his deposition and prepare."

Grosvenor stood behind the gate. I motioned him forward toward the witness stand. The judge said, "Let me see counsel at sidebar."

The court reporter picked her stenographic machine off its pedestal and followed Hackett and me to the side of the bench, where the judge had wheeled over for our conference. She said in a low voice, just above a whisper, "Mr. Nolan, why is this man not on the witness list? Who is he?"

I leaned forward. "Your Honor, Mr. Grosvenor is a Secret Service agent employed at the White House in the presidential detail. He was the head of security at Camp David. He will authenticate the photos that were discussed earlier, since he is the source, as well as provide additional testimony about who the president was going to see on the night of his death."

Hackett went absolutely red like he was going to explode. "Your Honor, this is potentially explosive testimony, and I am not prepared to cross-examine him. I need to take his deposition, explore whatever knowledge he has, and test that knowledge against reality. For all I know, this man could be a complete charlatan and a fake witness like Mr. Nolan has attempted to use in the preparation of —"

The judge wasn't having any of it. "Mr. Hackett, if he testifies under oath, you can test whatever theory you want. If Mr. Nolan only learned about his identity yesterday, he couldn't have put him on the witness list. Is that correct, Mr. Nolan?"

"That is correct, Your Honor. I didn't know his name until yesterday. My private investigator was murdered. The relationship that this Secret Service agent had with my private investigator was confidential and I was unaware of it. I knew he had information but I did not know his name. Mr. Byrd left an envelope for me in a safe-deposit box. Here is the note that was in that envelope that his wife gave to me yesterday."

The judge looked at it and nodded her head. "I'm going to mark this document as the court's next in order. It will not be admitted for the jury to see, but will be kept as part of the trial record. How did you receive this yesterday?"

"Mrs. Cherie Byrd, Tinny's wife. She came to my house. I had never met her before," I whispered. "And that's the first I knew of Mr. Grosvenor's identity."

"You may cross-examine him at your leisure, Mr. Hackett, and if there is severe injustice, we may provide time for you to take his deposition tonight or over the weekend if that's called for."

Hackett was furious. "This is completely irregular, Your Honor. I'm being sandbagged here."

"Not if what Mr. Nolan said here is true. Why don't you ask Mr. Grosvenor when he was first contacted by Mr. Nolan? You'll have time to cross-examine him. I'm going to allow this witness." With that, she turned her chair and moved back to the center of the bench. The court reporter picked up her machine and returned to her armless chair. Hackett sat down and I took my place at the center of the courtroom, in the center of the tornado.

The judge said, "You may take the stand, Mr. Grosvenor. Please swear the witness." The clerk swore Grosvenor in and he sat down in the seat.

I was glad that we were separated by fifteen feet. He looked as if he wanted to kill me. "Good morning, Mr. Grosvenor."

"Morning."

"You just told the clerk that your name was J. Mark Grosvenor. Is that correct?"

"Yes."

"Would you tell the jury your place of employment?"

"I'm employed by the United States Secret Service and I am assigned the White House detail."

"What is your particular area of responsibility?"

"Camp David."

The courtroom fell completely silent as everyone waited to hear his testimony.

"Sir, it's my understanding that on the night of the accident, the night that Marine One went down, you were at Camp David awaiting the president, is that correct?"

"Yes."

"We'll come back to that in a minute. First, I'd like for you to authenticate a few photographs for me." I went to the witness box and handed him the two photographs that showed the first lady with Collins. "Can you identify these photographs, sir?"

He refused to look at them. He refused to do anything at least initially. He stared at me with that look of complete contempt he had had ever since he realized what I wanted him to do. But he was also a professional and knew he couldn't make a scene, at least not yet.

"Sir, I need you to look at the photographs so you can identify them for me."

He shook his head. "I'm not really interested in photographs. I'm not a photographer."

A small chuckle in the room broke the tension slightly. I tried to reestablish that tension immediately. "I did not ask you to come here as a photographer, Mr. Grosvenor. I think you know that. You're here as a member of the Secret Service. You knew my private investigator, Tinny Byrd, did you not?"

"Yes."

"And sometimes you would talk with Mr. Byrd, wouldn't you?"

"On occasion."

"One of those occasions in which you spoke with Mr. Byrd, he asked you about issues pertaining to the White House, and you knew that he was working for me, or at least for an attorney defending World-Copter, right?"

"No. I didn't know he was working for an attorney. He asked me some questions about a possible relationship between the first lady and Colonel Collins."

"What did you tell him?"

"I told him I didn't talk about anything from inside the White House. That there was a rule in the Secret Service that you don't talk out of school."

"So you didn't tell him anything about any supposed relationship between the first lady and Colonel Collins, correct?"

"That's right. I didn't tell him anything."

"But you did provide him with something, didn't you? You gave him these two photographs, which you told him might be of interest. Right?"

Grosvenor picked up the two photographs. Put them down. He hesitated. Looked at the judge, looked at the jury, then said, "Yes."

The jury wrote quickly in their pads as they evaluated this witness and his unexpected testimony. They didn't know where it was going, but they were paying close attention. I heard the courtroom doors open behind me. I paused and turned. It was a man carrying a briefcase. At first I didn't recognize him, but then I realized it was Richard Packer from the Department of Justice. Our old friend who was heading the investigation of WorldCopter. And right behind Packer was Chris Thompson of the State Department's INR, the Bureau of "Intelligence and Research." Thompson stood behind the rail while Packer walked right through it. I looked at him in stunned silence. The judge said, "Stop right there, sir."

He stopped, completely unintimidated.

The judge continued, "Sir, you're interrupting a trial. What is your business here?"

Packer said softly, "I'm sorry, Your Honor. My name is Richard Packer, from the Department of Justice. Mr. Thompson behind me is from the State Department. I'm here on behalf of the United States, and the witness, Mr. Grosvenor. I am informed there may be areas of inquiry that intrude on national security information. I need to respond in such an eventuality."

The judge nodded. "Fine. Please take a seat behind Mr. Hackett." They did.

I turned around, slightly off-balance, and continued. "Mr. Grosvenor. Those pictures are authentic and they were provided to my private investigator, Tinny Byrd, by you. Correct?"

"Yes. I gave them to him on the condition that he not involve me in the case, and that he not disclose my identity. He has failed me in that regard. So I guess he's not very reliable."

I looked up, surprised at his tone. "Well, sir, he's been murdered. You understand that?"

"Yes. I've heard that."

"He didn't disclose any of this until after his murder. He left your name with his wife.

I think he believes that you have important information. Don't you agree?"

"I don't think those photographs are important at all."

I nodded. "Frankly, neither do I."

Grosvenor squinted at me in annoyance. "Then may I go?"

"No, sir. I have a few other questions for you."

I turned to Rachel, who handed me a large manila envelope. I opened it and pulled out four copies of a document that was twenty pages in length. I put them on my notebook in front of me. "Mr. Grosvenor, who was at Camp David the night that the president was killed?"

"I was, and the usual staff."

"Anyone else? Anyone, for example, who was not a U.S. citizen?"

Everyone in the room stared at Grosvenor, not even wanting to blink. He paused. "I'm not sure what you're getting at."

I nodded and put my hands in my pockets. "Yes, you are," I said, and paused. "Was anyone at Camp David to meet with the president on the night he was killed? *Other* than staff, other than U.S. government employees?"

Grosvenor looked at Thompson, then Packer, who stood up. "Your Honor, I would like to intervene at this point on behalf of the United States and instruct this witness not to answer this question. This question calls for matters that are state secrets. This is a matter of national security and is not subject to disclosure in a civil trial."

Grosvenor tried not to smile. "I'm going to follow the advice of my counsel."

I looked at the judge, who was puzzled. She knew this was leading somewhere important and was annoyed by the diversion of the Justice Department lawyer instructing the witness not to answer the most critical question of the case. She turned to Grosvenor and said, "Let me make sure I understand your testimony, sir. You have knowledge that there were people waiting for the president at Camp David on the night of his death, and you are now refusing to tell us who they were because of the instruction of the attorney who just arrived from the Department of Justice. Is that correct?"

"That is correct."

"So there were people there waiting to meet with the president? That's your testimony?"

"Yes —"

The DOJ lawyer stood again. "Your

Honor, again, this is over the line of national security matters. I would move at this point that this witness's testimony be suspended and that I be allowed to file a brief on behalf of the United States to preclude any inquiry into this area. These disclosures could cause irreparable national harm and must be dealt with outside of the presence of the jury and the press and after proper briefing. At the very least, we need to take the proper security steps for a trial that involves national security matters."

The judge sat back and considered. She could feel where the trial was going, she could tell where I was going, but she didn't know what was behind the door. She didn't want the whole thing to blow up, and the DOJ lawyer was now growing insistent.

She replied, "Let us find out first where this is going. I will take your motion under submission. You may continue for now, Mr. Nolan."

"Thank you, Your Honor." Packer sat down but on the edge of his seat.

"Mr. Grosvenor, let's just establish what it is you know. Let's set the parameters of your knowledge. You personally observed the people waiting for the president at Camp David on the night of his death, correct?"

"Correct."

"And you know who they are."

"Yes, I do."

"Mr. Grosvenor, one of the attendees was the premier of the People's Republic of China. Correct?"

A gasp went out in the entire room. Packer jumped out of his seat. This was exactly what he was trying to stop. "Your Honor, not only would it be inappropriate to allow Mr. Grosvenor to answer questions that could invade national security issues, but it's equally inappropriate for Mr. Nolan, who now claims to have classified information within his knowledge, to ask *questions* that implicate national security. I would move again at this time, immediately, and as forcefully as is possible for me to say it, that Mr. Grosvenor's testimony must be suspended until we are able to fully brief this issue."

Judge Betancourt said, "He hasn't answered the question. Attorneys' questions are not evidence. Overruled."

I looked at Grosvenor. "Your answer?"

"I'm not going to answer that based on instruction of the counsel from the Department of Justice."

"So you don't deny it. It might have been the premier of the People's Republic of China."

"I'm not going to answer that."

"And the other attendees, Mr. Grosvenor, were the president of Taiwan, and the prime minister of Japan, correct?"

Grosvenor remained frozen. "I'm not going to answer that." An ironic smile formed on his face. "He said you weren't reliable. That if I helped you at all, you'd wreck everything."

I looked up in surprise. "I'm sorry? Who said that?"

Grosvenor pointed at Thompson. "He did. Said you were unstable. Looks like he's right. You're reckless."

I pointed to Thompson. "Him? Chris Thompson?"

Grosvenor nodded.

I looked at Thompson then back at Grosvenor. "He wasn't properly introduced. He works for the section of Intelligence and Research at the State Department. Correct?"

"That's my understanding."

"Well, since we're putting it all on the table, did he tell you that he visited me very early in this case and threatened me? Told me to lay off you, and stop trying to find out what happened at Camp David on the night the president was killed?"

"No, he didn't tell me that. What he did

tell me is what happened in Iraq."

"That's irrel —"

Hackett said, "No, no, Your Honor. Mr. Nolan wants it all out, let's hear it all."

"Go ahead, Mr. Grosvenor," the judge said.

Grosvenor looked satisfied. There was no way to stop him. "He said you were flying Huey gunships in Iraq. He said you were on a mission and did a hard left turn to avoid fire and cut too close behind another Huey and your main rotor cut the tail off the other helicopter. Both the other Marine pilots died. You went back to the base and blamed some corporal for misaligning the flight-control linkages. You said you hadn't commanded a full left turn at all and the helicopter did it on its own. Then you came unhinged on the corporal. Took him behind the mess tent and beat him senseless."

The jury and the gallery stared at me.

"Then I'm sure he told you what the investigation's findings —"

"Sure. He told me what the investigation concluded. It was a mechanical problem, not pilot error. But he also told me that they did a psych eval on you and they determined you had an anger problem. Can't remember the diagnosis, but it doesn't matter. Your squadron commander covered it all up. He thought you were his best pilot, so that psych eval never saw the light of day. In fact, Mr. Thompson told me if the Maryland bar knew the entire story, you'd never be able to practice law. He said —"

"I am not the one on *trial* here, Mr. Grosvenor. If the Maryland bar or anyone else wants to know more, they can ask me at the appropriate time. Believe me, there is much more to tell. But the real point here is that Mr. Thompson used that information to keep me from digging into this question, right? The question of why the president was going to Camp David. And you're the one who can answer it. So answer it," I said angrily, trying to control my temper, which wanted very badly to come into play.

Grosvenor said nothing.

I picked up the four copies of the document, handed one to Hackett, handed another to Packer, handed one to the clerk for the judge, and handed one to the witness. The fifth copy was in my notebook. "Your Honor, I'd like marked as court's next exhibit in order the document I just handed to the witness.

"Mr. Grosvenor, have you seen this document before?"

He looked at the document, saw what it was, went white, and turned it over on the desk in front of him. He said nothing.

"Have you seen it before?"

He wouldn't respond.

I continued, "Mr. Grosvenor, this is a copy of a draft treaty that was at Camp David the night the president was killed, correct?"

"I can't answer that based on what I've been told by the Justice Department attorney."

"Sir, this treaty proposes to give Taiwan back to the People's Republic of China and states that neither the United States nor Japan will intervene or oppose it, correct?"

"I can't —"

Packer pulled out a brief. "Your Honor, I must insist that this trial be suspended immediately. I would also ask for the immediate return of the copy of the document that Mr. Nolan claims to have."

She looked at me.

"Your Honor, I didn't make this document up. I didn't print it. This document was in Mr. Byrd's safe-deposit box." I glanced back. "In spite of the efforts of Mr. Thompson, Mr. Byrd got it from Mr. Grosvenor. And in case he was unable to give it to me himself or convince Mr. Grosvenor to, he put it in a safe-deposit box, gave his wife the key, and she gave it to me. I retrieved it yesterday morning for the first time. Mr. Grosvenor, this is the treaty that you showed my investigator, Mr. Byrd, correct? You allowed him to have a copy in case anything happened to you. Correct?"

"I have no comment."

"In fact, you kept a copy even though you told Mr. Thompson here that you had given him your only copy. Right?"

"I have nothing to say."

"This treaty states that the United States, China, Japan, and the president of Taiwan agree to *return* Taiwan to China, in exchange for unfettered access to the Chinese markets . . ."

Packer began talking loudly, trying to stop me. I raised my voice. "With China agreeing to pay a huge tariff on everything exported from China to Japan and the United States for twenty years, correct?"

Packer demanded the court's attention. "Your Honor, this is completely improper. There is no evidence of any of this, it is just an attorney talking. None of this is admissible! You must put a stop —"

I raised my voice even more. "And it was Mr. Thompson's boss, the secretary of state, who was driving this entire thing, right? It was his idea. His chance to make a huge impact on the world stage, to set himself up to succeed President Adams. Right?"

"Your Honor!" Packer protested.

Judge Betancourt banged her gavel and demanded quiet. Everyone sat in stunned amazement. "Mr. Packer, if what you're wanting to protect are the things that Mr. Nolan already has stated, then you're motion is pointless; it is already in the public arena —"

I said, "Your Honor, I met with a reporter from the *Baltimore Sun* this morning and gave her a complete copy of this treaty. They will have a special edition at noon today that recites the entire text. It is completely unjust for the government to come in here and try to prevent the truth from coming out, to prevent the people from knowing what really happened to their president and why."

Hackett was beside himself. "Your Honor, this is outrageous. We've had no chance to discover any of this. All he has proved is that WorldCopter has killed the president through these defective tip weights, and the supposed political intrigue that surrounds it is irrelevant and unprovable."

"It is not irrelevant, Your Honor; it's the whole point. Marcel testified these tip weights were made in Taiwan. Someone in Taiwan discovered their president was about to betray them. I will prove that the owner of the company that makes these tip weights is the cousin of the chief of Taiwan's security agency. Your Honor, it seems almost certain that somebody from Taiwan was in Washington and transmitted the triggering signal when Marine One flew overhead. They found out this treaty was about to be signed and stopped it. The tip weights were there to be used whenever they needed to. If the treaty didn't go forward, no one would ever know, and the weights would never be discovered. It was the perfect murder weapon.

"So not only should this not be stopped, I request the court to enter a verdict in my clients' favor. No jury could possibly come to any other conclusion than that my client did nothing wrong. The president was assassinated by Taiwanese interested in preventing their country from being sold down the river. Plain and simple."

The judge put up her hands. She finally grabbed her gavel and hit it loudly. "Everybody be quiet and everybody sit down."

She took off her reading glasses, put her hands to the sides of her head, and remained quiet. The room continued to buzz as she looked around, demanding silence by her glare. Finally, she turned her gaze to Hackett. "Mr. Hackett," she said calmly. "If what Mr. Nolan asserts is true —"

Hackett rose with all the presence he could muster. "Your Honor, he hasn't proven anything. He has not authenticated this supposed treaty. He has not obtained *testimony* from this witness, who actually was attending the meeting that night —"

The judge put up her hand and stopped him. "Mr. Hackett, he has certainly raised enough of an issue in my mind that we will have to find out the answers to these questions. We have a witness who can answer them, but who is refusing to do so, on the instructions of the Justice Department." She looked at Packer, and not with favor. "We will need, at the very least, to suspend this trial and deal with the government's concerns." She sat back. After a minute she said, "Mr. Hackett, what I propose is a motion from you to dismiss your case — without prejudice — in exchange for a waiver of any statute of limitations, so that we can all give the federal government an opportunity to determine whether Mr. Nolan's assertions are true. If it turns out he's wrong, you may refile. If it turns out he's right, you would be foolish to do so. Are you in agreement?"

Hackett sat down and stared in front of

him. Finally he turned to the first lady and had a private conversation. She was visibly distraught and was responding to him slowly. He glanced back at his other clients, all of whom were subtly nodding to him. He stood and buttoned his suit coat. He took a deep breath. "We agree, Your Honor."

The judge looked at me.

I stood. "We agree as well, Your Honor."

She said, "Based on that agreement, this case is dismissed without prejudice." She then addressed Hackett: "Regardless of what you do, Mr. Hackett, now that the case is dismissed, I'm going to request that you be subject to an investigation by the Maryland and New York bar associations into the question of whether you participated in Mr. Braden Randall's, or Jonathan Dercks's, defrauding of Mr. Nolan's law firm and used it as an advantage in this litigation. I will also ask the district attorney to begin an investigation to determine whether you have committed criminal fraud or any wiretap violations. You may not leave the jurisdiction until further notice."

Hackett looked stunned. "Your Honor, there is no evidence I had anything —"

"Save it for the DBA, Mr. Hackett. I've heard enough." She turned to the jury. "Ladies and gentlemen of the jury, thank you for your Service. You are now dismissed and you may return to the jury room." They closed their notebooks, completely amazed at the turn of events. The judge looked over the rest of the people in the room. "This case is dismissed without prejudice." She banged her gavel down and stood. Everyone else in the room stood at the same time and the room erupted. Several of the journalists hurried for the door, others stood there absorbing what had happened and wondering if anything else would.

Hackett glared at me. "None of this will ever stick. You can't prove anything."

"Too bad you didn't accept two hundred and fifty million dollars a few nights ago," I replied.

Grosvenor stepped down from the witness box and crossed to me. He grabbed the podium directly across from me as I closed my notebook. Kathryn, Marcel, and Brightman approached me from behind with smiles on their faces. Jean Claude patted me on the back, waiting for me to turn around. But Grosvenor was furious.

He said angrily, "You have *no* idea what you've done."

I shook my head. "The Senate never would have ratified —"

"That's the whole *point*," Grosvenor said

menacingly. Journalists were starting to listen and take notes. "The heads of state had *agreed,* and now the whole world knows. When Taiwan realizes their president *turned* on them, it won't matter what the damned U.S. Senate *might* have done! China will take Taiwan now. And who's going to stop them? Us? No way. Not when our president agreed to the treaty you've just told the world about."

"Maybe if it had gone through, but now —"

"No! China had made concessions, to the U.S., to Japan, to Taiwan, in *writing.* Free access to their markets for twenty years and tariffs coming into our market, everything in the treaty. Now they'll get Taiwan for *nothing.* There *is* no treaty now. All because you had to win your case." Grosvenor pointed to my chest. "Think about that, lawyer boy. Think about your duties to your country and maybe the world next time, instead of tripping up the other side and showing everyone how clever you are."

I was taken aback. I looked directly at him. "I don't have to apologize for the truth. You should have told the FBI and the NTSB."

"I did! They all knew! You think the NTSB didn't find any tip weights? And they knew the implications if it leaked to the press. Now you've told the world. You really screwed the pooch, Nolan."

I looked into Grosvenor's eyes and understood. "You *wanted* all this to come out, didn't you? And probably just like this — a big drama with you dead center. You wanted everybody to know the president of Taiwan sold his country down the river because you thought it was wrong. And he's back in Taiwan right now pretending everything is fine. You wanted everyone to know that Adams had been willing to push Taiwan over the cliff as long as he got the right price. You despised President Adams, didn't you? Just like Collins did. Just like a lot of people who worked for him. And you wanted Adams to look bad, right here in this trial. You knew *exactly* what you were doing."

"You're full of —"

I leaned toward his menacing presence and lowered my voice. The press was trying hard to eavesdrop, but I didn't care. I even saw an arm extended with a tape recorder next to me. I said to Grosvenor, "I wondered about you when I saw you this morning. If you didn't want all this to come out, you wouldn't have come here at all. You would have had Justice fight your fight for you *before* you got on the witness stand. I mean, you weren't even supposed to *have* that treaty. You kept a copy just so it could get leaked. What better way to leak it than in a trial when you've been *subpoenaed,* where you've been *forced,* looking like the victim? You made sure Byrd got it to me."

Grosvenor looked over my shoulder at Packer, who was listening to every word, then said, "I've got nothing more to say to you," and walked out.

Jean Claude grabbed my hand and pumped it. Marcel stood behind him smiling. Rachel looked at me and nodded as Kathryn patted me on the shoulder.

I was exhausted. I gathered my papers and closed my briefcase. We walked through the mob toward our cars. People screamed questions at me from every direction. I didn't hear any of them. Debbie leaned against the Volvo with her arms crossed, shaking her head and smiling. Thompson stormed away in the distance, his neck visibly red. He wasn't done with me, I was sure of that. I wasn't done with him yet either.

We passed by a television production van. Through the open door I could see two of their monitors. I stopped to look, and Rachel stopped right next to me. One of the monitors showed people celebrating in

Paris. The other showed a mob forming outside the presidential palace in Taipei.

ACKNOWLEDGMENTS

Many people have been of inestimable help in putting this book together. But I would like to extend my particular appreciation and gratitude to my agent, David Gernert. I would also like to thank St. Martin's Press, and in particular my editors, Marc Resnick and Peter Wolverton, who have guided this book to completion and made it better.

Last, I'd like to thank my wife, Dianna, for her undying patience and support, who together with our children — Stephanie, Paul, Shannon, Colleen, and Scott — make my life rich and full of stories.

— James W. Huston

ABOUT THE AUTHOR

James W. Huston is the *New York Times* bestselling author of six thrillers including *Balance of Power* and *Secret Justice*. A graduate of Topgun, he served as a Naval Flight Officer in F-14s on the USS *Nimitz* with the Jolly Rogers. He is currently a trial lawyer for the international law firm of Morrison Foerster and has been involved in numerous high profile cases. He lives in San Diego, California.